Husband
Material

Also by Maeve Haran

Having It All
Scenes from the Sex War
It Takes Two
A Family Affair
All That She Wants
Soft Touch
Baby Come Back
The Farmer Wants a Wife

Husband Material

MAEVE HARAN

LITTLE, BROWN

A *Little, Brown* Book

First published in Great Britain in 2002
by Little, Brown

Copyright © Maeve Haran 2002

The moral right of the author has been asserted.

A CIP catalogue record for this book
is available from the British Library.

H ISBN 0 316 85972 9
C ISBN 0 316 85973 7

Typeset in Berkeley by M Rules
Printed and bound in Great Britain
by Clays Ltd, St Ives plc

Little, Brown
An imprint of
Time Warner Books UK
Brettenham House
Lancaster Place
London WC2E 7EN

www.TimeWarnerBooks.co.uk

For Alex

Chapter 1

Tinkle, tinkle, crash!

Amanda Wells tried to remember the words to 'I Love the Sound of Breaking Glass' as she posted yet another wine bottle into the bottle bank in Tesco's car park.

There were rather a lot of wine bottles, as a matter of fact. Yesterday had been her turn to host the book group. As usual they'd spent half an hour discussing the text of the month – a novel about suffocating relationships in a small town on the eastern seaboard of America – and then proceeded to get stuck into the plonk and discuss their own suffocating relationships in a seaside town in Britain. Or, in Amanda's case, the painful absence of a suffocating relationship ever since her husband, Giles the Bastard, had left her for Stephanie the Sylph, a ten-years-younger and considerably slimmer model.

'Mum!' accused her sixteen-year-old daughter Clio in wildly disapproving tones, as if Amanda had just stripped off in public or dared to dance to The Rolling Stones in front of Clio's friends. 'You didn't drink all that last night?'

'Of course not,' lied Amanda, deciding to leave the second carrier bag full of bottles in the car. 'There!' The final crash brought a smile of smug satisfaction to Amanda's face. There was nothing like expiating your guilt at having drunk too much

1

the night before by doing your bit, however small, to save the planet.

'You know it probably costs more to recycle each bottle than to make another one,' Clio pointed out meanly.

'You sound exactly like your father,' Amanda accused, trying to hang on to her planet-saving Wonder Woman mood.

Giles the Bastard, Clio's father, had in fact been something of a dual personality. Devastatingly handsome and charming in public, once in the boredom of his own home he'd become a world champion at nitpicking criticism and undermining comment. In the sixteen years of their marriage, Giles had made Amanda feel that everything from global warming to the element blowing up in the toaster was somehow her fault.

'Let's get home,' Amanda suggested, before the second carrier bag was spotted, 'or you'll miss *Hollyoaks*.'

'Wow!' Clio exclaimed, pointing at the gleaming machine that had parked behind them. It was a shiny, cobalt-blue, two-seater BMW sports car. 'Look at that! I bet that set someone back a few quid.'

In Amanda's view, the car, though beautiful, had 'Selfish Bloke' stamped all over it. No room in the back for children, ludicrously expensive and probably prettier than its owner's wife. It was no doubt a menopausal male like Giles's new toy, or the pride and joy of some spoilt yuppie with a City bonus instead of a brain.

'Come *on*, Mum,' Clio shouted, jumping into their own rather different car and pointing at her watch. 'We'll miss the beginning if we don't go now!'

Amanda, delighted at the success of her diversionary tactic, smiled affectionately and got into the car. Still smiling, she took off the handbrake, eased the car into reverse, forgetting the steep gradient of the car park, and put her foot on the accelerator instead of the brake.

Crunch, crunch, rip! The sound of a collapsing bumper and smashing plastic lights was unmistakable.

'Shit! Shit! Shit!' Amanda screeched, banging her head on the steering wheel and forgetting she'd been trying to curb Clio's habit of using four-letter words more often than commas.

'Jesus, Mum,' Clio hissed, sounding even more like her father, 'what on earth did you think you were doing?'

Resisting the desire to strangle her, Amanda looked behind her. The beautiful sports car now had a large crack in its bumper, just under its iconic BMW sign.

Red plastic shards, until recently Amanda's rear-light covers, littered the ground like space-age confetti.

Amanda prayed the driver was absent. Men, in Amanda's experience, turned into slavering psychos the moment they climbed behind the wheel, even the wheel of a Ford Fiesta. She hoped he wouldn't emerge, Giles-like, from its expensive interior and yell at her, all swear words and insults. If not at least she could leave a craven note, resisting the temptation to write 'The other drivers think I'm leaving my phone number but I'm not', and offer her insurance details.

Reluctantly she climbed out of her car to face the music.

The BMW driver was certainly no twenty-something yuppie. He was, Amanda guessed, in his early forties, clean-shaven, with dark wavy hair and grey eyes the colour of the North Sea in winter. He looked very angry indeed. He was wearing a soft polo-neck jumper with, of all things, a charcoal-grey cardigan over it – an outfit that reeked of money.

Probably just dumped the wife and kids and gone off with a bottle blonde, Amanda thought nastily. This status symbol of a car was no doubt to endorse his shaky virility, and she'd just crumpled it a little.

'Do you realise,' he demanded furiously, staring at the car rather than her, 'I only got this car three days ago?'

A disgraceful temptation to cling to his expensively trousered knees and apologise swept through Amanda, but something in his tone rescued her. It reminded her of Giles.

'Good,' she brazened, pulling herself up to her full height. That usually scared men for a start. 'Then at least it's under warranty.'

His steely eyes locked with her greeny-brown ones. 'I'm sure it is. But for mechanical breakdown, not for reckless reversing in supermarket car parks.'

'What about your careless parking?' Amanda was damned if she was going to give an inch. She gestured extravagantly. 'With a whole car park to choose from, you didn't have to stop so close to the bottle bank. Obviously cars are going to need to reverse out of this area.'

To her stunned amazement, he laughed with what seemed to be genuine amusement. 'You're not seriously suggesting this was my fault?' he asked, clearly struck by Amanda's comic capabilities. But before he could say any more, a commanding voice issued from the other side of the car.

'Don't you dare bully her, Angus! The girl was trying to do something useful at least.'

'Unlike me, you mean, Mother,' the newcomer breathed, only just audibly. 'I wouldn't dream of bullying her.' A hint of ironic humour softened his grey eyes. 'She's absolutely right. I'm far too near the bottle bank.'

'I don't suppose,' Amanda ventured hopefully, 'you'd like to settle this unofficially and not bother with insurance companies?' The truth was, though she'd rather die than admit it to him, in her suddenly single status Amanda couldn't afford to lose her no-claims bonus.

Should she offer him something towards the damage? She mentally rifled through the cash in her wallet. She had about a hundred quid on her, some of which she'd promised to Clio for a trip to the cinema while the rest was for the weekly shop. The depressing thought struck her that a hundred pounds probably wouldn't cover a windscreen wiper for this car. Then there was the cost of her own repairs.

The passenger door opened and a lean woman in what might have been anything from her late fifties to early seventies climbed out.

'Absolute nonsense,' she insisted briskly. 'Angus wouldn't dream of taking a penny from you. He's got far too much already.'

She made it sound as though her son's financial position was something rather shameful, a social stigma somewhere between halitosis and the plague.

'Shall we just forget about the whole thing, as my mother suggests?'

But this wasn't enough for the formidable matriarch. 'Don't be so mean, Angus. You must sort out her damage as well.'

For a moment Amanda thought he was going to say something extremely rude. He didn't look the type to do what his mother told him.

Instead, he reached for his wallet and extracted a card. 'Why don't you take it to my garage?' He scribbled a number on the back. 'Just tell them it's through me. They do all kinds of cars, from BMWs to . . .' He glanced at Amanda's scruffy M-reg vehicle.

'Honda Civics,' offered Clio helpfully.

'Quite.'

'It's fine,' Amanda insisted, wishing she could afford the pride in her tone. 'I'll take it to my own garage, thanks.'

'You will not,' insisted the imperious older woman. 'Or I'm not getting back into that ridiculous car.'

Amanda hesitated.

'They'll have it back with you in a day,' she added. 'They always did with mine when I was still driving.'

Amanda thought of the difficulties of being carless for days, maybe even weeks remembering her own rather inefficient garage, and the thought of taking her ten-year-old son, Sean, to football practice on the bus.

'All right then,' she agreed.

'Good.' Her job done, the grey-haired lady got back into the car, folding in her lisle-stockinged legs with the elegance of a debutante on a Lucie Clayton course.

'It's really very kind of you,' Amanda managed to say to the son, through only slightly gritted teeth.

'No problem at all. It'll serve me right for being a filthy capitalist, as my mother would be the first to point out. You planet-savers deserve the high moral ground, even in Tesco's car park.' She sensed that under the politeness he was laughing at her and she longed to tear up his card and kick his ripped and dented bumper, but the truth was she couldn't afford the option. 'Keep up the good work.' He held out his hand. 'Angus Day, by the way.' His grip was firm and disgracefully reassuring. His smile, when he allowed it free rein, was surprisingly warm.

Amanda shook herself. She wasn't going to fall for that old baloney again. If she'd learned one thing from sixteen years with Giles, it was that charm was a highly suspect quality.

'How patronising was that?' she whispered under her breath to Clio as Angus Day and his mother drove off.

'Mum,' Clio marvelled in an 'emperor's got no clothes' tone, 'it was your fault, remember? Just as well he didn't see how many bottles you had or he might have had you breathalysed.'

'They were from last night. Besides, serves him right for having such an outrageous car. You could probably house three families with the cost of that thing. And it's completely unrealistic for driving about in busy towns.'

'Or in the car park,' muttered Clio quietly. There was no reasoning with her mother when she was on her moral high horse. 'I thought he was really charming.'

'Hah!' snorted Amanda.

'Mum, tell me one thing. Why is it you're the one person on the planet who distrusts looks and charm?'

Amanda knew she shouldn't say things like this to her daughter, that she should never be spiteful, only neutral, but she couldn't help herself. 'The reason I distrust looks and charm, Clio darling, is because your father had both of them. In spades.'

She turned over the card he'd given her with the number of the garage. On the other side it read: Angus Day, Day Properties.

'Ah ha. That explains the BMW. He's only a bloody property developer.'

'What exactly *is* a property developer?'

'Someone who knocks down perfectly nice buildings and builds hideous new ones. And makes a fast buck on the way.'

'Mum.' Clio fixed her mother with a beady stare. 'Did Dad ever tell you you're just a teeny bit judgmental?'

Amanda ducked down and pretended to examine her bumper. Giles had indeed told her she was too judgmental. So had her mother. And her boss, Louise. Amanda liked to think they were wrong. She was simply someone who had strong instincts about things. Even if they occasionally let her down.

'Well, I think he was incredibly sexy,' Clio insisted defiantly.

'Sexy?' Amanda demanded, stunned. Clio had hitherto only ever thought members of boy bands sexy. Men of forty hadn't featured. She sincerely hoped this wasn't the start of a worrying new trend. 'How on earth can anyone be sexy in a cardigan?'

'Oh I don't know.' Clio half-closed her eyes and stroked the arm of her own jacket as if it were made of the softest, most sensual fabric possible. 'Use your imagination, Mum. You can if it's cashmere.'

'Not my cup of tea, I'm afraid. Men in cashmere are usually golfing bores, especially the ones with little polo players on their chests.'

'Get your prejudices sorted out, Mum. Surely the golfing bores'd have little golfers on them? Besides, he was logo-free. I checked.'

Amanda put her arm round her daughter. Clio was sixteen, and beanpole-thin and extremely conscious of the fact that her figure was more like a twelve-year-old's. This caused her immense grief, and no amount of assurances from Amanda that she might change overnight could assuage it.

'You can have him then,' Amanda teased. 'He's not my type.'

'Maybe I will,' challenged Clio. 'And aren't you forgetting something?'

'What?' Amanda asked, finally getting back into the car, extreme relief washing over her that she'd escaped not one car repair bill but two.

Clio grinned. 'The other bag of wine bottles in the boot.'

At home they were greeted by the unlikely sight of Amanda's mother Helen, often known behind her back as GG, short for Glamorous Grandmother, making cakes with Sean for a school party. It wasn't that Helen would have objected to the description glamorous, it was more the word grandmother she hated.

'They're eyeballs!' grinned a delighted Sean, wearing the pinny

Giles had given Amanda the Christmas before his departure, bearing the unflattering legend 'Never Trust a Skinny Cook'.

The kitchen was looking its usual chaotic self. No matter how often Amanda tried to throw away the array of old trainers, school bags, football boots, lunch boxes and copies of *Score!*, it never looked remotely tidy. When they'd moved in, she'd painted it yellow and blue, modelled laughingly on Monet's kitchen, and had imagined family suppers over the years discussing everything from Impressionism to whether there was a God. Well, if there was a God, he'd clearly changed his mind about all that 'Till death us do part' stuff.

Amanda tried to suppress a longing for shiny surfaces and glistening worktops, or at least gaps between the piles of objects. If a style magazine descended on her kitchen they would chuck everything out, add a splash of red velvet draped across a chair plus some wildly expensive flowers and label it 'shabby chic'. Without these touches it was plain shabby.

Sean added the last of the bloodshot veins to his cakes with a tube of writing icing and popped a glacé cherry on top. They did look remarkably like eyeballs; red, hungover ones, the kind Amanda got after a particularly heavy night discussing the Booker shortlist with her group.

'They're lovely, darling,' Amanda congratulated him.

'No, they're not!' Sean bristled. 'They're meant to be revolting. Gran says they make her feel sick.'

'Remember to put the top back on the writing icing or it won't work next time.' Amanda hated writing icing. It was one of those rip-off products that only ever worked the first time you used it. After that, no matter how many times you stuck a pin down the tube to unblock it, it remained infuriatingly jammed.

'Don't nag, Amanda,' her mother interrupted. 'No wonder Giles ran away with that girl. I bet she didn't keep on at him to put away his socks all the time. She probably told him he was wonderful.' It was Helen's theory that women should always tell their men they are wonderful, no matter how much they might despise them in private. Amanda had watched her mother minister slavishly to her father while secretly wanting to serve him rat poison. Amanda had made a vow she would not lead the same double life.

And where had Amanda's honesty got her? Giles had gone off with Stephanie, a modern incarnation of her mother who no doubt told him he was a perfect husband, not to mention a god in bed.

Sean, always the sensitive child, noticed her expression. 'Here, Mum, you have the first cake. You can be official taster.'

Amanda almost refused the thickly encrusted fairy cake. She loathed glacé cherries and the confection probably had more calories than the sylph-like Stephanie consumed in a week. But she knew the offer was an honour and so she bit into it, finding unexpected comfort in the sugar rush and even more in the love in Sean's eyes.

'Fabulous! Give a couple of those to Frankenstein and he'll turn into a pussycat!'

'You were a long time at the bottle bank,' commented her mother, who was dressed as usual in entirely neutral shades, from caramel to cappuccino, giving her the appearance of a very expensive toffee. The kind that smell glorious but stick in your teeth, Amanda thought bitchily. 'How many bottles did you take? A whole off-licence full?'

'That's because we had a crash!' Clio informed her gleefully. 'Or rather, because Mum backed into this man in the car park. You should have seen his car, Gran. It was the swishest thing. Till Mum bumped into it, that is, and dented his bumper.'

'For heaven's sake, Amanda! You always were hopelessly clumsy. Now I suppose this man's going to sue you. Haven't you got enough problems already now you're a *single parent*?' She issued the last two words as though they were wrapped in cling film to avoid contamination. 'Leper' or 'homicidal maniac' would have sounded less toxic.

'Well, as a matter of fact . . .' began Amanda.

'He said it didn't matter,' broke in Clio, 'and he even offered to get his garage to mend Mum's car.'

'Good heavens.' Helen sounded faintly disappointed. 'Why on earth did he do that?'

Amanda felt a sudden stab of irritation. 'Maybe he fancied me,' she suggested.

Her mother, Clio and Sean all fell about laughing.

'Actually, it was because his mother was with him and she told him to stop bullying Mum.'

'I hope you accepted,' Helen said. 'How old is he anyway, this paragon who still does what his mother tells him? Twenty-one?'

'Incredibly ancient,' Clio supplied helpfully. 'But very sexy.'

'About forty,' Amanda corrected.

'And still doing what his mother says. How sad.' As Amanda had noticed at regular intervals throughout her childhood, there was no pleasing Helen.

Her mother waited a beat before tossing her perfect platinum hair and adding, 'I hope you got his phone number. Even a man tied to his mother's apron strings is better than no man at all.'

Sean caught sight of Amanda's expression, which was similar to that of a volcano about to erupt. 'Mum doesn't need a man. She's got me.' He put his arms around her protectively, his head just reaching bust level. Amanda felt a great heave of tenderness. He'd been so brave about Giles's departure and so fiercely loyal to her, refusing to even meet Stephanie for months. Sometimes, Amanda had to admit, she was really pleased about that, even though she knew she shouldn't be. 'It takes two to make a marriage fail,' Amanda had announced piously, but with murder in her heart. 'No it doesn't,' Sean had insisted. 'Daddy was really mean to you.'

Amanda loved him for it.

When Helen finally went off to her beauty salon appointment, and Clio and Sean disappeared to see their respective friends, Amanda decided that what she needed was a comforting bath. She'd actually been more upset by the accident, and especially her own stupidity and carelessness, than she'd let on.

Taking a bath in the middle of the day always felt slightly wicked and indulgent. As she stripped off, the chill in the air made her shiver slightly. No central heating during the day was a necessary economy. She stood up straight and looked at herself in the bathroom mirror. She was taller than most women – Amazonian was the flattering word, though there were others.

Greeny-brown eyes stared back through a tangle of tawny-coloured hair which should have been to the hairdresser weeks ago. Her nose was large but straight and her cheekbones were surprisingly chiselled for a figure her mother had always referred to as 'big'. A faint tan still glowed from last summer. The cold was making her nipples stand to attention. Would anyone still fancy her at forty-one, with the baggage of a truculent teenager and a football-mad ten-year-old? Would anyone even be taller than her?

She had no bloody idea. After almost three years of singledom she'd thought her confidence would have returned by now. But confidence was a tricky beast and hers had stayed in the cave.

She needed to consult her hairdresser and go for a brand new look, even if it meant they all had to eat baked beans for a week. Sean would love that anyway. A make-over would be an extravagance, but her self-esteem needed a boost. In fact, it needed a rocket launcher.

She looked at herself in the rapidly steaming mirror and pouted, pretending to be Kate Moss, or rather one and a half Kate Mosses. 'Because I'm worth it,' she whispered, willing herself to believe it.

As she climbed into the bath she wondered fleetingly whether she should have thanked Angus Day for taking the business about his car so well. But, if she guessed rightly, life had given him a pretty easy ride. A bit of truculence from her would probably do him the world of good.

Chapter 2

She came down from her bath feeling better. Perhaps life wasn't over after all. But she'd forgotten about the mess in the kitchen. It looked like a war zone. The tray of eyeballs stared her out from the battlefield of flour, eggshells and icing sugar. The whisk, covered in cake mixture, sat stickily on the worktop. Kinky the cat, acquired to fill the hole caused by Giles's departure and about as much use round the house, was calmly licking the butter.

Amanda swatted the cat and debated whether to throw the butter away or remove the top layer and hope for the best. She decided on the latter. Economy was, after all, the order of the day. Her job at a small art gallery in town was enjoyable but not wildly well paid and Giles seemed to have forgotten how expensive bringing up children was. Anyway, she'd enjoy passing the butter to her mother.

Since Giles's departure she'd introduced a rota to cover household chores, which usually caused more trouble than it was worth, especially with Clio who considered squalor a style statement. Still, she had to instill some discipline now that she was on her own, though sometimes, weakly, she considered pouring herself a glass of wine and doing the chores herself. It would be quicker and a lot less emotionally exhausting.

To help out with sisterly support as she tidied up, she put on

Clio's Shania Twain CD. There was nothing like Shania belting out at maximum volume to get you through the washing up. Unfortunately for Amanda, the first track was 'You're Still the One', with its touching evocation of a happy marriage which had survived against the odds.

She had to wipe away a tear. What had gone so wrong in her own marriage that Giles could have left the way he had, insisting out of the blue that it was all over and that he was moving in with Stephanie? She'd asked herself the same question a hundred times over the last three years.

'It wasn't your fault,' her friend Simone had said when Amanda had announced Giles's departure at the book group. 'He was a bastard, plain and simple.'

They'd abandoned their text for the night (the title, Ian McEwan's *Enduring Love*, had hardly been appropriate) and seriously laid into men for their fecklessness, their irresponsibility, their incapacity to change the toilet roll, their mind-numbing selfishness and their sad, compartmentalised souls. Janine, a new member, had said limply that her husband was rather nice, and Ruthie, one of the longest-serving and extremely happily married, had kept her mouth shut.

'You should get your own back,' Simone had counselled. 'Slash his tyres.'

'Sew a kipper in her curtains,' Dale had suggested. Her husband had left two years earlier.

'Plant mustard and cress in her rug,' giggled Janine.

'Slash *her* tyres,' Dale had added.

'Tell his boss he's a wife beater,' gentle Anne had suggested, surprising herself.

'Have you ever tried talking to him about it?' Ruthie had enquired.

But Giles hadn't wanted to talk about it.

'Thank God he wasn't one of those hands-on fathers,' her mother had pointed out with her usual twisted logic. 'When hands-on fathers walk out it's a catastrophe. At least with Giles you'll hardly notice.'

Of course she had noticed. There was nothing like your marriage collapsing to make you feel terrible. Since then she'd whinged and binged, blamed Giles and blamed herself. Put on weight and lost weight. Been to a slimming class. Become their 'Slimmer of the Week' and then eaten a bag of fun-size Mars Bars on the way home. And that was before she'd asked herself how it would affect the children.

Now, finally, she was beginning to feel on an even keel. No dieting. No bingeing. Maybe a little whingeing, but that was understandable, she wasn't Mother Teresa. Maybe, miracle of miracles, she was coming out of the dark valley of divorce, if not exactly on to the sunny uplands of happiness then at least on to the flat plain of acceptance. She had even asked herself once or twice lately if it might have been partly her own fault.

With immaculate timing, the phone rang.

It was Giles the Bastard.

'Hello, Amanda, how's life in lovely Laineton?' Giles's smarmily engaging tones immediately made her hackles rise. Giles was only this charming when he wanted something.

'Come to the point, Giles.'

'I wondered if we could vary the arrangements for Christmas this year?' Normally Clio and Sean spent Christmas Day with Amanda and Boxing Day with their father. 'The thing is, I've had this incredible offer for Christmas in Val d'Isère.' Before she could protest, he rushed on. 'It's a freebie. The launch of TBL's new brochure.' Giles was a travel agent and always seemed to be departing for some exotic location. It was funny how none of the freebies were ever in Middlesbrough or Bognor Regis, but always somewhere with palm-fringed beaches or lavish après-ski. 'The kids'll love it. They've always wanted a white Christmas.'

Amanda's mouth had been open to protest, but as usual Giles had got in first. Sean was desperate to go skiing. Clio would adore it too. She was always saying she was the only one of her friends who hadn't been. She was just at the age where falling in love with her ski instructor would be one up on fancying the lead singer of Westlife.

Amanda was about to demand brusquely if Stephanie would be

going too when Giles jumped in yet again. 'Steph can't come. She thinks it's too risky.'

Amanda's heart felt as though it was being squeezed in a vice. She hadn't told Clio and Sean yet that Stephanie was pregnant, let alone that she was probably expecting twins. 'If I say yes,' she replied, trying to keep the hurt from her voice, 'will you promise to really talk to them about Steph?'

'Absolutely. And I'll be able to spend some quality time with them too, soften the blow.'

At least for once he had the insight to see it *would* be a blow that their father was having children with someone else.

'All right.' The offer was too good for Sean and Clio to miss.

'Holidays are great,' Amanda couldn't help adding, 'but getting the maintenance payment on time would be even more useful.'

'OK, OK, I promise.' Giles even sounded as though he meant it. But then sounding as though he meant things was one of Giles's greatest skills.

'And what about ski-wear? I could see if we could borrow some,' Amanda suggested, thinking of the wild expense.

'That's all right. I'm sure I can get a deal. We send enough people off on the piste. I'll talk to my contact at The Great Outdoors.'

Amanda shrugged. Giles always had a contact. They hadn't even known their honeymoon destination till they got to the airport because Giles had done a cheap deal.

When she'd put the phone down, the thought struck Amanda for the first time. This meant she'd be on her own for two weeks over the Christmas and New Year. It ought to be fabulous. Freedom at last. So why did she find the prospect so hideously depressing?

Clio and Sean were thrilled when she told them next morning. Sean even put down his copy of *Score!* magazine to practice slaloming through the kitchen, terrifying Kinky the cat. There were certainly plenty of obstacles to slalom round.

Amanda shouted upstairs to Clio, who was, as usual, running wildly late and was still in the bathroom giving herself a French manicure when she should have been strapping on her school bag.

'If you're not down here in ten seconds I'll throw away all your nail varnish!' yelled Amanda, trying to sort out two packed lunches and a slimming salad for herself to take to the gallery. She'd thought secondary school would mean the end of packed lunches, but both her children had demanded their reinstatement, Clio because she hated school food and Sean because he played football all lunchtime, missed the dinner queue altogether and otherwise made up for it with a Mars Bar and a Diet Coke.

'That's cool, Mum!' Sean enthused. 'Can I do ski-jumping?'

'I should start with just staying upright and not breaking anything,' Amanda suggested.

Clio rushed into the room, cheeks glowing with blusher. Make-up was supposed to be banned from school, but they all wore it anyway. 'Clio, you're wearing slap again!' Amanda pointed out.

'Just trying to highlight my cheekbones,' Clio grinned. She was always attempting to look more grown-up and it never worked. It was one of Clio's agonies that while her friends all looked eighteen, she hardly looked a day over twelve. She had a clumsy coltishness that would one day be stunning but now seemed simply gawkish.

The idea of the skiing holiday sent her into ecstasies. 'Jasmine's going to be so jealous when I tell her it. Will there be après-ski and Glühwein and cable cars?'

'I expect so.' Amanda's experience of ski resorts was limited to travel programmes on the telly. 'I'm sure there will be.'

'Just imagine, Mum. A white Christmas!' Clio's voice rang with excitement. And then, just as suddenly, the bubble burst. 'But what will you do? You can't spend Christmas on your own! Why don't you come too?'

It rankled with Amanda that Giles could so effortlessly produce such a treat while the most she could offer them was a trip to the pier or to the cinema. 'And leave GG? What would Gran do if we all swanned off on the piste?'

'I suppose. Why don't you both come then?' Clio asked hopefully.

'Because Gran would run off with a ski instructor, or manage to break her hip.'

'On the slopes?'

'In the disco, knowing Gran. Anyway, it'll be lovely for you. All that time with Dad.'

'Is *she* coming?'

'No. You'll have Dad all to yourself.'

'Cool. Although I bet, knowing Dad, he'll get ill and have all the chambermaids running after him with hot toddies.'

This sounded highly likely to Amanda, but she didn't say so. 'Come on, Clio, it's a lovely chance for you. You've always wanted to go skiing.'

'I wish you were coming.'

Amanda hugged her, sensing the hurt her daughter still felt about the divorce.

'I wish we were a real family like Jasmine's. Doing things together.'

'I bet they aren't going skiing.' Amanda tried to sound jolly.

'No. But I wouldn't mind not even leaving the house if we were all together. And, Mum,' she caught her mother's eye, 'spare me the lecture on how almost half of marriages end in divorce, will you?'

Amanda glanced to see that Sean was out of hearing. 'Right. The truth is it's a total fucking pain, isn't it?'

Clio laughed and looked happier than she had for days. 'Yeah,' she grinned, 'yeah, it is.'

The book group took a more proactive stand. 'It's time you found another man,' Ruthie announced after they'd finished discussing the latest Will Self novel in fifteen minutes flat. 'Someone the opposite of Giles. Someone who's really good husband material. And now you'll have almost two weeks of freedom to look. Perfect.'

The group was meeting at Ruthie's house, which had the feeling of a grown-up playroom, all bright colours and big cushions. Ruthie had once been a natural childbirth teacher and was still prone to lying on the floor and deep breathing in times of stress.

'Yes,' agreed Simone, who still had the long black hair and sultry looks of her college days, and liked men twenty years younger than herself. 'We all agree about that. But what *is* good husband material?'

'That's easy, at least in Amanda's case,' Louise chipped in. Louise was both a friend and Amanda's boss at the gallery. 'Someone who won't put her down in public or try it on with every woman under eighty like Giles did.'

'Louise,' Amanda snapped, not wanting the sixteen years of her marriage to be dismissed quite so brutally. 'He wasn't as bad as all that.'

'Yes he was,' corrected Louise. 'Worse. Charming though. But then charm is usually a commodity husbands save for other people.'

'OK, we'll rule out charm then, shall we?' Ruthie suggested. 'So what *does* make a good husband? How about unselfishness?'

'Steady on,' Louise chipped in, 'we don't want to disqualify the whole of the male gender.'

'I think kindness is important,' threw in Janine, 'and consideration.'

'Consideration?' Dale turned the word round as if she were unfamiliar with it. 'Does that mean not making you have sex when you don't want to?'

'And working out when you do,' Ruthie added.

'Well, I know what I like in a man.' Simone shook her black hair. 'Someone who's up for two hours of oral sex, then puts the rubbish out.'

'Thank you, Simone,' Ruthie corrected, 'but we're talking marriage here, not the porno version of *Brief Encounter*.'

'I know what I'd look for in a husband,' announced no-nonsense Anne, who very rarely spoke and always read the books in two days flat. 'Someone who will enhance, enrich and embolden me.'

'What's she talking about?' Simone asked.

'I just mean,' Anne blushed, unused to being the focus of attention, 'someone who'll allow me to really be myself and encourage me to give things a go instead of always stopping me like so many other men.'

'Good for you, Anne,' Ruthie endorsed.

'I agree,' smiled Amanda, remembering how often her own plans had collapsed once they threatened Giles's creature comforts. 'And thanks for all the advice on the husband front, but right now I'd be quite happy with a decent f—'

'Wouldn't we all?' cackled Simone.

'. . . fling, I was going to say. Forget the twenty years of consideration and commitment – someone to go to the cinema with who isn't my mother would be a start.'

'And I know just the man,' Ruthie grinned ominously, looking ludicrously pleased with herself. 'Adrian. He's a colleague of Mike's. Nice. Kind. Quite attractive.' She paused, as if to come up with the clinching point. 'And he's not at all charming.'

This, Amanda discovered when she met Adrian the following Thursday at Ruthie's insistence, was the understatement of the decade. Not only was Adrian not charming, he was dull. Not to mention mean. He nursed his half-pint of lager for over an hour and a half without even offering to replenish the wine glass Amanda had nervously downed in minutes. In the end she had to order her own. Twice. And had she wanted to write a history of the tax office where Adrian worked, by the end of the endless evening she could certainly have done so. And all without him even asking Amanda about herself at all.

'How was it?' Clio asked the moment Amanda escaped and crept back to her chaotic household. 'It's not ten yet. Was he that bad?'

Clio was slumped on the sofa. Next to her, a fast asleep Sean was curled in a ball in his royal blue boxer's dressing gown with Kinky the cat on top of him. This always happened when Clio was babysitting.

'Worse. I'd have been home at nine if I could have got away. The hardest thing will be trying not to confess how much I loathed him to Ruthie. He's their friend.'

'It is a truth universally acknowledged,' Clio grinned, 'that a woman who has recently been dumped by her husband will go out with anyone, no matter how pompous, dull or revolting. Tell Ruthie the truth. That he's boring as shit.' Clio jumped up from the sofa. 'Anyway, I've got a better idea.' She waved the local paper at her mother. 'There's a whole page of ads in here and all local to Laineton. There's women seeking men, men seeking women and, get this, men seeking men – though they all seem to be bisexual creeps cheating on their wives – and women seeking women. All that here in boring old Laineton! Who'd have thought it? There are also wrinklies seeking other wrinklies for fun and frolics.'

'Don't tell GG for God's sake or there'll be no stopping her. And with her luck she'd probably find someone on the first date. Let's have a look.'

Clio and Amanda retreated to the kitchen and spread the paper on the table, next to the late-night snack Clio had made herself of a toasted peanut butter and jam sandwich. The jam had oozed out all over the place and made the newspaper red and sticky.

Amanda was amazed at the sheer number of people prepared to take a risk on a total stranger like this. She read the first one out. '"Petite, feminine lady with an unusual hobby." Bloody hell, I bet she got a lot of calls. What do you think it could be? Chaining men to the bedpost and tickling them with a feather duster? Dressing up as a nun and making them say Hail Marys?'

'Probably something really dull like breeding sausage dogs. Look at that one. "Attractive, tactile brunette seeks tall, genuine biker." Do you think she's had a lot of fake bikers in the past?'

Amanda giggled. 'I love this. "Fifty-five-year-old female, six foot, seeks a man who is the real thing." And I thought I was past it at forty.'

'Forty-one,' corrected Clio cruelly, looking at the 'Men Seeking Women' section. '"Proud thoroughbred stallion, thirty, requires firm handling." Oooh, Mum, you should ring him up!'

'I don't think my handling'd be firm enough. Look at this one. "Housetrained male, GSOH. WLTM female for TLC and possible LTR." What on earth does that mean?'

'It tells you at the bottom,' Clio pointed out. 'GSOH is Good Sense of Humour, WLTM is Would Love to Meet, TLC – well, you know what TLC is – and LTR is Long-Term Relationship.'

'Or probably EFS, Extremely Fast Screw, and then you never hear from them again,' pointed out Amanda.

'Don't be so cynical, Mum. This one's cute. "Previously driven, forty-seven on clock. Good-looker. Excellent condition, seeks female model, thirty-five to forty-seven, to park alongside."'

'Oh God, I don't think I could bear a man who compared himself to a second-hand car. Of all the bloody nerve, look at this. "Tall male, thirty-two, likes pubs and clubs. Single mums welcome."' She ran her eye down the page of ads. About half of the women advertising in the paper announced they were single mothers.

'My God, I'm in a crowded market.'

'Come on, Mum. You've got to be more positive. Why don't we draft out an ad together?'

'Fine. How about "Old boiler, forty-one, likes flannelette nighties and early nights with a good book, seeks interesting man for cocoa and companionship.'

'Very funny.'

'But it's true.'

'You'll have to break it to them later then. Or change a few of your bad habits. Come on, Mum, I'll write it. After all, it affects me, too, what kind of man you find.'

'Maybe I shouldn't be looking for a man at all.'

'Of course you should. It's been three years now. And Dad's got Steph. You deserve someone nice. How about "Extremely attractive divorcee, forty-one, Catherine Deneuve type, seeks intelligent, solvent man to share coffee, conversation and maybe more."'

'That's brilliant. Am I really the Catherine Deneuve type?'

'No, but you can hardly put "Divorcee, forty-one, a bit like the mum in *2.4 Children*", can you?'

Amanda leaned backwards, looked in the kitchen mirror and pouted sexily. 'I preferred Catherine Deneuve.'

'Catherine Deneuve's probably a pensioner by now. Anyway, I'm sending it off!' Clio tore off the coupon, stuck a stamp on it and dashed out of the front door towards the postbox on the corner of the road.

'But it's eleven o'clock at night!' Amanda called after her.

'Yeah,' Clio replied, 'but by tomorrow morning you might have changed your mind!'

Amanda waited anxiously till Clio got back, marvelling at the spontaneity of youth but anxious she didn't get mugged on the way back. Five minutes later Clio was home. 'That's that then. Prince Charming here we come.'

Amanda hugged her and for once Clio let her. 'I'm not sure about that. More likely a lot of frogs.'

'Ever the cock-eyed optimist,' teased Clio.

Amanda laughed. She did tend to look on the black side. Anyway, what did she have to lose?

By the next morning she had indeed changed her mind. 'You didn't put our phone number in, did you? Tell me you didn't put our number in?'

'Of course I didn't put our phone number in,' mumbled Clio, who was simultaneously holding her toast between her teeth while packing her school bag. 'I don't want a bunch of saddos phoning us up.'

'And I'm supposed to go *out* with these saddos?'

'That's different. You're desperate.'

'Thanks a lot.'

'Anyway, we'll have to find a way of vetting the real creeps.'

'What are you on about?' demanded Sean who was, as usual, ready and waiting with his coat on ten minutes before either Amanda or Clio.

With unusual tact, Clio decided the subject of potential boyfriends for their mother was an unsuitable topic for a ten-year-old. 'Just some contest Mum's organising at the gallery.'

'Oh. Bor-ring.' Sean immediately lost interest and devoted himself to reading the sports page. It was amazing, Amanda marvelled, how Sean struggled with his reading at school yet could devour every word written about David Beckham's magical attacking skills.

Once Sean and Clio had departed for the bus stop, Amanda headed off to the gallery. It was only a ten-minute walk through the back streets towards the seafront. A few windows still sported pumpkin lanterns even though it was almost December. She breathed in the cold, clear air and hurried her step. This was the weather she loved best. There was a wonderful atmosphere about seaside towns in winter, something to do with the particular quality of the light, the way the brightness of the blue sea melted translucently into the soft grey of the winter sky.

Amanda stopped on the prom for a moment, watching the gulls wheeling. They were accomplished beggars, large and lazy, who clustered round every bus shelter waiting for old ladies to feed them. The town council, worried by their rampant fertility, and the hooliganism they showed in attacking the dustbins for tasty snacks, had put up signs exhorting the population not to feed them. These the old ladies studiously ignored. The birds' presence and the sharp *keee-ah* of their cries was as much a part of Laineton's charm as the pier or the prom.

Laineton was the town Amanda had grown up in. It was quite something to be a real Laineton local. Most people came here from other places, drawn by its shabby charm and its second-hand sophistication. Laineton was full of character. Relatively big for a seaside town, but not big enough for a city, it had always been a magnet for people of all types, usually flamboyant, who would have suffocated in a smaller place but despised the striving and stress of London living. It gave the place a lack of parochialism unusual outside a big city. Amanda loved it.

She leaned on the railings that separated the higher promenade from its lower deck. Two hardy old girls from the Laineton swimming club were striding across the shingle towards the freezing sea, as they did every day of the year, their shiny swimming caps making them look like a couple of boiled eggs.

Down on the lower deck she recognised Betty, one of the two old sisters who lived in a curious structure, half beach hut, half chalet, further down the strand. Betty was feeding the gulls and they swarmed round her. She clearly didn't watch Hitchcock films.

Amanda shouted a greeting to Betty and waved. Behind her, the houses ranged in their ice-cream colours up the hill. She pulled her coat tightly closed, shivering at the thought of the icy water, and how tough the ancient swimmers must be, and headed towards the gallery.

Over recent years the once harmonious town had become divided, its centre still prosperous but the eastern end full of bed and breakfasts and empty, boarded-up shops. It was declining into a scruffiness no one could even dignify with the description 'bohemian', the word so often used to capture Laineton's particular raffish appeal.

Amanda was about to turn towards the gallery when she had to make way for a large builder's lorry. She stepped back to the edge of the kerb and yelled several rude words at the vehicle. The driver simply grinned and sped on towards the council estate up on the hill, a series of drab, low-rise blocks which, Amanda reflected, would depress anyone who lived in them. Even more so because they were in sight of the seafront and the small harbour, which gleamed with polished prosperity. It was only this end of the town that was still run-down and charmless.

Now that she looked properly, there seemed to be some activity up on the estate: five or six lorries, a JCB and a crane were parked in its small forecourt and she remembered that there had been a row in the local paper over what some property developer was planning to do with it.

She'd be late opening up, Amanda realised, if she didn't stop staring at swimmers and builders. Louise was a stickler for opening on time. It irritated the hell out of Louise when shops stuck up little signs saying 'Back in Five Minutes' or 'Gone to Bank'. 'Those five minuteses, if you add them all up, could mean the difference between staying afloat or going out of business!' she would cry.

Slightly out of breath, and wishing for the hundredth time she were her own boss, Amanda pulled up the shutter and flipped over the OPEN sign.

The Wave Gallery was in a great position just off the promenade and specialised in scenes of Laineton, mostly in extremely bright colours. Laineton, with its piers and theatres and antique shops, was one of the most painted venues in the south of England. Most of the paintings were deeply conventional, almost paint by numbers, and quite hideous. Amanda wished Louise would be a bit more adventurous in her taste. 'Risk equals ruin' was one of Louise's favourite sayings, as she hung yet another sub-Impressionist view of Laineton beach, children in straw hats digging sandcastles in the dappled sunlight in front of a sea so bright it was more Greek island than south coast. Occasionally, when the gallery was empty, Amanda fantasised about what she would hang if it were her own.

'Excuse me.' A rather scruffy young woman with a very large bag had come into the gallery and was lurking near one of the gaudiest of Louise's beach scenes. 'I wondered if you ever show any sculpture?'

Amanda was on the point of explaining that her boss thought it too uncommercial but the girl was already down on her knees opening her bag. It had to be a magic bag, like Mary Poppins', because she had already removed two large sculptures wrapped in cloth before Amanda had time to stop her.

'I'm afraid I really don't think . . .' Amanda began.

The girl, whose previous rejections had clearly toughened her up, ignored Amanda and went on unwrapping. A moment later two perfectly carved white herons stood facing each other, both about two feet high.

'That's their courting ritual,' explained the young woman. 'They stretch their necks and put their beaks into the air.'

'They're beautiful,' Amanda replied, forgetting completely that Louise would hate them. There was something enchanting about the utter simplicity of the white-painted shapes that Amanda couldn't resist.

'They're based on observation,' the girl rushed on. 'I studied natural history at university and I still go birdwatching all round the world.' Sensing Amanda's enthusiasm, she delved into the Mary Poppins bag again and pulled out a wonderful wood carving of a seabird. 'These are nesting seagulls.' The carving had the same magical simplicity of the herons, stylised yet capturing a reality and a beauty that couldn't fail to move.

'The gulls are from Laineton,' she added, taking in for the first time that everything in the shop seemed to feature the town. 'They were nesting outside my window.'

Amanda examined the birds. Their white chests, the greeny-yellow of their beaks and the pale grey wings with their dramatic black and white tips were astoundingly realistic. The polished wood felt soft to the touch. Amanda realised how much she'd like to own one herself. 'It's extraordinarily lifelike . . .' she began.

'. . . but not our cup of tea at all,' cut in Louise's crisp tones. She had just come in the door carrying a particularly hideous painting of the bandstand which looked as if it had been executed by Oskar Kokoschka on speed. 'Too subtle for our audience, I'm afraid. They think seagulls ought to be poisoned or put on the pill.' She noticed Amanda's pained expression and pointed to the canvas tucked under her arm. 'This was painted by Mrs Wilson at the Over-Sixties art class. It'll go very well. Local subject. Local artist. I get a lot of work from the Over-Sixties. And it's very reasonably priced too.' She fixed the young sculptor with an eye beadier than the seagull's. 'How much did you say you were asking?'

'A hundred and fifty pounds,' faltered the girl. 'Though I suppose I could go a bit lower.'

If you starve, thought Amanda, furious with Louise. Louise exploited the Over-Sixties and paid them a pittance. The old dears were too thrilled to find a buyer to quibble when Louise offered them twenty pounds for something that had taken them months.

'Quite. Sorry, but we couldn't afford that price.'

'The herons are less,' blurted the girl. 'A hundred pounds the pair.'

'I'm sorry . . .'

'Go on, Louise,' Amanda interrupted, knowing Louise would give her a bollocking later, 'it's Christmas soon, remember. Our best time. Besides, you don't pay the Over-Sixties nearly enough. Remember Scrooge. He'll come and haunt you and show you all those poor pensioners knocking out oils in freezing rooms with icicles dripping off their noses. Just take one carving. See how it goes.'

Louise, who was dressed nearly as colourfully as her scenes of Laineton, pursed her jewel-hued lips in disapproval and sighed. 'I'll give the herons three weeks. Sale or return. You organise it, Amanda. It's your call. They'll never sell so you might as well fix a day for collection with the artist before she goes. I don't want to be lumbered with two fucking herons.'

Amanda deliberately misunderstood her. 'They're not fucking herons, Louise. They're courting herons. They haven't decided about the fucking bit yet. There's a difference.'

'Actually,' blushed the young woman, taken aback by the direction the conversation was taking, but concerned with accuracy all the same, 'by this stage they *have* decided to, er, you know. Herons don't tend to change their minds, like people, at the eleventh hour.'

'I don't care if they wear bloody condoms,' Louise shouted. 'I just want them collected if they haven't sold in three weeks, that's all.'

'Three weeks then,' Amanda smiled. 'I'll do my damnedest to sell them.'

'This isn't Cork Street, you know,' hissed Louise as the girl packed away the nesting seagull. 'And, by the way, there doesn't seem to be any coffee on.'

If she hadn't needed the money so badly, Amanda would have enjoyed throwing the Kenyan light-roast over Louise when she finally got time to make it. If only she could work for herself. But working for herself would need capital and she didn't have any. Louise was divorced too but in totally different circumstances from Amanda's. After fifteen years of being married to a man she disliked he finally left her, but he was so grateful she didn't seem to have noticed that he gave her fifty thousand pounds as well as the marital home. So she opened up a gallery with it. Giles, on the other hand, had given Amanda nothing, quite often failed to pay the maintenance even though his company was booming, and fiddled his income to appear one step up from a tramp if the question of the Child Support Agency ever arose. As a matter of fact, she'd yearned to open her own gallery while they were still married but Giles had always told her it was crazy.

The conversation at the book group drifted into her mind. Who was it who'd said a good husband would be one who encouraged you and made you feel you could do anything if you tried. Hah!

Amanda made the coffee, avoiding Louise's eye, and put the herons in the window, moving a gaudy plaster model of a Parisian street café out of the way.

'Not there!' protested Louise. 'Put it at the back somewhere. It'll frighten off all the customers.' She took a gulp of the strong black liquid. Louise had an asbestos throat and liked her coffee strong enough to keep Sleeping Beauty awake. 'You do make excellent coffee, Amanda. Now go and sell some scenes of lovely Laineton. Plus the window needs polishing. I distinctly saw a hand print on it.'

'We can't have that,' Amanda replied brightly, resisting the temptation to hit Louise with the plaster model. 'By the way, what are all those lorries doing up at the Eastcliff Estate?'

'God knows. Knocking it down, I hope. The place is an eyesore.'

'And home to a thousand people.'

'Yes, well, they should never have put a council estate this close to the seafront.'

'Better at the back of the town. Better still beyond the bypass?'

'Don't sound so bloody disapproving.' Louise lit up a fag and brandished it. 'Just because you've started doing a bit of recycling it doesn't make you a parliamentary candidate for a greener future.'

Louise's dig brought the image of the bottle bank and the damaged BMW sharply into focus. Amanda found her face suddenly a fiery red. 'You don't know anyone called Angus Day, do you?'

'Angus Day,' repeated Louise, blowing three smoke rings and grinning with smug satisfaction at their round perfection. 'Now you're talking. He could be my type all right. Rich. Nasty. Or at least a property developer, and they *have* to be nasty. Lives with his mother but nobody's perfect.' She fixed Amanda with a beady stare. 'Used to be married. No kids, sensible people. I don't suppose children would have fitted in with the lifestyle. Why do you ask?'

'As a matter of fact,' Amanda tried to make the whole thing sound boringly normal, 'I backed into him in Tesco's car park.'

Louise cackled with laughter. 'Oh, Amanda, you do lead an exciting life. What do you do on Saturdays, go all-night shopping?' She choked on her Marlboro. 'Anyway, what an extraordinary place for Angus Day to be. Maybe he's advising them on an out-of-town development.'

'He seemed to be taking his mother shopping, actually.'

'In Tesco's? Mean bunch, the Scots. You'd think he'd at least go to Marks and Spencer.'

'Anyway, I backed into his BMW and his mother told him to stop bullying me, so he ended up paying for all the damage to his car and mine too, except that there wasn't as much as I thought.'

'I hope you pretended there was.'

'Of course I didn't. I couldn't believe how generous he was.'

'Probably thought you'd go to the local paper if he made a fuss. "Property Spiv Leans on Single Mum." Not good.'

'You do have an extraordinary way of looking at life, Louise.'

'Besides, isn't that taking your desire to meet a man a little too far? Backing into his BMW? Angus Day definitely isn't the type you're after. You need one of those nice "New Men". I don't suppose he even knows where the kitchen is. Why else would someone his age live with his mother, except to be waited on hand and foot?'

Amanda didn't have time to speculate on Angus Day's motivation. The bell rang on the door and a customer arrived, enquiring about the price of the plaster model. To Amanda's irritation, they even bought it. Louise didn't even need to say, 'There, I told you so,' about the average Laineton customer's artistic preferences.

Chapter 3

Amanda couldn't believe how quickly the Christmas rush had descended upon them. Once December had arrived, Louise had extended their opening hours to meet the seasonal demands. The shop part of the gallery was doing a brisk trade in charity cards, musical Father Christmases and gifts for under a fiver. One party of pensioners had travelled fifty miles by coach to shop in Laineton, and by the sound of them had stopped at a pub or two on the way, and had noisily selected Beryl Cook reproductions of large ladies stripping off their even larger lingerie. For one nasty moment Amanda had thought they might follow suit and remove their own.

She was deeply grateful when Saturday closing time finally came, for once rather relieved that, as usual, she wasn't going to a wildly exciting dinner date but staying in with Sean to eat pizza and watch telly. This was their Saturday night ritual, while Clio went out with her friends.

During this busy period she was paying Clio extra pocket money to look after Sean till she got home, which Clio did extremely grudgingly and only after screwing an extortionate pay rise out of Amanda. Sometimes Amanda wondered why she bothered to work at all. The money only just covered the extra expense of paying Clio plus the childminder to supervise Sean in the holidays. But if – apart from the money – she didn't work she'd go mad sitting in all day contemplating the wreckage of her married life. Besides, at forty-one she was too young for an impoverished retirement.

Since Clio normally greeted her with, 'It's such a pain. Jasmine wanted me to go to her house but I couldn't because of *him*!', pointing to her brother as if he were the spawn of the devil when actually he was a very nice ten-year-old immersed in his Game Boy, Amanda was stunned to find her waiting in the kitchen with a cup of tea ready and a broad grin on her face.

'Hello. Not going out tonight?' Amanda enquired delicately. Clio, though sixteen, hadn't yet discovered boys. However, she did hang out with a group of girls, who watched the boys from a safe distance and mocked them.

'You've got some replies from your ad, Mum!' Clio waved three letters excitedly.

'How do you know they're from the ad?'

'Because I pass the paper's office on my way home and I couldn't resist checking. You had three letters waiting. Go on, open them!'

Amanda put down her bags and sat at the kitchen table. She felt oddly reluctant to open them now that the letters were here. It was so humiliating. 'I'll just drink this cup of tea first.'

'No! No! I want to know what they're like. This is so brilliant!'

'I'm not a live version of *Blind Date*, you know, laid on for your entertainment!' Feeling like a foolish teenager herself, Amanda opened the three letters. A photo fell out of one of them and Clio leapt on it.

'Oooh, look! He's really nice-looking.'

It was true that the face in the photograph was surprisingly attractive. At least he didn't have two heads, 'Loser' stamped on his forehead or look even vaguely like the killer in *Psycho*.

'I think he's really sweet,' Clio insisted. 'He reminds me of my gym teacher, Mr Butler, and we all fancy him rotten.'

'Which letter did it come with?' Amanda asked, picking up all three.

Clio made a face. 'Oh shoot, I don't know. Maybe he's written his name on the back.'

But the other side of the photograph was entirely blank.

'Sorry, Mum.' Clio looked stricken. 'We must be able to tell from the letters.' She grabbed them and read them all out.

'They all sound the same. Over thirty-five with a good sense of humour, own homes, divorced or widowed. Oh, this one sounds nice. Listen. "My friends tell me I've bored them long enough with why my marriage went wrong. It's time to close that chapter and open a new one. I sincerely hope it might be with you." Ah, Mum, he sounds just like you! He's bound to be the one in the photo. Look at those nice big eyes. His wife must have been mad to let him go. You've got to meet him. I mean, what harm could it do? If you didn't like him you'd never have to see him again.'

'I suppose that's true.'

'Come on, Mum, why did we bother to put in the ad if you're not going to follow it up?'

'Good question. Anyway, who's *we*, Paleface? I'm the one who's got to go and meet them all.' At that moment she couldn't think of anything worse.

The phone rang, distracting Clio from her mission. She ran to get it. 'It's Dad. He wants to talk about the travel arrangements for skiing.'

Giles was in a hurry. She could hear Stephanie in the background, shouting that they'd be late for some party. 'Hello, Amanda. I've got the tickets. I'll meet you at the airport at three p.m. on the twenty-second. Could you have them packed and ready with passports in their hands? The Great Outdoors will fix them up with ski suits and send me the bill and I'll do the spending money. If you could just sort out suncream and make sure they've got stuff for the evenings, that would be great. Got to dash. Sorry.'

Amanda felt a small and ignoble flash of satisfaction at how annoyed Stephanie probably felt at Giles going on holiday with Sean and Clio. She was being left behind too. Or maybe she felt relief at not having to be nice to Giles's children. Two weeks without Giles's bulldozing energy would probably be a blissful relief. She could relate to that.

Amanda put the phone down. Giles was being surprisingly

generous. She'd rather she got regular maintenance to pay for necessities instead of luxuries like this, but still.

The two weeks of their absence yawned miserably ahead. Two weeks of her mother telling her that she should get out more, meet a man, with only the book group to keep her sane. Their next read was Jilly Cooper's *How to Survive Christmas*, which Ruthie had found two copies of in a second-hand bookshop and was passing from reader to reader like some proscribed text in the former Soviet Union.

Amanda went back into the kitchen and looked once more at the Lonely Hearts letters. Now would be a perfect time to answer them yet somehow she didn't feel like it. Clio's voice echoed in her ears, asking why they had bothered to send off the ad if she wasn't going to follow it up. Then Louise's bossy tones chipped in, a Greek chorus reminding her that the days of freedom coming up were the perfect moment to look for a man. It *was* true that while Clio and Sean were away it might be easier for her to see what she thought of the senders, free from her children's second opinions.

Clio was right. Now had to be the moment. What did she have to lose?

Her dignity, that's what, she reminded herself as she went back to the phone and lost her nerve for the third time. She'd be a sad person who'd resorted to advertising herself, a social outcast reduced to meeting strange men under clocks. People would guess and point.

'Of course they won't,' she told herself firmly. 'People are far too caught up with their own lives to notice yours. Are you a woman or a mouse?'

Kinky the cat came and sat on her feet and rubbed herself against Amanda. 'You wouldn't be so friendly if I *were* a mouse, would you? You think I should go too, don't you?'

Kinky meowed.

'OK. Let's do it before I change my mind.'

The first question was where should she meet the first candidate?

She finally decided that the wine bar in the piazza of Laineton's shopping centre would be ideal. It was brightly lit, very busy and full of exit routes. Besides, if he didn't turn up she could pretend to be having a quick glass of Chardonnay before hitting the shops. There were always lots of other women in there. At least she wouldn't be chopped up into small pieces and posted back to her family. The biggest risk was not that of being diced into a julienne but of meeting someone she knew. Still, it was a risk she'd have to take. She certainly wasn't going to meet him anywhere dark, romantic and dangerous.

The second question was what to wear. 'Not too smart,' counselled Clio, who'd decided, to Amanda's annoyance, that she knew everything about dating via a newspaper ad. 'Men can't stand businesslike women. How about your pink angora?'

'I refuse to look fluffy on a first date,' Amanda had insisted. 'I'm not the fluffy type.'

'You don't have to tell him that. Men adore fluffy women.'

In the end she settled for a sea-green chenille jumper which did great things for her eyes and a pair of soft loose trousers. Clio would have told her to show off her excellent legs, but by this time Amanda had banned her from the bedroom.

'Where are you going, all dressed up?' Sean asked her suspiciously. He hated it when she looked smart because it meant she was going out. On this occasion, sensing the excitement in the air, he decided to be generous. 'You look beautiful,' he conceded.

When Amanda and Clio both chorused 'Aaah,' he retracted it slightly. 'For a mum.'

What Amanda felt was ludicrously nervous.

Thank God the wine bar was reasonably busy without being too crowded. Amanda found herself a corner where she could see the whole piazza, thereby ensuring she could check that Tony, for that was his name, looked reasonably OK before she confessed to being Amanda. They'd already talked briefly on the phone. He'd sounded nice; maybe it really *was* the beginning of a new chapter, as he'd put it rather sweetly in his letter. For both of them. And, best of all, Tony didn't sound even the tiniest bit like Giles.

It was corny, she knew, but she'd suggested he carry a copy of the local paper so she'd know it was him. She just hoped the place wouldn't be bursting with men carrying the *Laineton Evening Post*.

It took ages to catch the waitress's attention. The girl had obviously been on an advanced 'How to Avoid the Customer's Eye' course. Especially if they were single and female. Eventually, when there were no other customers left to serve, she graciously descended on Amanda.

'What can I get you? A glass of house white is it?'

Amanda, who had been on the point of ordering just that, felt nettled. 'Which white wines do you do by the glass?' she asked. She was damned if the girl was going to slot her into a category. 'Is the Chardonnay dry?'

The girl shrugged as if to say, 'I don't drink the stuff, not on my wages.'

'Hello there,' a male voice interrupted, making Amanda jump. 'Are you waiting for someone, or could I join you for a moment?'

Amanda flushed a fiery red. This was her worst nightmare come true. The man who'd greeted her wasn't Tony from the ad, it was Angus Day.

With typical property developer insensitivity, he sat down without even waiting for an answer. Admittedly, Amanda was too busy choking to come up with one. 'The thing is,' Angus continued, 'you were obviously in such a tearing hurry the other week that I didn't really get the chance to apologise properly.'

'Look,' Amanda began, desperate to get rid of him before Tony arrived, 'it really wasn't your fault. I reversed into you. You were extremely generous not to make a claim against me.'

'My mother said I was rude and overbearing.'

It was on the tip of Amanda's tongue to say maybe he should think for himself, but the twinkle in Angus Day's eye told her that he hadn't paid too much attention to his mother's remarks anyway. Then why *had* he been so generous?

Angus had already ordered not a glass but a whole bottle. Amanda noticed how willingly the waitress took *his* order, even adding a smile for good measure.

'So, how's life working in Laineton's premier art gallery?' he asked.

She might have argued with this description of The Wave, or

even wondered how on earth he knew where she worked, when she choked on her drink again.

Tony from the ad had arrived. His face had the familiar smile from the photograph, except for one difference: he was tiny. Not small, but *tiny*, about four foot ten inches in height. Amanda was exceptionally tall for a woman, and was at least a foot bigger than he was.

Surreptitiously she hid behind Angus, hating herself, telling herself there was nothing wrong with short people, that the seven dwarfs were utterly charming, while in her heart she knew that she and Tony would never hit it off.

She ducked behind Angus, only to find he was studying her face. He leaned back, delving into the pockets of his cashmere cardigan, ungallantly exposing her to Tony's gaze.

Tony, for his part, was trawling the tables, clutching his copy of the local paper and looking eager.

Oh shit! The paper was deliberately folded open on the Lonely Hearts page for easier identification. Amanda wanted to die. She was powerless to stop the telltale flush that covered her face and neck, giving her the look, she was sure, of a parboiled lobster. Her hands felt wet and clammy. Tony paused for a moment, near their table, and fixed his gaze on Amanda. Thank God the photo she'd supplied was so ancient. Even so, she should never have sent it. Oh God, she wanted to roll over and die.

Tony had obviously made his mind up. He strode, insofar as anyone of his restricted growth could, towards her.

A sudden spark of understanding flashed into Angus's eyes. She was sure he'd worked out what was happening. Amanda waited for the crack of laughter.

Instead, Angus turned and fixed the newcomer with a smile. 'Are you looking for something? Could either my wife or I help you?'

'I'm fine, thanks.' Tony looked from one to the other suspiciously, wondering whether to challenge Angus. He'd clearly decided Amanda was the woman in the photo. 'But if I were you, I'd keep an eye on your other half.'

Amanda yearned for the floor to open up, or for her body to be atomised into the ether so that she never had to face Angus Day again.

'Difficult, isn't it,' he said with surprising tact, pouring her another glass of wine, 'when your spouse suddenly ups and leaves you in the lurch.' There was no trace of a mocking smile, just straightforward sympathy. 'Mine walked out four years ago, ran off with my business partner so I never saw him again either.'

'How awful. Did you have any children?'

'Thankfully not.' Amanda thought she caught a shadow of pain in the words.

'Did she tell you why?'

'I was married to my job, apparently. Like Charles and Di, there were three players in our marriage, Laura told me. Me, her and my mobile phone.' He smiled ruefully, small grooves of laughter or pain appearing at the sides of his eyes. 'She had a point, as a matter of fact, though I didn't see it at the time. I'm now the only property developer you'll meet without a mobile. And I don't take calls at home. A bit late for my marriage unfortunately.'

'It must have been a shock.'

'Yes. How about you?'

Amanda felt suddenly embarrassed. 'Oh, the usual story, my husband left me for someone ten years younger. A colleague. She thinks he's wonderful. For now. And the worst thing,' Amanda realised she hadn't even told Ruthie or Louise this yet, she knew what their reaction would be, 'she's going to have a baby. Twins, in fact.'

'Not much variation in the range of human dramas, is there?' Angus replied.

'That doesn't stop them hurting like hell,' Amanda bristled. 'And each of them seems different to the people involved.'

'Sorry. I didn't mean to trivialise your situation.'

Amanda noticed that with gentle subtlety he'd avoided the word 'problems', and also that he was a surprisingly empathetic listener. She'd thought, given his reputation as a tough businessman, he'd only be interested in himself, but here he was pouring her another glass of wine and she was telling him things she'd hardly acknowledged herself.

'So.' He seemed to sense that she'd said enough. 'What's it like working for the dragon lady?'

Amanda smiled at this description of Louise. 'Oh, OK. It pays the bills – just. The only thing is, she and I have such different tastes.'

'Not easy in an art gallery. Doesn't having the same taste matter rather a lot?'

'Not in our position. She owns it, I'm the employee. She bought the place with her divorce settlement. She wanted to call it the Alimony Gallery. I don't suppose too many of our customers would have got the joke.'

'Now, now. Don't underestimate your public.'

'I don't!' Amanda felt instantly needled. What did someone as rich as Angus Day know about the common man anyway? 'In fact, it's the other way round. I believe the public has perfectly good taste, it's Louise who's convinced things won't sell. Only last week a young artist came in whose work I loved, but Louise refused point blank to take her on.'

'What was it like?'

Somehow, without her noticing, Angus had ordered another bottle and the waitress was pouring it out, smiling flirtatiously at him. Maybe he was a regular, on the look-out for unattached women. She flushed again, almost sure he'd worked out why she was here. How sad was that, as Clio would say.

'It was incredible. She'd carved some wooden birds, naturalistic yet abstract at the same time, if that isn't a contradiction in terms. She'd done the most fantastic nesting seagull drawn from one she'd seen on her roof right here in Laineton. I thought Louise might go for it for that alone, she loves the local touch. But no. And a wonderful pair of courting herons. We've actually taken those – on sale or return for three whole weeks! Generosity itself.'

'And if it had been your gallery you'd have done it differently?'

'If it had been my gallery I'd have given her a show!' Amanda hadn't even realised herself how passionate she felt about the girl's work.

'Then why don't you get your own gallery?'

Amanda laughed hollowly. 'Unfortunately my ex-husband isn't quite as generous as Louise's. In my case it'd have to be the Please Pay My Maintenance Gallery.'

'What about borrowing?'

'Who'd lend *me* money?'

'You're passionate enough. Combine that with a sound business plan. There are plenty of cheap premises about.'

'But surely I'd need capital?'

'I started with five hundred pounds.'

Amanda glanced at him. Somehow, from Angus Day's ease with himself, the way he wore expensive clothes so casually, she'd assumed he'd been born with money. And here he was encouraging her to take a punt. It was funny but no one, not her mother, certainly not Giles, not even Clio, had ever suggested that she go it alone, take a risk on what she believed in.

The discussion at the book group of what made a good husband flitted into her mind. Someone, Ruthie perhaps, or had it been mousy Anne, had said that a good husband was someone who encouraged you to spread your wings.

The sudden sense that the man sitting opposite was interesting and attractive made her self-conscious. She reached up to touch her neck in a familiar childish gesture of reassurance and managed to knock her glass of wine straight into Angus's lap.

'Oh God, I'm really sorry,' she blurted, Giles's constant accusations of how clumsy she was ringing in her ears. She was so embarrassed that she dabbed at him with a paper hankie before she realised that the wine was all over his crotch.

Angus laughed. 'Don't worry, I've got dozens of these trousers. I hate shopping so I always wear the same combination. My assistant says I should go and work in China. I'd look the same as everyone else there apparently.'

'I really must go.' Amanda realised how long she'd been sitting there. Clio would be sure she'd been murdered by now. She glanced round to make sure Tony the Lonely Heart wasn't still lurking.

'I think he's gone,' Angus said, his face deadpan.

He really had guessed that she was a sad, desperate woman

reduced to advertising in the paper for a date. Amanda wished she were anywhere else on the universe. Any moment he was bound to say, 'I can't think why someone like you would need to advertise for a man.'

Instead he grinned at her, ignoring the embarrassing damp patch on his trousers, and said, 'Anyway, it's been very pleasant sharing a glass of wine with someone as charming and intelligent as you.'

He really was quite something. Instead of humiliating her he'd actually managed to make her feel flattered. A small flame of excitement, a distant memory of how it felt to be in the company of an attractive man who clearly found *you* attractive, lit up Amanda.

'At least let me pay for that last bottle of wine,' she insisted and beckoned the waitress over, offering her credit card.

'Fine,' he shrugged, smiling, 'only I don't think they take Blockbuster video cards.'

Amanda looked away, feeling foolish. How could she have muddled her cards up like that?

'By the way,' Angus added, 'you know the herons you mentioned? I might come and look at them.'

Amanda bit her lip. Was he saying he wanted to see the herons or her? 'Of course, here's our card. We're open till six most nights.'

'Thanks. Perhaps you could advise me. I've got to get a special present for a very special person. And I think the herons might really mean something to her.'

His words were like a vicious wind, blowing out the tiny light of attraction in Amanda. How stupid of her to think that someone like him would be unattached. He was rich, straight, charming. And he had a very special someone in his life.

'I'll look forward to it,' she managed to say before scuttling off towards the car park.

'And don't forget your idea about the gallery,' he called out.

But that, like Angus Day fancying her, had just been a silly notion too.

Chapter 4

'Jesus, Mum, where have you been all this time? I mean, you met the guy at six. It's almost eleven now!'

'I am forty-one, you know, and just about able to take care of myself.'

'Yes, Amanda.' Her mother's disapproving tones rang out from the sitting room. 'I really do think you could have let us know you were safe!'

'What's Gran doing here?' Amanda mouthed.

'Sorry,' hissed Clio. 'I called her up because I really was getting a bit worried. I didn't think she'd come steaming round.'

'GG would never miss out on a crisis. Especially one involving me being murdered by a man I picked up through a Lonely Hearts ad. I expect she's rubbing her hands with glee.'

'Anyway,' Clio whispered, 'he must have been quite something if you spent this long with him. I *knew* I was right to get you to advertise.'

'Actually,' Amanda gave her daughter an affectionate hug, 'I never met him. I could see from first glance he wasn't my type so I pretended not to be me.'

'Oh.' Clio's disappointment was touching. 'I really wanted you to meet a nice man.'

'And the funny thing is, I did. Only he's obviously involved with someone else.'

'Only involved? Not married?'

'I don't think so.'

'Time you were in bed, young lady,' Helen announced, appearing from the sitting room, an expensive-looking coat draped over her arm. Helen had sickeningly good taste in clothes.

'Yes,' said Amanda, deliberately misunderstanding her mother, 'at forty-one I need my beauty sleep.'

'I don't mean you,' sniffed her mother. 'Anyway, I don't know what you were thinking of. Meeting strange men in wine bars. Men loathe desperate women, you know. They can sniff it. Not that I had any problems. I only had to bat my eyelashes and doors would open for me.'

'How amazing,' Amanda replied, opening the front door with a flourish. 'Look, it still works.'

Helen swept grandly through. 'Why don't I ask around at the golf club? Anything would be better than my middle-aged daughter hanging round wine bars. How do you know they're not serial killers using the paper to find their victims? Lonely, sex-starved women with no families . . .'

'I'll be all right then. I'll just tell any serial killer I've got a bossy mother, a son who's a black belt in karate, and a daughter with a mobile phone who can reach a dangerous gang of sixteen-year-olds in ten seconds flat.'

'I don't think you're taking this very seriously.'

'I'm trying not to. Look, it was only going to be a chat in a very public, brightly lit wine bar.'

'Oh my God, did you see anyone we know?' The shame of having a daughter who was that desperate occurred to Helen and she shuddered. 'These men who advertise in newspapers, how do you know they aren't just after sex? They probably know single women of your age will do *anything* to get a man.'

'Now you mention it, that's an excellent idea. Maybe I should reword my ad. "Attractive forty-one-year-old seeks adventure and fun. A free screw with every date."'

She shut the door before she could hear her mother's protests.

Back in the cosy sitting room where the last embers were dying down in the fire, and Kinky the cat was pretending to be a hearthrug, Clio flopped onto the sofa and giggled. 'How was it really?'

'Apart from the fact I was a foot taller than him? To be honest, I don't think Lonely Hearts columns are for me. I need to get to know someone a bit before I can fancy them.' Actually, Amanda reminded herself, this wasn't strictly true. She didn't know Angus Day very well at all and she'd managed to fancy him. 'Maybe I'm just not quite enough of a saddo yet.'

'Some hope for the future then. We'll just have to find another way of meeting men. Actually, our new PE teacher's quite tasty; why don't I put in a good word for you? You could blow his whistle.'

'Come on,' Amanda pretended not to hear her comment, 'time for bed. School tomorrow. Was Sean OK?'

'Yep. I made sure GG didn't yap on about sex-starved serial killers in front of him. He thinks grown-ups are pretty weird about love anyway.'

'Not surprisingly.'

Clio glanced at her mother. 'Do you miss Dad?'

'I miss the early years. We had some very good times. But not recently.' Maybe this was the time to broach the subject she'd been putting off in the hope that Giles would bring it up first. But Giles wasn't the most tactful person. If she didn't tell Clio and Sean soon he'd probably blurt it out and spoil their entire holiday. 'Clio, love, I wanted to tell you, Dad and Stephanie are going to have a baby. Maybe even two.'

'Oh really?' Clio's voice was shaking slightly and had a sharp edge of bitterness. 'Dad so enjoyed being a father first time round, did he, that he can't wait to repeat the experience? How sweet.' Amanda reached out to her.

'When?'

'Not for a few months yet.'

'Is that why she isn't coming skiing?'

'Yes.'

'Pity. I could have pushed her down a mountain and killed the little brats.'

Amanda was taken aback by Clio's venom. She had tried to protect her children from the violence of the emotions swirling around during their break-up and be as civilised as she could. Maybe that hadn't been such a good policy after all.

'Go on,' Clio instructed, 'say you hate the bitch and you hope she has a two-headed monster.'

Amanda laughed and pulled Clio into a big, loving hug. She was such a fantastic child and Giles, never interested in children, had always failed to see it. 'I hate the bitch and I hope she has a two-headed monster.'

'Hey, how about if they *do* have twins? Then they'd have *two* little two-headed monsters. That'd serve Dad right.'

'I love you, Clio.'

'Thanks, Mum. I know you do.' She started going upstairs, then stopped. 'And Dad? What do you think about him?'

This was the question she dreaded. She couldn't admit to Clio that her father was vain, silly and weak; that seeing his own children start to grow up had made him jealous instead of proud, and that he'd had to go out and prove he was still young in the most obvious way possible.

Rubbishing the mistress was permissible in this situation but rubbishing their father seemed somehow unfair.

Astonishingly, Clio seemed to understand. 'Don't worry,' she whispered. 'His secret's safe with me.'

Several more replies to Amanda's advertisement came in over the following week but she decided to ignore them. At work, Louise was driving her mad. She kept suddenly interrupting Amanda when she was talking a customer through a painting, just at the very moment they were about to make a purchase, then taking the credit for having made the sale. She even had the gall to criticise Amanda for not selling enough paintings. Angus Day's advice about setting up on her own kept coming back to her, but despite the irritations of Louise, she wasn't sure she felt confident enough to go it alone.

Then a very curious thing happened. Out of the blue, with no apparent explanation, an estate agent's flyer arrived, addressed to her. It featured a boathouse at the very edge of the town, near the small harbour next to the run-down beach huts. It had already been converted by the previous occupant, a tyre replacement company, who'd stored all the spare tyres in the large roof space and used the ground floor as a reception area. Amanda felt suddenly dizzy with possibilities. Was Angus behind this? She went on reading, her mind fizzing with possibilities.

Then there was the catch. One year's ground rent was required. A sum she couldn't possibly afford.

All the same, she couldn't resist looking, so during her lunch hour the next day she walked down to the water's edge.

The boathouse was in a quiet backwater at the far end of the harbour, immediately beyond the Eastcliff council estate. The view would have been picturesque except for the boarded-up shops and overflowing dustbins that marked this end of town. Just below the boathouse was the chalet belonging to the Miles sisters, as well as the rows of beach huts, once brightly painted and attractive, now faded and peeling like glamorous old ladies who'd lost all their money and gone into decline.

Still, Amanda reminded herself, if the area were picturesque like the rest of Laineton, the boathouse would be three times the price. On the down side, there was a chance that browsers and tourists, maybe even the locals, wouldn't bother to walk this far along and that would be commercially disastrous.

The building was locked and unoccupied but one glance inside made Amanda's heart race. It was dull and peeling now but the interior was amazing, full of light and beams and with an almost church-like quality. It would need hardly any structural work to convert it into a workable space. She would simply have to reduce the size of the ugly reception area until it was just big enough for a till island, paint the whole thing a dazzling white, perhaps with Shaker-blue paintwork . . . Amanda had to pull herself down to earth. She hadn't even come to a decision about starting up on her own. Did she really want the risk and the worry when she was already struggling to pay all the bills, run a car and keep up the mortgage payments with only erratic help from Giles? She could end up in a far worse financial mess than she was already. It would be mad. She shouldn't even be fantasising about it.

It was the end of her lunch break and Louise was in a clock-watching mood; Amanda had better get back. On her way she passed the edge of the Eastcliff Estate. She knew the builders had been working on it for months, but the activity seemed more frantic today. It was strange. Half of the flats appeared to be empty and the bulldozers stood by, as if ready to gobble them up.

'Have you found out any more about what's going on up at the estate?' she asked Louise when she got back to The Wave Gallery. 'I've just seen about three lorries go up there in the last five minutes.'

Louise looked as smug as Puss in Boots. 'Didn't you know? It's your friend Angus Day. He's done some deal with the council and the tenants are up in arms about it. It's been terribly hush-hush. He showed them lots of plans to make improvements, but they think it's all a front, that he just wants to get his hands on it for the location. I must admit it was weird of someone to build a council estate on top of the cliff, in full view of Laineton seafront.'

'Maybe they thought council tenants deserved a nice view too.'

'They haven't exactly shown their appreciation then. It's a tip. Graffiti everywhere. Broken glass in the bus shelters, old ladies frightened to go out at night. Anyway, the tenants are convinced he's going to turn the place into luxury flats and charge rents they'll never be able to afford. Good thing too, in my view, but he's the big bad bogey man up there.'

'Surely he couldn't do that if they all belong to the council? Where have all the old tenants gone, anyway?'

'They've been rehoused. Pity it's not in John O'Groats.'

Amanda was appalled. Didn't Angus have any scruples at all about taking away people's homes for his own profit? No wonder he could afford a new BMW. She wished she'd done more damage now.

'Well, what I think he should do is . . .' began Louise in her usual Wagnerian tones. She cut herself short, conscious that the object of her advice, Angus Day himself, had just walked into the shop.

Amanda looked round to see what irresistible force had stopped Louise mid-sentence. 'Good God,' Amanda greeted him, as if the devil himself had jumped off a gargoyle and come to life in front of her. 'What are *you* doing here?'

'I've come to look for that present I mentioned.' Angus looked less like a big bad property shark and more like a small boy being told off by his teacher.

'Terrific,' purred Louise, descending on him like a hawk on a field mouse. 'And what sort of budget did you have in mind? Four hundred? Five hundred? Silly me, that sort of sum probably doesn't really worry you.'

'No, obviously not.' He caught Amanda's eye and winked. 'What with my being such a chronic exploiter of the poor. But it would worry the person I'm giving it to. I think she'd prefer something more modest.'

Louise's feathers drooped a little. 'Ah. So you wouldn't like that fabulous oil of "Laineton Sands in Summer" then?' She pointed to a hideous pink and red, four-foot-high creation. 'It's a snip at five hundred. He's Laineton's very own Matisse.'

'I'm a bit of a Picasso man myself,' Angus replied.

If she hadn't been so furious with him, Amanda would have giggled. Instead she busied herself with sorting out cards. She thought of the council tenants, all of them families and probably a lot of lone parents, as she was, who had been shoved into smelly bed and breakfasts to make way for Angus's luxury flats.

'How about this adorable watercolour?' Louise suggested. 'It's called "Dusk Over Downland". Is the lucky lady a country lover?'

'No,' Angus smiled wryly. 'She hates the country. Give her the city any day. The busier the better.'

Despite herself, Amanda couldn't help building up a picture of Angus's lady friend. Sleek. Sophisticated. Urban. She probably found even Laineton, a place most city dwellers loved, too provincial for words.

'Actually,' Angus finally interrupted as Louise reached for a sub-pointillist evocation of Laineton's Pier, 'I gather you have a sculpture of a pair of herons.'

Louise scowled at Amanda. She'd hoped to sell him something far pricier than those. 'Perhaps you'd better get them, Amanda.'

Louise had hidden the carvings on the highest shelf in the shop, so that Amanda had to stand on a chair to get them. As she did so, she sensed his eyes linger on her legs and felt a crazy and quite unsuitable longing that he reach out and touch her.

Instead she said, matter of factly, reminding herself that he was a bully and maybe even one step away from corrupt, 'Do you mean these?'

He took the pair of herons and studied them. 'These are beautiful,' he said. 'Absolutely perfect. They'll remind her of home. I couldn't have found her a better present. Thank you.'

Even though she still felt angry with him, Amanda couldn't repress a flash of jealousy at the excitement in his voice. What would it be like to have someone who went to so much trouble for you? Giles's presents, even for her birthday, had tended to be flowers hastily bought at a service station or Ferrero Rocher chocolates. In all their years of marriage, he'd never taken in the fact that she hated the things.

She folded the herons into crisp white tissue paper with quite unnecessary brusqueness.

'For heaven's sake, Amanda,' snapped Louise, her coloured glass earrings wobbling with irritation, 'ask Mr Day if he'd like them gift-wrapped.'

'Would you?' Amanda asked. 'They're very awkward.'

'Rather like you,' Angus Day said so softly she couldn't be sure she'd heard him correctly.

He was flirting with her! What kind of man would flirt with one woman while buying a particularly special present for another? No wonder his wife had left him. He was the type who probably chatted-up the air hostesses on his honeymoon.

'Here's a box,' Louise offered, looking daggers at Amanda, 'wrap them in this.'

Amanda undid the original wrapping, made a nest out of more tissue paper, then added a top sheet of bright blue paper before tucking the herons snugly in. They looked blissfully comfortable.

'By the way,' Amanda added in a low voice when Louise disappeared to deal with another customer, 'did you get the estate agent to send me details about the Old Boathouse?'

Angus shrugged. 'Would I encourage you to give up your stable, if badly paid, job,' he asked in a low voice, 'to do something wild and risky?'

'Probably.' Amanda put the box in a Wave Gallery carrier bag and tied a blue bow on to the string handle. She thought suddenly of all the people whose homes he was taking, while he idled away his time buying presents and flirting, and she felt furiously angry with him. 'By the way,' she retorted, 'I'd probably lose my badly paid yet stable job if Louise heard me saying this, but I'm going to anyway. I think what you're doing to the Eastcliff Estate is terrible. Not everyone in the world can afford BMWs, you know. But the one thing they all want, even the poorest ones, is a decent home!' Without her noticing, Amanda's voice had risen in volume. 'So I hope you're ashamed of yourself, turning their homes into luxury townhouses!'

Angus looked at her through narrowed eyes, his flirtatious manner evaporating. 'I don't think I need you to tell me what people want from a home,' he snapped, his voice as sharp as flint on granite. 'At the risk of sounding like a *Monty Python* sketch, when I was a kid I lived for ten years in a tenement block. My bed was behind a curtain in the kitchen. Perhaps that's what people like you would call en-suite?'

From across the other side of the shop, like Boadicea in blue velvet, Louise strode over. 'Is something the matter?'

'No,' Angus replied smoothly, 'I was just asking to be kept informed if you get any more pieces by this artist.'

'Oh.' Louise looked almost disappointed.

Together they watched Angus walk out through the door of the shop, which had been wedged open by a man delivering picture-framing materials. Angus, Amanda noticed, had the top of his car down even though it was December.

'How pretentious,' Amanda announced, far too loudly. 'He probably looks at himself in shop windows while he's driving it.'

'They do say,' Louise added, fortunately in a less penetrating tone than Amanda's, 'that only men with small cocks drive cars like that, but I can't believe it's true of Angus Day.'

'I have no idea,' Amanda said primly, 'and absolutely no desire to find out.'

'Then you're the only woman in Laineton who doesn't,' Louise sighed.

Angus Day drove off, aware that the two women were still watching him. He felt furious with Amanda. There was nothing he loathed more than people who made moral judgments when they didn't know the facts. Until that moment he'd warmed to her, felt she had a natural sympathy, and the incident with the Lonely Hearts advertisement had touched and amused him. She was clearly such a novice. But perhaps he'd been wrong in assuming she was different from most of the women he met. Small-town disapproval was one thing he couldn't stomach.

He drove too fast, knowing he shouldn't be doing it but enjoying the feeling of speed all the same, out of Laineton and into the countryside behind. He loved driving with the roof down, not because he liked looking at himself in shop windows as Amanda had suggested, but because he took a small boy's pleasure in the beauty of his machine. After his father had gone bankrupt, suddenly, overnight, they'd had to move from relative comfort to a tiny, cold flat. There'd been no money for extras, only for survival, and he'd longed, so badly he could still taste it, for a cobalt-blue remote-control sports car. Now he had a real one.

After ten minutes of cleansing speed, he drew up outside a pretty gatehouse next to two impressive flint gates, each with a stone globe on the top, which heralded the start of a long sweeping drive through parkland to the large, square, Georgian farmhouse he lived in alone. He'd bought this place because he liked the solid proportions and because his mother could be near but have her own home.

Isobel Day was fiercely independent. Even now she insisted on doing all her own cooking and cleaning, even though her son could more than afford to pay other people to do it. And while he longed to make her life cosy and comfortable, a chintzy view of things was the last thing Isobel wanted.

Instead she had let him furnish her house simply, and perhaps a little austerely, in muted greens and blues that echoed the sea surrounding the Hebrides where she'd grown up. As a concession to her past she'd allowed him to cover her wing chair in wildly expensive, silky-soft, lavender tweed, which would have been equally at home as a Chanel suit. It was in this chair that Isobel was sitting when Angus arrived. Even now, when she'd been diagnosed with cancer, Isobel told everyone not to make a fuss and pretended nothing had changed.

Angus had let himself in with his own key because he knew that at this time in the afternoon she'd be having her rest, tucked up in her favourite chair with a rug and a cup of Earl Grey, a hot-water bottle behind her back, watching *Countdown*. She affected to dislike television but took huge pleasure in getting the answers before the contestant did.

'Hello, Maw.' He affected this special pronunciation from a favourite song she'd sung him as a child. It started, 'There were three craws greeting for their maw . . .' He couldn't remember the rest. He must ask her some time. He kissed the top of her short grey crop. 'You missed that one.' He pointed to the clue on the television.

Isobel swatted him with her magazine. 'You put me off.'

'Ah ha,' he teased, grabbing it, 'the *Daily Telegraph* TV guide. For a woman who never watches the box, it looks pretty well-thumbed.'

'I was just recording a few programmes for Marjorie.' Marjorie was Isobel's golf partner. 'The pathetic woman can't even set a video machine to save her life.'

'Of course you were.' He glanced round at the log fire, the polished wood of her small dining table, the small footstool she'd embroidered in lavender and the greeny-blue velvet curtains.

Unconsciously, the thought occurred to him that they were the same colour as Amanda Wells's eyes.

All the same, he admired his mother's quiet efficiency. She would never let something as trivial as a video machine get the better of her. She'd study the handbook. Just as she'd struggled to give him and his father a clean shirt, and decent clothes, and not let anyone feel sorry for them just because they'd slipped down the social scale. Isobel Day believed in getting on with things with a quiet stoicism.

The only trouble was, there were some things not even Isobel's willpower could control. And he wished she'd be a bit less bloody stoical about those.

'How're you feeling today?'

Isobel stiffened.

'Did the Macmillan nurse arrive on time?'

'Yes.'

'How did she say you were?'

'She said I was as well as could be expected.' A small ironic smile crossed Isobel's lips. 'For someone with terminal cancer.'

Angus winced. 'She didn't.'

'No. She didn't. She said to take things day by day.'

Angus lifted her hand and squeezed it. Life had been unfair to Isobel. 'Don't. You've never given up on anything. You'll live to ninety.'

'I wouldn't count on it. Or even my next birthday. Luckily you aren't the type to buy things ahead.'

'And that's where you're wrong,' Angus grinned, delighted that for once she'd read him incorrectly. 'I have bought you something and it's not even for your birthday.' He produced the carrier bag from its hiding place in the hall.

'You know I don't like presents.' Isobel shook her head. 'Besides, what's the point? I won't be here long to appreciate it. Complete waste of money.'

'Look at it first.'

As she unwrapped the gift, Angus noticed how transparent her skin had become, thinner even than the tissue paper she was unwrapping.

She undid one layer of paper, then the next. 'Is this pass the parcel or something?' she asked testily.

Angus just smiled.

Finally she got to the two carvings nestling inside. 'Herons!' A thin thrill of excitement lit up her voice. 'I used to watch them all the time when I was a girl. They'd stand in the river for hours on one leg, then catch a fish and swoop off into the sky with their great wings beating.' A smiling glow had warmed her drained-out features, giving them more colour than he'd seen for months. 'These are beauties! Look at the smoothness of the carving.'

'You stand them like this.' He placed the two statues face to face. The birds were looking upwards, as if contemplating the stars, their necks outstretched. 'They're courting. It's part of the ritual, apparently.'

'That I never saw. I suppose it's the same the whole world over, man or animals or birds. The continuation of the species is what drives them.'

Angus saw the drift of the conversation and tried to head it off. 'There are other things in life besides procreation, you know.'

'Hah!' said his mother. 'Tell the herons that. Or the great crested grebes or any other species you care to name. Or your cousin Flora, for that matter. She's about to have her sixth, did you know that?' She fixed him with a focused gaze. 'I wish you'd meet some-one. Since Laura left, you only seem to be interested in cladding and ready-mixed concrete.'

Angus shrugged. 'Safer maybe. As a matter of fact, I did meet someone I liked.' He wondered if he should mention that his mother had already met her and decided against it. He'd rather give the thing more time to grow. 'It was she who told me about the herons.'

'Ah ha.'

'But I don't think she has too high an opinion of me. She thinks I'm a scourge of the underprivileged and that I only take the roof of my car down so I can look at myself in shop windows.'

Isobel smiled a pure, wide grin of amusement. 'I like the sound of her. And do you?'

'Do I what?'

'Take the roof of your car down to look at yourself in shop windows?'

Angus looked wounded. 'Of course I don't.'

'I wouldn't blame you,' she said surprisingly. 'We didn't have mirrors in our house. My father thought it was ungodly. So I used to put my lipstick on staring into the kettle.'

Angus cracked with laughter at this unlikely image of his mother.

'You'd be surprised how many polished surfaces there are, even in a God-fearing house. Metal teapots. Glass picture frames. My father used to go on for so long about polishing your shoes till you could see your face in them that I even used those once.'

'You put your lipstick on using his shoes as a mirror?'

'It gave me particular pleasure, I can tell you.'

'Maw, you're wonderful.' He hugged the once-strong body. She'd always been lean and lithe and proud of her looks when she was young. 'I love this picture of Isobel, the wilful make-up addict,' Angus said.

'It was only a bit of lipstick. Anyway, don't change the subject. I'd like to meet her, this girl of yours.'

Angus almost told her she already had, but hesitated. 'Well, she's not exactly a girl. She's about forty.'

'Forty! An old maid!' Isobel was shocked. 'She'll be fixed in her habits and make you fit in with her spinsterish ways.'

'Actually, she's not a spinster. She's been married . . .'

'A divorcee . . .!' Isobel's tone couldn't have been more disapproving if he'd brought Lucrezia Borgia home. 'Probably a gold-digger into the bargain. I suppose she's got a brood of some other man's children she'll be wanting you to support!'

'I think she has a son and a daughter. But their own father supports them.' He didn't add that their father wasn't the most reliable provider of maintenance. 'Look, Maw, this is mad. I hardly know her really . . .'

'Perhaps you'd better leave it that way. Work's a great consolation, I always say.'

Angus shrugged at his mother's contrariness. She wanted him to find a wife yet was convinced every woman he met had designs on her son's hard-won wealth. 'Time for your sleep now. The herons are here on this table so you can remember your girlhood when you look at them.' He tucked her in and put the remote control where she could reach it. 'Not that you'll be watching any TV, of course.'

'Wisht!' said Isobel, smiling faintly. 'As sons go, I suppose you aren't too bad.'

'Why don't you move in with me then, where I can really look after you?'

'I want to die in my own home,' Isobel insisted waspishly. 'I waited long enough for it.'

Angus hesitated. 'I hate leaving you like this.'

'If the Grim Reaper comes to call I'll offer him some Earl Grey and a shortbread biscuit, how's that?'

'I'd rather you told him you don't let in callers. Especially suspicious-looking ones in long black robes with no faces.'

'Get on with you. You've been watching too much Bergman. Just because you had to leave university and save your father's business, you like to be one up on the ignorant masses.'

'You're a wicked woman, Isobel Day.'

'I have to have some pleasures left to me. Off with you.'

'By the way,' Angus suddenly said, just as he was going out of the door, 'you have met her, the woman I was talking about. She's called Amanda. She's the person who backed into my BMW in the car park.'

'As long as it wasn't her daughter. Too young for you.'

'Ma, really. I do have some judgment.'

'You're a change from most men then,' announced Isobel, and put the TV back on.

The next two weeks passed in a blur for Amanda. The gallery was packed with gift hunters and in her lunch breaks she had to buy and wrap Clio and Sean's Christmas presents so they could take them skiing, as well as sort out their ski gear and get them packed for their holiday with their father.

'What do you want for Christmas, sweetie?' she asked Sean in the five minutes between him waking up, getting dressed and leaving for school.

'A David Beckham haircut,' Sean replied without a blink of hesitation.

Amanda gulped. The thought of her precious curly-haired choir boy submitting himself to the Number One razor and coming out looking like a skinhead made her feel sick.

'No, darling, not at the moment.' She searched desperately for a convincing reason.

'All my friends've got it. They say I'm a sissy.'

'You'll catch cold skiing,' Amanda offered lamely, wondering if she wasn't being mean to deprive her son of the approval of his peers. When you were a lone parent you either had to give up on authority altogether or be strict enough for two. But then Giles had always given in anyway.

'No, darling. You shouldn't just follow the herd.'

Sean slammed his cereal bowl down on the table so that the contents jumped out, his usually sweet-natured face contorted with anger. He'd inherited his father's good looks, blond and blue-eyed. 'You always say no!' he accused. 'None of the other mothers do!'

Amanda snapped. She always had to be the bad guy because there was no Giles to share the difficulties of bringing up children with.

'Tough. Talk to your father about it.'

This was a tactical error. Giles never listened to the children when they talked to him. He'd probably say yes without even meaning to and then her lovely boy would come home with a shaven head and probably a swastika tattoo for good measure.

Sean grabbed his school bag. The scowl disappeared like the sun coming out from behind storm clouds. 'Love you, Mum. That was all crap about everyone having Beckham haircuts. Only Baz does.' Baz was the class cool guy.

Sean's honesty was so endearing that she had to overlook the language. This was what made him so easy to love. Even when he was a screaming, kicking ball of aggression one minute, which fortunately was very rare, the next moment he'd be his usual sunny self again.

She pulled him into her arms. Even though he was ten he still let her do this on occasion, provided none of his friends were looking. If they were, he treated her like a highly infectious plague-carrier.

After Sean had left she leafed through the Manchester United catalogue. The away strip Sean yearned for was ludicrously expensive. Amanda told herself she shouldn't be swayed by wanton commercialism but sent off for it all the same. She'd economise during the two weeks she had on her own. Two weeks! What would she do with herself? Her life revolved around Sean and Clio so entirely that she sometimes resented it, but now that she was faced with some time without them all she felt was panic. She'd just have to discover the old Amanda. The girlie, flirty person she was before she'd met Giles. Funny how Giles had been drawn to her party-girl personality, then, after they were married, had done everything he could to stamp on it.

Bloody Giles. Why did he and Stephanie have to go and have twins? Stephanie was the least maternal person Amanda had ever met, forever counting calories and going to step classes. It was impossible to imagine her with baby goo on one of her pastel jumpers. Surely Clio and Sean would feel second-best? She laughed at the memory of Clio wishing for two-headed monsters. At least Clio talked about her feelings. Sean was far harder.

Out of anger at Giles she added a Manchester United backpack to her order. Giles could pay for it.

But what could she get Clio? Amanda thought about her daughter while chewing on the tip of her biro. Clio was tall, like her mother, but wand-like instead of large-framed. Although very much a child in body, she was given to occasional flashes of such maturity that she sometimes seemed about thirty-two.

Clothes were always a no-no for Clio. She was incredibly fussy and Amanda always got it wrong. Sometimes Amanda longed for the days when she'd bought all Clio's outfits, lovely frilly, brightly coloured frocks, and Clio had put them on obediently and twirled round for everyone to admire her. Distant memories. Besides, Clio didn't like surprises. She preferred to be given the money and to buy it all herself. It was easier, but it still made Amanda rather sad.

She'd spent so long dawdling around and wondering about Christmas presents that she was going to be late opening up the gallery if she wasn't careful, and Louise would be livid. She put on her warm coat, pulled on her gloves and scarf and walked briskly towards the seafront.

The air was clear and cold – perfect winter weather. The gulls wheeled around her, hoping for bread. She decided to take a short cut along the lower promenade, partly because it was quicker and partly because the sea was so beautiful today, pale green and pellucid, like painted Venetian glass.

'Hello, dear, lovely morning, isn't it?' It was one of the Miles sisters, calling up from their chalet near the beach. Amanda sighed. It was Betty, the chatty one. Rose, the other sister, was almost entirely silent, just filled in the odd gap in Betty's speech. Not that there were many.

'I'm going for a swim,' Betty announced and opened her towelling robe to reveal a puckered and saggy floral costume, made up of small elastic sections, giving her the air of a sponge cake that had been left for decades on a cake cooling tray.

Amanda shivered. It was mid-December and however inviting and calm the sea looked it would be blood-chillingly cold. 'Doesn't it look lovely?' trilled Betty, striding off in her ancient plastic beach shoes, tucking her hair into a pink bathing cap.

'It'll be a bit warm for her,' announced Rose, appearing from inside the chalet. 'She likes breaking the ice.'

Amanda waved goodbye, wondering what had become of all the famed British toughness that characterised these sisters. Once upon a time Britain seemed to produce ladies like this by the score. Memsahibs, lone female explorers, butterfly hunters who consorted with their bearers, blue-stockinged Cambridge dons. Maybe central heating and too much daytime television had sapped the will of succeeding generations, but they didn't seem to make ladies like this any more.

Amanda arrived at the gallery at precisely 9.27 a.m., having sprinted the last few yards. By 9.30 she was behind the cash till with the door unlocked and the coffee on. So far there were no customers.

Only Ruthie, who suddenly rushed into the shop bearing a pile of books. 'Book group meeting early January. I've bought it for you since you're stuck in the shop. My little gift.' She plonked down a bright pink, stocking-filler-sized version of *Men Are from Mars, Women Are from Venus*. 'Should be food for thought.'

Louise arrived at that moment. 'You'll come too, Louise, to the next book group, won't you?' Ruthie pressed. Louise sometimes turned up with Amanda, but never if something better was offered. 'We're discussing whether men and women come from different planets.'

'I haven't got time for reading at the moment,' Louise replied. Her numerous necklaces and earrings tinkled with superiority. 'This is my busiest time. I make a third of my turnover in the next two weeks.'

'You should stay open twenty-four hours. Like Tesco's,' Ruthie teased.

'Don't encourage her,' shuddered Amanda.

'Actually, that's not a bad idea . . . only joking!'

'When are Clio and Sean off skiing?'

'I'm taking them to the airport on Thursday afternoon.' Amanda busied herself with sorting out the card stand, to cover up the sudden wave of pain. What if there was an accident or a ski-lift disaster? She'd be miles away. She told herself to calm down. The greatest risk for them would probably be spending too long on arcade games while their father drank in the bar.

'How long will they be away?'

'Two weeks.' Actually it felt like two years.

'Excellent. I hope you're going to make the most of it.'

'My mantelpiece is thick with invitations,' Amanda replied loftily. This was true but they were all to carol concerts, parents' evenings and yet another performance of *The Sound of Music* by Clio's school.

'So you won't be able to make it to my New Year's Eve party

then?' Louise asked, her head jauntily to one side. 'That's a pity because I've just met the most perfect man for you. He's here organising the Laineton Festival. Scores one hundred per cent on the anti-Giles-ometer. Handsome, intelligent, helps old ladies across the road and he's incredibly empathetic with women.'

Amanda listened suspiciously. 'Bound to be gay. Sounds gay to me.'

'Nope,' Louise winked lasciviously. 'I've got references.'

'What do you mean, you've references?' Amanda couldn't help being intrigued. 'What kind of references? "A truly marvellous orgasm," Mrs F. Ward, Sunningdale. "I now know the meaning of 'the earth moved'," Susan Brown, Walton Forest.'

'Not quite. He went out with a friend of mine. Let's just say he's definitely straight.'

'And what's this paragon of modern manhood called?' Ruthie enquired.

'His name's Luke Knight. So you'll come, Amanda?'

'Maybe.'

'By the way, how's the big bad property developer? Did he get in touch again?'

'Of course not,' Amanda said, rather too quickly. 'I didn't expect him to. Anyway, all he's interested in is profit. What he's doing up at Eastcliff is diabolical.'

'Oh, Amanda, stop being so *worthy*,' Louise said. 'Besides, it was obvious from the way you were being rude to him that you fancied the pants off him.'

'I did not.'

'Good. Because he'd only hurt you. What he needs is a woman who doesn't have any scruples about being nasty to the underprivileged and would help him spend his lovely money.'

'Like you, you mean? I can't see the Scottish mama approving.'

'Mmmm. But then men love women their mamas wouldn't approve of.'

'So, are you inviting him to your party?'

'Maybe. Providing you stick to the lovely Luke, or Angus might decide he prefers you. And I am not risking that. In fact, I may weave a spell in private.' Louise, with her dark curly hair and her red lips and clanking jewellery, did have a witchy air about her. Not a black old crone but a ripe, red-blooded woman in her prime. The question occurred to Amanda now, looking at Louise, whether in medieval times some witches might have been burned at the stake not because they were evil but because they were competition.

'A funny thing struck me about your two suitors,' Louise smirked.

'Angus Day is *not* a suitor, and I haven't met Luke whatshis-name,' interrupted Amanda.

'You will. Knight. His name's Knight. And the other one's Day. Knight and Day, geddit?'

Chapter 5

'Bye, Mum!' Clio hugged Amanda tightly, knocking the breath out of her. 'No more meeting strange men in wine bars while I'm away.' They were all standing in an emotional huddle at the airport.

'I promise.' Amanda tried to hide how devastated she felt at their departure. 'Have a wonderful time and mind you take advantage of all the facilities. I gather the ski instructors are particularly gorgeous at this time of year.'

'Bye, Mummy.' Sean threw himself into her arms, close to tears. He never called her mummy. 'We'll ring you as soon as we get there.'

Giles looked at his watch impatiently. 'Don't worry, love, I'll look after them. We'd better check-in with plenty of time.'

Amanda knew what that meant. He wanted a couple of whiskies in the bar before they took off.

He treated her to one of his special smiles. Age hadn't dimmed his golden attractiveness. But maybe a new baby – or even twins – at forty-five might add a few worry lines. He'd be sixty when they were at their most aggravating. What a satisfying thought.

Giles, she noted, had a slim hardback novel with him. The annoying thing was he'd actually manage to read it. Fatherhood had never intruded on Giles's habits.

At the check-in desk, Giles was already flirting with the ground stewardess. Thank God it wasn't Amanda's problem any longer. Now it was Stephanie who had to worry whether Giles was safe with any pretty woman under eighty. She had to admit it was a great relief.

'Goodbye!' As Giles lifted the luggage on to the check-in counter, Amanda noticed that his suitcases were new and expensive with wheels and an extending handle to pull them along effortlessly while Clio had Amanda's ancient, pick-up-and-carry Delsey and Sean had a rather grubby Adidas sports bag. Divorce, Amanda realised, wishing it wasn't so, made you notice things like that. 'Have a fabulous time. I'd say break a leg, but maybe not. Send me a postcard. And don't do anything stupid.'

'It's all *right*, Amanda.' Giles's tone had taken on an edge of irritation. 'I'm with them, for God's sake.'

It was on the tip of her tongue to add, 'That's what I'm afraid of.'

Sean ran back for one last hug. 'You will be all right, won't you, Mum, when we're gone?'

'Me?' Amanda said in mock amazement. 'Without all that bedroom tidying and packed-lunch making? I'll put my feet up all day and watch daytime television with a big box of chocolates.'

Sean tried to smile. 'You won't have anyone to nag.'

'Yes I will. Kinky.'

'Poor old Kinky.'

She waved at them furiously and then walked back to the car. It was only forty minutes back to Laineton. She drove faster than usual, even though there was no hurry with nothing waiting for her.

It was stunning how different an empty house felt. The untidiness, the sense of their house being one giant lost property depot, which normally irritated the hell out of her, suddenly didn't seem to matter at all. She picked up one of Sean's Wellingtons and found herself holding it to her chest as if it were some precious memento. Thank heavens Clio had made her put up the Christmas tree and had decorated it with all the scruffy ornaments they'd accumulated over the years, or she wouldn't have bothered. And that would have been genuinely sad. At the top of the tree perched the fairy with the squashed face from where someone had sat on her years before. Amanda had tried to throw it away but Clio wouldn't let her. The fairy was part of Clio's childhood, the part before her parents had split up, and she was determined to cling on to it.

Amanda had just sat down at the kitchen table and wondered what the hell she was going to do with the next week or so when the phone rang.

'Amanda.' Her mother's commanding tones hardly needed the benefit of the telecommunications system. 'I'm at the golf club and there's a very nice young man here I'd like you to meet. He's Mr and Mrs Worthington's nephew and he's just down from Fulham. He works in the City. He'd love to take you out to dinner.' She could almost hear her mother give the 'young' man a knowing smile. He would be jowly, full of self-importance, wearing a pale-pink Ralph Lauren polo shirt and too-tight jeans, probably called Gordon.

'He's called Gordon,' her mother added. Amanda tried to suppress a giggle.

'Sorry, Mother. I'm afraid I'm whacked. I've promised myself an early night.'

'Really, Amanda, you are hopeless.'

'Why don't you go instead?'

The trouble with her mother was, she probably would.

In bed that night Amanda found it hard to sleep. 'You've got a nasty case of empty nest syndrome,' she told herself. This was what it would be like when her children left home. Clio would be gone in the wink of an eye. Sean would need her for longer but eventually he'd be off too. You need a real interest, she told herself, something more than just a family and a job you only half care about.

As she fell asleep, her thoughts drifted to the empty boathouse which could be a wonderful gallery, and to whether it really was Angus Day who had sent her the flyer.

If it was, it was a surprisingly thoughtful thing to do. Angus Day obviously believed she should take the risk. But then he was the risk-taking type. She found herself softening, but then remembered the angry tenants on the Eastcliff Estate he'd moved out of their homes and also the way the waitress had smiled and flirted with him in the wine bar. Angus Day was another version of Giles, charming but ruthless and without moral scruples. And falling for someone like Giles was one mistake she was never, ever going to make again.

She was almost asleep when she realised Clio and Sean hadn't phoned from Val d'Isère. She sat up, images of burning aeroplanes filling her mind. The more probable explanation was that Giles had been in too much of a hurry to get to the hotel minibar to wait for them. She wondered if she should ring but decided it was being over-protective.

A telltale bleep issued from her handbag. It was her mobile telling her she had a message. She pushed the button for text and it appeared in the tiny frame. LOVE YA MUM. It was their special greeting. ARRIVED SAFELY CLIO.

Slowly fumbling with the keys she keyed out the words LOVE YOU CLIO GONE TO BED SAFELY MUM

It was two days before Christmas and the tills at the gallery were singing the 'Halleluiah Chorus'. Louise's stock of Beryl Cook prints, framed in dark-blue stained wood at £9.99, had proved a wild success, as had the two Italian cherubs with a lovely mischievous look in their eyes, framed in gold. Some small sculptures of plump nude couples embracing had been unexpectedly popular. As she wrapped the last one in tissue paper, she wondered what the recipients would make of it. Hopefully they'd see the roly-poly pair as a celebration of their love, but if they didn't it'd make a handy doorstop.

When she'd closed up the shop, Amanda found herself taking the route home via the boathouse and peering in. A moon was rising over the sea and its shimmering path, in Amanda's hopeful eyes, seemed to lead straight to the boathouse.

'Terribly cold in there.' A voice startled her; it was Betty Miles. 'My father used to take me there to buy fish. The fishermen had a big table with the fresh catch all laid out. I liked sprats best. Do you like sprats?' Betty never waited for an answer to a question. 'Shake them in a paper bag of seasoned flour, then fry them in sizzling hot oil and eat them with bread and butter and vinegar. Delicious! You don't see sprats often nowadays, do you? Mind you, I used to feel a bit sorry for them. What is it they say? Use a sprat to catch a mackerel. Everyone eats sprats, people *and* mackerel. Not a happy state for the sprat.'

'Betty!' called her sister Rose from the deck in front of their chalet. 'I hope you're not chattering on to Mrs Wells. She probably wants to go home.'

'As a matter of fact,' Betty sniffed, 'I found her peering in the window of the boathouse and I was just filling her in on its history. I wasn't boring you, was I, dear?'

'Absolutely not.'

'Rose isn't interested in people, only blessed crosswords,' Betty confided. 'Goodnight.' Betty tripped off home, the frilly feminine foil to Rose's severe dress sense and manner to match.

'I hope she wasn't annoying you,' Rose shouted, 'only sometimes she's like a gramophone record. Except that you can't turn her off.'

Amanda smiled. How on earth those two had spent fifty years living together in the tiny space of their chalet, hardly bigger than a beach hut, Amanda couldn't fathom.

On Christmas Eve, Louise opened a bottle of champagne to celebrate how well the gallery had done. Someone had even bought the hideous painting of Laineton Sands in the ghastly pinks and reds.

'Hope your husband likes it,' Amanda had murmured as she wrapped the enormous four-by-three canvas.

'Too bad,' had been the spirited reply. '*I* like it. He's colourblind anyway.'

Amanda had had to bite her tongue not to add, 'Just as well.'

'So where are you spending Christmas?' Louise asked, replenishing their glasses.

'With my mother.'

'How ghastly.'

'Not as ghastly as her suggestion that we have Christmas dinner at the golf club.'

'Where are you going to have it then? Are you cooking? Seems rather a waste without Clio and Sean. All that work.'

'Which is why we're going to lunch in splendour at the Grand.'

'Amongst all the geriatrics?'

Amanda grinned. 'Only the *best* geriatrics. It gives my mother a chance to wear a hat. She loves wearing hats.'

'You'll be glad to know we've had such a good Christmas I'm shutting up shop till New Year,' Louise beamed. 'That'll give you plenty of time to beautify yourself and go shopping before you meet the lovely Luke.'

'Look, Louise, I know you're trying to be helpful but I'm beginning to loathe the sound of this Luke.'

'That's because you haven't met him yet. He'll be your best Christmas present yet.'

'I hope you're not getting him gift-wrapped.'

'Now there's a thought. Bollock naked with just a red bow round his . . .'

'*Louise!*'

'Have a lovely one, anyway. Here's a little present. Open it tomorrow.' She handed Amanda a small gift box. Louise was usually so unsentimental that Amanda almost felt moved to tears.

'That's really kind of you. I'm afraid I haven't . . .' She trailed off in embarrassment.

'Don't worry, you were too busy with the kids. Happy Christmas and see you at my New Year's Eve party.'

Waking on Christmas morning without her children was the oddest sensation. She realised how many rituals they'd built up over the years. Everyone piling into her bed to open their stockings, sharing out their chocolate money, going downstairs at the crack of dawn to put the ham on to boil or the turkey in the oven, the usual arguments over whether to go to church. She'd stuck to these rituals even more since Giles had left, trying to make things seem safe and solid for Clio and Sean. Now, without them, Christmas seemed meaningless.

She made herself a cup of tea and took it back to bed, listening to the silence of the house. The phone made her jump, slicing through the stillness that almost felt like a snowfall except that it was only in her mind. She reached for the receiver, already smiling, guessing who it would be.

'We wish you a Merry Christmas!' warbled two off-key voices. 'We wish you a Merry Christmas! We wish you a Merry Christmas and a Happy New Year!'

'Hi, Mum!' Sean shouted. 'Have a good one!'

'Hope you're not moping,' Clio added, a hint of protectiveness in her voice.

'Me? Mope? GG and I are about to do a Christmas tango round the Grand Hotel.'

'She would too, given half a chance,' Clio laughed. 'Good old Gran. How's the manhunt?'

'I don't think she's found Mr Right yet.'

'I mean you.'

'I know you do. On hold. How can I search without your advice and assistance?' Amanda changed the subject. 'Is it snowing?'

'I'll just pull the curtains. Oh, Mum.' She could hear the awe in Clio's voice. 'I wish you could see it. It's amazing! All white mountains and frozen lakes. And it's started snowing!'

Amanda closed her eyes. If things had been different then she would have been able to share it all. For a split-second she let herself imagine them throwing snowballs and laughing in that wide white landscape, laughing and loving, perhaps on a sledge like in some happy family scene by Norman Rockwell.

She dragged herself back to earth. 'How's Dad been?'

Clio's tone tightened. 'He bumped into an old work friend on the second day, so we've been pretty much left to get on with it.'

That sounded like Giles all right. The reality was oddly reassuring, as if she hadn't made a mistake in letting Giles walk out of their marriage, only in ever believing he could be different. On the other hand, without him there would have been no Sean and Clio.

'Happy Christmas, darling! I miss you.'

'I miss you too.' There was a tiny break in Clio's voice. 'I wish . . .' she tailed off.

'I know, darling, so do I.' Amanda could read Clio's thoughts.

She wished they could all be together, but she knew it would never happen.

Sean, on the other hand, seemed far more accepting of the situation. 'We're going to watch the downhill racing this afternoon,' he enthused when Clio handed him the phone to say goodbye, 'and then we have a Glühwein reception and Santa's going to come.' He paused. 'Well, actually it won't be Santa but one of the waiters dressed up. Dad's coming too. If we can get him out of the bar.'

He might only be ten, but Sean seemed to have a pretty firm grasp of reality already.

When they'd rung off, Amanda forced herself to get up, shower and make at least a slight effort. It was Christmas Day after all. Only an hour or two till she was due to meet her mother.

The Grand Hotel, Laineton's most famous establishment, had summoned all of its faded splendour to provide its guests with a happy Christmas. The enormous marble and wrought iron stair-case was draped with swags of fake fir decorated with gilded balls. A giant fir tree stood in the lobby, covered in white fairy lights, with a mound of tinfoil presents heaped at the bottom.

'I think they're trying to out-glitz Harrods,' commented Helen in a piercing tone.

'Don't the presents look lovely?' Amanda pointed to the heap of prettily wrapped gifts under the tree.

'They're not real, you know.' Trust her mother to point that out. 'Just empty boxes.' Amanda realised people were staring and rather wished her mother hadn't chosen a hat that made the millinery in *My Fair Lady* seem modest by comparison.

Amanda, knowing her mother would enjoy hogging the spot-light, had decided on her cosy sea-green chenille jumper with a short velvet skirt and her one extravagance this winter – high-heeled black lizard-look boots which had been so reduced in the sale it would have been a crime not to buy them. She'd also blown her Christmas bonus on a pair of sleek, black leather trousers, also in the sale, ignoring Clio's voice in her head saying, 'My mother in black leather trousers! How weird is that?'

In the bay window nearest the promenade, an ancient string

quartet played 'Winter' from Vivaldi's *Four Seasons* so many times Amanda decided they had to be robots with a tape installed in their backs.

She let her mother walk in first, not wanting to steal her thunder. Helen swept into the dining room as if it were a first night at Covent Garden. The waiter led them to a table by the window. 'A sea view!' Helen gushed, 'thank you!', as if it were a special gift from the waiter in acknowledgement of her beauty and status. Actually Amanda had booked it.

The waiter darted for Amanda's napkin, determined she shouldn't get there first, and shook it out with such a flourish that Amanda half expected a rabbit or a bunch of fake flowers to appear. 'Would you like to pull your cracker now or later?' He made it sound like a faintly forbidden activity.

'Now,' said Amanda. 'Let's live dangerously.'

'Later,' said Helen. 'What I'd like now is a drink. A Pimm's please. You'll have one, Amanda?'

Even though to most people Pimm's conjured up parties on summer lawns, for Amanda the pungent, fruity taste always made it seem like Christmas Day. When her father had been alive he'd always made it on Christmas morning. Every year he'd forgotten to buy the mint and fruit that was supposed to garnish it and they'd ended up raiding the neighbour's greenhouse and drinking their Pimm's spiced with a handful of stolen mint.

The memory made her think of Clio and Sean again. How magical to have a white Christmas and listen to carols in the snow and sip hot Glühwein and stamp your feet to keep warm. Her thoughts were rudely interrupted by her mother's voice. 'Who on earth's that man over there? He's staring at you.'

Amanda looked round.

Three tables away, tucked in the corner near the string quartet, Angus Day sat with his mother. He raised his glass to her in a Christmas toast.

'Just a client of the gallery's.' Amanda failed to mention that he was also the owner of the damaged BMW.

'He looks mad, bad and dangerous know, just the way I like

them,' Helen commented. 'I might have a go myself if you're not interested.'

'I'm afraid he's already got someone in his life,' Amanda informed her. 'He came in and bought her a beautiful sculpture of a pair of herons.'

Isobel Day followed the line of her son's gaze. 'How extraordinary. It's your gold-digger, or did you arrange for her to be here? Perhaps she's following you around. In fact, maybe she bumped into your car deliberately. Stranger things have happened when a woman's after a man's money. She soon let you pay for her damage, as I remember.'

'Maw, you're outrageous! You almost forced her to let me pay. And I'm nothing like as eligible as you think. Laura said she'd be a happy woman if she never saw me again, remember.'

'Laura was beautiful but selfish. And who on earth's the catastrophe in the hat? Who does she think she is? Gertrude Shilling?'

'I'm not absolutely sure,' Angus replied, 'but I suspect that's her mother.'

'Good heavens!' Isobel choked on her whisky. 'She doesn't look much older than her daughter. How very undignified to be trying that hard to hang on to your youth.' It was beneath Isobel's dignity to stare. 'What are her hands like? Hands always show your true age.'

'Maw,' Angus marvelled, 'I didn't know you could be so bitchy.'

'That wasn't bitchiness,' Isobel corrected primly, 'it's a simple fact.'

Amanda pushed Angus's presence out of her mind, determined to enjoy herself. The food was surprisingly good. Despite her svelte frame, Helen ploughed her way through smoked salmon cornets, fillet of turkey with cranberry coulis, roast potatoes, sprouts that she declared to be satisfactorily crunchy, two angels on horseback and a chipolata, followed by a large helping of Christmas pudding with brandy butter *and* cream.

'Does the pudding have any sixpences in it?' Helen demanded of a passing waiter. 'Only I don't want to break a tooth, do I?'

Amanda knew her mother had dentures but kept quiet.

'Just lucky charms, madam. A bachelor's button, a wish-bone for good luck, a wedding bell, or a coin for wealth.'

'Thank you.' Helen attacked her pudding with the wild enthusiasm of a prospector hunting for gold. 'Damn! I've got the bachelor's button,' she announced with all the petulance of a little girl who hadn't won the prize at her own party.

Isobel Day studied her son across the white linen with its festive crackers and tasteful table decorations. She was beginning to feel very tired. This would be her last Christmas and Angus was refusing to acknowledge it, which was why he'd bought that foolishly extravagant present for her. She who had always measured her life out carefully, even in her movements and her choice of clothes, as well as in the way she lived, felt suddenly reckless, as if the chance of happiness must not be allowed to slip away due to caution but should be grabbed at once.

'Angus . . .' she said with sudden urgency.

He looked up, surprised at the change in her tone.

'You're behaving like a mental defective. You've been staring at her for fifteen minutes now. To save all our embarrassment, why don't you just go and say something? Happy Christmas? Or better still, would you like to have dinner with me?'

Angus threw back his head and laughed. 'You're a wonder, Maw.'

'I know.'

'I thought you disapproved.'

'Being right is a very annoying habit.'

He began to push his chair back.

Amanda unwrapped the tiny greaseproof parcel she'd found in her Christmas pudding. Inside was a coin. 'Oh, bad luck, Amanda darling.' Helen's tones rang out with hideous clarity through the sudden silence that greeted the end of the Vivaldi. 'You haven't got a wedding ring, you've got a coin. Maybe that means you'll meet some lovely rich man who'll marry you anyway!'

For the second time in her brief acquaintance with Angus, Amanda wished the floor would open up and swallow her. How could her mother be so embarrassing and crass? And just as Angus started across the room towards her, Amanda, flushing like a traffic light, grabbed her handbag and fled from it.

Chapter 6

New Year's Eve dawned blue and beautiful, a perfect clean slate for all the good resolutions Amanda should be starting tomorrow. This year would be different, she told herself. There must be no more looking back, only forward. She hated people who moaned about their lives and did nothing to change things. She would be bold. She would be brave.

She just wished she had someone to be bold and brave with, to make her bolder and braver.

The last week hadn't been as bad as she'd expected. What with visits to the cinema, a pantomime with Ruthie's boisterous family where she'd found herself shouting *'He's behind you!'* with the best of them, and a quiet drink with Simone who was in love with another unsuitable and unavailable man, the time had passed surprisingly quickly.

The phone on the bedside table rang and Louise's bugle tones filled the silence of her bedroom. 'Just ringing to check. You are coming to my party tonight, aren't you? I haven't been doing all this advance PR with Luke Knight for nothing?'

Amanda's heart sank. What would Louise have told this man about her?

The day passed pleasantly enough with a brisk walk on the seafront to clear her head. She climbed down across the shingle towards the water's edge and began skimming stones. To Giles's annoyance, while his pebbles always sank like the *Titanic*, she had a particular talent for this small art. Perhaps it was on such tiny triumphs that her marriage had foundered.

As she walked back from the beach, she passed Betty Miles. 'Are you doing something nice tonight, dear?' asked Betty, who was sweeping the sand off their small deck.

'Going to a party,' smiled Amanda, feeling faintly self-conscious.

'I'm so glad, dear,' Betty smiled back. 'You're far too young and pretty to stay in on New Year's Eve. How I used to love it! All that champagne and dancing and the resolutions you knew you were never going to keep.' She lowered her voice and leaned towards Amanda. 'Of course, Rose never got any invitations to parties. I was the beauty, you see. That's why she hates New Year's Eve still. But tonight,' she confided gaily, as though it were the social gathering of the decade, 'we're going to a party at the community centre. Hogmanay for the Over-Sixties. Rose says it should be Over-Eighties, but that's just Rose. Sometimes she makes Scrooge look cheerful. And I, for one, intend to dance the night away.'

Amanda hoped the assembled beaux at the Over-Sixties would be equal to the challenge. She could almost hear the rattle of Zimmer frames.

Behind them, a sudden crash made them jump. A large section of clapboard had fallen off one of the beach huts in the row beside the Mileses' chalet. When Amanda had been a child the neat line of pastel beach huts had reminded her of Neapolitan ice creams, but over recent years they'd been neglected and were quickly falling into disrepair.

'They're getting so dangerous,' Betty complained. 'Rose was hit by a piece of wood the other day. It nearly knocked her over.'

'It used to be so lovely down here when I was little,' Amanda said. 'I longed for a beach hut. I remember my friend Elizabeth had one and her mum and dad sat in it every day from June to October, brewing cups of tea.'

'There used to be a waiting list for a beach hut longer than for an allotment. It was pretty as a picture down here, but now all the young people want to go to the amusement arcades and the cinema. No one wants beach huts any more and this is what happens to them. Talking of cups of tea, dear, would you like one?'

Fond as Amanda was of Betty, she knew if she accepted she'd be there for another hour.

'I'd better be getting on. The hairdresser awaits.'

'Of course.' She took Amanda's hand in her own gnarled one and gazed at her with sudden alertness. How old was Betty, Amanda wondered? Eighty? Certainly over seventy-five.

'Do you know, dear, I think you're going to meet someone special tonight. And when you do, give him a run for his money. I always did that. That was why I got all the boys and Rose got none.' She winked, her curled eyelashes suddenly reminding Amanda of an octogenarian Betty Boop. 'Apart from the fact that I was prettier anyway.'

'Well, we're both alone now, aren't we?' came Rose's voice from inside the chalet.

Amanda suppressed a smile. She loved Rose's laconic humour.

Amanda waved goodbye. Behind the chalet she glimpsed the empty boathouse. It too added to the dilapidated and mournful air that had descended on the area. It was hard to believe that just around the corner the prosperous lights of Laineton town centre winked away alluringly.

Amanda's hairdresser, Sandy, was wasted in Laineton. He had the leonine looks of a young Nicky Clarke, the listening skills of Sigmund Freud and could have taken over an agony aunt slot in any national newspaper at the drop of a hat. He was also an extremely good hairdresser.

'Why do you stay here in the sticks?' Amanda often asked him.

'Because Laineton isn't the sticks. As my friend Billy puts it, it's the outback without the drawbacks. Only an hour and a half to London but without all the hassle. Laineton's the most tolerant place on earth.' He winked at Amanda.

Amanda wasn't sure the residents of Laineton would welcome this epithet, but it was true, Laineton was a lovely place. In summer it had a pure candyfloss and deckchair appeal and in winter a misty, washed-out, pared-down charm of its own.

'Now, what are we going to do today?' Sandy grinned at her. 'The usual half-inch so no one knows you've been?'

Some devil of adventurousness took Amanda over. 'No. I think I'd like something new.'

Sandy pretended to fall off his stool. 'Here everyone,' he yelled to Amanda's enormous embarrassment. 'The lovely Amanda's going for a new look. Give her a round of applause!'

Amanda sank into her chair and tried to hide inside the black gown.

'What do you fancy? Gamine and feathery? Layered?'

I've never seen myself as the gamine type,' Amanda replied. 'What do you think?'

He considered her face for a moment. 'Right. Trust me.'

'Do you know,' Amanda laughed, 'my mother always told me never to trust a man who says that.'

'Your mother was absolutely right. About every other man on the planet. You shouldn't trust any of them, the lying bastards, I never do, but she was wrong on this occasion.'

'Go ahead then.'

Amanda sat back in her chair and gave herself up to the luxury of being pampered. She hadn't been to the hairdresser for far too long. Clio, desperate before a party, had nicked her last appointment on the grounds that Amanda's life was over and Clio's just beginning.

Just a few more days and they'd be back. It had seemed a lifetime without them, though she had to admit she'd finally got used to and even started to luxuriate in the space and solitude of having the house to herself, safe in the knowledge that it was only temporary.

'How about a few highlights?' Sandy tempted, his smile more seductive than Milton's Lucifer. 'Just a few. To bring up the contrast with your natural tawny?'

Amanda knew she shouldn't. She knew highlights would double her bill, but after all, she'd missed her last appointment thanks to

Clio. Giles could pay for Clio's. That meant she had twice as much to spend today.

'Go on then.'

Sandy smiled beatifically. He liked Amanda and thought her extremely attractive. He even liked her strong practical streak. He sensed there was more to Amanda's life than just her appearance, unlike a lot of his clients. Plus, she'd had a tough time since that bastard of a husband had left her. Sandy had never liked Giles. Giles had come to the salon once, without an appointment, and demanded they fit him in, then complained loudly that they'd made him look like Rod Stewart. He should be so lucky. He didn't have enough hair.

Giles, Sandy decided, was one of those men who loved being exceptionally handsome and couldn't handle it when they lost their looks. Often, Sandy had noticed with satisfaction, it was men like that who lost their looks the fastest.

While he chatted away to Amanda, Sandy added a few more highlights than were normally included in the cost.

'Right, Shezre,' he said to the junior when he'd finished putting on the foils, 'a cappuccino for Amanda, please, and a nice magazine.'

He wrested the copy of *Good Housekeeping* from Shezre's astonished grasp, clearly deciding this was not Amanda's market, and instead handed her a raunchy men's glossy featuring a busty blonde draped over a Harley Davidson while holding, of all things, a palm organiser.

'They give her the gadgets to make it seem respectable. You'd better read it, though, if you're going to understand the male of the species.'

Amanda, absorbed in page after page of computer wizardry and erotic titillation, paused at an article entitled 'Twenty Ways to Make Her Come'. A pity Giles hadn't read this, but then other people's pleasure hadn't exactly been Giles's top priority.

Amanda glanced in the mirror, wishing she'd put on some make-up. With a hundred silver foils sticking out of her head she looked like an anaemic Dalek. Why on earth did she think this Luke Knight would look at her twice?

Before she knew it, it was time to have the foils taken off and her hair washed. Amanda actually felt rather regretful. She was in the middle of a double-page spread in *Hello!* She never bought it, of course, but always leapt on it at the hairdresser or dentist.

'Shezre, over here please. Shampoo Mrs Wells's hair, would you?'

The scent of the shampoo was delicious. A fruity and luscious aroma filled Amanda's nostrils as the girl massaged her scalp with firm and practised fingers. If only life were always this luxurious.

The girl wasn't the chatty type, which Amanda appreciated. Silence was much more restful than being asked for the nine hundredth time where she was going on her holidays. Especially as she didn't know. Probably nowhere unless her finances looked up.

'Would you like conditioner?' The girl's words penetrated her daydream of being on a tropical island, lying in the sun, with a waiter standing at her elbow ready for her cocktail order, while beside her on the adjoining sun bed was . . . for an instant Angus Day's face leapt into her mind. She quickly shoved it out.

'Yes. Conditioner would be lovely.'

The comb slipped through her conditioned hair like silk. Normally her hair was tough and tangly with a mind of its own. 'It'll never do as it's told,' her mother used to say when she washed Amanda's hair as a child, 'just like you.'

'Now, how about putting on a bit of eye make-up before we blow-dry?' Sandy suggested. 'Just so that you can judge the effect properly.'

'I didn't bring any,' Amanda apologised. 'I was going to do it later.'

'Sandy,' called out the receptionist, 'your three o'clock's here.'

'Old trout,' Sandy mumbled. 'Nothing short of a miracle could make her lovely. Don't worry, Shezre here is training to be a make-up artist at college. Come on, Shez, I give you enough time off for this so-called block release. Show us what you can do.'

Shezre's somewhat wilted manner instantly transformed. 'I'll get my stuff.'

For twenty minutes, Amanda's makeover became the focus of the salon. Customers were left unshampooed while Shezre wielded more brushes than Monet and the other junior, Tia, painted Amanda's nails a deep plum.

'Don't look,' insisted Sandy when the effect was finally finished. 'Under pain of turning into Mrs P over there, keep your eyes closed while I finish your hair.'

Sandy added some mousse, which Amanda didn't usually bother with, then blow-dried her hair using a round hairbrush. 'The brush will give it some height and a bit of volume.'

Finally he stood back to assess his work.

To Amanda's disappointment, instead of praising it, he swore. 'That's not right!' he announced and then clapped like some Eastern potentate. 'Bring me the heated rollers!'

Amanda hadn't used heated rollers since she was sixteen. It all came back to her. Those heady, girlie days when getting ready for the party with your friends was every bit as important as the party itself; in fact, quite often *more* fun.

Sandy left the rollers in for five minutes, then took out the pins and combed it through. Finally, he fluffed it with his fingers before standing back to admire his handiwork. 'Right,' he invited archly, '*now* you can look.'

Amanda opened her eyes and gaped. She looked like a completely different person! Sandy had blended blonde and tawny together so that it looked totally natural and had styled it much shorter than usual, but at the same time had given it such a lift that it looked more luxuriant than when it had been longer.

'Toss your head,' commanded Sandy.

Amanda did so.

'Wow,' commented Tia, the junior, 'you look . . .' She hesitated, searching for the right word for someone of Amanda's age.

'Sexy.' Sandy filled in the gap for her. 'Sexy is definitely the word for you. Not to mention stylish. I almost wish I was straight, but not quite. I hope they're going to appreciate you at this bash tonight.'

'So do I. But what on earth am I going to wear to come up to this standard?'

'Something new,' insisted Sandy. 'You can go over there and have your snap taken for our styling book, then you won't have to pay for the hairdo. With the money you've saved you're going out right now to buy something nice.' He reached for his wallet and for one embarrassing moment she thought he was going to hand her a note, but instead it was a business card. 'Try here. He's a beast but he's got wonderful taste. Mention me and he'll try harder.'

The shop Sandy had suggested was called Green. Amanda, although she embraced recycling with enthusiasm, hoped it didn't mean the clothes would all be made of bin-liners and sensible, earthy flax. In fact, she couldn't have been more wrong. Green stocked only the softest, clingiest silks. The owner, who looked at her levelly when she mentioned Sandy, had developed a technique which owed a debt both to Fortuny and to Issey Miyake, but was fortunately a lot cheaper than either of them. His garments were all made of narrowly pleated pure silk and hung in figure-hugging emphasis on the display dummies. Amanda almost turned around and walked out. The clothes were far too attention-grabbing, not to mention probably wildly expensive. These dresses, she decided, were made for women with wand-like bodies, Kate Moss types, not real, living, breathing size fourteens like Amanda. If she hadn't already mentioned Sandy she would most certainly have left. There was a price to be paid, she found, for exploiting contacts.

'I'm not sure these are quite my style,' she began.

'Hang on a sec,' instructed the owner and disappeared into a tiny office adjoining the shop. He came back holding a dress inside a plastic cover. Amanda couldn't really see it from this angle.

'What size is it?' she asked, expecting the humiliating answer to be size eight.

'My clothes don't have sizes,' was the unexpected reply. 'Try it on and see.'

Amanda retreated to the tiny changing room and slipped on the dress. It slithered over her wide shoulders and down her body with surprising ease. Looking in the mirror, Amanda bit her lip. For the first time in her life, even to her own self-critical standards, she could see that she looked beautiful. The dress was sea-green, her favourite colour, and was shot with iridescent shades of blue like a moonlit tropical ocean.

The shop's owner pulled back the curtain. 'Good heavens.' He blinked. 'I don't think I've seen it look that good on anyone. Certainly not the anorexic racehorses we usually sell to.'

'How much is it?' Amanda asked finally, holding her breath.

The owner paused, his head on one side. 'A hundred pounds.' And then, with the smallest of smiles, he added, 'And tell Sandy not to send me any more beautiful customers. I can't afford it.'

Amanda knew she had to have it. It was much more than she'd intended to pay but, dammit, she'd just spent Christmas on her own and this was her only party.

'Thank you, I'd love it.'

'Good. It matches your eyes.'

He folded the dress into a swathe of pale pink tissue paper and put it in a handmade paper bag that had real flowers woven into the paper. 'Have fun.'

To her amazement, it was nearly six by the time she got home. She carefully covered up her hair with a bath-hat, patted her new make-up and ran a bath. A glass of wine was the final indulgence. She lay back and watched the steam frost up the mirror, all the excitement of her teenage years flooding back. Clio would laugh at her. But then Clio wasn't here.

It struck her with a frisson of excitement that the house would be hers tonight. For the first time she could ever remember, there would be no fear of interruption.

After the soak she rubbed her skin with body lotion and painted her toenails to match her fingers. She stood for a moment, naked, in front of the steamy bathroom mirror. 'Come on, sea goddess,' she challenged her reflection, 'let's see if you hook yourself a catch tonight.'

It was then that she hit a problem. Tights. She rarely wore dresses, especially not sea-green silk ones. Her drawer was stuffed with sensible black opaques but she couldn't find any fine denier ones anywhere. 'I could have sworn I had some,' Amanda muttered. 'I bet that beast Clio has pinched them.'

Briefly she considered bare legs, but hers were not recently waxed, silky smooth, lightly tanned ones. They were winter white and lightly tufted with hair. Not goddess standard at all.

In a rare act of role reversal she raided Clio's chest of drawers, where she discovered a whole new three-pack of her favourite black silk opaques, unfortunately not suitable for tonight but welcome anyway, several pairs of her missing trouser socks, but no pale tights at all. She was about to give up when she spotted Kinky the cat asleep on Clio's bed. Kinky was sleeping on the half-finished pillow Clio had been making for her pet.

'Hello, you pampered animal.'

Amanda lay down on the bed next to the cat to cuddle her, with her head half on the bed and half on the pillow. She put her hand behind her to inspect the strange consistency of Kinky's pillow. No wonder it was weird: apart from one lone and fragrant pair of Clio's hockey socks, it was entirely stuffed with Amanda's expensive tights.

Much to Kinky's annoyance, Amanda chucked her off it and emptied the tights on to Clio's bed. There, at the very bottom, were three pairs of ivory ten-denier ones.

'I'll kill that child,' muttered Amanda wrathfully as she pulled on the delicate, almost transparent mesh, being careful not to put her fingers through and ruin them.

The only shoes that went with the outfit were some bronze summer sandals, but what the hell, at least with the tights her toes wouldn't go blue.

Finally she reached for the carrier bag and shook out the dress. From inside its crisp tissuey folds, a single strand of beads fell on to the bed. How had those got in there?

She looked in the bag again and took out the bill. The owner had scrawled a message on it:

The final touch. Have fun at the ball.

Amanda laughed delightedly. She really did feel a bit like Cinderella. She slipped on the necklace. It was made of tiny sea-green gems threaded on the narrowest of silver threads. It was perfect. She hoped this Luke was worth the effort.

At 7.30 p.m. she squirted a spray of Dune behind her earlobes. She had considered Opium, but Clio always said it reminded her of something you'd spray after an outbreak of the plague.

At 8 p.m. the doorbell rang. She'd booked a minicab even though it was only a ten-minute walk because, after all, goddesses didn't arrive on foot. She supposed they probably arrived in winged chariots and the battered red Vauxhall Astra that waited outside didn't much resemble that, but at least she would turn up undishevelled.

She hadn't reckoned on getting the only chain-smoking minicab driver in western Europe. And the one who was dead to all requests to put out his fag. In the end she had to fully open the window to avoid choking to death, and became just as windswept as if she'd walked, except that she was six quid poorer.

Louise had decided that there was no point in owning your own large open space and then hiring another, so the party was in the gallery, although tonight it was unrecognisable from its usual brightly lit self. Louise, who had a lot of style when she needed it, had blacked out all the glass windows and decked the gallery with yards of material suspended from the ceiling to form three different tents. Round the edge of the tents she'd built a seating area covered with exotic velvet cushions borrowed from her friend in the soft furnishing shop down the road. She had promised faithfully that no one would (a) be sick on them, (b) drop ash on them, or (c) baptise them in red wine.

The floor was covered in borrowed Turkish rugs, and Louise had added some Spanish stained-glass lights shaped like stars she'd found in a flea market and lit a few joss sticks to add to the atmosphere. It might not be ethnically authentic, as one of her guests pointed out, but it certainly added to the whole harem mood.

'Louise,' Amanda congratulated, hardly able to recognise the gallery in its new guise, 'the place looks fabulous!'

Louise took Amanda's hand and held her at arm's length. 'My God, Amanda, forget the gallery, what have you *done* to yourself? You look absolutely stunning.'

'I sold my soul to the devil,' Amanda replied, enjoying the fuss.

'Cheap at the price. So you're going to be behaving like a wicked angel tonight, are you? Luke should enjoy that. Where is the naughty boy?'

It was only nine o'clock but the room was beginning to fill up so fast that in another half-hour it would be positively uncomfortable.

'Have a drink while you can,' Louise counselled, putting a large Sea Breeze in her hand. 'You never know when it's going to run out.'

But her drink never did seem to run out. Louise returned at regular intervals and topped it up. Everyone was in a happy mood. A lot of Louise's friends were shop owners too, antiques dealers and other gallery owners, and they'd all had a bumper Christmas. Ruthie was there, and Simone from the book group, so Amanda had plenty of people to talk to. Suddenly it was eleven o'clock and there was still no sign of Luke.

'I don't know what's happened to him,' hissed Louise every time she came back. 'He promised he'd be here and he *really* wants to meet you.'

Oh yeah? Amanda thought. So much so that he couldn't be bothered to turn up. All the stupid preparation was wasted. The hairdresser, the dress, the make-up. Had she really thought she'd come along here tonight and find Mr Right Mark II, gift-wrapped and willing? How naive was that?

She took a large sip of her Sea Breeze. She was actually feeling a bit wobbly; she normally stuck to wine. Vodka wasn't her drink and although Louise had promised there wasn't a lot of it in the cocktails, Amanda was beginning to doubt the truth of that. Luke would hardly come now. He'd probably had a better offer and gone to another party. Anyway, wasn't she old enough to know that life didn't work out as easily as that?

A few minutes later Louise sidled up again with the jug of Sea Breeze. 'Darling, I'm so sorry. Luke's not coming. At least he rang to apologise. He's been delayed at the Over-Sixties Hogmanay. He's organising it as part of the Festival.'

'Oh dear.' Amanda took a large gulp of her cocktail. 'I hope Betty hasn't got her claws into him.'

'At least he rang,' Louise consoled as she turned away again. 'Giles would never have done that, would he?'

'Hello.' A voice behind Amanda startled her and she turned to find herself staring up into a pair of glinting kohl-lined eyes. To her stunned amazement, Angus Day had come dressed as a sheik. Louise must have invited him after all.

'Good God,' she gasped, 'I didn't know it was fancy dress!'

Angus shrugged. 'Louise's little joke. She thought I would cut a dash like this, apparently, and I assumed everyone else was dressing up too. I don't think your friend is that subtle on the sexual symbolism.'

'No,' agreed Amanda, trying not to laugh. 'Or the ingredients of her cocktails. But she's right,' she took another sip, 'it does suit you.'

'Careful,' Angus answered, his kohl-eyes only half joking, 'or I'll have you brought to my tent in a rug and rolled out on to the carpet at my feet.'

A devil possessed Amanda. Maybe it was too many Sea Breezes, or the disappointment that Luke hadn't turned up, or the fact that she felt beautiful for the first time she could remember. 'Is that all?' she asked provocatively. 'How very disappointing.'

Without waiting a second, Angus took her by the wrist and led her, laughing, through the crowded party and out into the air.

'Where's your stallion?' Amanda demanded. She'd hoped the sea air would sober her up but if anything it was having the opposite effect.

'It's over there.' Angus pointed to his cobalt-blue car. 'Just back from the blacksmith. It had a little accident. Shall we ride off into the sunset? Or would you rather stay and wait for midnight?'

Amanda realised he was being chivalrous and was giving her the chance to sober up and change her mind. But, un-PC though it was, she wanted him to make the decision for her. 'Can we put the roof down?' she asked, climbing into the car.

He pushed a button and the roof glided effortlessly and expensively into a slot behind the seats. They drove along the cliff top, the wind dishevelling her expensive new haircut, but Amanda didn't mind. A few people stared at the sight of a sheik driving a BMW, but it was New Year's Eve after all. Maybe he was a real sheik with Arab oil money.

They passed the Eastcliff Estate, which reminded Amanda for a brief and sensible moment that this was the man she disapproved of, that he was a wicked money-making capitalist with no compassion for the people he'd evicted.

They parked on top of the cliffs, facing out to sea, a ludicrous moon dangling in front of them like a baby's mobile, and told each other their histories. Amanda could hardly believe it when Angus looked at his watch and started to count. 'Twelve, eleven, ten,' began Angus.

'The New Year!' interrupted Amanda, suddenly feeling extremely drunk. 'Well done for remembering.'

'I am Scottish you know, we invented Hogmanay . . . three, two, one, zero!'

Without giving her time to protest, he turned her face to his and kissed her.

'Happy New Year!' he said when he finally let her go.

Amanda gasped for breath. Her body was on fire. She couldn't remember feeling like this since she was a frustrated teenager longing for her first taste of the delights of the flesh.

Yet this was also the moment she'd dreaded, the first man she'd kissed other than her husband in nineteen years. She'd expected to feel embarrassed, conscious of her ineptitude, of the shortcomings of her body. Instead all she felt was desire; a shameless, all-encompassing, heady desire.

This was a man she hardly knew – a man she disapproved of and who was capable of callous behaviour. And all she wanted to do was rip his clothes off and drag him to bed.

He leaned towards her again, a slow smile in his eyes as if he could read her thoughts and understood them because he felt the same.

'I just wondered,' Amanda began, some of her sudden boldness deserting her, 'if perhaps you might like to come back to my house? Everyone's away and I've got it all to myself.'

Angus Day fixed her with his kohl-dark eyes, which at that moment seemed far more sheik than Scottish capitalist. 'I can't think of a better way to start the New Year.' And he raised her hand to his lips and kissed it.

The drive home passed in a blur of excitement and music. Angus didn't try to talk but instead pushed another button and Ella Fitzgerald filled the car with 'A Foggy Day In London Town'.

In what seemed like moments they were outside her front door. Amanda giggled. 'I wonder what the neighbours will think,' she laughed. 'Me arriving home with a sheik.'

'Let's really give them something to talk about.' Angus had swept her into his arms and carried her up the front path before she'd even had time to protest that she was too heavy, or that it would be undignified. 'Next time I'll have a lackey posted at the tent, but for now we'll need your key.'

Amanda rummaged in her evening bag and handed it to him.

Seconds later they were in the darkened hall and he was kissing her with a passionate intensity that made her blood sing.

'Well, my delicate English rose,' he muttered, only half joking, 'I think perhaps we should go upstairs to your boudoir . . .' He took one step towards the staircase and stumbled on something piled at the foot of it.

Still in his arms, Amanda, confused by strong desire and too much vodka, reached for the light switch.

At the bottom of the stairs, in a jumbled heap, was Sean and Clio's skiing gear.

At that precise moment Giles appeared, holding a glass of her expensive brandy. 'Hello, Amanda, I was going to offer you a night-cap but I can see you've skipped that stage. How about introducing me to your sheik?'

Chapter 7

'Giles! What the bloody hell are you doing here?'

Angus slid her gently to the ground, for once in his life devoid of his usual self-possession.

'They were predicting nasty weather,' Giles grinned. 'Heavy snow that might close the airport. So I pulled a few strings and got us out early.'

'And you didn't think to ring me and let me know?'

'As a matter of fact,' Giles beamed, obviously enjoying the situation hugely, 'I think you'll find several messages on your answering machine.' Amanda could see the wretched thing flashing. 'Maybe your mind was on other things?' He held out his hand to Angus. 'Glad to meet you. I'm Giles Wells, the previous incumbent.'

Amanda could have wrung his self-satisfied neck. How had he managed to make the whole situation sound so sleazy? As if he'd just found Angus with his trousers round his ankles in a broom cupboard.

'Angus Day. Amanda and I have just been to a New Year's Eve party.'

'So I see. Fancy dress?'

Angus shrugged. 'It's a long story.'

'Anyway.' Giles glanced from one to the other. 'I can guess what your New Year's resolution was. I'm sorry to have interrupted. Her boudoir's at the top of the stairs, second on the right.'

'Actually,' Angus's smile was pleasant and even, 'it's time I watered my camel. Goodnight, Amanda. It was a delightful evening. Perhaps I could call you at a more opportune moment.'

'You're not leaving on account of me, I hope?' Giles insisted blandly. 'I'm just off and the children will sleep through anything. Although there was that time – do you remember, Amanda? When Sean walked in just as we were . . .'

If she'd had an axe to hand, Amanda would have swung it at her ex-husband. She could see how much he was relishing the situation. There was no way that the fragile flame between her and Angus could survive this onslaught.

'Well, you're a dark horse,' Giles commented as soon as Angus had left. 'We're gone for five minutes and you're off with a wily Arab.'

'Actually,' Amanda cut in furiously, 'he's from East Fife.'

'You know what I mean. Though now I think about it, you do look rather stunning, much more stunning than you have for years, in fact.' He walked towards her with a glint in his eye that she remembered from their marriage, though it wasn't usually aimed in her direction.

'Oh, for Christ's sake, Giles! Pull yourself together. You're about to be a father. Of twins. Have some dignity.'

'Still as waspish as ever,' Giles commented with some satisfaction. 'Hope your sheik doesn't find that out too soon. Even a new hairdo and a dress that costs hundreds can't make up for a shrewish nature.'

If she hadn't been so angry she would have laughed. The truth about their marriage was that she hadn't been shrewish, she'd been far too long-suffering. But Giles's interruption had had one positive effect. It had reminded her – at the eleventh hour plus fifty-ninth minute – that she'd been in danger of getting involved with another charming but faithless man. Angus was already involved with someone else and she knew it. When would she ever learn, for God's sake?

'Anyway,' Amanda changed the subject brusquely away from the subject of tonight's encounter, 'how was the skiing holiday?'

'A great success. Sean turned out to be quite a nice little skier. I bumped into Simon Langham from Sunblaze Travel – you remember Simon?'

Amanda swept through a mental list of Giles's travel cronies, an unmemorable lot who seemed mainly drawn to their chosen career because they couldn't think of anything else to do rather than for an intrinsic love of travel. Simon Langham was a burly, rugger-bugger type whom Amanda couldn't quite picture on skis.

'Anyway, old Simon felt the same way about the snow as I did. Stupid stuff. Wet and cold. Who'd want to go out in it when you've got a nice cosy bar with hot Glühwein and cold beer?'

'Your children perhaps? Where were Clio and Sean while you two were sinking steins of lager all afternoon?'

'Sean was happy with the other kids in the ski school and Clio . . .' Giles suddenly grinned in an ominous way. If anything, Amanda decided, he'd become more leering since they'd split up. 'Clio had a little adventure.'

'What kind of adventure?'

'There was this very handsome boy, French, a ski instructor, who singled her out. He was eager to teach her more than how to slalom, if you ask me.'

'But Clio's never been the slightest bit interested in boys.'

'And neither have they in her. The extraordinary thing was, she changed. She grew up in front of our eyes. You know she's always been as flat-chested as an ironing board. She suddenly sprouted tits! And the boys all started looking at her.'

Upstairs, on the landing, a sudden sound alerted them to the fact that they were being overheard. Amanda hoped it was Sean, but the small sob that echoed from the top of the stairs confirmed it was Clio and that she'd definitely overheard the latest outbreak of her father's celebrated tact.

'You'd better get off, Giles. Thanks for taking them.'

'I hope you'll be nicer now that I've done my bit. They all know it's my ex-wife when you call at work, you realise, ringing me to nag.'

Amanda winced. She hated this vision of herself as a mean old bag, especially as it was so unfair. 'I only call about the maintenance. You know my salary can't cover all the expenses.'

'Then maybe you'd better think about getting something better paid.'

Amanda was so furious she almost pushed him out of the door.

On the threshold, Giles hesitated. The old, slightly wolfish smile appeared and, without warning, he suddenly stroked her face. 'You really do look stunning tonight. Quite a different Amanda altogether. I was quite jealous of the sheik.'

Amanda's palms itched to slap his self-satisfied face. Her ex-husband was flirting with her, something he hadn't done for years. Furious, she looked round for something to throw at him, but all she could find was a bowl of scented pot-pourri, Louise's Christmas present to her. She grabbed it and upturned it over his head.

Giles's outraged expression, emerging from a waterfall of green and red dried flowers, a wooden Christmas tree decoration looped over one ear, would live with her for ever. God only knew what he'd be like when slim Stephanie was heavily pregnant and then busy with the twins. No woman in the county would be safe.

Once he'd gone she massaged her neck, stiff with tiredness, and removed the earrings that had been pinching all evening but were far too pretty to take off. Then she went to look for Clio.

Her daughter was lying face down on her bed with her head stuffed under the pillow.

'I hate them!' Clio announced tragically, her head still under the pillow.

Amanda sat down on the bed and stroked her. 'Who do you hate? Dad and Stephanie?'

'No,' was the muffled answer.

'Who then?' Amanda asked gently.

'Not who, *what*.' Clio turned over, her pretty face red and puffy. 'These!' she spat, looking down at her chest where two distinct mounds were clearly visible through her thin Snoopy nightshirt.

Amanda had to fight back a smile. Knowing it would be the worst possible response, especially after Giles's tactlessness, she didn't remind Clio of the hundreds of occasions she'd wept piteously that she was the only girl, *the only girl*, in her class who didn't need a bra.

'It must have given you a fright, finding you'd suddenly grown so much.' Amanda stroked her hair.

'Oh, Mum, it was *awful*! It was OK during the day when I was wearing my ski suit but at night all these boys kept leering at me.'

'But you managed to meet someone nice,' Amanda began, then wished she hadn't. She'd only had it from Giles after all, not the most sensitive of sources.

An even more heartrending sob hiccupped out of Clio. 'Gilles!' she sobbed. 'The same name as Dad, only French; he loved that.'

'What happened?' Amanda went on stroking her hair quietly.

'He dumped me, Mum. On the last day. And he'd been so keen till then. He rang me all the time, bought me flowers even though they cost a fortune in a place like Val d'Isère. Lilies of the valley. He said they were sweet and shy like me, the nearest thing he could find to the wild flowers in his valley in spring.'

Amanda hated the sound of him already.

'Did you see a lot of him?'

Clio buried her head again. 'You mean did I go to bed with him?' She blurted each word out, banging her head on the pillow.

Amanda didn't know if that was what she meant. Probably.

'Stupid, aren't I? Really sodding stupid. Silly old Clio, who goes and sleeps with the first male who chats her up.'

Amanda's heart turned over. Clio had seemed so innocent. She'd had the usual mother-daughter chats about emotion and the need for taking precautions, but with Clio it had seemed so academic. Now it sounded as though she'd gone ahead and had sex. 'Oh darling. How awful for you.'

'Yes. And it's all right. To answer your next question, we did take precautions. He was very well organised. In fact, just as we were about to do it, it struck me that he'd probably done it a hundred times before with a hundred silly girls who'd all kept their lilies of the valley to remind them of him.'

By the side of the bed was a tiny vase containing a wilting bunch of white flowers. Their perfume was strong, sickly and just a shade sinister, like the flower arrangements in a funeral parlour.

'You don't know that,' Amanda tried to soothe. 'I'm sure he thought you were very special.'

'So special he blanked me on the last day's skiing.' The hurt in her voice made it sharp. 'And spent all day with a sixteen-year-old from Stuttgart. She had a rich daddy so she may have got a bigger bunch.'

Amanda wanted to fold Clio in her arms and protect her from all the hurt that would ever happen to her. But Amanda hadn't even, she reminded herself bitterly, protected Clio from the pain of her parents' marriage breaking up.

'And do you know what Dad said when I tried to tell him about it?'

Amanda braced herself.

'He said, "A froggy would a wooing go . . ." and went off to the bar, laughing at his own joke.'

Bloody Giles, Amanda vowed silently. Bloody, *bloody*, Giles. If thoughts could kill he'd be dead meat.

'Go to sleep now, darling. Do you want to come into my bed?' This was the ultimate antidote, used only in emergencies but whose powerful magic usually wrought miracles.

'No thanks, Mum.' Amanda could hardly believe it. 'After all, I am sixteen.'

This was almost as telling a rite of passage as the episode with the ski instructor.

'All right, darling. Why don't you ring your friend Jasmine in the morning and have a heart-to-heart?'

If her own teenage heartbreaks were anything to go by, a long no-details-spared chat with her best friend would be a big help for Clio.

Amanda suddenly realised how physically exhausted she was. The late night, the champagne, the unexpected encounter with Angus Day, so disappointingly – yet obviously sensibly – interrupted, had worn her out. She stood up and stole one last glance at Clio.

Giles was right about one thing. Clio had changed. A gawky, blushing child had gone to France and a shy but beautiful girl had returned.

She slipped into Sean's room and drew comfort from the fact that her son was still exactly the same. The same floppy blond hair she loved, still intact, the same big eyes full of fun. She kissed him, feeling herself melting with love as he looked up and kissed her back. He was sitting up in bed reading a book entitled *The Definitive History of Manchester United FC*.

'Hi, Mum. It was fab. And I found this great book at the airport. It has stuff about Man U even I didn't know!'

'It must be good then.' Trust Sean to go skiing and be more excited about finding a book on football.

Finally she headed back to her own room. She took off the beautiful dress and the necklace and laid them on her chair. Too tired even to remove her make-up, she flopped into bed.

For just a split-second before she fell asleep, she remembered the thrill of Angus's mouth on hers, the touch of his hand on her breast and the way he had expertly undone her zip before she'd even noticed. Years of practice, she told herself, ignoring the jolt of excitement that was running through her.

Angus had clearly been an accomplished lover. Rather like Gilles the ski instructor, perhaps. She reminded herself sternly what a lucky escape she'd had and wished she could feel more grateful.

Chapter 8

'Who's a dark horse, then?' Louise demanded with more than an edge of irritation as soon as Amanda set foot in the gallery. 'I didn't have you down as an easy lay, but one whiff of Angus Day's aftershave and you were Kim Basinger on heat.'

'I think it was the Sea Breezes. And the sheik's outfit. Was it that obvious?'

'You could have stripped off and lain on the floor *during* the party, I suppose.'

Amanda closed her eyes to blot out the graphic image. She'd obviously had more to drink than she'd thought.

'The mean thing was,' Louise shook out her hair petulantly, 'I asked Angus for me. Luke was supposed to be your Christmas present.'

'So what happened to him then? My Christmas presents always seem to be bum ones. Probably because I have to buy them myself. Anyway, Angus Day's got someone already, the one he bought the herons for. Remember?'

'What's a girlfriend here and there? It's not the same as a wife, is it? Anyway, Luke rang to apologise, don't you remember? No, I don't suppose you do, too busy eyeing up the sheik of Araby. He got stuck at the Over-Sixties Hogmanay.'

'Sounds like an excuse to me.'

'Bollocks. Luke's the genuinely nice type. He wouldn't dream of throwing old ladies out on to the street like your wicked property developer. Anyway, whether he came or not, the party's over. Time for stocktaking. Starting with all the Christmas cards. I want them dusted and put away for next year. And all those Nudes in Art cards need putting back in the right place. We've just had some silly schoolboys in giggling at them.'

Amanda took herself off to the L-shaped end of the gallery where all the cards were kept. Louise was right. There were nudes everywhere. She got out a duster and polished up their privates with unusual vigour.

Now that the Christmas rush was over the gallery looked a little bare and forlorn, like a grocer's shop during rationing. 'You have to admit,' Amanda insisted to Louise, 'those herons went within a week.'

'Only because you offered Angus Day a free feel with each heron.'

'I did not!' Amanda snapped. 'I just recommended them to him, that's all. Why don't I see if the artist's got some more?'

Louise shook her head. 'They just aren't our market, Amanda. Face it.'

There wasn't a gloomier time of year than January, Amanda reflected as she put on her coat to go home at the end of the day. Even February at least heralded March and the first daffodils, with their promise of spring and sunshine. Amanda huddled into her warm wool coat, reminding herself that Sean and Clio were home now and that next week she was hosting the book group on *Men Are from Mars, Women Are from Venus*. She had plenty to look forward to.

The wind was particularly bitter down by the beach huts. To her surprise, Betty Miles stood on the decking outside their chalet, her face peering anxiously through a forest of washing optimistically hung up to dry, wearing only a thin cardigan.

Betty, normally a tough old bird who swam right through the year, was looking pale and shivery.

'Betty, what's the matter? You don't look well at all. Where's Rose?'

Although Betty was the one who struck the outside world as the extrovert, it was Rose, in Amanda's opinion, who held their life together. Betty always twittered on like a young girl at her first party, while Rose made sure they were both warm and fed. Tonight, without Rose, Betty looked cold and confused.

'She won the dancing contest the other night and she's gone to give a display.'

'Rose?' Amanda asked, staggered. Rose was both shy and stern in equal measures, entirely unlikely as a candidate for *Come Dancing*. It was such an improbable picture, like hearing Margaret Thatcher had gone in for a Miss World contest. It made you question all previous judgments about the person.

'She's down at the Pier Pavilion. I wish she were here, Amanda. To be quite honest with you, I'm not feeling myself. I had a funny dizzy turn a moment ago.' Betty was well-known for her various ailments, which often coincided with events Betty would rather didn't take place. But this time she did look vulnerable.

'I didn't know Rose was a dancer.'

'Neither did I!' She sounded part scandalised, part jealous. Betty might be almost eighty but she was used to being the centre of attention. 'It was that young man, the one who's organising the Festival. Peter? Paul? I know it's something biblical. John perhaps?'

For some absurd reason Amanda felt herself smiling, as if an unexpected shaft of sunlight had moved across a floor, illuminating everything in its path. 'You don't mean Luke?'

'Yes, that's the boy. Rose had been having dancing lessons, the sly old hen, and Luke found out about it. All the times she told me she was popping to the chemist and I thought she was a long time. Dancing lessons! So he made her get up and demonstrate, for heaven's sake. The tango!' From Betty's tone you could almost imagine an act of public indecency had taken place at the Over-Sixties. But maybe it had in Betty's eyes. Her sister had outshone her for the first time in their eighty years together.

'Amanda, dear, I know it's a lot to ask, but do you think you could possibly go and fetch her for me?'

Amanda looked at Betty keenly. If Betty was simply trying to sabotage her sister's moment of glory, she could forget it. But, actually, she did look pale and disorientated.

Concerned that Betty really ought to see a doctor, Amanda agreed. She hoped Clio and Sean would understand why she was so late. Anyway, the Pier Pavilion wasn't far out of her way.

'All right, I'll go and tell her what's happened. Now you go inside and keep warm.'

The chalet, though no bigger than a large beach hut and with room for only two single beds, a couple of chairs, a table by the window where they took their meals, plus a tiny kitchenette and a bathroom, was actually quite cosy.

From the door, Betty pointed to the electric fire which had all three bars blazing. She grinned, already looking less ill now she knew her sister was to be summoned. 'Rose only lets me have one bar so I'm making the most of it while she's out tripping the light fandango.'

Amanda pulled her coat tightly round her, did up all the buttons so that it created a warm funnel for her breath and hurried her steps. Her feet were bloody freezing. Her own fault for choosing shoes with heels that made her legs look thinner instead of comfortable boots suitable for standing in all day.

It would have been a pleasant walk apart from the shoes. The sun had gone down hours ago but the sea still reflected a glimmer of light from the bright decorations on the pier. Amanda loved piers. There was something about them that was always adventurous and faintly wicked, like an all-year fairground. Perhaps it was because they were to do with pleasure and holidays and chips and candyfloss.

The home-made doughnut seller was still on duty and it suddenly struck Amanda that she hadn't had lunch or dinner, that the pier's doughnuts were the single most delicious food known to man, and that she would die if she didn't have one now. Two, in fact, since they were fifty pence each but two only cost eighty pence. Put like that, it was almost a duty.

Amanda scoffed them greedily as a particularly pushy seagull watched her from three feet away. 'Get lost,' Amanda told it with Marie Antoinettish hauteur. 'You can eat bread.'

'Kee-ah!' replied the seagull and flapped off disdainfully.

The Old Tyme Dancing display was in the main hall. Amanda just had to follow the music. The tune was haunting and mournful and sounded as though it were being played on an ancient gramophone, so she was surprised when she pushed open the door and found the music was coming from a state-of-the-art CD player.

Amanda glanced around. About three dozen Over-Sixties sat next to the dance floor, some of them in evening dress but most wearing their normal clothes, drinking tea and orange juice. Two couples held the floor, one consisting of a very nifty elderly lady who looked as though she'd sewn every sequin on to her dress herself and was partnered by an ancient bolero-wearing escort. The other couple contained Rose.

Amanda stared. She'd never seen Rose look soft or feminine, but now, doing the tango on a freezing winter's evening, on the equally freezing pier, she was blooming like a flower in June.

The music stopped and the two couples broke away. For the first time Amanda caught a glimpse of Rose's dancing partner.

He was dazzling – tall and fair-haired yet with eyes so rich and brown you could warm your soul by them.

'Have you met my own personal lounge lizard?' Rose asked, putting her head on one side coquettishly. 'Amanda, this is Luke Knight.'

'Hardly a lounge lizard, Rose,' teased her dance partner, kissing the old lady's hand. 'More a state-funded gigolo. I'm running the Festival and this is part of the Festival, remember.'

'Absolutely. That's why you've spent two hours here today with an old bat of eighty when you probably have a million things you ought to be doing.'

'None of them as pleasant as tangoing with you, Rose.' He grinned again. His slightly long fair hair flopped into his dark eyes and he pushed it away. He was about four inches taller than Amanda and slim, yet lightly muscled, like a dancer who lifts weights in his spare time. His skin was a glorious un-British gold and it shone against his black T-shirt and Levi's.

Amanda wondered how old he was. Early thirties perhaps? Certainly younger than her. But not *too* young she found herself thinking before she could censor the thought.

Rose excused herself, saying what she needed now was a cup of tea.

'You're very good at the tango,' Amanda commented, wanting the conversation to continue and yet feeling suddenly self-conscious.

'Some of my family lived in South America,' Luke replied.

That explained the touch of exoticism which made him seem so different from the pasty Brits. 'And I spent a couple of years in Argentina on VSO when I was a student.'

God, he even had a conscience. VSO didn't attract the ruthlessly ambitious types.

'I love the music,' Amanda said. 'I could hear it all the way down the corridor. I was expecting something more "Fernando's Hideaway".'

'Tango isn't all roses in the teeth.' Luke's tone was light and teasing. 'It's about love and loss and betrayal and all sorts of deep stuff. I'll play you some more another time if you like. Knowing about tango is one of my many useless founts of knowledge.'

Amanda laughed. There was something amazingly intimate, almost caressing, in his tone that made her spine tingle. She felt a sudden rush of excitement, and then a guilty pang that only a few nights ago she'd almost gone to bed with Angus Day. Thank God she hadn't or meeting Luke might have been too complicated.

She'd been attracted to Angus, there was no denying that, but it had been the old caveman-cavewoman thing. Luke was different. He seemed so honest and unexpected. 'Well, you've made Rose very happy. It's usually her sister who hogs the limelight.'

'She's a wonderful woman. Full of amazing stories about the past. I had a grandmother like that. She was always trying to tell me things about life in the Depression and I never listened to her. Then she died and it was too late.'

Amanda nodded; she'd felt the same about her own grandparents, and even her father. There was no point asking her mother about the past. GG pretended it hadn't happened. Talking about the past was so ageing.

'Are you the Amanda I was supposed to meet at the gallery party the other night?'

Amanda flushed. She hoped to God Louise hadn't portrayed her as some desperate no-hoper who couldn't even find a man through Lonely Hearts ads.

'You know Louise . . .' She shrugged.

'Not really. I know a friend of hers who insisted I get in touch when I came here.'

Of course. The friend of Louise's. The one who'd given the glowing testimonial of sexual satisfaction.

'Louise has a God complex,' Amanda ran on, trying not to sound nervous. 'She likes everyone to fit in with her plans.'

Luke looked at her, a gleam of flirtation in his conker-coloured eyes. 'And what would her plans be? For you and me, I mean?'

Amanda looked him straight in the eye. She could dive into that warm brown gaze and never want to come up for air. 'Maybe that should be up to us to decide.' She'd never been so outspoken to a man she'd met barely five minutes ago.

Luke leaned forward so that his lips were close to hers and for a moment she thought her heart would grind to a complete halt. Surely he wasn't going to kiss her, right here in front of Rose and the Over-Sixties!

Instead he licked his finger and rubbed her face at either side of her mouth. Then he put the finger to his lips.

'Hmmmm . . . Sugar.'

Amanda flushed. The doughnuts! That served her right for being greedy.

Luke just smiled, as if he found it wildly sensual. 'So it's true then, what little girls are made of.'

All the way home with Rose, Amanda felt in a daze. She'd never met a man who'd had an effect on her like this.

'Would you like me to come in?' she asked Rose once they got to the chalet. 'To see that Betty's all right?'

'Betty will be absolutely fine,' Rose replied crisply. 'She'll be tucked up in a rug with a cup of Lapsang Souchong and only one bar on the fire, looking martyred. She'll have turned the other two off the moment she heard us coming. Thank you all the same, dear. And I'm glad you've met Luke at last. Otherwise I would have had to start wondering how on earth I could get you two together.'

Amanda could only laugh at Rose in the unlikely role of Fairy Godmother.

'You go for him, dear. They don't often come together in one package – sexy *and* kind.'

'No,' Amanda agreed, making no pretence at misunderstanding the old lady. 'And they're a pretty dynamite combination.'

'Whoosh!' Rose made a gesture like a Roman candle.

'Whoosh!' agreed Amanda, wondering when she'd get the chance to see him again. Tomorrow wouldn't be too soon. Luke Knight was the most exciting man she'd met in years.

Chapter 9

'Angus, when's that screed arriving to finish off the kitchen floors in the flats?' Laddie Smithson, Angus's foreman, yelled. They were assessing progress on the Eastcliff Estate, where the work was now almost finished. 'And we're fresh out of those poncy bricks you love so much, the reclaimed ones.'

'Order some more then. That reminds me of a funny story I heard when I was in Oz.'

'Jeeze, Angus.' Laddie rolled his eyes, knowing what would come next. 'Do we have time to listen to stories?'

'Only if they're funny.'

The building crew enthusiastically downed tools to listen. They loved Angus's stories.

'Angus, mate,' Laddie interrupted rudely, 'we do have a job to do here.'

Angus ignored him. So did the building crew. When he reached the punchline everyone collapsed helplessly. Even Laddie grinned.

'Now lead me to the mason who built that wall straight when I told him to do it cock and hen.'

Laddie Smithson took Angus through the building site to the last house on the estate. He didn't like the stone mason and was glad he was going to get screwed. But if anyone could get a good job out of him it'd be Angus. In all the building sites Laddie had ever worked on, no boss had had the common touch like Angus. He might have a posh car and expensive clothes, but he hadn't forgotten where he came from.

The building work was now virtually over. Another few weeks and they could reopen the place. Angus hadn't, despite the scare stories in the local paper, turned the estate into *chi-chi* townhouses to sell. He'd refurbished it, in partnership with the local council, at little or no profit, for its existing tenants.

'You're barmy, you know,' Laddie pointed out laconically. He threw his arm out in an expansive gesture to take in the estate. Before the refurbishment it had consisted of row after row of drab, unprepossessing low-rise flats, whose only advantage was their views over the harbour.

Angus had brought in a young architect, not long out of college, and given him the brief of making the estate the kind of place he'd like to live in himself. The architect had added pitched roofs and folksy porches to the communal front doors which were made of white clapboard. Finally he'd fixed cladding to the drab grey exteriors and painted them a duck-egg blue. It had been Angus's idea to make some of the other blocks different colours, a pale yellow and a mint green. He'd even wanted one block in pink but Laddie had drawn the line. Finally he'd had the scruffy gardens landscaped so that the flats would enjoy large communal green spaces. Angus was delighted with them.

'Why am I barmy?' he asked his foreman, suspecting he already knew the answer.

'They won't appreciate it.' Laddie shook his head. 'They may not put coal in the baths, your modern council tenant's too bone idle to even make a coal fire, but they'll let their pets crap in the garden and their kids crap anywhere they fancy. They'll complain about the poncy colours and tell you they preferred it before and you'll wish you'd stuck to what you know, which is selling fancy properties to people who appreciate them.'

'Some of them'll complain, a few will take liberties, but most of them will enjoy living somewhere decent for a change, and they'll look after the place, you wait and see, and they won't be scared to let their kids out.'

'It's their kids who do the scaring,' Laddie harrumphed.

'I think we should have a party to celebrate the opening.' Angus, if he was honest, wanted to show off not just to the tenants but to someone else. Someone with greeny-brown eyes and a fighting spirit who thought he was a filthy capitalist. It was ridiculous how much he found himself wanting her good opinion.

To think he'd got so near the other night and then her loathsome ex-husband had appeared. He knew men like that. He was sure there'd been a glint of satisfaction in Giles's eyes at sabotaging Amanda's encounter.

For the last two days or so he'd been agonising over what to do. Should he call her? Maybe the whole situation was too complicated. Was he being stupid in risking rejection? And when he had finally plucked up courage last night and dialled the gallery, Louise told him Amanda had just left.

'Why did you do it, Angus?' Laddie broke in to his thoughts. 'You're going to lose money hand over fist on this place.'

Angus grinned. 'To redeem myself in my mother's stern Calvinist eyes.'

'Bollocks,' Laddie dismissed. 'Your mother's too much of a canny Scot to approve of this nonsense.'

Angus laughed, his grey eyes crinkling at being caught out. 'You're probably right. Call it an altruistic impulse.'

'Tell you one thing.' Laddie pulled his woolly hat down over his ears against the cold. 'I hope you aren't going to have too many more of these here altruistic impulses or we'll all be out of a bleedin' job.'

'I won't. I promise.'

'And one more thing. You know what's going to happen?'

Angus steeled himself against Laddie's next onslaught.

'Now that you've been kind enough to spend all this dosh on them, the tenants'll only sell them, won't they, now they're allowed to, and what a fool law that was. And who'll be making the fat profit then, eh? Not you, for sure.'

Angus patted him and shrugged. You could always rely on Laddie to think the worst of people. The trouble was, he was probably right. Some tenants might well sell up.

Angus walked briskly back to his car, shouting greetings to the various chippies, brickies and ground workers he employed and asking about their families. Laddie was always amazed that Angus remembered their names. Laddie was right about one thing, though. He had their livelihoods to think of too.

"Ere,' shouted a woman with a strange orange hairdo whom Angus recognised as one of the tenants who'd been most vociferously critical of the whole scheme. His heart sank. He didn't feel like a slanging match at the moment. 'Are you the bloke who's behind this lot?' She gestured towards the estate.

Feebly, Angus considered directing her to Laddie, who would take no lip from a bolshy council tenant. But he decided to bite the bullet.

'Yes,' he admitted reluctantly. 'I am.'

She paused, her heavily mascaraed eyes holding his. 'It ain't too bad, as a matter of fact.'

Angus almost laughed with relief. 'Thanks,' he answered, keeping the ludicrous pleasure he felt out of his voice. 'Then you'll be coming to the opening party?'

The woman looked at him suspiciously. 'When is it?'

'Whenever you want. We're almost finished here. Just the landscaping to do.'

'What, grass and that?'

'All round here.' He indicated the untidy scrubland dotted with rubbish and builders' skips.

'That'll be an improvement,' she conceded.

'Yes. Maybe you'd organise it? With our funds of course . . .'

'What?'

'The party. Here's my number. I'm Angus Day.'

'Lou Wills. Thanks. I might. I'll give you a call.'

Angus walked back to his car feeling cheered. It would give him the greatest possible pleasure to prove Laddie wrong.

When he dropped in to see his mother later that afternoon she was looking better than she had for weeks. Isobel was sitting in her favourite chair, a book on her knee, staring out at the wintry garden.

'Hello, Maw. You're looking fit.' He dropped down to kiss her bony cheek.

'Probably because these narcissi you bought me have been cheering me up. Just smell them.'

As he leaned over to take in the scent of the pale yellow flowers on the table next to her chair, she dropped a light hand on to his dark wavy hair in a rare gesture of physical affection.

She lifted it again quickly, but smiled. 'You need a haircut.'

'I know,' Angus smiled. He'd been about to say he'd been too busy with the Eastcliff Estate, then he remembered Laddie's words about what his mother would think. Laddie was probably right. 'I should get a short back and sides.'

'No, don't do that. I like it. It makes you look rather buccaneering. Errol Flynn with a touch of Mel Gibson.'

'I didn't know you liked Mel Gibson.'

'All women like Mel Gibson. But only some of them admit to it. As a matter of fact, I fell for his bottom in *Braveheart*. Did you see it?'

Angus laughed. 'I'll take your word for it.'

He puffed up the cushions behind her back. 'Have you eaten today?'

'I've been stuffed to the gills. Mrs Northam brought me one of her famous chicken pies.'

'Good.'

'And I've taken my medicine. How about you? Have you seen any more of your Amanda?'

Isobel Day knew her son well enough to notice the slight flicker of disappointment in his eyes. She suspected her son was falling in love with Amanda, but that things weren't going as smoothly as he'd hoped.

'It occurred to me –' Isobel paused for a second, a glint of amusement creeping into her expression – 'that I'd really like another sculpture. By the same artist that did the herons. I'll pay for it. But I wondered if you and Amanda could choose it for me.'

'Isobel Day,' Angus grinned, 'you're a wicked, calculating old woman.' He kissed her again, struck once more by the incredible fragility of her frame.

'I know,' Isobel admitted, 'and I'm enjoying it no end.'

'Go on, admit it,' Louise demanded the next day before Amanda had even had a chance to take off her coat, 'you've met Luke at last!'

'What makes you say that?' Amanda tried not to grin as she unbuttoned her coat.

For once Louise had made coffee herself and was taking down canvases in preparation for a show they were having entitled 'A Summer's Day in Lovely Laineton'. Amanda knew it would bring out the very worst of the Sunday painters but Louise insisted it was just what people needed to cheer them up after Christmas.

'Call it women's intuition,' Louise said over her shoulder. 'Or the fact that you've done your hair and are wearing make-up and fuck-me shoes. Assuming you haven't turned lezzy overnight, I can only guess that it's for Luke's benefit rather than mine.' She paused tellingly. 'Plus the fact that I bumped into Rose Miles at the green-grocer and she told me all about it.'

Louise stood back to admire the empty walls. 'Rose was very struck. She made it sound like the plot of *Romeo and Juliet*, only hopefully with a happier ending.'

'And leaving out the fact that I'm old enough to be Juliet's mother; no, make that grandmother.'

'Tsk, tsk, such details! So where did you bump into him? I've been trying to get you two together for weeks.'

'At the Old Tyme Dancing. He's amazing. You know how but-toned-up Rose is. She hardly says a word and has disapproval stamped all over her forehead. Luke found out she'd been having tango lessons and got her to give a demonstration. She's a changed person! And Betty's absolutely furious!'

'So it's his way with old people, is it, that primarily attracted you to Luke Knight?'

Amanda sighed. 'That and the fact that he's fabulously, daz-zlingly, jaw-droppingly fanciable.'

'And it sounds as if, from what my friend says, there's more delights to come in the trouser department.'

Amanda giggled guiltily. There was no point trying to explain to Louise that something had also clicked with Luke on a deeper level, that in the brief moment she'd met him she'd felt at ease and had sensed that he had a complexity that was at least as fascinating as his superficial attractions. Though she certainly wasn't complaining about those either. She could hardly tell Louise she was attracted to his soul too – she would have a field day with that bit of information.

'And what's more,' Louise winked at her, 'from what I can gather, he's absolutely and completely different from Giles.'

'He must be.' Amanda could hear the excitement in her own voice. 'Rose says he's kind *and* sexy.'

'So, come on,' the ever-subtle Louise demanded in a voice that could have been heard the other side of Laineton, 'let's have a bet. How long do you think it's going to take you to get this thrusting example of glorious manhood, this dark-eyed Lothario with his firm and glowing flesh, into your bedroom?'

They were so caught up with their joke that neither of them had noticed the unexpected arrival of Angus Day in the gallery.

'I hope it's not me you're describing or I'll have to call my lawyer. The firmness of my flesh is privileged information.'

Amanda flushed like an overripe tomato. Even her neck went bright red.

Angus quickly realised his mistake. How naive of him to imagine it was he who was the subject of their conversation just because of what had almost happened a few days ago.

'Sorry, Angus,' Louise drawled, 'you were last week's dish of the day. We've moved on now.'

'I came in,' Angus began, trying not to show the pain and humiliation he was feeling, 'to see if you had any more carved birds like the pair of herons I bought from you.'

Amanda was just about to cover her embarrassment by saying that she was sure the artist had some more pieces when Louise beat her to it. Louise had spotted the real reason for Angus's visit – he obviously wanted to see Amanda, dammit.

She cut in swiftly. 'I'm afraid we don't show that particular artist's work any more. The herons were a one-off. But I'm sure I could arrange to take you to visit the artist if you were really interested.'

Angus hesitated. It was obvious that this wasn't at all what he had in mind. 'Well, maybe I'll—' he began.

'Quite,' Louise nodded. 'Anyway, I trust you'll come to our new show in two weeks' time? "A Summer's Day in Lovely Laineton".' For a brief moment Amanda and Angus's eyes locked in shared amusement. 'Perhaps you could find something for your special lady at that.'

Angus was about to say that his mother would hate summer scenes of lovely Laineton but thought Louise might be insulted. 'I'd better leave.' He cheered up for a moment. 'And you could both come to our party.'

'Oh yes?' Louise said guardedly. She didn't like the sound of this 'our' stuff. 'When's that?'

'For the reopening of the Eastcliff Estate.'

Louise visibly shuddered. 'I'm not sure that's really my kind of thing.'

'Louise is worried the tenants might realise that she'd prefer them to be transported,' Amanda pointed out.

'She and my foreman both. He says the only reason they won't put coal in their brand new baths is because they're too idle to make a fire in the first place.'

'Sound man,' seconded Louise.

'I'll send you an invitation,' Angus insisted and headed for the door. Through the window he noticed that one of the two old ladies who lived in the beach hut was standing outside rummaging in her bag. He was about to open the door for her when a tall, fair-haired man got there first. The newcomer swept open the door to the gallery with a flourish, bowing like an Elizabethan courtier as he did so. The gesture should have been charming but somehow, to Angus's eyes, it seemed condescending instead. *I don't really mean this*, was the message, *but you and I can pretend I do.*

Angus wondered why his instinct was to dislike so intensely

someone he hadn't even met. He glanced back at Amanda. Her face had suddenly come to life like a flower after a sudden shower of rain.

A sharp pain winded him. Amanda had fallen in love all right. But not with him.`

Chapter 10

'Hello, Rose.' Amanda was deeply grateful that Rose's arrival in the gallery gave her a distraction from the embarrassment of Angus bumping into Luke. In fact, glancing out at the pavement, she saw that Angus was still standing watching them. However, while Angus had certainly noticed Luke, Luke seemed sublimely indifferent to Angus.

'We don't often see you in here, Rose,' Amanda greeted her. 'What can we get you?'

'Actually, I wanted a card for Betty's birthday. I don't suppose you do any "Happy Birthday, You're Eighty-one" cards?'

'I think the card manufacturers see it as a dwindling market,' Louise pointed out with her usual sensitivity.

'We do have some lovely flower paintings.' Amanda took her over to the card racks. 'Or what about this one?' Amanda selected a card of Michelangelo's David which played 'Happy Birthday to You' when the fig leaf was lifted.

'Perfect,' pronounced Rose.

Amanda turned to catch Luke, who was pretending to discuss an exhibition with Louise, following her movements with his eyes. He treated her to his dazzling smile. 'I was just wondering,' he said, 'since it's almost lunchtime and the weather is so glorious, if you'd like to come for a walk? I'm sure your kind employer will appreciate that on a day like this life has to be grabbed with both hands.'

'Just don't grab Amanda with both hands,' Louise barked. 'I want her back here at two.'

'Pier or prom?' asked Luke. And then, without waiting, 'I'd prefer prom myself. Fewer people. We'll have it to ourselves.'

Going for a walk on a January lunchtime wasn't something Amanda usually considered. It was so cold that she could easily have been persuaded to have a bowl of hot soup instead of a stroll, but Luke was striding past the cafés on the lower deck of the promenade, laughing at the arctic wind blowing in his face and whipping up his fair hair.

'Come on,' he shouted, grabbing her hand. 'What you need is to warm up a bit, get your circulation going.'

Amanda's circulation was screaming for a log fire but she'd freeze to death rather than admit it.

'Let's walk up towards the harbour.'

'On one condition,' Amanda laughed. He'd made no attempt to let go of her hand, she noticed with a secret thrill. 'You tell me all about yourself. I hardly know anything about you.'

'All right. Luke Knight, This Is Your Life. Born in Shepherd's Bush, father a vicar . . .'

'Ah, that probably explains the social conscience.'

'You've heard of being poorer than a church mouse?'

Amanda nodded.

'Church mice were millionaires compared to us. Three older sisters who both doted on me.' He grinned engagingly. 'Ditto mother. Fortunately I had two assets which got me into Choir School, so at least my parents could relax about my education. They didn't want to send me to the local comprehensive but knew it was snobbish to say so. So they said it didn't teach Latin. That sounded suitably devout. Anyway, I looked sweet in a choir boy's outfit and I have quite a good voice. You should hear my "O for the Wings of a Dove". Not quite what it was since my balls dropped, of course. It brought tears to the choirmaster's eyes. Not to mention a hard-on.'

For a moment the laughter in Luke's dark eyes faded, but then he carried on gaily, leaving Amanda to wonder whether she'd imagined it. 'So I became an angelic boarder, cried my eyes out at first because I missed my mum and learned just about enough, God knows how, to get to university.'

'What did you study?'

'All right, let's get it over with . . .' He grinned broadly, mischief lighting up his conker-brown eyes. 'Divinity. My father was eager, no passionate, that I should follow in his footsteps.'

'Hard footsteps to follow. Not everyone is suited to being a vicar.'

'And certainly not me. You know what they say about a vicar's children . . . they either become saints or sinners. I chose the latter path, you'll be relieved to hear.'

By this time they'd reached the row of flaking beach huts. 'Come on, let's run down to the beach.' Luke squeezed her hand. It was a wonderful feeling. His grip was warm and firm despite the freezing weather, and contained a hint of unexpected strength. Excitement fizzled through her, and to her embarrassment Louise's voice rang through her head. *You know what they say about a firm handshake* . . .

Feeling slightly shamed by her thoughts, she concentrated on not falling over on the slippery shingle. The tide was in so there was no sand today, just the pale blue sea lapping at the pebbles.

'Perfect,' announced Luke, throwing himself down into the shelter of the breakwater and pulling her after him. 'You, me, the glassy sea . . . and this.' He reached down to where the breakwater met the edge of the sea and pulled out a bottle of champagne.

'How on earth . . .?' began Amanda. 'You put it there!'

'Ever the optimist, me. I wanted to celebrate that we'd finally met.' He began expertly unscrewing the cork. 'Damn, I forgot glasses.'

'Never mind. I'm happy swigging from the bottle,' Amanda reassured, laughing, enjoying the adventure far too much to care about such details.

'Here you are,' said a voice behind them. They both turned. Rose Miles was standing on the shingle, holding out two glasses. 'Only tumblers I'm afraid. I saw Luke putting the bottle here and worked out the rest. Happy Tuesday, both of you.' She departed as quickly as she'd arrived, smiling to herself.

'You've certainly charmed Rose,' Amanda admired. 'She used to be the dourest, most disapproving old bat.'

'Don't jump to conclusions. There's fire and passion in Rose.'

'And you're good at detecting those?' Amanda asked.

'I like to think so.' Luke stopped smiling for a moment. 'You, for instance, are capable of being shameless but no one's spotted it.'

Amanda didn't understand what had got into her. All she knew was that her life was so trammelled, so caught up with responsibilities, and Luke represented a crazy, careless alternative. 'Except you.'

He leaned forward and kissed her hard on the lips, champagne fizzing from his mouth to hers. He kissed her for so long she could hardly breathe, and yet she didn't want him to stop. When he did pull back she could hardly believe where they were, sitting here on Laineton beach, in January, on a Tuesday lunchtime.

He touched her lips lightly with his finger. 'There. I knew I was right. And, yes, I know it's time you got back. What are you doing after work?'

She almost said, 'Cooking tea and doing the ironing like every other night', but she stopped herself. She didn't want him to know how predictable her life was. Instead she said, 'Why, did you want to do something?'

'There's an incredible film showing at the Festival. Ozu's *Early Summer*. It's Japanese, black and white, about a young couple going on an outing to look at the cherry blossom and falling in love against their parents' wishes. It's a wonderful metaphor for everything coming alive, both outside and inside. I know you'll love it.'

Amanda's heart somersaulted. He was talking to her about ideas. He recognised that she actually had a brain, and even thought she was capable of deep passion. Giles had never talked to her about ideas. Giles didn't *have* any ideas apart from how to look after Giles Wells. Even Angus hadn't talked to her about ideas. Amanda, was outrageously flattered.

'I'd love to come. What time is it?' Her mind raced through the possibilities of asking Sean's friend's mum to collect Sean from football practice.

'Not till eight-thirty. Shall I pick you up?'

'No, thanks.' She didn't quite feel ready to introduce him to Clio and Sean. She'd prefer to prepare the ground a little so it wasn't too much of a shock. 'I'll meet you there.'

They clinked glasses. 'It's at the Corn Exchange. Maybe we could eat afterwards.'

Those few little words showed how different his life was to hers. Luke could do precisely what he wanted, without consulting anyone. How blissful. And, in her case, how impossible.

'I'd love to another night. A Saturday perhaps?'

'Of course, you've got kids. Louise did tell me. How old are they?'

'Clio's sixteen and Sean is ten.'

'Can't the sixteen-year-old look after the ten-year-old?'

'Normally yes, but Clio studies at her friend's house on Tuesdays.'

The tiniest irritation flickered in his dazzling dark eyes. 'Can't you just *tell* her?'

She could see Luke didn't have a lot of experience of teenagers. She didn't explain that she wanted her children to like Luke, not see him as the enemy, and that it would be better in the long run if she played this sudden new relationship tactfully. But that sounded too presumptuous. She might still be wrong about the level of his interest in her.

Luke seemed to sense her indecision. 'Up to you, I shouldn't interfere. Let's go for a meal another time then, if you can arrange it. We'll just do the cinema tonight. You'd better be off. I've got a meeting in town anyway. I'll walk you back.'

She was actually rather grateful that he didn't kiss her again, especially in front of Louise. Not that she didn't want to be kissed. She did. All over, if possible. Very slowly. But Luke wasn't attuned to small-town, or even medium-town, habits. He was used to London ways and London anonymity. She had to slow him down without seeming to.

Just as she said goodbye, he asked nonchalantly, 'By the way, who was the man leaving as I arrived, the rich-looking one? He seemed rather interested in you, I thought.'

'Oh.' Amanda feigned nonchalance. 'That's Angus Day.'

'The property developer? The one who's turfed out all the tenants from the estate on the hill?'

'Yes, but . . .' For reasons she didn't fully understand, Amanda, who had made precisely this accusation herself, felt the irrational urge to spring to Angus's defence, but Luke didn't leave her time.

'Tsk, tsk, Amanda. Consorting with property developers? I'm surprised at you.'

Amanda could see Louise inside the shop watching them and tapping her watch in irritation.

'Sorry, got to dash. Louise is in one of her clock-watching moods. See you at eight-thirty.'

Luke smiled at her indulgently and blew her a kiss.

'So,' Louise asked, torn between jealousy that Amanda was glowing with fresh air and a fresh man and the desire to know everything that had happened, 'did you really go for a walk? It'd freeze a dog's bollocks off out there.'

'Not only did we go for a walk but he'd hidden a bottle of champagne down by the breakwater.'

'What does he think this is? Laineton on a Tuesday or a bloody Lanson advert?'

'You're just envious.'

'True.'

'Wait, there's more. He's asked me out tonight. To see a Japanese film!'

'That sexy one? The Japanese Kama Sutra? Only I can't remember the title. Something about a corridor.'

'*Ai No Corrida*? No, this one's about people falling in love against their parents' wishes.'

'He's met your mother, has he?'

Amanda grinned. She didn't know what her mother would make of Luke. Dislike him probably. Call him an intellectual snob. Unless he decided to charm her of course.

'And he wanted to go out on Saturday too.'

'Bloody hell, Amanda. Why don't you just save all the hassle and ask him to move in straightaway? Now look, there's a couple been staring at that painting for ten minutes. Go sell it 'em, girl.'

'Come on, Clio, cheer up! I'm sure he really liked you,' Jasmine, Clio's best friend, tried to console her. They were both at Jasmine's house revising for their mock GCSEs, or rather not revising but running through, for the nineteenth time, the possible motivations of Gilles.

Clio sat on the bright-red lip-shaped chair near Jasmine's bed. She was wearing the hugest, most camouflaging old jumper she could find, which had been left behind by her father. She didn't want anyone to notice her breasts, or make remarks about them. She wanted to be safe and sexless again.

The problem was, she hadn't told Jasmine the whole truth. Or her mother, for that matter. What Clio felt really bad about was that she'd allowed herself to be bullied. The first night she'd gone out with Gilles he'd tried to get her into bed, and she'd fended him off by telling him she was a virgin.

'And you're proud of that?' Gilles had asked her in amazement. 'Most girls of your age would be embarrassed.' Clio had flushed with shame. She hadn't been ready for this. It had all happened so quickly, boys suddenly being interested in her. She'd had no defences and no practice. Until six months ago she'd worn braces on her teeth and been beanpole thin, not to mention taller than ninety per cent of the boys she'd met. She was also still reeling from the breakup of her parents' marriage. A walking disaster zone. Fortunately, apart from Jasmine, people had left her alone and she had been able to wander around, unhappy but anonymous. Then the breasts had appeared and suddenly boys were looking, but inside Clio was the same.

If her mother had been there it would have been all right. She could have talked to her about it. But her father had been hopeless. Still, she'd got through the holiday with a bewildering mixture of fear, excitement and dawning sexual arousal. At least her skiing, with all the individual attention, had come on a dream. On the second from last day Gilles had taken her on a terrifying mountain ski trip designed, she suspected, to make her feel frightened and turned on in equal measure.

That night, Gilles had come to her room. He'd told her that Gudrun, the girl from Stuttgart, was gagging for him but that he'd resisted because he liked Clio so much. And Clio, who had always hated bullying tactics and been the first to stand up to them at school, had given in for some reason she couldn't understand.

She hadn't told Jasmine this. Or that her period hadn't come yet, despite the fact they'd taken precautions. Maybe it had been the flying. She'd heard that flying could affect your cycle. All the same, she desperately wanted to talk to her mother about it. She just wished Amanda would ask her, but Amanda wasn't her usual sensitive self at the moment. Her mind seemed permanently elsewhere.

'I think I'll go home now,' Clio announced. It was no good, she just couldn't concentrate.

'But we haven't started our English Lit.'

Clio was in no mood for revising Jane Austen tonight.

It was six o'clock by the time she'd walked slowly home, and already as dark as midnight. The sight of the house, small, narrow and painted pale pink, in a row of others in similar pastel colours, always cheered her. Their whole street reminded her of the Neapolitan ice cream they sold in the corner shop near school. They were friendly houses.

Unusually, the light was on in her mother's bedroom.

As soon as she'd turned her key in the door, Amanda, who'd obviously been listening out for her, came bounding down the stairs wearing her dressing gown. 'Clio! Thank heavens. I've got a favour to ask you. I've put a lasagne in the oven – don't worry, not one of mine, a Marks and Spencer one.' Clio always thought shop-bought lasagne wildly superior to her mother's. 'And there's a salad to go with it. I wondered if you could make sure Sean has his after football practice and goes to bed at nine.'

'Why? Where will you be?' Clio asked suspiciously.

'I'm going to the cinema,' Amanda answered primly. 'With a friend.'

Clio grinned. 'A friend with a bright-blue BMW?' she asked teasingly.

This time it was Amanda's turn to smile. 'No, as a matter of fact. A new friend.' Her mother, it seemed to Clio, was lit from within. There was a brightness to her smile and her eyes and a fizziness in her manner that Clio had never seen before, like a child hugging a secret. Not to mention a new self-absorption. Normally Amanda would have remembered that Clio had been going to Jasmine's to revise this evening, and would have asked her, her voice all tender concern, if everything was all right, coming home early like this. But Amanda had obviously forgotten she was going to Jasmine's at all.

Bloody hell, Clio thought furiously, my mother's behaving like a teenager.

So much for a heart-to-heart about her worries over Gilles and her late period. Her mother was too busy to listen. Well, maybe she'd regret that.

The film was entrancing. Amanda's usual film diet was action-adventures selected by Sean or the mildly funny romantic comedies Clio enjoyed – both hired from the video shop because cinema trips were too expensive. *Early Summer* was both beautiful to look at and profoundly moving. Amanda was amazed she could enjoy a black and white film, with subtitles, made forty years ago, so much more than modern Hollywood offerings.

'Well, did you like it?' Luke asked as they walked towards his car.

'I thought it was wonderful, absolutely fantastic.'

'What did you make of the symbolism of the cherry blossom and their relationship?'

He was actually asking her her opinion. Amanda realised how long it had been since anyone had asked her to stretch her mind beyond shopping lists and school calendars. Giles wouldn't have dreamed of soliciting her views on anything remotely intellectual. Giles found anything even faintly arty-farty threatening. Louise occasionally asked her what she thought of a picture, but since their tastes were so different, she'd stopped even doing that.

This felt heady and wonderful, like being a student. Having never been to college herself, Amanda imagined it to consist of passionate arguments about philosophy and art and stretching intellectual experiences.

'Sure about not eating? What about a quick drink?'

There was nothing Amanda would have liked more than to discuss the film over a curry, but Clio had been a little strange earlier and she had to be fair to her children. It was important that they didn't take against Luke if she were to see more of him. Clio could be an awesomely destructive force when she wanted to be, and she didn't need her daughter aiming a nuclear missile at whatever might develop between her and Luke.

'I ought to get back. I'm sorry.'

'Ah well. I could have fallen for fancy-free Louise, but Louise with no responsibilities can't hold a candle to you. I'll just have to join the queue, I suppose, somewhere below your kids and the cat.'

'Above the cat,' Amanda reassured, smiling.

He stopped at the end of her road, sensing that she wouldn't want to say her goodbyes in full view of her house.

'Mrs Wells,' Luke said softly, melting her insides with his inviting brown eyes, 'you're the loveliest surprise I've had for a long time,' and he pulled her into his arms and kissed her till she could hardly breathe.

When he let her go, she pushed him reluctantly away. Every bit of her was tingling with longing. If only she didn't have such a complicated life, she'd drag him to bed and never let him get up.

'I must go,' she said gently.

'Saturday week. Would that be giving you enough warning?' Luke asked, his voice soft with teasing. 'There's a rock concert on as part of the Festival. Quite a few big names. As Festival Organiser I happen to have tickets.'

'That'd be Fantastic.' She'd been on the point of telling him that Clio would be spitting with jealousy, but it sounded so mumsy.

'Great.' He blew her another kiss. He really was the most gorgeous man she'd ever met. She tore herself away, wishing her life were different, more like his, that she didn't have to worry about homework and football practice and whether Sean had his lunch or Clio was doing enough revision for her GCSEs.

Clio was still up when she got back, sitting at the kitchen table eating ice cream and watching television.

'I thought you'd be in bed.' Amanda dropped a kiss on to Clio's hair.

'Got to keep an eye on my mother. Make sure she gets home safe,' Clio announced, showing no signs of going to bed.

'Want a cup of tea?' Amanda asked, aware that Clio didn't usually hang around like this in the kitchen. She was normally asleep by this time, or reading a trashy novel or texting her friend Jasmine. The kitchen was a mess, as usual, with schoolbooks propped all over the table, empty cereal bowls from late-night snack attacks littering the work surfaces and unwashed dishes soaking in the sink. She was about to yell at Clio, but something stopped her.

'Everything OK?' Amanda asked, pretending to be casual.

'Everything's fine,' Clio replied in the tone of faint outrage she reserved for her mother's nosiness. 'Apart from mocks next week.'

So that was it. 'I'm sure you'll do fine. You've worked hard.'

No I won't, Clio wanted to scream, not if I'm worried to death about my sodding period.

Amanda, with a mother's sixth sense, guessed there might be more and tried to tread the tricky, occasionally impossible path between being concerned and being intrusive. 'Are you sure? You would tell me if anything serious was worrying you?'

Clio hesitated. It would be a huge relief to share this with her mother. 'Well, I . . .'

The phone rang, cutting into Clio's words.

'Who the hell could that be?' Amanda said, irritated. 'It's far too late for your father or GG.'

'Hi.' His voice was as caressing as molten chocolate – dark, rich and incredibly sexy. 'It's Luke. I'm in bed. I just rang to say that I had a glorious evening and that I wish you were here.'

Amanda smiled in spite of herself. 'Me too.'

'Tell me what you're doing now.' She wondered if he had some Mrs Robinson fantasy of her stripping off black stockings.

'Actually, I'm sitting at the kitchen table talking to my daughter.'

'Oh.' His tone changed gear abruptly. 'You'd better get back, then. See you very soon.'

'Who was that?' Clio was sitting bolt upright, her narrow body tense.

'A friend.'

'The friend you went to the cinema with?'

'Yes. His name's Luke.'

Clio crinkled her nose. 'Poncy name. Makes him sound like an angel or something.'

Unconsciously, Amanda smiled. 'He's hardly that.'

Clio had never heard that tone from her mother before, all melted and vulnerable and sexy. She hated it.

'What happened to the other one? I liked him.'

'He already has someone. Anyway, you were saying . . .'

Clio removed her teabag, squeezed it out into her cup, then put it on the table.

'Clio, don't do that, it marks the wood.' Although this habit of Clio's drove her to distraction, Amanda wished, just for once, she could have resisted nagging her daughter.

'Don't worry,' Clio announced huffily, 'I'm going to bed.' She stumped off noisily.

Amanda sighed, her pleasure at the evening draining away. Was something important worrying Clio? Maybe it was just that the timing was bad. This should be Clio's time to be thinking about boyfriends, not Amanda's. And yet it had been Clio who had encouraged her to look for a man in the first place. Perhaps Clio hadn't stopped to think what life would be like if her mother actually found one.

From the corner of her eye, Amanda noticed Kinky the cat sneaking into the room. Suddenly desperate for affection, Amanda swooped on her and held her tight. But for once Kinky was having none of it. She jumped out of Amanda's arms and began to yowl piteously, dragging her back legs and bottom across the peasant-tiled floor.

'Whatever's the matter, Kinky?' Amanda asked, studying this peculiar behaviour. And then she realised.

Kinky was on heat.

'Tough luck, fluffball.' She stroked Kinky's furry tummy in sympathy. 'Believe me, I know exactly how you feel.'

Chapter 11

'Mu-um!' Sean's voice penetrated Amanda's dream just at the point where she and Luke were walking, hand in hand, along a white sandy beach towards a deserted olive grove. Moments later they would be sinking down together and . . .

'Mu-um! Where are my goggles? I need them for swimming today.'

Amanda sat up. What the hell was the time? She leapt out of bed, grabbed yesterday's clothes and hopped towards the bath-room, which of course was occupied by Clio. Amanda's slot had been twenty minutes earlier.

Downstairs everything was chaos. School gear was strewn over the hall, no packed lunches were ready and Kinky was sitting on the breakfast table calmly lapping the milk from Sean's cereal bowl.

'Off!' Amanda shouted, sweeping the cat from the table. Kinky shot her a reproachful look, as if to say, 'If sex is out, at least leave me food.'

'Clio!' Amanda yelled, chomping a piece of toast while simulta-neously searching for her house keys. She glanced at the family organiser calendar on the wall. God, she'd almost forgotten – tonight it was her turn to host the book group on *Men Are from Mars, Women Are from Venus*. Knowing the views of most of its members, the session would probably end up as Men Are Complete

Bastards, Women Are Far the Superior Gender. Until a week or so ago she might have agreed, but now she'd met Luke she was prepared to give men another chance.

Clio finally appeared in an extremely short skirt and jumper so enormous that any sign of her newly arrived bosoms was hidden from view. She had, Amanda noticed, purple smudges of sleeplessness under her eyes.

'Is anything the matter? You don't look as if you've slept a wink.'

'Maybe that's because I haven't,' snapped Clio unhelpfully.

Sean rolled his eyes to heaven. His sister was in a sulk again. Didn't she realise that if you sulked all the time people stopped paying attention?

'Perhaps she's got PMT,' suggested Sean.

'PMT?' snorted Clio, wishing desperately she *did* have it because at least it would mean she had a period coming. 'What do you know about PMT, squirt?'

'We had a lesson on puberty yesterday. A lady from some tampon company and a man flogging acne stuff came to talk to us.'

'How outrageous,' Amanda protested, forgetting about Clio for a moment. 'You mean your school has people in from commercial companies to tell you about spots and periods?'

'Better than hearing it from Mr Henderson. He's got spots *and* dandruff. When he told us about S-E-X Duffy asked him if he'd ever had it himself and he went bright red and sweaty which means he hasn't, according to Duffy. Anyway, he can't give us a booty bag with anti-spot stuff in it like this bloke did. It was full of all these great free samples.' He produced a plastic carrier bag of potions and creams.

'Isn't it a bit soon for all this stuff?' Amanda asked. She'd found her keys, they'd been under Kinky. Now all she needed was her purse.

'Puberty happens younger and younger now, Mr Henderson says.' Sean pulled himself up to his full ten-year-old height. 'There was even one boy,' he announced grandly, 'who fathered a child at ten.'

'Oh, for God's sake!' Clio exploded, banging her fist on the kitchen table so that Kinky, who'd climbed up again, was bounced into the air. 'You really ought to complain, Mum. They shouldn't be filling his head with all this crap!'

'It's not crap,' Sean insisted. 'The tampon lady did this really cool experiment.' He picked up a jug of water. 'You take the girls' thingamebob,' Sean began, as if he were demonstrating a new football kick he'd just learned.

'Sanitary pad,' supplied Clio loftily.

'And you pour in the liquid, thirty-five millilitres a day they said. And look!' He waved the pad at them with all the enthusiasm of a vacuum cleaner salesman. 'The gel in the layers stops it coming through. Feel.'

'God, this is revolting. Mum, you're going to have to complain.' Clio grabbed the soggy pad and flung it on the ground.

Amanda picked it up, wondering if Sean was right about the cause of his sister's moodiness. 'Clio, for God's sake. What on earth's the matter with you?'

Clio picked up her school bag. 'And don't look at me like that!' she screamed as she stomped out of the room. 'I haven't got PMT. I only wish I bloody well had!'

Amanda rushed round the kitchen, doling out bus fares and gathering up the things she needed for work. What had Clio meant by that?

On the way to the bus stop, Clio softened. 'Sorry Mum. Maybe we should have a chat later. I know,' she brightened, 'why don't you ask Gran over to look after Sean and you and I can go out for a pizza?'

Offers like this from Clio were unheard of, and it wrenched Amanda's heart to say, 'Fabulous. But not tonight. The book group's coming round. How about tomorrow instead?'

'Oh great!' Clio's pretty face darkened. 'So the house will be full of man-hating harpies, will it?'

'Clio,' Amanda teased gently, 'you sound just like your father.'

'Yes, well, no wonder he went off with Stephanie. At least she likes men.'

'Preferably for breakfast,' Amanda murmured, trying not to show how hurt she was. 'Now come on or you'll be late for school.'

For a moment Amanda wondered whether she ought to put off the book group. But there were eight of them and she probably wouldn't even be able to get hold of them at this short notice. Louise would kill her if she spent the morning on the phone.

Amanda smiled secretly. Should she tell them about Luke? No, maybe not. It was too soon. Better to keep him as her delicious secret.

No matter how hard she tried, she'd never be able to convey quite how attractive he was. But it would be fun to give it a go.

As everyone had been so busy with Christmas, Ruthie, the group's unofficial organiser, had decreed they could read the pocket-sized version of *Men Are from Mars, Women Are from Venus*.

'Hi!' Ruthie swept in, all dungarees and certainty. 'Where shall I put the vino?' It was custom that everyone brought a bottle. That meant a bottle each, except for stingy Myra who brought water which they suspected she'd filled up from the tap, and arty Simone who swore by Aqua Libra but pinched several glasses of wine from other people's bottles. The group, though ostensibly devoted to literary self-improvement, had at least two other functions: part relationship counselling and part let's-get-out-of-the-bloody-house.

'Hey, everyone,' announced Simone, flicking back her long black hair to reveal her row of ear piercings. 'We got the title wrong. It's really *Women Are from Mars, Men Have a Penis*.'

Everyone laughed except Anne, who looked deeply puzzled. 'But I thought . . .' she began.

'Say it to yourself out loud,' whispered Ruthie.

They'd all just poured a glass of wine and sat down when Louise arrived, bracelets jangling and shawls swirling.

'God, Louise,' Ruthie commented rudely, 'you look like a cross between Clint Eastwood's poncho and the *Country Living* spring fair.'

Louise smiled narrowly. Her expression, which looked jolly and life-embracing when she was in a good mood, could switch to granite cliff-face when she was irritated. She sat down. 'All right.' She smoothly took on Ruthie's role of group organiser, much to

Ruthie's annoyance. 'What did we think of the text? Are men and women really from different planets?'

'Different galaxies, if you ask me,' Janine offered.

'But aren't these a lot of ludicrous generalisations all strung together without any regard for individual men?' Anne suggested.

'No,' said Ruthie. 'Twenty reasonably happy years with Tom have convinced me he really does work differently. Like this book says, men pride themselves on being experts at practical things, and if anything like that goes wrong . . . kerpoww! He explodes. He feels good about himself if he can tick off a list of achievements in life. And it drives him insane that I don't see life as a series of goals.'

Amanda listened, fascinated. 'What do you see life as then?'

'Being open to things. Valuing the moment. Being there for my friends.'

'And what do you do while you're being open and spontaneous,' Amanda asked, ' and your husband goes off with someone who could goal-set for England? Someone who needed a man because she wanted a baby, took yours, and is having twins?' Amanda realised how angry she still felt at Stephanie who had stolen her husband and was about to make Clio and Sean feel second-best.

Everyone laughed, except Ruthie. 'In your case, I'd ask myself why I'd wanted that particular man in the first place. Especially if he was a complete shit.'

Amanda stopped, shocked. Ruthie had never actually said out loud that Giles was a shit.

'Why do you looked so stunned? You call him Giles the Bastard.'

'Because he left me.'

'So until that moment he was the perfect husband, was he?'

'You know he wasn't.'

'And so do you,' Ruthie insisted, the intensity of her tone taking Amanda by surprise. 'So why did you choose him in the first place?'

'I don't know. I was young. He was handsome and decisive.'

'You mean he made all your decisions for you. As soon as you met decisive, for which read overbearing, Giles you gave up thinking for yourself and just did everything he told you to do.'

'Ruthie,' Simone interrupted. 'Why are you being so foul to Amanda? This is supposed to be a book group, not gestalt therapy.'

'Ah,' Ruthie persisted, 'but this is a book that's trying to get us to challenge our assumptions. Amanda blames Giles for her marriage going wrong. I'm trying to get her to see her part in it. I mean, for Christ's sake, she married Giles in the first place. He's not just from Mars, the man's from the planet Ego. But Amanda didn't see that. How's she ever going to judge the next man if she doesn't learn by her mistakes?'

Louise, with the air of the messenger who knows she's about to change the course of the play, threw in, 'Actually, she's already met the next man.'

Ruthie gawped. 'Since when?'

'Since a few days ago.' Amanda tried to stop herself smirking and failed.

'So what's he like?'

'He's really lovely. He's kind and funny, and loves old people – he's transformed Rose Miles from a bitter old bat into a tango goddess. He's fun but he's also got a social conscience. He thinks of other people, unlike Giles who only ever thought of himself, and he isn't career-obsessed like most men, at least not to the exclusion of everything else in life.' Amanda ended with a little shrug of happiness and surprise. She hadn't meant to come out with any of this. She'd meant to keep Luke hidden quietly away from the gaze of her friends until their relationship was more solid.

'Wow,' said Simone.

'Wow, indeed,' seconded Ruthie. 'What's his name, this paragon of alternative male virtue?'

'Mr Knight,' Louise shrieked, eager to hang on to her role as the major informant. 'Isn't that a hoot? Not Mr Right. Mr *Knight*.'

'Or maybe Mr *Nightly*?' winked Simone.

'I always loved *Emma,*' endorsed Anne.

'Not Mr Knightley . . . Mr Nightly . . . as in *every night*. Oh forget it . . .'

'You didn't tell me,' Ruthie said, a touch sadly.

'No. Well, Louise introduced us and I was trying to keep it quiet.

It's very early days. I wanted to get to know him properly first. Clio and Sean haven't even met him yet.'

'But he knows about them?'

'Of course he knows about them,' Amanda replied, a shade tartly. 'You don't think I'd spring a fully formed family on him, do you? "Oh, by the way, I thought I'd just mention it. I've got two kids."'

'Right,' Louise interrupted bossily. 'We are here to discuss the text. Maybe we should leave Amanda's love life for another moment. What did you think of chapter two?'

Amanda didn't feel like joining in. Ruthie had hurt her feelings over the subject of Giles. And yet, why *had* she fallen for someone so controlling? Was it really all Giles's fault, as she liked to think?

The next hour turned out to be one of the liveliest sessions they'd had. The wine flowed and Amanda had to say, 'Girls! Girls! Quiet down or we'll wake Sean!' Clio, she noticed, had stayed safely up in her bedroom, away from the maenad throng.

When it was time to go home, Ruthie sought her out. 'I'm sorry. You looked hurt when I had a go at you about Giles. I probably went too far. It's just that you're such a fabulous person, Amanda. You're generous and funny, and brave and competent, and a fantastic mother. And yet you put up with all that shit from Giles. I just couldn't bear you to make that mistake again. You deserve someone who really appreciates you.' She hugged Amanda with so much affection that Amanda couldn't help forgiving her.

'I don't know why I did put up with it. I could try and tell myself I didn't know it was happening, but I did. I knew Giles always wrong-footed me and made me feel things were my fault.'

'Sometimes it's the little things that matter as much as the big betrayals like affairs.'

Amanda reached up for Ruthie's coat. It struck her that the reason she'd chosen Giles in the first place, and the reason that she'd put up with him for so long, even when she'd known he wasn't making her happy, was that she'd been frightened of making her own choices. She'd fallen for his certainty. But people who were certain about life were often controlling. The thought of

Angus Day slipped into her mind. He was just the same. The kind who took charge. Thank God Luke wasn't like that. Not like that at all.

'So what's his Christian name, this exciting Mr Knight you've met?'

'OK. I'll tell you as long as you don't make any knights-in-shining-armour jokes. His name's Luke.'

'Luke,' repeated Ruthie. 'Luke Knight. How funny. I've heard that name before.'

'Probably because he runs the Laineton Festival.'

'I expect so,' agreed Ruthie and she hugged Amanda again. The name was definitely familiar. And for some reason she couldn't understand, a small bell rang in Ruthie's mind. And it wasn't one of pleasure at her friend's announcement, but of warning.

Chapter 12

So far the day had passed in a real 'I don't like Mondays' mood. Sean had lost his football boots *and* his lunch box, Clio had been surly and withdrawn, and the house was deep in its postweekend chaos. That and she'd been late for work. Only by five minutes, but it had been enough to earn her a dirty look from Louise. Then the phone rang.

'It's for you,' Louise had shouted. 'Mr Right.'

Amanda shot her a furious look.

'What did she say?' asked a laughing voice on the other end of the line.

'Mr Knight,' Amanda insisted, making a face at Louise. 'She said it was a Mr Knight.'

'But I didn't give my name.' Luke sounded puzzled.

'Louise knows everything. That's why some people in Laineton have her down as a witch.'

'I was just ringing about the concert. Are you still able to come?'

'Absolutely.' She'd even remembered to book her mother in to look after Sean. Asking Clio to babysit on a Saturday night, even if she paid her, would be pushing her luck.

'Do you think your daughter would like tickets too?'

Amanda felt like declaring her infatuation on the spot. Ruthie's suspicion as to whether Luke was prepared to take on her children came into her head. How wrong could she have been – he was actually being considerate about them.

'I'm sure she'd love tickets. As long as they aren't next to ours. She doesn't like having anything to do with me in public.'

'Why's that?'

'She thinks I might embarrass her with inappropriate maternal behaviour.'

'What kind of inappropriate maternal behaviour?'

'Saying hello to her.'

'My God, I didn't think having teenagers was such a minefield.'

Amanda had to stop herself from saying, 'You'll learn.'

'And your little boy? Would he like to come too?'

Amanda could have kissed him. Even though she hadn't mentioned it to Ruthie, Luke's slight impatience about her family ties had been worrying her and had even struck her as faintly Giles-like. But it would never have occurred to Giles in a million years to think of what children might want, not even his own.

'No thanks. My mother's coming round. They'll be happier watching the wrestling. Seeing The Rock in action is something my mother and Sean enjoy as much as each other.'

'That's all right then. I've been missing you.'

Her heart almost flew around the room. 'Me too.' She felt a sudden jolt of desire and a longing to skip the getting-to-know-you stage and tear each other's clothes off. 'Not long now.'

'Too long for me.' The faint suggestiveness in his tone made her tingle.

'All right, all right,' Louise tutted when Amanda handed back the telephone. 'Don't melt all over the gallery floor. So he's asked you to a concert. It happens all the time. No need to leak out of every orifice.'

'Actually, I was just touched that he's asked Clio along too.'

'Is that a good idea? Clio's absolutely gorgeous all of a sudden.'

'Louise.' Amanda shook her head, as if talking to someone who didn't quite get things. 'Clio's just sixteen.'

'Sixteen and stunning,' Louise reminded her.

Amanda shrugged. Sometimes she thought her friends, even if they meant well, had some very odd ideas.

'Anyway, let's postpone the soap opera of the Wells family for the moment. Could you take this lot to the bank and cash up for me?' Louise handed Amanda that week's takings. 'And nip into Safeway while you're in town, would you, we're almost out of coffee. Oh, and could you pick up a couple of lamb chops? I'm rushed off my feet here.'

'But you live next door to the deli,' Amanda reminded her, convinced that there were more useful things she could be doing. 'You could at least get the coffee from there.'

'I could indeed get the coffee.' Louise gave her a 'Me Boss, You Employee Who'd Find It Hard To Get Another Job At Your Age' smile. 'But not the chops.'

'Come on, Clio, we'll be late for DT!' Jasmine pulled Clio's arm. They were both in the girls' toilets, which were smelly and fairly disgusting but one of the few places at school where they could get away from boys. Jasmine studied her friend. Despite the baggy jumpers she'd taken to wearing all the time, Clio still looked incredible, like one of those barely grown-up models with pouty lips and enormous eyes who look out from under their fringes in the magazines.

It wasn't fair, Jasmine couldn't help thinking, that only a few months ago Clio had been no more attractive than she was. Now all the boys, and even some of the male teachers, had started to steal furtive glances at her.

'Why are you wearing that horrible old jumper?' Jasmine asked. 'Even if you were pregnant, it'd hardly show yet.' Even to her own ears this sounded a bit unsympathetic.

'Because I can't bear people looking at my tits,' Clio replied, crossing her arms across her chest for double protection.

'They're not exactly Pamela Anderson's.'

'They are when you're used to being flat as a pancake.'

'Anyway,' Jasmine blurted, hating herself for it, 'isn't it a bit late to be covering up your tits?'

Clio burst into tears.

'Sorry, sorry, I'm a right cow.' Jasmine patted her. 'How late are you?'

'About ten days.'

'That's not the end of the world. Have you done a test?'

Clio raised huge, tearful eyes to her friend. 'No. If I don't do a test then it isn't real.'

'Have you told your mum? Got her advice?'

'She'd go spare. She thinks I'm sensible, a good little girl who'll get As for all her GCSEs, not get banged up by a sodding ski instructor!'

Jasmine got a bit of loo paper and handed it to her friend to wipe her eyes. 'I don't know. She always seems really nice, your mum. Not like my dad – he'd kill me. Take me down the abortion clinic faster than you could say "unprotected sex". What about *your* dad? Could you talk to him?'

'He'd probably think I'd done it to upstage his girlfriend. She's only having bloody twins.'

'Shit, I'd forgotten. Look, why don't *I* go and buy a test? We could do it together. At least it'd put you out of your misery.'

Clio clutched herself even more tightly. 'Or start it.'

Outside the toilets they could hear the shouts and giggles of their classmates. The boys had stolen a girl's folder and she was chasing them, laughing.

'You've got to do *something*.'

'Why? I think hiding my head in the sand's quite a good idea.'

'Except that while your head's in the sand, your body might be getting bigger and bigger.'

'OK then. You buy the kit and I'll come round to your house next weekend and do it.' Clio picked up the enormous backpack they had to carry everywhere with all their school books in it. She rummaged around for her purse. In the back, behind the photo of her mum and dad and Sean taken several Christmases ago when the family was still together, her emergency tenner was tucked away. 'I was saving for a push-you-up bra. I don't need it now. Funny thing is, if I hadn't suddenly got boobs, I don't suppose Gilles would have noticed me.'

'Well, he did, girl, that's for sure.'

*

'Have you taken your medication?' Angus Day gently eased his mother forward while he straightened her cushions and tucked in her rug.

'Unfortunately, yes. Raspberry flavoured. Why does it have to be raspberry? I hate the things.'

'Maybe they're Scottish raspberries.'

Isobel came up with a small smile. It reminded Angus of an exhausted walker struggling round one more bend. 'Maybe they are.'

Isobel's illness seemed to him to have moved up a gear lately. She was breathless and permanently exhausted. But there was one question she'd made as clear to him as a Hebridean stream: when the end came she didn't want to die in some unfriendly hospital. She wanted to die at home. He just hoped, when the time came, he could keep that promise.

'One thing that would cheer me up. Those carved birds you promised me.'

Angus replied with a mock salute. It might be embarrassing for both of them, but he needed to talk to Amanda Wells.

'I'll see you later.' He kissed his mother gently. 'Mind you remember the medication.'

'Don't worry. Mrs Northam will force it down me if I resist.'

He just had time to drop in to The Wave Gallery and ask about the carvings before meeting the tenants to finalise the arrangements for the reopening of the estate.

To his intense disappointment, Amanda wasn't there.

'She's just popped to the bank,' Louise explained.

'I might wait then,' Angus replied.

'And the supermarket.'

'Ah. Oh well, maybe I'll call back later.'

'Can't I help you?' Louise injected as much huskiness into her voice as she could. The effect was Fenella Fielding with bronchitis.

'The thing is . . .'

The door opened behind them, ringing its customer warning bell. 'Hello, Angus.' It was Amanda with the shopping. Safeway's had been empty and for once there hadn't even been a queue in the bank.

'Oh, great.' Louise could have kicked Amanda for her timing and for the warmth in Angus's tone at seeing her.

'I'm sorry to keep badgering,' Angus said, 'but I really do need another bird carving. At once. Otherwise it could be too late.'

'Right.' Something in his tone told Amanda that this was no ordinary gift-buying exercise, nor was it the frenzied madness of a frustrated collector.

'If it's that important, why don't we go now?' She ignored Louise's look of disapproval. 'It's my lunch hour in a moment.'

'I'd be incredibly grateful.'

'I'll expect you back at two,' Louise announced. 'There could be a rush this afternoon.'

Angus and Amanda avoided looking at each other. The gallery was entirely empty.

Angus's car was parked directly outside. 'I've got the roof up,' he smiled, 'so I can't stare at myself in any shop windows.'

Amanda flushed as she climbed into the car. She hadn't realised that Angus had overheard that particular comment.

'It really amused my mother when I told her about it,' Angus teased. 'She said you reminded her of herself.'

Amanda felt surprised and oddly touched that he'd talked about her to his mother. She'd also forgotten how small and intimate it felt inside his car and wondered if he was thinking of New Year's Eve too. She'd behaved outrageously.

'Your mother sounds great.' Amanda forced herself to stop thinking about that night. 'But then I knew that when she made you pay for the damage I caused to your car.'

'She always takes the side of the underdog. Partly because she's had a tough life herself.' He almost told her about Isobel's cancer and that the carved birds had been the one thing that had really meant something to her, but his mother was so proud and private. She hated people feeling sorry for her as much as she hated people who complained. From Isobel's point of view, the fewer people who knew she was dying the better. Maybe it was the Calvinist streak again, but Isobel Day believed dying was between her and God alone, and certainly not to be shared with a bunch of people she hardly knew who were only concerned because it made them grateful to be alive.

They were already driving out of Laineton when Amanda realised she didn't have the sculptor's address with her. She remembered that Natasha lived on the road out of town beyond the harbour. But when they got there, she recognised it at once. Natasha's flat was on the ground floor of a house a few streets back from the seafront. It was a red-brick building with peeling paintwork and didn't seem at all like an artist's home.

'We should have phoned ahead,' Amanda said as she rang the bell for the third time. They were about to leave when Natasha, wearing a blue overall with the unlikely claim of 'Masterchef' on the front, opened the door.

She recognised Amanda at once. 'Oh, hi. Excuse the pinny. They don't do one with "Master Sculptor" on it.' She led them through a shabby but cosy sitting room to a lean-to at the back. 'My studio!' She gestured around at the large porch-like room with peeling paintwork and condensation clouding up its windows. 'Not much,' she said, gesturing towards the sitting room where the TV was on, 'but at least I can watch *Jerry Springer* while I'm carving.'

'This is Angus Day,' Amanda introduced him. 'He's a real fan of yours.'

Angus was about to say that it was really his mother who was the fan, but he didn't want to offend Natasha. 'I bought a pair of your herons.'

'They were lovely, weren't they?' Natasha smiled delightedly.

'Angus was wondering if you had anything else? I was telling him about the nesting seagulls you'd carved.'

'Gone, I'm afraid.'

Amanda was conscious of an intense disappointment. She hadn't realised how much she'd wanted Angus to buy the beautiful seagulls.

'I gave them away as a present. I thought I might as well since they weren't selling. I've been doing a lot of painting lately.' She gestured behind her to a series of small pieces of reclaimed driftwood, each framing a brightly coloured tropical fish.

'They're fabulous,' Amanda enthused. 'Don't you think they're great, Angus?'

'Yes, but I particularly wanted a carving.'

'There's this, I suppose.' Natasha picked up a half-finished wooden bird, about three feet long, its great wings just emerging from the block of driftwood as if it were being born right in front of their eyes. It had a stark simplicity that Angus knew instantly would appeal to Isobel.

'It's a Trumpeter swan. They're over on the marshland by the river.'

'It's perfect,' Angus turned it over in his hands, caressing the smooth wood. 'There's an almost Shaker quality to it. She'll love it.' Amanda experienced that familiar, yet totally irrational, splinter of envy for the recipient of the swan.

Natasha glowed at his appreciation. 'I love the Shakers. There's only the purest, clearest lines in all they did. Everything had a function, even their art.'

'How long until you could finish it?'

'A couple of days should do it. I could deliver it to you if you give me your address.'

Angus looked thrilled. 'That would be fantastic. I know she'll love it.'

Amanda watched him surreptitiously. How wonderful to have someone who wanted as much as Angus did to make you happy. Yet how much did it really mean if, even while he was buying that special person a gift, he could flirt with Amanda and Natasha? Maybe his presents were to say sorry. While most erring lovers bought flowers when they got out of another woman's bed, Angus Day bought Shakeresque carvings.

Thank God Luke was so straightforward. She could at least know with Luke that what you saw was what you got. She smiled to herself. And he even came recommended.

'You look happy.' Angus's words drilled into her reverie as they drove back into town.

'Yes. Yes, I am.'

'No more ads in the paper?'

She froze, while Angus, seeing the embarrassment on her face, wished he could kick himself. 'Not for the moment, no,' she muttered.

'You're seeing the man who came to the art gallery?' His gaze was almost accusing. 'He seemed very charming.'

Amanda stiffened. Charming was the one thing she didn't want Luke to be.

'Not charming. Straightforward. Caring. Unselfish.'

'He sounds a real paragon.' But not, Angus guessed, though he made sure he said nothing, much like the man he'd glimpsed outside the art gallery. There were different words altogether he'd use to describe that character. But why? He didn't know the man at all. All he had to operate on was instinct. And even Angus had to admit that his instinct, though usually pretty accurate, was in this case more than a little clouded.

Natasha was even better than her word. The next day she arrived with the swan at Angus's office. 'Thank you so much.' He carefully put the carving into his car boot and decided to take it to Isobel straightaway. 'You don't know what this'll mean to her.'

'And to me. It feels fantastic to be appreciated.'

He was halfway to his mother's house when he remembered he had promised to drop in and see Laddie about some crisis that had come up at the Eastcliff Estate.

Laddie was waiting in the forecourt at the back of the estate, his usual knitted beanie hat with a St Andrew's cross on the front pulled down over his ears. It was so cold that he got into Angus's car for their discussion.

'Mind out!' Angus moved the swan just before Laddie sat on it.

'Buying swans now, are you? Not for these dratted flats? Flying ducks would be more up their street than that thing.'

'That, Laddie, is a work of art.'

'And how much did they take off you for it? It doesn't even look real. They have better ones in plaster of Paris with nice yellow beaks down in the Everything's-A-Pound shop.'

Angus considered offering Laddie an explanation of the principles of Shaker carving and wisely thought better of it.

'It's like some child's toy, if you ask me,' Laddie added.

'Which I didn't. It's for my mother, as a matter of fact.'

'Your mother's a sensible Scot. She wouldn't want you wasting good money on something like that.'

'As a matter of fact, she asked me to get it.'

'Then she's going as mad as you are. More money down the drain. Just like this crazy project.' He gestured around him at the refurbished blocks of flats which gleamed invitingly in the wintry sunshine.

'You could always go and work for someone else. Bill Neil at Goldhill would take you on tomorrow.' Goldhill was their only serious rival in the property field and Bill Neil was as sharp as a razor blade. And it was true that he would take Laddie on instantly – foremen like him were as rare as gold dust.

'Och,' Laddie grinned suddenly, 'without me you'd be offering en-suite bathrooms to council tenants and building five-star studio flats for the homeless.'

Angus grinned at how well Laddie knew him. 'Now that you mention it, there is a half-way house in town that the council would like me to refurbish . . .'

'You see what I mean!' Laddie choked.

'Only joking,' Angus grinned. 'Actually I'd better get back to a few profit-making schemes.'

'Thank the Lord he's seen the light.'

'For a man of the people you make a pretty good capitalist.'

'I'll take that as a compliment, shall I? Now about these here ten-ants that are moving back in. The lady in number twenty-one says you promised her a pink bathroom. I was going to say, "Look here, missus, no sane developer is going to let people choose the colour of their bathrooms," and then I remembered we were talking about you . . .'

By the time he had finished his discussion with Laddie, Angus realised that he only had half an hour between meetings to take the swan to his mother. He hoped she'd think more of it than Laddie had.

He wasn't disappointed.

'Angus, it's beautiful!' Isobel exclaimed the moment he showed it to her. 'This artist's got a real feel for the natural world. Put it over there on the mantelpiece. There! How lovely is that? I can sit here and imagine I'm back in the Hebrides.'

'I thought you were a city-lover, and too much peace drove you mad?'

Isobel smiled at him lovingly. 'It does. And before long I'll have more of it than I'll know what to do with.' She took his hand. 'When I'm gone you can look at that swan and think of me. I hope that's how I'll be feeling.'

'For God's sake, Maw.' Angus tried to hide his emotion in matter-of-factness. 'Don't be so pessimistic.'

Isobel smiled. 'What's the difference between an optimist, a pessimist and a realist?'

'I don't know.'

'A pessimist says the glass is half empty, an optimist says it's half full and a realist says, "Make mine a whisky." So why don't you pour me a small glass of the Macallan?'

'I'd be delighted.'

'Did your Amanda come with you to choose it?'

Angus raised an eyebrow. 'She's not my Amanda, but yes she did.'

'Why isn't she your Amanda? You like her enough.'

'I was too late. Someone else seems to have claimed her first.'

'And you call *me* a defeatist? What do you do if one of your business rivals steals a march on you?'

Angus grinned. 'I search for a sneaky way in round the back.'

Isobel drank her whisky, suddenly looking exhausted. 'My point exactly.'

'You're looking very nice,' Helen told her daughter.

Compliments from Helen were so rare that Amanda studied herself in the mirror. She *did* look good, as a matter of fact. Her hair was glowing (it ought to, she'd borrowed some of Clio's Australian shampoo instead of her usual supermarket own brand), her eyes sparkled with excitement, and even her legs looked thin since she'd crammed her feet into slimming stiletto-heeled mules which she'd teamed with a girlie skirt from the Boden catalogue.

'Wow, Mum,' Sean commented, looking up from his FIFA football game. 'You don't even look like a mum.' Amanda could only assume this to be a compliment. 'Can I watch the *DragonBall* Zee I taped while you're out?'

Amanda knelt beside him and whispered, 'I think Gran's been looking forward to the wrestling. She hasn't got cable TV at home. You might have to make sure she doesn't get too excited.'

'OK.' Sean clearly took his responsibilities seriously. 'What do I do if she *does* get too excited?'

'Tell her that if she doesn't act her age you'll have to turn the TV off.'

'But Mum,' Sean pointed out reasonably, 'she never acts her age anyway.'

A ring at the doorbell brought Amanda to her feet but not before Clio had swooped down the stairs and into the hall.

She reappeared a moment later, flushing like a ripe tomato, with Luke a few steps behind her. 'Sorry,' she mumbled, 'I thought you were my friend Jasmine.'

'Sorry to disappoint you.' Luke's smile was heart-melting. 'My name's Luke. You must be Clio.' He held out his hand but Clio kept her arms firmly clutched across her chest, a gesture she'd adopted almost constantly since her breasts had appeared.

'Hi.'

'Hello, Luke.' Amanda was struck again by his careless grace, and by the naturalness of his smile. No wonder Rose Miles had crumbled after eighty years of one-woman resistance towards the male sex. Luke was irresistible. 'Luke, this is my mother, Helen.'

Luke took Helen's hand. 'I can see where you get your looks from.'

'Actually,' Clio corrected insolently, 'Mum always says she takes after her father.'

Luke raised a lazy eyebrow. 'It must be just in the stylishness they both share then.'

Helen visibly purred, like a great caramel-coloured cat.

Amanda found herself in sympathy with Clio. Did Luke *have* to be so consciously charming? She was about to add something waspish when Sean got in before her.

'What team do you support?' he demanded, getting out his encyclopaedia of the *World's Greatest Football Teams*.

'I'm not much of a football supporter, I'm afraid.'

Sean looked at him in disgust and decided to abandon him to the caramel clutches of his grandmother. It would serve him right.

'Amanda tells me you're rather a whizz at ballroom dancing.' Helen patted the sofa beside her invitingly.

'Only the tango. I lived in Argentina for a while. I'm afraid my polka lacks pizzazz and my samba has no sparkle.'

'I doubt that. Amanda says you've put the spring back into Rose Miles's step, if she ever had one that is, and that it's all thanks to the tango.'

'It's a very powerful influence, the tango. Love, deceit, betrayal, adultery.'

'Sounds like *EastEnders*,' commented Clio.

'Sounds boring,' amended Sean.

'I think we should go,' pointed out Amanda. 'Are you in tonight?' she asked Clio. 'I thought the reason you couldn't come to the concert was that you were busy.'

'I am.' Clio reddened, thinking of the pregnancy test she planned to do tonight with Jasmine's help. 'I'm going round to Jasmine's. Her mum's coming to pick me up any minute.'

'Yes,' Amanda replied with a touch of sarcasm, 'I can see that's more exciting than a concert.'

'Oh for God's sake, Mum,' Clio flashed with sudden venom, 'leave it alone. I don't have to come to some stupid concert just because your new boyfriend wants to impress me with his generosity.'

'Actually, the tickets are free. Luke runs the Festival.'

'Then you won't mind if we don't use them, will you?'

'Clio,' Amanda began, 'there's no need to be so bloody rude.'

'You two get along.' Helen tried to smooth things down. 'Clio will be fine.' The sight of Helen simpering at Luke was a terrifying one. 'Perhaps you'll take me out for a tango?' she asked him coquettishly.

'Perhaps I will,' promised Luke and kissed her hand.

As they walked down the street, bracing themselves against the January wind, a thought struck Amanda. For the first time she could ever remember, her mother seemed to approve of her boyfriend.

There had to be a catch somewhere.

Chapter 13

The concert was wonderful. Amanda had half expected to be the only over-thirty among a sea of trendy young things, but the hall was packed with people of all ages. The famous Irish band that headed the bill played a mix of their current hits and haunting traditional folk songs, some of which were so moving Amanda found herself sniffing quietly into her hankie. And she couldn't believe it when, as a surprise second act, they announced that they'd be joined by Bann McGaffrey, one of Amanda's all-time heroes.

'Bloody hell!' Amanda blurted. 'I've got every single one of his albums, right back to *Planet Days*.'

'Ah ha,' Luke teased as they walked back along the empty seafront after the singer had finished his fourth encore. 'A closet McGaffrey fan, eh?'

Amanda was still pinching herself that she'd actually just experienced Bann, her hero, in the flesh in Laineton.

Luke suddenly took her in his arms and began to dance with her along the prom, singing Bann McGaffrey's most famous hit and sounding astoundingly like the singer himself.

'My God,' Amanda breathed, loving the feeling of his arms round her, 'you can even sing!' She was conscious of the fact that they were being watched by various respectable Laineton residents taking their dogs for walks, but realised she couldn't care less.

'Up to a point,' Luke shrugged in mock modesty. 'But then there are lots of things you don't know about me.' He stopped under the light of a lamp-post. 'And a lot of things I don't know about you.' He looked at her intently, suddenly serious, as if he could tell the secrets of her soul just by staring into her eyes.

'Libra,' he pronounced.

Amanda laughed, taken aback. She was indeed Libra. 'You've looked at my driving licence! You don't believe any of that nonsense, do you?'

'OK, I admit it. But yes, I do, I'm Scorpio . . . self-assured, dominating, sexy . . . so I have to believe it.' They started walking, his arm around her. Next to them the moon beamed a white path of optimism towards the dark line of the horizon. 'Tell you what, let's play the Luke Knight patented compatibility test – guaranteed to tell us absolutely nothing but fun to play all the same. First question. Favourite book?'

'*Far From the Madding Crowd* by Thomas Hardy.'

'Hmm. So you identify with a self-centred coquette playing fast and loose with the emotions of a good and honourable man while being seduced by a faithless but sexy one, eh?'

'I wouldn't put it quite like that,' Amanda protested.

'Favourite film?'

'*Don't Look Now.*'

'Spooky goings-on in out-of-season Venice, with one of the most famous erotic scenes in cinema. I think I'm beginning to build a picture here.'

Amanda laughed, enjoying the flirtatiousness of the game.

'Favourite singer? Well, we know one of them. Famous Irish singer and drunk. Favourite sexual position?'

Amanda bit her lip.

'No, perhaps we'll get to that one later. Favourite painting?'

'Anything by Matisse.'

'Ah ha. Colourful, stylish, but just a little bit safe?'

'How dare you!' Amanda chided, just as Luke pulled her into his arms again and kissed her hard on the mouth. Amanda felt her body responding despite the coldness of the night and the unsuitability of a forty-one-year-old mother of two snogging on the seafront.

As Luke slipped one hand inside her jacket she forgot everything: where they were, the fact that Rose or Betty or any other respectable resident might wander past at any time, even the fact that it was so cold she was losing all sensation in her stilettoed feet.

'Hey,' she said finally, while she could still speak some sense. 'You didn't tell me your favourites.'

'Chekhov. *Casablanca*. Jacques Brel. Hockney. Now,' he tried to kiss her again, but she ducked away, laughing, 'where were we?'

'I can't find out what you're really like from that.'

'Maybe you'll have to dig a little deeper then.' He took her hand and slid it downwards.

'It'd be a pleasure, but my mother always told me not to do it on the first date. Especially in public on freezing promenades.'

'It isn't our first date. Besides, I feel I've known you for weeks, months, before we even met.'

'A courtship on the astral plane? Nonetheless,' she shivered suddenly, 'it's absolutely bloody freezing here.'

Luke smiled devilishly. 'Then I'd better take you home.'

They walked quickly, partly because it was cold but also because Amanda felt she needed time to think. In that moment underneath the lamp-post, she'd experienced more excitement than she'd felt for years. Another face swam briefly into her mind, dressed as a sheik, with kohl-lined steel-grey eyes. All right, so she'd felt aroused with Angus too, but surely that would have been a disastrous one-night stand? For once, she felt grateful to her ex-husband for interfering in her life.

'Would you like to come in?' she asked as they reached her house. 'My mother's here, I'm afraid, and Clio may be back.'

Luke looked as if he were about to decline, then suddenly accepted.

'Hello, Mum,' Amanda greeted Helen. 'Everything all right?'

Helen was watching *Sex and the City*. 'This programme is outrageous,' she greeted them with relish. 'I'm amazed it isn't banned. What channel is it on? I might write and complain.'

'Channel Four,' replied Amanda, knowing her mother very well. 'Don't worry, you've got it.'

Helen drew herself up with great dignity. 'I'll make a point of ringing them to complain. Did you have a nice evening?'

Amanda noticed that one half of the sitting room was unusually tidy. Helen must have decided it was too much to bear and begun a sort-out, but the tidying had stopped abruptly, probably coinciding with the beginning of the programme. Faced with a choice between fumbling down the back of the sofa for lost objects and watching *Sex and the City*, there hadn't been much contest.

'Was Sean all right?'

'Fine. He spent most of the evening devising some wretched football league.'

There was a thundering on the stairs and Sean appeared in his red and white Manchester United dressing gown. 'Hi, Mum! I made the most amazing chart measuring Barthez's goals conceded versus goals saved over a whole season.'

'Wow. That sounds complicated.'

'It took me hours. Do you want to see?'

Amanda felt faint. 'Not now, thanks, darling. In the morning.'

Sean, knowing his number was up, tried one last desperate tack. 'Are you sure you don't like football, Luke?' he asked hopefully.

'Not a lot.' Luke grinned his boyish grin. 'I could never master the offside rule.'

'I'll explain it to you if you like,' Sean offered kindly.

'Another time, maybe. Isn't it time for bed?'

'It was his time for bed hours ago,' Helen threw in waspishly. 'If only Amanda had any discipline he'd have been there too, but she's let them both run wild. What they need is a father's . . .'

Helen stopped, noticing Amanda shaking her head furiously. 'I think it's time I left. By the way, Clio's not back yet. You should watch out for that girl. She's behaving very oddly.'

'What do you mean?' Amanda didn't want to discuss Clio's problems with Luke there, but she was so worried about her daughter she couldn't stop herself.

'She's moping about like Ophelia on a wet Wednesday. Wouldn't eat any supper. Hardly spoke. Still wearing that jumper that looks like a giant Hoover bag. She hasn't been the same since she came back from skiing, if you ask me. Anyway, time I went home.' She surveyed Luke with a challenging glint. 'Can I give you a lift, Luke?'

'No thanks,' Luke said with a reassuring lack of hesitation. 'I love walking.'

'Aren't you going to offer me a cup of coffee?' he asked after Helen had gone.

Amanda put the coffee in the top of her Italian coffee maker, then screwed on the lid.

Luke followed her into the kitchen and pinned her against the worktop, his eyes a heady mixture of laughter and promise. He took her hand and kissed the soft skin inside her wrist.

Amanda shivered.

Luke pulled her into his arms.

Neither of them noticed when the front door banged and the coffee boiled over simultaneously.

'What the hell's that smell?' Clio demanded as they jumped apart. She leaned across and turned off the gas ring. 'Next time you're going to stick your tongues down each other's throats, remember to turn the gas off. You might kill the lot of us.' And she turned and ran up to bed.

'Sorry about that. My mother's right, she is behaving oddly at the moment.'

'On the other hand, maybe she isn't. It could be galling to find your mother, what did she say, sticking her tongue down someone's throat, especially if you're a teenager.' He paused fractionally. 'Does she have a boyfriend of her own?'

'Not really. She's never been interested in boys. She was always very, you know, underdeveloped physically.' She stopped, not sure it was fair to discuss Clio in this intimate way. But she needed to talk to someone. 'Then, while she was away skiing she suddenly found she was changing, that men and boys were looking at her.'

'Did she enjoy it?'

'No. I think she hated it.'

'Oh, come on.'

'No, really, she hated being looked at in a sexual kind of way. Except for one boy. A young French ski instructor. She seems to have really fallen for him. But I get the impression she was just another notch to him. He dumped her for a German girl with a rich daddy.'

'It's the same the whole world over. Poor kid. She's very pretty.'

'Yes.' Amanda smiled with sudden pride. 'Actually she's absolutely gorgeous, if only she'd realise it.'

Luke seemed to register that they'd spent a long time discussing Clio. 'Then she takes after her mother.'

Amanda stretched, suddenly tired, wishing her life were less complicated and that she and Luke could just go to bed together like other people did. She kissed Luke briefly on the lips. 'Time for you to leave, I think.'

'All right. I know when I'm not wanted.'

'Stop fishing.' She pushed him tenderly to the door, and then lingered for one last kiss.

After he'd gone, she turned out the lights and went upstairs to look for Clio. She knocked softly on Clio's door. Clio's room was usually strictly off-limits, a fact asserted by the enormous red and black NO ENTRY sign she'd made and pasted to her door. An arrow pointed to the centre where the words ESPECIALLY TO MUM had been added.

Clio's room was a constant source of friction between them. It drove Amanda mental that Clio should leave her clothes on the floor, under her bed, behind the curtains, anywhere but in the drawers or wardrobe. Her desk, where school work was supposed to be done – and especially revision for her mock exams – was littered with make-up, teen magazines, CDs out of their cases and chocolate wrappers. The final sign of the Teenager in Residence was the suffocating *eau de trainer* which hit Amanda the moment the door was opened.

'Clio! Clio, love. Can I come in?' Amanda knew she ought to be angry with Clio over her rude outburst downstairs but some instinct told her to tread carefully. Clio was already in bed with the duvet pulled right up so that only the top of her head was visible. She was cuddling an unwilling Kinky, who was meowing in protest and showing a general lack of feline sensitivity. On the pillow next to Clio was the pink rabbit she'd had since she was a baby and which was usually relegated, unnoticed and unloved, to a spot on the bookcase.

Amanda sat down on the bed. 'Clio, darling, is everything all right?'

The answer was a sob.

Instantly feeling guilty that this might be because of Luke's arrival in her life, Amanda reached out and stroked the top of Clio's head. 'What's the matter, Clio love?' Her mother was right, Clio had been different ever since the ski trip. 'Is it something to do with Gilles?'

At the mention of Gilles, Clio sat up, her face crumpled with tears, and flung herself into Amanda's arms, squashing an outraged Kinky as she did so. 'Oh Mum, I was so bloody stupid! I didn't really want to go to bed with him at all, but he was horrible to me and called me a silly little virgin and said most girls my age would be embarrassed to even admit they'd never slept with anyone.'

A cold, gnawing fury at this arrogant young man came over Amanda, along with an even greater fury at her ex-husband for not appreciating that any of this was happening under his nose and even going as far as to turn the whole thing into a joke.

'It doesn't matter, darling. He was a bully, that's all. Most boys aren't like him. It's all over now.' She rocked Clio against her chest like she'd done when Clio was a baby.

Clio was still crying. 'I'm sorry I was so rude to you, Mum.'

Amanda felt a surge of love for her coltishly beautiful daughter. 'It doesn't matter. I should have been more considerate of your feelings too. I mean, you hardly know Luke and it must be a shock to suddenly see him kissing your mother.'

'It isn't that, Mum.' She sobbed again, her face streaked with tears. 'It's because my period's late.'

Amanda's heart lurched as if she were on some terrifying roller-coaster. Clio had said they'd been careful. What the hell would they do if Clio were actually pregnant? Clio had always been a girl of strong principles; she would never, Amanda suspected, agree to a termination. Oh God, what a mess. She felt another flash of anger, this time directed not just at Gilles and her ex-husband but at Clio herself. How could she have been so stupid?

Yet one glance at Clio's hollow eyes and tear-stained face pushed all thoughts of losing her temper out of the window. 'You poor, poor girl.' She patted Clio's lank and unwashed hair. 'Are you sure? Have you done a test? You can do them when you're only five minutes late nowadays.'

'I was going to do it tonight but Jasmine's sister spent the whole night in the bathroom.'

'Do you want me to help you?'

Clio shook her head. 'No, I'd rather do it on my own. I'll do it soon.'

Amanda almost responded with, 'Why not now?' but she knew she mustn't interfere.

'Fine. Are you OK? Want to sleep in my bed?'

'It's all right. I'd better get used to the fact that you might want it to yourself. Now that you've met the luscious Luke.'

'We wouldn't . . .' Amanda found herself flushing with the inappropriateness of discussing this with Clio at this of all moments. 'I mean, I wouldn't dream of . . .'

'Going to bed with him when we're around?'

'Clio . . .'

'It's all right. Just because I've been stupid doesn't mean you have to forswear sex for the rest of your life.' Clio produced the tiniest of heartbreaking smiles. 'Even the Reverend Mother in *The Sound of Music* knew that was a bad idea.'

Clio slipped under the duvet again and reached out to turn off the light. 'By the way,' she halted mid-gesture, 'what happened to that nice Angus? The one with the social conscience. I thought he fancied you and you fancied him back.'

'I think you've got your facts a bit muddled. Angus Day hasn't got a social conscience. All he's interested in is making money. Luke's the one who cares about changing society.'

'Ah.' Clio turned the light out suddenly. If she hadn't just been so incredibly upset, Amanda might have taken Clio's sceptical tone as a deliberate insult. 'I must have got it wrong. I thought Angus was actually rather caring.'

Amanda stayed on the bed for another couple of minutes, listening to the silence. Clio, despite her worries, had fallen into a deep sleep in seconds, with Kinky purring noisily beside her like an ancient outboard engine. They looked the picture of childhood innocence.

Except that Clio's predicament was anything but childish.

Amanda asked herself where she'd gone wrong. Clio had let herself be talked into having sex when she didn't want to. All her rudeness and strongly held convictions hadn't stopped her from giving in to a combination of charm and bullying. Perhaps Amanda hadn't prepared her well enough for the situations she might find herself in.

And then a shameful thought struck her. Hadn't Giles used rather the same tactics to get her into bed too? The only difference was that Amanda had been almost twenty-two and Clio was only sixteen with a bright future ahead of her. So was it the getting pregnant Amanda really minded about, or the having sex part?

Sitting on Clio's bed, Amanda remembered when Clio was a baby. She'd hated being put to bed and would only fall asleep if she could see her mother's adoring face through the side of her cot. So Amanda had got into the habit of waiting till Clio had dropped off, then getting down on her hands and knees and backing out of the room without making a sound.

Quietly she slipped to the floor and did the same tonight. She'd just got to the door when Clio's voice rang out through the darkness. 'Mum, what are you doing crawling about on the floor, for fuck's sake?'

Amanda shuddered and climbed stiffly to her feet. Clio certainly wasn't a baby any more.

'Goodnight, darling,' she said softly and went to her own room, where she quickly got ready for bed, then lay wide-eyed for hours, wondering what would happen next if Clio's pregnancy test turned out to be positive.

Chapter 14

Amanda sat up in bed and reached for her clock. Shit. They'd overslept. She'd lain awake again worrying about Clio for half the night, desperately wishing she had someone she could share the anxiety with. She knew Giles would be useless and furious, neither of which would be a blind bit of help.

It was almost time for Clio and Sean to leave for school. She jumped out of bed and put on the same clothes she'd worn yesterday to save time.

Downstairs, Sean, always the organised one, was sitting at the table and calmly eating his Cheerios. Naturally there was no sign of Clio. Amanda wondered whether she should suggest Clio take the day off, but moping at home might be the worst possible thing for her.

She was about to go up to Clio's room to discuss it when Clio herself came downstairs. She looked like a different person. Her pretty face was beaming, and her eyes were shining like the sun on a shiny sea. She almost skipped into the room.

'It's OK, Mum,' she gushed, hugging Amanda tightly. 'I don't need to do the test. My period's just come.'

'Oh Clio.' Amanda felt all the worry of the previous night lift from her shoulders. 'Thank God. How absolutely bloody wonderful!'

Sean watched this interchange between his sister and mother

with growing mystification. 'Excuse me?' He looked from one to the other. 'Haven't you got something wrong here? The lady who gave us the talk said having a period is painful, and Ben Summers says his sister calls it "The Curse", so why on earth are you and Clio over the moon 'cos she's got hers?'

Clio and Amanda clung to each other and giggled with relief. 'Believe me,' Amanda said, 'no matter what Ben Summers' sister says, there are times when it ought to be called "The Blessing".'

'You're in a good mood,' Louise remarked later that morning. Amanda had not only made the coffee, polished the display cabinet and even tidied the stockroom before it really needed it, but she was humming too.

'I know.' She was damned if she was going to tell Louise, the biggest gossip in Laineton, that it was because her sixteen-year-old daughter wasn't pregnant by a ski instructor after all. 'I feel spring is in the air.'

'You must be the only person who does. It's absolutely freezing if you ask me.'

'All right. Spring's round the corner then.'

'I wish I had your optimism.'

Amanda almost laughed. Last night she'd been so depressed that even Eeyore would have seemed cheerful by comparison.

For once the morning flashed by. Amanda even volunteered to go to the bank, usually the job they both hated most. Paying in all the five pence pieces the pensioners counted out in exchange for their cards always brought on an attack of tutting and sighing from the tellers. 'For God's sake,' Amanda always wanted to yell at them, 'you'll be broke one day and I hope no one bothers to send you a bloody birthday card.'

She'd just finished paying-in and was about to head back to the gallery when she bumped into Luke, who was talking intently to someone on a mobile phone. When he saw her he stopped abruptly and smiled. It was an incredible smile. It conveyed pleasure and warmth and excitement at seeing her. It was the kind of smile that could light up your entire day.

'Hi, what a lovely surprise. Not flogging works of art to the unappreciative hordes today?'

'Just paying in our meagre rewards, as a matter of fact.' She loved it when he held her arm and she took a wicked pleasure in the envious glances other women gave them as they walked along, hand in hand.

'Hope I didn't interrupt you.' She gestured towards his mobile. 'It looked as if you were having a heavy conversation.'

'Oh that,' Luke said dismissively. 'Just discussing my contract. The Leeds Festival's leaning on me to accept a contract for next autumn. Planning festivals is getting earlier and earlier, especially if you want to book big names.'

The word 'Leeds' jolted and jarred in Amanda's brain. Leeds was hundreds of miles away. Selfishly, she'd never really thought about what Luke's job entailed. Obviously it would mean moving from area to area whenever there was a festival on. Amanda suddenly felt no older or more mature than Clio faced with abandonment by the horrible ski instructor.

'Don't look like that.' Luke put his arm round her. 'I haven't said yes. But my contract here does run out in a couple of months. I'll see if I can play them along for a while. The council mentioned something about needing a permanent arts officer. The money's crap so I hadn't really considered it.' He stopped and looked into her eyes, his warm brown ones beaming out a tenderness that was infinitely reassuring. 'Until I met you.'

Amanda found she could breathe again, even if it was only a temporary reprieve. At least in a couple of months she would have had time to see what they really meant to each other. But the best thing was that he did care about her. He wanted to stay in Laineton if he could.

'That would be great,' she said, meaning that would be fabulous, fantastic, completely and utterly gobsmackingly brilliant. And then, taking the plunge, 'I mean that'd be fabulous, fantastic, completely and utterly gobsmackingly brilliant.'

'That's all right then,' Luke laughed. 'I'd better go and see them soon. So,' he asked, his eyes still teasing, 'how's the wayward daughter?'

Amanda, wafting on a cloud of relief and happiness, wanted to share everything with him. 'She's not wayward, she was just worried about something.'

'She seemed pretty rude last night.'

Amanda struggled with herself. Would it be an abuse of Clio's trust to tell Luke the truth? On the other hand, if he was to be a serious part of Amanda's life, he would have to understand and get to know Clio too.

'The thing was, her period was late and she thought she might be pregnant.'

Luke's hand on hers tightened. 'Pregnant? You mean she sleeps around already?'

'Not around. She slept with one boy. The ski instructor on holiday. It was an awful mistake and he dumped her for another girl. From what I gather, he took advantage of her innocence and bullied her into it.'

'Poor Clio. There are some evil people in this world.' There was a surprising venom in his tone.

'Yes. Though I don't think this Gilles was evil, just young, male and selfish.'

'Don't they go together inevitably?'

'Hey,' Amanda laughed, hoping she hadn't told him too much, 'you're beginning to sound like the women in my book group.'

'God help me. I'll walk you back to the gallery,' Luke offered, laughing. 'My next meeting isn't for twenty minutes.'

Louise was waiting for her, looking out at the street.

'I was wondering how long it could possibly take to pay the takings in,' she commented. 'Now I know the answer. Your friend Mr Day's just been in. Wanted to remind us about the party for the reopening of the Eastcliff Estate at lunchtime.' Louise waved the invitation and accompanying press release at Amanda.

'God, I'd forgotten all about that. Are you going?'

'Not my cup of tea. I can't stand the poor close up. But you can go if you want. Providing it's only for an hour. I think we should keep in with Mr Day. At least he buys stuff.'

'I wouldn't mind seeing capitalism in action,' Luke said, studying the press release. 'Find out what this so-called "imaginative joint venture between the private and public sector" really means. What's the betting it should be called "How the fat cats manage to screw the council yet again"?'

'You're such a cynic, Luke Knight.' Amanda blew a kiss at him. 'And I love it.'

'I've just seen it happen too many times over sponsorship. Some stupid businessman who knows shit about art or the community puts in a couple of hundred quid and manages to grab all the publicity.'

'I'm not sure Angus Day's as bad as that,' Amanda defended.

'Amanda's got a little bit of a soft spot for Mr Day,' Louise confided.

'I'd definitely better come along then.' Luke put his arm round her meaningfully. 'Just to keep an eye on her.'

There was just a hint of possessiveness in Luke's tone. In one way it thrilled Amanda, but it opened up a small door of doubt too. Giles had gone spare if another man took even the most passing interest in her and she'd absolutely hated it.

'What time is this do?' Luke enquired.

'Twelve-thirty for one p.m.'

'My dears, is it canapés and champagne, then?'

'More likely sausage rolls and a half of lager and lime, knowing council tenants' tastes,' Louise trilled.

It was on the tip of Amanda's tongue to point out that Louise probably had as much experience of council tenants' tastes as she did of betting shops or travelling by bus.

'I'll pick you up at twelve-thirty, then, shall I?' Luke waved goodbye.

Angus decided he had good reason to feel pleased with himself. He and Laddie had come for a final inspection before the official opening and had found the place looking fantastic. All the building work was finished, the new gravel had been laid, and there were tubs of winter pansies and cyclamen outside each entrance to the six blocks of refurbished flats.

The young architect who'd helped with the design had just declared that he wouldn't mind living in one himself.

'Tough titties, my lad,' Lou Wills, the tenants' rep, snapped back. 'There's already a waiting list to move here. Fancy that, eh, people actually *wanting* to live on the Eastcliff Estate?'

'You heed my words,' Laddie muttered darkly, 'they'll muck the place up in no time.'

Angus just laughed. His instinct told him that Laddie was wrong.

'OK, Lou,' Angus asked, 'who have you rounded up to come to the party?'

'All the pen-pushers from the council are coming,' Lou replied, 'and the busybodies from social services.'

Angus wondered if there were any groups of people Lou approved of.

'I almost forgot,' she grinned back, 'that troublemaker from the local rag's coming too. And the tenants, of course. They can smell free drink a mile off. 'Ere!' Lou shouted at a shaven-headed youth who was crossing the newly laid turf, or rather being pulled along it by a ravenous-looking bulldog in a studded collar. She handed him a plastic bag. 'Leave that animal's business on the new grass and I'll stick the turd down your trousers personally!'

Angus caught Laddie's eye. 'What was that you were saying about tenants and their dogs?' he asked his foreman.

'The novelty'll wear off in five minutes, you mark my words,' Laddie warned mournfully, pulling his woolly hat down over his ears.

'Not if I have anything to do with it,' growled Lou. 'The women are going to take over this estate and we'll be fiercer than any tosspot security guards, I can tell you.'

'You'd better watch it, Laddie. Or they'll have you before the women's tribunal.'

Laddie gave him a nervous look. 'They can't do that, can they?'

'It's an idea,' grinned Lou. 'Now, Mr Day, would you mind if I have the Portaloo put behind the tent? And on the drinks front, I decided to stick to sherry and lager; anything stronger and number seven will start accusing number twenty-one's son of getting their daughter pregnant again.'

'You've been fantastic, Lou,' Angus thanked her. 'I really wanted this to be the tenants' party. It's amazing you've got them all to come.'

'With free drink and free food on offer? It would have been more of a miracle to keep them away.'

'See you at lunchtime then.' Angus waved her and Laddie good-bye and walked towards his car. He'd almost reached it when Lou ran after him. From inside her sweatshirt she produced a BMW icon and handed it to him. 'Sorry about this. It was one of the kids from fifty-three. I hope you'll be able to stick it back on all right.'

Angus studied his car. The icon was indeed missing. How on earth had the kid managed to lever it off? Angus opened the boot and put it away till he could find time to take it to the garage. Seeing it reminded him of the last time the icon had been damaged – in Tesco's car park by Amanda Wells.

He realised how much he hoped she was coming today. *You just want to show off to her that you're one of the good guys*, he told himself ironically. And it was true. He wanted her to see for herself that property developers could do the occasional good deed.

'Come on, Clio, show us your tits!' One of the spottiest boys in her class leapt out on her from behind the toilets, making Clio jump.

'I will if you'll show me your willy,' she answered. 'So that I can laugh at it.'

'Forget her,' the boy's friend advised. 'She'll never show you her tits, she's such a fucking snob. Just because her mother works in an *art gallery*. It's just a jumped-up gift shop. I mean, who'd call their daughter Clio anyway? Sounds like Cleo-fucking-patra.'

Clio ignored them. She was still feeling such a wave of relief that she didn't have to consider either an abortion or bringing up a baby at sixteen that nothing these berks said could touch her. In fact, she'd had a good morning drawing up her GCSE revision plan. From now on it was going to be work, work, work.

Part of the reason she intended to study hard was to thank her mum. She knew Amanda could have gone berserk over the pregnancy scare, and also that she'd been foul to her mother lately, and she wanted to make it up. They were finishing early today and she'd decided to stop by at the gallery to show Amanda her work chart and maybe even get her a little bunch of flowers.

Clio walked across the tarmac playground, wishing for the hundredth time that she went to school with just girls. Then she wouldn't have to put up with all this stuff about her tits. It wasn't as though she had enormous boobs that knocked people out every time she turned round. Jasmine said it was because they were round and perfect and because she'd been flat as a pancake before. It was the difference everyone noticed.

Hugging herself in a manner she hoped would camouflage her chest but which only served to draw attention to it, she scuttled off to the next class. Double biology. It would be.

'Right, everyone,' their biology teacher, Mr Van der Wyck, said with the air of exhausted inevitability that resulted from fifteen years of teaching children about procreation. 'We're doing Human Reproduction, remember?'

One of the few studious girls from Clio's class put up her hand to ask a question.

The spotty boy leaned towards Clio's ear. 'I'd stick my sperm up your urethra any time you fancy.'

'Witty,' remarked Jasmine, who was sitting next to Clio.

''Ere, Jason.' The spotty boy nudged his mate and indicated Jasmine. 'Don't fancy your egg.'

'Want to come back to my house for a Diet Coke?' Jasmine invited Clio when their class finally finished. They were supposed to go home for study leave. 'We could have a laugh in an internet chat room with that one who calls himself "The Whopper".'

'I thought I'd drop in on my mother, actually,' Clio said. 'She's been really nice over, you know.' She shrugged in embarrassment. Jasmine had been nearly as relieved as she had to hear that the scare was over. Pregnancy could be catching.

'Wow, Clio, are you feeling OK? Your mum'll probably die of shock. Anyway, I wouldn't be *that* grateful. She's probably told all her friends. Mums always do.'

'Not mine. She wouldn't tell a soul, I swear. She'd know I'd never forgive her if she did.'

'Then she'd be the first mum on the planet to keep her mouth shut,' shrugged Jasmine. 'Mine even told my auntie when my periods started, how much I weigh, and that I stuff tissues down my bra to make my boobs look bigger.'

'Jas, that is seriously out of order.'

'I know. But she did it all the same.'

For once there was a bus waiting outside the school gates, and since Clio was leaving early it wasn't full of giggling girls, BO, revolting boys and so many backpacks it resembled a cut-price flight to Thailand.

It was only a few minutes from the bus stop near the pier to The Wave Gallery. On the way, Clio stopped at a flower stall and bought a tiny posy of snowdrops. They were wrapped in ivy leaves which set off their delicate whiteness. Her mother would love them.

'Hi,' she greeted Louise, suddenly overcome with shyness.

Louise studied her. Until recently, Clio, despite her exotic name, had always struck Louise as rather mousy. Perhaps it was because Louise herself was such an exotic bloom, given to clothes in vivid colours and jewellery that made other people pale by comparison. But Clio wasn't mousy any more. The puberty fairy must have appeared overnight and waved a magic wand. The girl's hair, usually tied back, was loose today and fell in a dark-gold sheen. It wasn't as tawny as Amanda's, more a pewtery blonde, and the stick-like thinness of the child's body was ripening into the rounder curves of maturity.

If a model scout clapped eyes on Clio now she would be snapped up overnight. She was at that precise moment of youth, poised between waif and woman, that so appealed to the fashion business. But then, even if she were spotted, Amanda would never let her go. She was very hot on childhood innocence.

'Are you looking for Amanda?' Stupid question, but beauty made even sensible adults stumble. 'If so, I'm afraid she's gone to a party up the road at the Eastcliff Estate.'

Clio's face lost its look of happy anticipation.

'I'm sure you could go and find her there,' Louise offered in a rare moment of generosity. There was something about the way Clio's emotions reflected so clearly on her face that touched even Louise's cynical heart. 'It's just an informal party to mark the end of the refurbishment. You wouldn't need an invitation. It's only ten minutes up the road.'

Clio hesitated.

'I'm positive your mother would rather you gave her those flowers yourself.'

'All right,' Clio smiled. 'I'll go and look for her. Thanks.'

My God, the girl was even prettier when she smiled. Louise wondered if Amanda had registered the power of so much innocent beauty. Louise was grateful for the hundredth time that she didn't have children. In her opinion, based on years of observation of her friends, children were a major cause of heartbreak. Even though she was still of childbearing age, Louise had decided they were a risk she was never going to take. Even if they were as lovely as Clio. No, rephrase that, *especially* if they were as lovely as Clio.

The walk took Clio along the promenade and then up a steep hill. The weather was turning into a real patchwork of an afternoon, with dark rain clouds scudding across a clear blue sky and patches of bright sunlight that turned the sea to shot silk.

Clio breathed in the sharp salt air and stood for a moment feeling the happiness of intense relief. She wasn't pregnant. Her life wasn't over before it had begun. She was sixteen, she'd weathered her parents' divorce – just – and had her first heartbreak. Now she was ready to make her way into the world, to see what she alone could give it. It was almost exciting.

Lost in her thoughts, she hadn't noticed that she'd arrived at the estate. She stopped, astonished by the change in it. The Eastcliff Estate had always been part of the Laineton landscape. It had been the scruffy backdrop to her childhood, perched up on the hill, grey and unappealing and used by parents as a strange and unsettling threat: If you don't do well at school/listen to the teacher/do your homework/you'll end up a no-hoper living on the Eastcliff Estate.

Clio looked around her. The six Gulag-style blocks, previously faced with grey pebble-dash, had been transformed. But equally amazing was the change in the setting. Gone were the overflowing bins and piled up black plastic bags with dogs pulling them apart and spewing the contents on to the pavement. Clio remembered the threadbare grass, the abandoned car parts, even – on one thrilling and frightening occasion – the car that was set alight just like cars on the news in Beirut or Bosnia. She also recalled the groups of scruffy children, much too young to be out alone, hanging round bus shelters or skateboarding in the road. Clio had been grateful she'd got a nice, if untidy, home to go to where someone actually cared about her and worried if she were home late. But the whole place looked fantastic now.

'Are you looking for the party?' asked a voice behind her. Angus had instantly recognised Clio from the day he'd met her in Tesco's car park. 'It's round the corner in the marquee. We're just going there, aren't we, Laddie?'

Clio looked round. Two men were standing behind her, one in a woolly hat and donkey jacket, the other smartly dressed. The man who'd spoken, she realised with a start, was Angus Day, the owner of the BMW her mother had backed into.

'I was just noticing how different it is here. The architecture's changed and everything.'

'It's more of a facelift, in fact. Less dramatic than it looks.'

'But it's the atmosphere that's really different. It used to feel quite frightening.'

'Thank you,' Angus beamed.

'Are you involved in it, then?' Clio asked.

'My company's been doing the refurbishment, yes. Are you interested in architecture?'

'I'm interested in the way people live. I hadn't seen it as architecture.' Clio laughed.

'No more it should be,' Laddie couldn't help chipping in. 'Property developers should stick to what they know. Not start tinkering in social engineering.'

Clio raised an eyebrow. 'Are you tinkering in social engineering?'

she asked. 'Only my mother says property developers are people who knock down nice buildings and replace them with horrible ones and make a fast buck on the way.'

'Laddie would certainly approve of that. Wouldn't you, Laddie?'

Laddie grunted. 'I just hope our next project makes us a profit. It'd be a nice change.'

'Look,' Angus pointed out, 'there's your mother.' Amanda had just appeared out of the crowd. Clio waved and was about to shout when Luke materalised at Amanda's side. She darted a glance at Angus and saw his face harden.

'Excuse me.' Angus turned away. 'I won't be long. Someone's bringing *my* mother along and I want to make sure she's arrived safely. The speeches will be in about fifteen minutes.' He winked suddenly. 'In case you want to get away first.'

A waiter appeared. 'Would you like an orange juice?' Angus enquired of Clio. 'Unless you'd prefer a glass of wine?' He held one out to her.

Clio laughed. 'Maybe not in school uniform.'

Clio watched her mother and her mother's new boyfriend walk towards her. He was incredibly good-looking, it was true, but there was something about the way that Luke had his arm around her mother, holding tightly on to her waist, that seemed strangely inappropriate at a gathering like this. As if he were trying to tell the world: Look, we're lovers. Do you have a problem with that?

'Hello, Clio,' Amanda greeted her. 'What a lovely surprise.'

'He was in a bit of a hurry to get away,' Luke commented, watching Angus shake hands as he moved through the tent. 'And was that a glass of wine he was pressing on you? I wonder what his game is? He must know you're under age.'

'Actually,' Clio pulled herself up until she was almost as tall as Luke, 'I'm sixteen and my mother allows me to have an occasional glass of wine.' She noticed Laddie standing a few feet away. 'Excuse me, I just need to ask that man something about the refurbishment. I've decided to do urban renewal as my special geography project.'

Amanda looked stunned. 'But you've never shown the slightest interest in geography. You've always said it was boring. That it had nothing to do with real life.'

'Maybe I've just realised I was wrong.'

'I wonder what's the matter with her,' Amanda said softly.

'As far as I can gather, there's always something the matter with her,' Luke commented.

But Amanda knew her daughter a lot better than that. For some reason Clio had taken against Luke. Maybe it was straightforward jealousy. She might resent the fact that Amanda, by finding herself a good-looking man, wasn't behaving like a mother but drawing unseemly attention to herself. Well, Clio was going to have to get used to it. Men as delicious as Luke only came along if you were very lucky indeed.

On the other side of the tent, which backed straight on to one of the porches belonging to the flats, a ribbon was tied between two bay trees. Someone who looked like the mayor tapped his glass with a fork to get silence.

'Thank you everybody. Firstly we'd like to thank Mr Day for all his hard work and imagination in completing this project – in partnership with the council of course – both on time and on budget. It would have taken a miracle to get the council's own building team to do the same.'

There were cheers and nervous laughter from the audience. 'I have to say that certain council members were sceptical about the idea of Mr Day getting involved at all. There were suggestions that we would have to produce used fivers in brown envelopes to get the job finished. And the fact is, we did have to hand over envelopes of used fivers – but to the council's own drainage department when the brand new toilets started packing up! Mr Day, on the other hand, has asked for no kickbacks, palm-greasers, or even, as footballers so genteelly put it, bungs. And he's still finished the project on time. And now I believe Mrs Isobel Day is going to cut the ribbon and declare the refurbished Eastcliff Estate officially open!'

Angus appeared, pushing his mother in a wheelchair.

From her position towards the back, Amanda was horrified. Isobel was so pale she had an almost wraith-like quality, accentuated by the spots of colour on her cheeks. They were almost at the ribbon when Isobel made Angus stop and insisted on walking the last few feet unaided.

Amanda held her breath. Would Isobel be all right?

Unexpectedly, Isobel took the microphone from the mayor. 'Please forgive me, but as you see, I'm not too steady on my pins. But I want you to know it's old age, not too many halves of lager and lime. I just wanted to pay tribute to my son, which he'll hate me for, but frankly, Angus, I'm too old to care.'

The audience laughed, while Angus shrugged.

'When Angus was a boy his father's business collapsed and we had to move from a large house to a council flat. From East Fife we came here and my husband started again. When he became ill he asked Angus to take over and Angus agreed – reluctantly, because he was halfway through his university course. Angus made a big success of the business. You've all seen his car outside.' There was a big laugh from everyone at this. 'That's why he was so committed to improving this estate. He's never forgotten how important it is to have a decent home. But that wasn't enough for Angus. He wanted people to *care* about where they live. To feel that home really is where the heart is.'

Luke nudged Amanda and raised a cynical eyebrow. But Amanda found herself curiously moved. Isobel wasn't the type to play the sentimental card.

'Anyway. Enough about us. I declare the Eastcliff Estate officially reopened. And I hope all the tenants will greatly enjoy living here.'

'We will,' Lou Wills shouted, 'and I promise I've left no coal in the bath. I don't need to. Thanks to Angus we've got underfloor heating!'

Most of the tenants joined in the laughter as Isobel cut the ribbon.

'A bouquet!' the mayor announced. 'We have to have a bouquet for the lady!'

Angus almost swore out loud. In all the arrangements, this was the one thing he'd forgotten.

Suddenly, from the middle of the crowd, Clio appeared holding out the small bunch of snowdrops she'd bought for her mother. She knew Amanda would understand.

Isobel took the posy tenderly. 'Snowdrops. The first flowers of spring.' For a moment she faltered. Only Angus knew why. These would be the last snowdrops she'd see. The last spring.

'Thank you,' he whispered to Clio as he helped Isobel back to her chair. 'I owe you one.'

'No you don't,' Clio mouthed back. 'But I might think of something all the same.'

Amanda and Luke were waiting for her at the back of the crowd.

'What a lot of sentimental tosh,' Luke announced. 'I'd like to see how much profit he actually made out of it.'

Behind them, Laddie loomed into the picture. 'How much he lost, you mean. And it'll be more than you earn in a year or two, sunshine!'

'Sorry,' Luke apologised smoothly. 'I've obviously underestimated the man.'

'You have that,' Laddie snarled. 'and I hope he returns the favour. It wouldn't be too hard.'

'Time we went,' Amanda said brightly. 'I've got to get back to the gallery. What are you doing, Clio?'

'Oh, I'll get the bus home. I want to do some revision on the way. And I might start thinking about this geography project.'

'I thought you said Clio wouldn't do any school work,' Luke grinned as they walked back.

'She wouldn't. But something's obviously changed. I wonder what.'

'So how was the fabulous opening party?' Louise demanded as soon as Amanda got back to the gallery. 'All Scotch eggs and spam fritters? And did Angus Day finally bring this mystery girlfriend of his?'

'Not a glimpse. Just his mother. She cut the ribbon.'

'How touching,' Louise commented sarcastically. 'I declare this subsidised shit-heap duly open.'

'Hardly a shit-heap. You should go and have a look. It looks smarter than half the hotels on the seafront.'

'Yes, but how long for? And did you bump into Clio? She came looking for you.'

'Yes, thanks. Though in some ways I wish she hadn't come. She was incredibly rude to Luke.'

Louise concentrated on changing the till roll, one of her least favourite tasks. 'Maybe she's jealous. Luke's almost got pop star looks. Perhaps she thinks he should prefer her.'

'Don't be ridiculous, Louise. I'd better talk to her later.' Amanda felt every sympathy for her daughter's recent scare, but she had to live her own life. And Luke was becoming part of it. She suspected he would become more so. He'd asked her to come away with him for the weekend. And Amanda had a good idea why.

A sudden flame of excitement ran through her and she had to turn away in case Louise noticed. She couldn't wait to go to bed with Luke Knight.

When she got home, Sean and Clio were both sitting at the kitchen table studying.

'Wow!' Amanda struck her forehead in mock amazement. 'Have I come to the right house? My home doesn't have co-operative children sitting round a table doing their homework. My children fight with each other, make a complete mess of the kitchen, then play computer games in their bedrooms.'

Clio smiled angelically. 'I've turned over a new leaf. I'm going to work like fu— . . . like a Trojan from now on so that you'll be able to relax about my grades. Then, for my work experience, I've fixed up a week's stint with Day Properties.'

'That was quick work.'

'You're supposed to be impressed by my enterprise and self-motivation.'

Amanda knew it was irrational but she felt a little hurt that Clio should want to work with Angus rather than Luke. 'I am. But won't property development be rather dull? I could ask Luke if he could find you something in the theatre, if you like.'

'Can't stand arty types. All up their own bums, daaaahling.'

'Your decision, I suppose.'

'Yes, it is.'

Amanda swiped at Kinky the cat who was trying to lick the butter again. 'Bad cat!' Kinky purred furiously.

'Maybe she doesn't speak Human,' Sean offered. 'By the way, what's for supper?'

'We-ell . . .' Amanda answered in her best 'I know we shouldn't be doing this but . . .' tone. 'I thought maybe fish and chips.'

'Wow. You must be guilty about something.'

'She is,' Clio supplied. 'She's going away this weekend with the Love God. Gran's looking after us. She just rang and told me.'

Typical of Helen to blow the whole thing before Amanda got the chance to break it tactfully. Tact was a gift that her mother considered overrated.

'It's only Saturday night, actually.'

'Why not go for Friday too?' offered Sean generously.

'Do we really need Gran?' Clio asked sweetly. 'I can look after Sean.'

'You just want the babysitting money because you've spent your allowance again,' Sean pointed out.

'You'd be fine for the evening,' Amanda replied. 'But not the whole night. I'd worry too much.'

'And we don't want you worrying. It might dent the passion.'

Amanda actually found herself blushing. What the hell was the matter with her?

The next few days passed in a flash and already it was the weekend. As Amanda packed her overnight bag, she was attacked by a nasty case of second thoughts. Shouldn't sex be some wild and elemental force that made you throw manners, convention and even your knickers to the wind? The idea of booking a weekend break with the express intention of making love suddenly seemed as much of a turn-on as a night with Cliff Richard.

What if it was all a ghastly disappointment? What if he looked at her thighs and imagined them in ten years' time? Now that they were in the realms of reality rather than fantasy, she was losing her nerve. And Amanda realised that far from being carried along on a yearning tidal wave of passion, she rather wished she was staying at home with Sean and Clio for a pizza and a video.

Chapter 15

'Have you packed your passport?' were Luke's first words when he picked her up on Saturday. It was a freezing February morning but Luke's obvious excitement was more thrilling than the brightest sunshine. 'We're going to Dieppe for the night. The ferry leaves at half past nine.'

'Go on, Mum,' Clio grinned, happy that her mother was having a treat for once, 'here's your coat. You'd better run or you'll miss it.'

'But Gran's not here yet.'

'I'll look after Sean. Just go.'

Naturally, she couldn't find her passport. Clio came to the rescue again. 'It's in your bedside drawer – I saw it there when I was looking for tights.'

Under any other circumstances Amanda would have wanted to know why Clio was stealing her tights yet again when she had a perfectly good allowance. Today she was just grateful.

She'd been worried as to how Sean would take it when his mother disappeared with a suitcase and a relatively strange man, but Sean didn't even look up from the football pull-out that had come free with the Saturday paper.

'Bye, Mum. If you see any Man United sweatshirts will you bring me one?'

173

'Absolutely. Though I doubt they'll be thick on the ground in Dieppe. Bye, darling.'

The ferry port was only a half-hour drive away. Somehow, getting on board a ship and heading for France was absolutely the right thing to do. It instantly felt like an adventure.

It was almost one by the time they got to their hotel and the owner showed them up to their room. It was small but pretty, with a narrow double bed covered in a faded flowery bedspread, a small bathroom and a shuttered window that overlooked a quiet street.

The intimacy of it, the idea of showering and going to the loo with Luke in earshot, suddenly overwhelmed Amanda.

'Sex or lunch?' enquired Luke.

'Lunch. No contest.' Amanda laughed, relieved that he saw the funny side. 'I've just realised I'm absolutely ravenous.'

'Then I know just the place. They do the best *steak-frites* in Dieppe.' He hesitated, considering her. 'Unless you're a nouvelle cuisine fan as well as being green?'

The restaurant was packed with Saturday shoppers taking a couple of hours out to eat a vast meal. 'You have to start with the seafood platter,' Luke insisted, waving his hand at a three-tiered metal platter stacked with mussels, oysters, scallops, crab claws, langoustines and tiny black shellfish.

It was the best fish she'd ever tasted. Amanda even tried the oysters, slurping them down just as they did in the sexy eating scene in the film of *Tom Jones*. Luke knew all about wine and ordered a bottle of delicious *Entre Deux Mers* to go with it.

'Right,' Luke announced when the seafood platter had been demolished, 'here comes the steak. Forget the Eiffel Tower or Rodin's *Kiss*. Prepare yourself for a real French masterpiece.'

He was right too. The steak was thick and juicy, with a tangy, freshly made Béarnaise sauce. The *frites* were thin and salty and melted in her mouth.

'Even better than McDonald's,' Amanda sighed, sipping the red wine that had replaced the white. 'And that's a pretty high accolade.'

'You sophisticate, you,' teased Luke tenderly. While they had been eating, a guitar player had come round singing ancient French ballads of knights and ladies. It all seemed ludicrously perfect.

'And now, how about completing the cliché with some crème brûlée?'

And it wasn't just any crème brûlée. Underneath the layer of burnt sugar and delicious creamy custard lay a sharp coulis of passion fruit.

'How appropriate,' whispered Luke. 'How about going back to the hotel for a siesta?'

Amanda's nervousness was back. 'What about all the sightseeing we'd planned? The cathedral? The famous open-air market?'

'I think I can live without them.' His smile was so inviting that she felt a delicious tightening in her knickers, which, in a rare moment of planning, actually matched her bra.

With impressive speed, Luke ordered the bill and went to get their coats. Amanda glanced at the receipt the waiter had left on the table. The meal was the price of a rather average pizza at home. What's more, Luke had left a generous tip.

She liked him more for knowing somewhere so good and cheap. It wouldn't have impressed her half as much if they'd gone to a fifty-pounds-a-head place, dripping with waiters, where everyone talked in hushed voices, worshipping at the altar of food.

The whole of Dieppe seemed to be out on the streets, haggling over the fish, filling their baskets with mud-covered leeks or buying their baguettes to accompany the evening meal.

'Why are they selling stones?' Amanda stared into a *confiserie* window where grey pebbles were tied up in small pages priced at twenty francs each.

'They're sweets, silly. Let's buy some chocolate for later.'

They scuttled back to their hotel like kids, laughing and holding hands. Once inside, Luke pulled the curtains and turned to Amanda.

'And now, Mrs Wells, that we're finally alone together . . .'

Under normal circumstances she would have swooned at the silky suggestion of pleasure in his tone, but suddenly sex was the last thing on her mind.

'God, Luke, I'm so sorry, but I think I'm going to be sick . . .'

She ran into the tiny bathroom, just making it to the loo in time, and heaved up the wonderful meal they'd just eaten.

Luke, thank God, didn't try to tenderly hold her head but left her in peace.

She imagined him lying on the bed and listening in irritation as their romantic weekend turned into a disaster. No, that was Giles, she reminded herself. Luke was different.

Finally she emerged, shaken and hideously embarrassed.

'Come on, get into bed,' he said with no apparent sign of annoyance. 'You must have had a bad mussel. It gets you like that. Have a nap and you'll feel fine in a few hours.'

Amanda, clad in her dressing gown, climbed into bed and fell almost instantly asleep.

It was dark when she woke up, with just the beam from a street light illuminating the room. Luke was on the bed next to her, fully clothed. She sat up gingerly.

'Here, this'll make you feel a whole lot better. French chocolate is known for its miraculous powers.'

Amanda was about to say she could never eat again when she realised that the pain in her stomach was actually hunger. She took the chocolate gratefully.

Whoever the patron saint of chocolate was, they were clearly on overtime because she did, almost immediately, start to feel better. After another couple of squares it was as if she'd never been ill.

'Wow!' Amanda conceded, 'you were right about the miraculous powers.'

'In that case,' Luke began to undo the belt of his blue jeans, 'perhaps we should give thanks in our own particular way.'

Amanda giggled and lifted the bedclothes to let him in.

'For God's sake, Mum!' Clio banged her mug of morning coffee down on the counter. 'Stop humming!'

'Was I humming?' Amanda asked infuriatingly.

'Yes. And as a matter of fact, you haven't stopped for the last two weeks. Ever since your night of passion in France.'

176

'Ah.'

'And maybe you don't know *what* you're humming but perhaps, in case it frightens him off, you ought to know that it's Pachelbel's *Canon*.'

'So?'

'Which is most generally known as the tune to which brides come down the aisle.'

'Oh my God!' Amanda was appalled. It had been entirely subconscious. But still, if Luke had heard her, it could be extremely embarrassing. She'd try and stop herself.

On the other hand, explaining how wonderful it felt to have a man who cared about you after sixteen years of emotional autism from Giles was like describing the taste of a dry martini to someone who'd never touched alcohol. It made no sense.

How could Clio understand what it meant to her mother to be phoned twice a day, to have funny text messages left on her mobile, to be given bunches of exotic tulips, 'because they were as beautiful as she was' and, instead of producing endless demands, to have found a man who tried to think up ways of making her happy.

As Amanda walked to work she decided that nature was trying to make her happy too. The chill and depressing greyness of winter had surrendered, without a protest, to a startling explosion of spring. Almost overnight (she fancifully wondered if it had been *that* night) the daffodils had burst into bloom, the wood pigeons had begun cooing and people had started loitering in pavement cafés.

Gradually Luke was becoming part of her life, arriving every lunchtime for their stroll – Amanda was actually getting quite fit – meeting her after work, taking her to more concerts, asking her opinion on films and books.

He'd been round to supper three or four times when Clio and Sean were there, although Amanda and he had agreed he shouldn't stay overnight. But she missed him terribly when he went.

He was, in Amanda's book, almost perfect.

'You're looking smart today,' she commented to Clio the next morning at the breakfast table. 'Are you going somewhere nice?'

Clio had done excellently in her GCSE mocks and was now out as often as possible.

'Thanks. Actually I'm going for my interview at Day Properties.'

Amanda repressed another sliver of annoyance that Clio had chosen Angus over Luke. 'Do you have to have an interview for work experience?'

'Of course I do. I'm not just going there to open the mail and make tea, you know. I want to learn about property development.'

'But I thought you wanted to do something useful. Work for a charity or something. Property developers are in it for the money.'

'There's nothing wrong with making money if you use it well,' Clio announced.

'I wouldn't know. I work in an art gallery. For someone else.'

'You don't have to. You could try your own gallery.'

'Not you too. I suppose I'll be getting more of this if you're going off to work for Angus Day. I'm quite happy as I am, thank you.'

The headquarters of Day Properties weren't at all what Clio expected. For a start, although the building was old-fashioned outside, its interior was startlingly modern. The entire space was open-plan and contained a truly vast semi-circular desk that stretched along an entire wall.

'Yours?' Clio asked Angus.

'Who else's?' said Laddie, who appeared at Angus's side.

'I've never seen such a big one,' giggled Clio.

'Right, young lady, no coarse sexual innuendo in this office,' corrected Angus sternly.

Clio was taken aback.

Laddie grinned. 'We save it all for the site.'

'As a matter of fact,' Angus sat down on his office chair and whizzed up to the other end of his desk to get a file, 'we're rather worried about having a young lady like yourself visiting sites at all. The language may not be what you're used to.'

'Mr Day . . .' she began.

'Angus,' he corrected.

'Angus. Have you visited a secondary school lately? I think you'll find a building site is a lot more genteel.'

Laddie whooped with laughter. 'She could be right, Angus.'

'And don't tell me the toilet facilities are a problem or I'll take you on a personal tour of the school bogs. You may never be the same again. Speaking of which,' Clio suddenly looked embarrassed, 'could I use yours now?'

She'd suddenly had a bad period cramp, but even the embarrassment of having to ask for the loo couldn't wipe out the relief of having her next period arriving on time.

'Nice lass, eh?' Laddie approved when she was out of earshot. 'I wish the lads who want to do work experience were half as keen as she is. Or as on the ball.'

Angus nodded. As it happened, if Clio did her work experience with them she would spend more time in meetings and doing paperwork than on site. Which was just as well. Clio seemed to have no idea of just how attractive she was, which, of course, served to make her even more alluring. She was like a pale new shoot tentatively pushing its way through the winter earth. *Oh for God's sake*, Angus told himself, *forget the poetics; it's just that she reminds you of her mother*.

Laddie seemed to be following his thoughts. 'Don't worry. I'll look after her. Besides, the lads on the site prefer the barmaid type. Just don't send me Pamela Anderson on work experience.'

'I think she's got all the work experience she needs.'

They both laughed. Clio, coming back into the room, coloured faintly.

'Right, Angus, I'll be off. There's some roof trusses I have to chase up.'

Clio giggled. 'Are they really called roof trusses?'

'I'm afraid so. And guess what,' Laddie laughed, 'you nail them to the stud.'

'I'd better be getting home, I suppose. If you could sign this form.' She handed it to Angus. 'It's for my school. So they know I'm not just bunking off. And do those dates suit you? A week at the beginning of April?'

'Fine. I'll see if we can think up some interesting projects for you.'

'That's really kind of you,' Clio said gratefully. 'Most people treat work experience students as either a nuisance or unpaid post-openers.'

'Funny you should mention it,' Angus said straight-faced, 'we've got a vacancy for an unpaid post-opener.'

'I'd better be going then.'

'Would you like a lift? I'm just heading over to my mother's. She gets a bit low in the afternoons.'

'I really liked your mother,' Clio said as she climbed into Angus's car. She'd never been in anything as swish as this before and was surprised at how low-slung and like a racing car it felt after their dented old Honda. 'The way she made you pay for Mum's damage.'

'I'm very hen-pecked.' Angus's smile implied he was anything but.

'No you're not, you're kind.'

'How *is* your mother, by the way?' Angus changed the subject swiftly. Clio got the impression that he would have loved to have asked ages ago but was holding back.

'Fine.' She waited a moment, unsure of what to say. His tone had held an intensity that betrayed more than just a friendly interest. The news that her mother was behaving like an eighteen-year-old in love would not, she suspected, exactly make his day.

'Is she still seeing Luke Knight?'

Clio's hesitation told him everything.

'Is it serious, do you think?'

'Hard to tell.' Clio knew she sounded like a matron in a boys' school explaining a match cancellation due to flu.

'Send her my regards.' He grinned ruefully. 'No, don't bother. What does she think of your work experience idea?'

'She suggested I go and find out about the arts with Luke.' She raised an eyebrow and they both laughed.

'I said I preferred the idea of builders' bums to arty-farty people who're all up themselves anyway.'

Angus tried not to laugh. 'It's not all builders' bums, you know.'

'Yes, Mr Day – Angus. I do know.' She pulled a copy of *Quantity*

Surveyors Weekly out of her backpack. 'I've even started doing a bit of background reading. I really am interested, you know.'

'You're an amazing person, Miss Wells.' He wondered how it would feel to have a daughter like this; bright, intelligent, funny, eager to soak up her father's wisdom. And then he remembered Giles, who'd seemed a rather boorish, insensitive individual. Amanda had said he was having twins with his new wife. That must be tough for Clio. Life wasn't easy or kind, even to people who deserved for it to be. The thought led him to his mother, and how much she'd wished for grandchildren. She would have loved a granddaughter like Clio.

'I just wondered,' his tone had taken on an unfamiliar hesitation, 'if you might come with me and visit my mother. She loves young people and hardly ever gets to see any. Old people are boring, she says – always complaining.'

Clio was touched. Her own gran was always busy. And the funny thing was, her own gran didn't like young people, she wanted to *be* one. 'I'd love to.'

Clio felt very grand and grown-up as they drove through the town. She rather wished they'd go past her school so that one of her friends might see her in this flash car, but they went the other way, out of Laineton and on to the bypass. Angus drove quite fast here and she felt a sudden thrill at the car's powerful engine.

'I don't suppose,' she asked shyly, 'we could have the roof down? Only I've never been in a sports car before.'

Angus laughed, remembering New Year's Eve when Amanda had asked the same thing, even though it was freezing. And then her earlier remark.

'Why're you laughing?'

'Because your mother accused me of having the roof down because I'm vain.'

Clio looked puzzled. 'Why would it be vain to put the roof down?'

'So that I could look at myself in shop windows, apparently.'

'What a good idea! Pity there aren't any shop windows here so that I could do it now.'

'I'll have to see what I can do another day. I'm sure we'll have to do some driving during your work experience.'

'Cool. I'll remember to bring my shades.'

By now they were in the countryside, approaching a set of huge and impressive gates.

'My mother lives in the lodge.'

'Wow!' Clio studied the large house in the distance. 'And I wonder which fat cat lives in that place?'

'I do, actually. But I don't suppose you'll believe that I bought the house because of the lodge. So I'd be near my mother and yet she could be independent.'

'Haven't you ever heard of granny flats?'

'I have, as a matter of fact,' Angus replied, trying not to grin, 'but my mother hated the idea. This seemed a reasonable compromise.'

'I'm sure. And you get to live in the mansion.'

'I don't like it much. Too big and empty.'

'Oh well. Could be worse,' Clio grinned. 'You could be selling the *Big Issue* and sleeping on the street.'

Angus cracked with laughter. 'That's true. I must try to remember that.'

Isobel Day was dozing in her usual chair. The television murmured quietly in the corner.

'Hello, Maw.' Isobel jumped when Angus kissed her. 'I've brought you a visitor. It's Clio Wells. Amanda's daughter.'

Clio took in the lovely peaceful rooms, the walls painted a pale sea-green, the colour Amanda loved so much, the skirting boards picked out in Shaker blue. The softly patterned curtains, in the shape of shells, framed a glorious vista out over the garden to the lush landscape beyond.

'What a wonderful view,' Clio admired, shaking Isobel's hand shyly.

'Yes. The daffodils and the crocuses are beautiful this year. I used to do all the gardening myself and then have a sleep under that apple tree.' She pointed to a wonderfully gnarled old tree, on which delicate leaf-buds were just beginning to appear. She looked at Angus. 'It's the tree I want to be buried under. None of

182

this churchy nonsense. I've had enough of that to last me a life-time.'

'Don't be so morbid,' was Angus's brisk response.

'Angus, face facts.' Isobel's tone was one of exasperated tenderness. 'You ought to start thinking about it. If I'm prepared to, I don't see why you can't be.'

'Cup of tea?' Angus replied, changing the subject. He knew she was right but he couldn't be as stoical about it as she was. She was all he had, apart from some distant cousins in New Zealand.

'I'll make it,' offered Clio. 'My mum says I make the best tea. Which is just as well, she says, given how I never do any tidying, spread my make-up everywhere and use up all her tights.'

Angus busied himself with looking for the Earl Grey, surprised at how painful this sudden glimpse into the everyday life of the Wells family was. He had always envied domestic chaos, perhaps because he'd never experienced it. Laura had believed one dirty coffee cup turned a home into a hovel.

'Is your mother very ill?' Clio asked quietly when she joined him in the kitchen.

'I'm afraid so.'

'Isn't there anything they can do?'

'Not to cure it. It's gone too far. But there is a drug that would probably prolong things. It's just that being my mother, she won't take it.'

'Why not?'

'Because you have to pay for it and she says it isn't fair that she should be able to buy life at the expense of younger people who can't.'

'God,' Clio whispered, 'that's incredibly principled.'

'And incredibly infuriating. Here I am, having made a bit of money, and the one person who might benefit from it won't use it to live longer.'

'I am sorry.' She was beginning to see that the adult world was more complicated than she'd realised. For instance, if she'd really been pregnant it would have affected her family as well as herself, just as Isobel's attitude to treatment affected Angus.

'She likes these shortbread biscuits too.' Angus laid some out on a plate.

Clio carried in the tray. Isobel was staring intently at two carved herons on the windowsill.

'Aren't they wonderful!' Clio admired. She'd hardly ever seen anything so beautiful.

'Angus bought them for me,' Isobel said with simple pride. 'And the swan too.' She pointed to the carving on the mantelpiece. 'They remind me of growing up in the Hebrides.'

'In fact,' Angus added with a soft smile, 'I have your mother to thank for them. She told me about the artist.'

'I've never seen anything like those in the gallery. It's all chocolate-box pictures of lovely Laineton.'

'Louise didn't think they'd sell, apparently.'

'Oh God. Louise. Mum's taste is so much better than hers. How Mum can bear to work for someone who looks like one of those ancient hippies who hang round Glastonbury, I don't know. She should get a gallery of her own.'

'Just what I told her,' Angus agreed. 'Why don't you think she listens?'

Clio paused, remembering her thought about the complexity of adult life. 'Probably because of us. We don't have a hell of a lot coming in. She probably feels it wouldn't be fair to take the risk.'

She felt hotly embarrassed talking about money to someone who had so much. And yet, all his money couldn't help him save his mother. No one has a charmed life. Money couldn't buy everything.

She sat down next to Isobel. 'So what's it like in the Hebrides? I bet it's really cool.'

'Yes,' Isobel smiled over Clio's head at her son. 'It's really, really cool.'

Clio was amazed when she glanced at her watch and found an hour and a half had passed. 'God! I'd better rush. I thought we'd only been chatting five minutes.'

'Angus'll drop you back, won't you, Angus? It's far too dark now for you to be thinking about buses.'

Clio remembered how Isobel had bossed him over the business of Amanda driving into him. But it was a nice kind of bossiness. It wasn't controlling, more the outward recognition of their closeness.

'Of course,' Angus smiled. 'It'd be a pleasure.'

'Perhaps I could come again when I'm doing the work experience?'

'You don't have to wait for that,' Isobel said. 'You can come whenever you like. As long as I can fit you in between jetting to Cannes, shopping in Harrods and my couture fittings.'

Fifteen minutes later, just as Angus slowed down outside Clio's house, Amanda climbed out of her battered old Honda. Angus lowered his electric window to explain their late arrival and saw Luke following her. He pressed the button again and decided to let Clio tell her.

'Where on earth have you been all this time?' Amanda asked Clio, half irritated, half anxious. 'I thought your interview was at eleven?' They both watched Angus drive off.

'It was. Angus asked if I wanted to come and visit his mother. She's the nicest woman. Only, did you know, she's got cancer and she won't take the drug that would help her because you have to buy it and it wouldn't be fair to people who haven't got the money.'

'How very saintly,' commented Luke.

'Yes, but the funny thing is, she's not like that at all. She's very witty and nice.'

'Yes,' echoed Luke, 'but isn't her son a bit old for you?'

It should have been a joke, but there was an uncomfortable edge to the remark. Amanda shot him a look. Not for the first time in their relationship, she felt a flash of exasperation with Luke. 'That's a very weird thing to say.'

'Why? It's true, isn't it?'

Somewhere in Amanda's mind a warning bell went off, faint and disturbing. Surely there couldn't be anything between Clio and Angus Day?

Chapter 16

Amanda was horrified at herself. How could she distrust Clio like that? Or Angus for that matter. He was old enough to be her father. For a moment, the thought flashed through her mind that Clio had just lost her father and might be vulnerable to an older man, especially now that she feared she might be replaced in Giles's affections by twin babies.

She dismissed the thought. The idea was absurd. In fact, it would never have crossed her mind if Luke hadn't made the suggestion. She forced herself to treat the situation as it was – perfectly straightforward. 'So, how did the interview go?'

'Fine. I'm doing a week, starting in April.'

'Good for you for showing so much initiative.' She meant it too. Clio sometimes struck Amanda as more grown up than Amanda felt herself. She switched her mind to what Luke had said earlier, that he needed to talk to her tonight about something important. She was dying of curiosity to know what it was.

She didn't have long to wait. Clio immediately disappeared up to her room to text Jasmine, and since Sean was out at football practice, they were alone for once.

Amanda poured them both a glass of wine and started to make supper.

Luke put his arms round her. 'Here, you sit down. You've been at the gallery all day. I'll do that. My pesto is famed across six continents.'

Amanda sighed with pleasure. This was bliss. A man who actually did some cooking. 'I thought there were only five.'

'Pedant. Geography was always my worst subject.'

'And what was your best?' Even though they'd been almost inseparable for the last few weeks, and here he was making her supper in her own kitchen, and it felt natural and wonderful, not to mention amazing after her years with Giles, there was still so much she didn't know about him.

'Drama. My parents tried to overlook the fact.'

Amanda laughed. 'I'll bet they did. Not the sort of subject that leads to the church. You should have been deep in Latin, with a bit of divinity thrown in.'

'God, how I hated divinity.'

Amanda grinned.

'Why are you laughing?'

'"*God,* how I hated divinity." I was just laughing at your choice of words.'

He put down his measuring jug and came over. '*God,*' he imitated her tone, 'how I love you, Amanda Wells.' He leaned over and kissed her, hard on the lips.

'Excuse *me,*' Clio's voice interrupted sarcastically from behind them, 'I'm just going over to Jasmine's to do some homework.'

'What about supper?'

'I'll have it there. Wouldn't want to spoil the party.'

Amanda was about to say, 'The rule is we all eat together,' when it occurred to her that Clio going to Jasmine's would probably be for the best. Then she and Luke could talk, and there wouldn't be this horrible edge between Clio and Luke.

'All right. Be back by ten.'

Amanda turned back to Luke. His handsome face had hardened.

'You shouldn't let her talk to you like that. She'll think she can get away with anything.'

Even though he had a point, Amanda felt an urge to remind him that Clio was her responsibility. 'I know. It's just that it's hard for her with you and me getting together, and her father soon to have twins . . .'

But Luke wasn't listening. 'I mean, do you *want* her to hang round with older men like that, especially after the business with the ski instructor?'

'Drop it, Luke.' The steel in her voice surprised herself, but she felt Clio's behaviour really wasn't anything to do with him.

Luke shrugged. Amanda struggled to keep her annoyance under control. She didn't want to quarrel with Luke. He was trying to be helpful, after all. And Clio's behaviour had been out of order. 'Now what was this important matter you wanted to discuss?'

Luke bristled. 'Doesn't matter. It may not happen anyway. Let's just leave it, shall we?'

It was the first time he'd ever pushed her away emotionally and it reminded her of a party game she'd particularly loathed as a child. Someone put a blindfold on you and you waited. You might get a kiss, or be tickled with a feather, or maybe get a slap. The fun came in not knowing which. Except that Amanda had never found it fun in the first place.

'This pasta's ready,' Luke said.

Amanda found that she wasn't hungry. Luke was different from Giles in almost every way she could think of. So why on earth was she feeling the same sense of frustration and resentment that Giles had induced? Maybe the problem was hers, as Giles had always insisted. But whereas, whether out of cowardice or habit, she'd let Giles get away with it, she was damned if she was going to repeat her mistake.

'Look, this thing you were going to tell me obviously matters to you. I'd rather we talked about it now.'

'All right, then.' Luke's most charming smile was back. It was almost as if she'd imagined the atmosphere of a moment ago. They sat down together at the kitchen table and he refilled their glasses of wine.

'Do you remember I told you about the job offer I'd had in Leeds?'

Amanda's heart lurched. She did indeed remember, but since he hadn't mentioned it again, in a stupid head-in-the-sand manner she'd hoped it had gone away.

'They're pressing me for an answer. It's a fabulous opportunity, running a new arts festival there. Everyone's saying Leeds is fantastic these days. Vibrant. Energetic. The university's the most exciting in the country.'

'Leeds,' Amanda repeated dully.

Laineton to Leeds was over 300 miles. But it wasn't just the distance. Their relationship was still new, it needed feeding and watering. It needed nearness and intimacy. What it didn't need was hundreds of miles of bad rail connections. 'I see. When would you start, if you took the job, that is?' She tried to gauge his enthusiasm, whether this was a job he desperately wanted. But Luke was waiting for a reaction.

'You don't seem overjoyed,' he said eventually.

'No. Well, I hardly would be, would I? I know it's selfish but I suppose I hoped you'd stay here.'

'My contract finishes soon.'

'Of course it does.' For God's sake, she'd known a job like his would involve moving about.

The inevitability of it all suddenly struck her. Luke would go to Leeds. They would try to stay involved but it would be impossible because her life was so complicated. Clio was doing important exams. Sean was only ten and needed attention. Her mother would help, but she couldn't look after the children full-time.

'Maybe you could all come too?' Luke took her hand.

Amanda smiled limply. Luke had no idea of what relocating would mean to a family that had all its complicated roots in another place. Especially after the instability of the divorce. The one thing she'd tried to do when she and Giles had split was to keep Clio and Sean's lives exactly the same in every other way.

Luke raised his glass and looked at her over the rim. 'There is one other alternative,' he smiled, like a magician who knows he still has the white rabbit left in the hat.

Amanda felt like a prisoner given a last chance of parole. 'What's that?'

'I mentioned that there might be a permanent job here. Of course, it's nothing like the Leeds offer, and normally I wouldn't have considered it, but . . .' His words trailed off tantalisingly.

'But what?' Amanda prompted.

'I've fallen in love with you.'

Her heart was looping the loop now. The prisoner had got parole.

'I'd be happy to accept the job in Laineton. On one condition.'

Amanda held her breath. 'And what would that be?'

'That we try and make a real go of it, you and I. That I move in here with you. That we try to be a proper family.'

Amanda didn't have to hesitate. She would have liked to talk it over with Clio and Sean first, but this was an emergency. Luke would be out of her life if she didn't act now. Clio and Sean would just have to learn to accept him.

'All right.' She raised her own glass and clinked his. 'Let's do it. To us. Wishing us all the luck in the world.'

'Do you think we need that much?'

'We do with Sean and Clio. Promise me one thing – that you let me break it to them gently.'

'You make me sound more like a threat than a lover.'

'I'm sorry,' she touched his face, 'let me rephrase that. It's the most wonderful, glorious surprise and I know we'll all be very happy.' She smiled tenderly at him. 'Eventually.'

By the time Angus looked in again Isobel had got out of her chair and made herself a pitiful supper of half a piece of toast and a poached egg. 'I'd invite you to dinner,' she said, 'but as you see, it won't really go around – unless you're good at miracles.'

Angus hugged her gently, pushing away the thought of his own empty house. He hadn't even considered what he was going to eat.

'By the way, something I wanted to say.' She sat down with the tray on her knee and took a deep breath to quell the pain that had suddenly attacked with a cruel sharp blade in her abdomen. 'The party for the estate.'

'I wondered when you'd get round to that. You didn't approve, despite your speech.'

It had taken a while for Angus to understand his mother's complex response to things. She loathed what she called the 'hand-out culture'. Having lost her own home, she had little time for those who were housed by the state and abused their good luck. 'No, I didn't approve at first. I don't see why people feel they can have something for nothing.'

'Laddie thinks I'm mad too.'

'But I don't think you're mad. I joked about miracles, but I think the Eastcliff Estate almost qualifies. You've done an amazing job there. When I came here it was a no-go area. You've given people some pride in their homes and I don't think they're taking it for granted. You could feel it the other day. Now I'd better eat this egg before it turns into India rubber.'

Angus had to turn away, astonished at how much his mother's words meant to him.

She took a mouthful of egg, but being Isobel, couldn't resist one parting shot. 'You're still in love with that girl's mother, aren't you?'

Angus shrugged.

'I don't understand how you can be so in charge of every other aspect of your life but this.'

'You're out of date, Maw. Women don't like men to be in charge any more.'

'Codswallop,' commented Isobel in her stern Scots tones.

Angus tried not to look shocked. 'Are you suggesting I stride in there, grab Amanda by her hair and hit Luke Knight with a cudgel?'

Isobel took a minuscule bite of her toast. 'It'd be better than your current strategy of doing bog all.'

'Look, Maw,' Angus fired up suddenly, 'if I want your advice on my love life, I'll ask for it.'

True to form, Isobel couldn't resist having the last word. 'Then you'd better bloody well hurry up. That young man is a fast worker and he doesn't share your scruples. I recognise the type. Play by the rules if you will, but *he* won't.'

If she hadn't been dying, Angus reflected grimly, he would have felt like strangling her. Besides, it was all very well for his mother to accuse him of doing bog all about Amanda. It was a lot less clear what he *should* be doing.

On the other hand, maybe he ought to do something. Maybe he should forget about Luke Knight and just tell her his feelings, that he thought of her constantly and endlessly fantasised about what would have happened if her husband hadn't returned that night.

Angus was fairly level-headed, but he knew one thing with every inch of his being. If Giles hadn't interrupted them, it would be he, not Luke, who was in her arms and in her mind. But how could he persuade her of that now?

No matter how likely the risk of painful rejection, he had to tell her.

In fact, he'd do it tomorrow.

For the first time in weeks, even though his house was huge and echoey and painfully empty, he slept as soundly as a baby.

'You seem very cheerful,' Rose Miles congratulated Luke when she saw him walking along the seafront near their chalet.

She'd been watching him for several minutes before she'd spoken. He'd selected a pebble from the beach and thrown it carefully on to the hopscotch pitch some children had drawn in chalk, then skipped to the top number and back again. It was such an exuberant, unadult gesture that it had made Rose smile.

'I am, as a matter of fact. Fancy a waltz, Rose?'

Rose's face broke into a smile. Her skin was so ancient and sunburned from decades of lying out on the beach that she resembled a happy alligator. Glancing round to check that there was no one to see them – or maybe hoping there was – she and Luke waltzed along the boardwalk that led from the promenade to the row of beach huts.

At the back of the boardwalk was a row of shabby lock-up shops, more like stalls, that operated only in summer and sold cheap seaside tat. They were still closed for the winter. Two men were staring at them speculatively, one of them with a small palm-top computer in his hand.

As they waltzed closer, Luke saw that it was Angus Day and his Scottish foreman.

Angus had seen Luke too. Despite his feelings, he smiled at the incongruous sight of Rose Miles, at probably eighty-five, twirling like a young girl along the empty seafront.

'Hello, Rose,' Angus said. He knew he should acknowledge Luke, but some childish streak prevented him. 'You look happy.'

'It's not me who's happy.' The couple stopped next to them, breathless and laughing. 'It's Luke.'

Angus felt a dead thump of premonition in the pit of his stomach. 'And why is that?'

Luke smiled lazily, with the gleam of victory in his eye. 'Because the woman I love has just asked me to move in with her.'

Rose, innocent of the swirling waters she was paddling in, smiled at Angus. 'Isn't that good news? I've always said the woman who got Luke would be a lucky lady. He's the handsomest young man in the whole of Laineton.'

'Ah,' Angus replied, his voice heavy with irony, 'but as my mother always says, handsome is as handsome does.'

'Thanks for that, Angus.' Luke raised an eyebrow mockingly. 'I'll try to live up to your mother's touching homily.'

'Yes.' Angus's eyes narrowed and his voice took on a steely tone that cut through the sunny morning. 'You'd better bloody do that.'

'Well,' said Rose as she and Luke turned abruptly away, 'that wasn't very well-mannered of Mr Day.'

'No,' agreed Luke, suppressing a grin, 'it wasn't very well-mannered at all. But then, what do you expect? Angus Day's just a property spiv who pretends to have a conscience. Sometimes the real man shows through.'

'How very odd,' Rose confided to her sister Betty, when she got home. 'I was out on the promenade with nice Luke Knight and we bumped into Angus Day. They almost came to blows.'

Betty looked at her sister as if she were simple in the head. 'Of course they did.' Betty went on hanging her nighties out on their small line in front of their beach hut home. It was a lovely drying wind. March but with the promise of a warm April.

'Why *of course*?' Rose replied, prickled. She prided herself on being the sensible one who'd acquired the wisdom of age, while Betty went through life making silly remarks and generally behaving like a young girl at her first party.

'It's obvious, isn't it? There's only one reason men behave like that towards each other.'

'And what's that, pray?' Rose pushed her sister's flowery nightie to one side and waited.

'They must both be in love with the same woman.'

'Oh for heaven's sake, Betty, what possible evidence have you got for that?'

'Only a lifetime of men falling in love with me.' Betty threw her scarf over her shoulder like a wrinkled Isadora Duncan.

'So how come you're a lonely old lady, living in a glorified beach hut with your crabby old sister for company, then?'

'Because I felt sorry for you and didn't want to leave you alone. And by the way, Mr Day popped in while you were waltzing ridiculously along the promenade.' She paused grandly, savouring the thrill of knowing more than Rose twice in one morning. 'He's got a proposition to make to us.'

'What kind of proposition?'

'I've no idea.' Betty pegged up the last pair of bloomers. 'But if he's proposing to set us up as octogenarian ladies of the night, then I for one think it's a brilliant idea.'

'What on earth are you doing?' Clio watched her mother tidy the house for the second time that week.

The truth was, ever since Luke had suggested he move in with her, Amanda had seen the house differently. Suddenly the piles of newspapers, unidentified plastic objects and cat hairs that littered the kitchen seemed less the inevitable chaos of family life than just plain depressing. She wanted the place to feel clean, even if tidy were an impossible goal.

'What the hell's the matter with you?' Clio demanded as she made herself some sandwiches for school. 'You're turning into a one-woman ad for rubber gloves. Go on, reassure me. You've been drinking household fluids or sniffing furniture polish, haven't you?

This isn't my real mother scrubbing the kitchen sink and bleaching teacups?'

'I wasn't bleaching teacups. I just thought I'd tidy up a bit, that's all.' Amanda tried not to sound defensive. 'You can get tired of living in a rubbish tip. It's called spring cleaning. All sorts of people do it.'

'All sorts of people may do it, but you never have. I bet this is something to do with your knight in shining armour, isn't it?'

Amanda didn't reply. She wanted to be in control of the conversation when she broke the news about Luke. She'd planned to take Sean and Clio out tonight and tell them over a pizza.

'It is, isn't it?' Clio insisted. 'Are you worried he'll catch something nasty off the worktops?'

Amanda ignored the comment. 'Actually,' she said with more emphasis in her voice than she'd intended, 'there is something I need to talk to you about.' She stopped, not quite knowing how to break the news.

'Shit.' Clio stopped loading up her school bag and faced her mother. 'It's more serious than that, isn't it? A quick shag would merit ten minutes of shoving everything under the sofa. You haven't asked him to move in?'

Amanda flushed. 'Clio, look, everything got very difficult. He's been offered a really good job up North, but he's turning it down because of me. The only thing he asked was that if he stayed in Laineton it wasn't in some crummy, lonely flat. He wants to live with me. With us.'

'He doesn't even know us, Mum.' Clio's voice was shredded with hurt. 'He knows you. He's interested in you. He didn't choose us and he probably doesn't want us either. We're just the price he has to pay if he wants a relationship with our mother. Well, I don't want a relationship with him. I don't even like him.'

'Clio,' Amanda started to reason with her daughter, 'you don't know what it'll be like. Neither do I. I promise you, if it doesn't work out I'll ask him to leave. As a matter of fact, I'd rather it wasn't quite so soon either . . .'

'Oh, really,' Clio cut in sarcastically.

'I'll lose him, Clio.' Amanda felt torn in two. Luke was the first man since Giles she could contemplate having a proper relationship with. Angus Day had just been a brief mistake, another man in Giles's mould, but Luke was something different. He could be irritating, of course, but he was still the best she was ever likely to get. 'You know how lonely I was. You helped me with those ads. Luke wants to make a proper commitment.'

'Do you know what,' Clio yelled, 'it sounds to me as though he's blackmailing you. Don't you ever learn, Mum? That's exactly what Dad did, all the time. And you let him. It was your fault too that the marriage failed. You should have stood up to him. And Luke'll do it all over again. Only this time I might not stay around and watch.' She shoved her sandwiches into her school bag and slammed out of the house before she heard Amanda shout, 'No, you've got it wrong! Luke's not like Dad at all!'

Amanda turned, fighting back tears of pain and exasperation that she'd handled things so badly. Sean was standing behind her, his hair standing up like a Seventies punk's, his blazer buttons done up in the wrong holes.

She hugged him to her, hoping he hadn't overheard the fight with Clio.

'Here, take your blazer off.' She undid the top button. 'You haven't even had breakfast yet.'

'It's all right,' Sean jerked his shoulder back into the blazer, 'I'm not hungry.'

Amanda knew she should probably insist he ate something, but she didn't feel up to another confrontation. She quickly made him a peanut butter and jam sandwich, his favourite, and even cut the crusts off the way he liked it. 'Here. You can eat it on the bus.'

'No thanks, Mum. I'll wait till break.' He picked up his backpack which suddenly looked too heavy for his small frame, and walked towards the front door. Just as he was going out, he turned. 'He doesn't even like football, Mum,' Sean said quietly. 'He'd never even heard of Barthez.' And then, shaking his head sadly, 'Even Dad had heard of Barthez.'

'You can teach him,' Amanda called after him, but it was too late, Sean had gone too.

Amanda sat down at the kitchen table, fighting back the tears. Children didn't understand how devastatingly lonely it was when your husband left you. Everyone trusted you to survive, to pick up the pieces. No matter how much hurt you felt, you had to hold it all together. Everyone expected it of you, even your husband – even his new lover, for Christ's sake. Good old Amanda. She's strong enough to cope. Well, this time she wasn't. Someone had come into her life who loved her, someone she loved back, and she wasn't going to let him go.

Clio's accusation flashed into her mind, angry and corrosive, that Luke was just as controlling as Giles had been. But Clio was wrong. She might be bright and intelligent but she didn't know everything. And she'd never really bothered to get to know Luke.

When she did, she'd realise that he was nothing whatsoever like Giles.

All she had to do was find ways of helping Clio and Sean discover that for themselves.

The trouble was, she hadn't made a very good start.

Chapter 17

The day that Luke moved his stuff in, Clio made sure she was out. 'I'll be at Jasmine's if you need me,' she informed her mother.

Amanda didn't argue. She couldn't force Clio to welcome Luke and besides, given the mood her daughter was in these days, it would be easier for everyone if she *was* out. 'Just be back for supper this evening. I'm planning something special.'

Clio was obviously about to say something rude, but decided against it. 'Look, why don't you and Luke go out together? I'll mind Sean for you.' She produced a small smile. 'I won't even charge you.'

Amanda reached out to touch her daughter's arm. She guessed that Clio was trying to avoid them all sitting down together. 'I'm doing roast chicken with stuffing and roast potatoes. Your favourite.'

'Mum,' Clio shook her off angrily. 'I know you want to be happy, that you're even *entitled* to be happy after the way Dad treated you. It's just that this is my home too and I don't know Luke. I've only met him a few times, and all of this seems so sudden. You don't know him either, really. What happens if he turns out to be violent, or have some secret past? I mean, has he ever been married, or lived with anyone? Doesn't it strike you as odd that he's in his thirties and yet he can up-sticks and move in with you like a student?'

Amanda bit her lip. It *was* all sudden, much more sudden than she would have liked. But wasn't that because Luke was so sure, even if she would have liked a bit more time to get used to the idea?

'He loves me, Clio, and I'm not going to lose him.'

'But don't you care about losing me, that I don't feel comfortable in my own home?'

'Of course I do. But you'll be eighteen in less than two years. You'll be going off to college. You won't need me any more.'

'And you'll turn my bedroom into an office for Luke, no doubt.'

'Clio, that's not fair. Maybe it would be better if you stayed at Jasmine's for supper.'

'Don't worry. I'll stay at Jasmine's for the night!' She slammed out without looking back.

After she'd gone, Amanda sat down and wept at the kitchen table, surrounded by supermarket bags, like Ruth weeping amid the alien corn. She didn't feel like roasting a chicken any more. Roast chicken was a symbol of happy family life. It conjured up images of Christmas and Easter and endless meals gathered together round a table, laughing and teasing each other.

'It's OK, Mum.' The slight figure of Sean appeared in the kitchen doorway. 'I love roast chicken. Especially the way you do it with all the garlic.'

She smiled palely at him.

'Don't worry about Clio. She's just a teenager. They're quite like toddlers, you know. Always having tantrums to get attention. Shall I peel the spuds for you?'

She pulled him into her arms. Normally he said, 'Yuk! Mum!' in disgust whenever she tried to kiss him but today he seemed to understand that greater tact was required.

'What would I do without you?' she asked, nuzzling his soft blond hair, the hair he'd wanted shaved into a bald Beckham cut.

'Probably go climbing in Nepal or camel-riding round the Pyramids,' he announced sagely. 'That's what Ben's mummy says she's going to do the moment he goes off to university.'

'Well,' she swept back his fringe and kissed his forehead, 'that'll be something to look forward to.' And she got out the roasting pan and started dividing up garlic cloves to roast them with the chicken, just the way Sean liked them, soft and sweet.

In fact, the supper went better than she'd expected. Luke arrived with one small suitcase, which he stowed discreetly in her bedroom and then came down to find the table decked with candles and colourful paper napkins which Amanda had dug out of the drawer. 'I'm sorry they say Happy Birthday,' Amanda explained. 'They were all I had, I'm afraid.'

'They're perfect.' He moved to kiss her, then realised it might embarrass Sean and stopped. 'Thank you both for going to so much trouble.' She noticed that, diplomatically, he didn't mention Clio's absence.

After supper they did the clearing up together, then Sean asked, 'Would you like to see my Manchester United folder?'

There was a beat of silence. *Please say yes*, Amanda silently willed him.

'Fantastic,' Luke replied, touching her hand lightly as she passed.

Sean spread out the contents of the precious file on the kitchen table. There were programmes, photos of the team and an ancient season ticket someone's granddad had donated to the collection. 'Alex Ferguson – he's Manchester United's manager,' Sean explained loudly and slowly to Luke as if Luke had a limited grasp of English, 'believes in a four-four-two formation.'

'I have heard of Alex Ferguson, actually,' Luke protested, sitting next to Sean. 'He's a Scot, isn't he? I'm not very fond of Scots usually.' He winked at Amanda, in case she missed the reference to Angus.

'I don't see what that's got to do with being a football manager,' protested Sean, flummoxed at the weirdness of adult behaviour. 'Some of the greatest football managers ever are Scottish.'

'Just a personal prejudice.' His inviting chocolate-brown gaze rested on Amanda. 'I shouldn't worry about it.'

Amanda watched them both tenderly. She could have kissed Sean for making this effort to get to know Luke. Except that he would have loathed it.

'Didn't you play football at school?' Amanda asked Luke.

'Football was for the plebs. We were rugger-buggers. I was quite good actually.'

Amanda considered him. His build was tall and slender rather than bull-necked and vast in the way she associated with rugby players. 'I can't see you as a prop forward.'

'I was a winger. I wanted to keep my ears. Players in the front line have a nasty habit of losing theirs. Meanwhile,' he smiled lovingly and her heart felt as if it might melt all over the worktop, 'back to Man United.'

Amanda made some coffee. It was strange for all of them having Luke here. She'd felt really quite odd when she'd made space for his clothes in the closet she'd shared with Giles, and then there was the question of which side of the bed he slept on.

'Do you prefer right or left?' she asked as he unpacked his things. She'd always slept on the right, the side nearest the door, so that she could get up for the children in the night. On the other hand, why did things always have to stay the same?

Luke's answer was completely disarming. 'I hope we'll both be in the middle.'

She held out her hands to him. 'I'm really glad we're doing this.'

'No, you're not,' he said, pulling her close to him. 'You would much rather things carried on as before – just seeing me occasionally, pleading parents' night if you didn't feel like it – but habits are there to be broken. Look, I know this is strange for you; it is for me too, as a matter of fact. Let's work it out as we go along, shall we?'

Amanda felt a warm wave of gratitude and relief that Luke seemed to understand the situation so well. He was the sweetest, most sensitive man. Not to mention the sexiest. She found her eyes straying towards the bed.

'Hey,' he nuzzled her ear, so that a sudden thrill of delight shot through her body. 'Don't let's frighten the children. When do they go to sleep?'

'Clio probably won't be back tonight. Sean around nine o'clock.'

'Then roll on nine o'clock.' His eyes were full of wicked promise.

'Oh, and don't forget the cat. She's liable to jump on you. She's very protective of her mistress.'

'So that's why the cat's called Kinky. She likes to join in a three-some.'

Amanda looked round the room. It looked good with Luke's dressing gown besides hers. She couldn't see any pyjamas. 'What do you wear in bed?'

'Guess.'

'Hmm,' Amanda giggled, 'that's a tricky one.'

'Silk boxer shorts from a grateful admirer.' He held up a pair of underpants adorned with dozens of tiny boxer dogs.

'They weren't really from . . .'

'I bought them myself. By mail-order. How suburban is that?'

Clio's words that she knew nothing about him flashed into her mind. 'Have you ever been married?'

'No.'

'Lived with anyone?'

Luke looked as if he wanted to change the subject. 'A couple of times.'

'Why didn't it work out?'

'Why is the sea blue? It's a long story. Anyway, that was then. This is now. And I'm really happy to be here, Amanda.'

Amanda felt a surge of happiness.

'And I'm really glad to have you here.'

'So what have you got against him?' Jasmine asked Clio as they both settled down for a night of chatting, Jasmine in her single bed with its pretty, flower-embroidered duvet cover and Clio next to her on a mattress on the floor.

'The fact that we hardly know him. Mum's only been going out with him for five minutes and suddenly he's living with us. I think it's fishy. The other thing is, I'm sure Mum didn't really want him to move in. I think he bullied her into it, just like Dad used to do. I'm never going to fall for a man who makes me feel guilty. And Mum's so guilt-prone.'

'So you never make her feel guilty when you want something then?'

'Of course I do, but that's different. I'm her daughter and I'm a teenager. Teenagers always make parents feel guilty to get what they want. The trouble with Mum is, where men are concerned she's a bad picker.'

'What does she say about it? Does she see that he's like your dad?'

'Absolutely not. She thinks he's sweet and caring. One of these "New Man" types. The polar opposite of Dad.'

'And isn't he?'

'So far all he's done is buy her a few bunches of flowers. He *looks* different. Good-looking, trendy, charming.'

'Sounds like quite an improvement on your dad to me.'

'Yeah, but who wants their dad, or even stepdad, to be like that? I'd rather he wore a cardigan and cared about her.'

The thought of Angus Day, who did indeed wear cardigans, much to Clio's vast amusement, and even managed to look halfway decent in them, invaded her mind. Why couldn't her mother fall for him instead of Luke?

'Does your mother love him, do you reckon?'

Clio considered this gloomily. 'Probably. Given her record.'

'Then maybe you're stuck with him. Unless –' Jasmine brightened at the thought of the potential drama ahead – 'you decide to deliberately screw it up?'

'No,' Clio sighed. 'I love Mum. That wouldn't be fair.'

'Then maybe you should try being nice to him.'

For some reason, this suggestion filled Clio with panic. She didn't want to be nice to him. She didn't want him there. Her house wouldn't be her home any more. Even using the bathroom would be embarrassing. She'd have to hide away all her personal stuff and never run around in a bath towel or nightie.

The truth was, the thought of Luke Knight permanently in her home gave her a sick feeling in the base of her stomach, worse even than having the curse.

And yet she had no real idea why.

*

'Have you heard?' Louise demanded of the rest of the book group, 'The Knight in Shining Armour's moved in with Amanda!'

It was Ruthie's turn to host the meeting and they were all in her sitting room, draped over the brightly coloured beanbags that she'd used in her natural childbirth classes. Anne always said she felt like practising her breathing the moment she lay down on one.

'What? The new man?' Anne was shocked. 'But she's only known him a few months.'

'They obviously made the most of their time then,' suggested Simone lewdly.

'Things do move fast when you're our age, I suppose,' suggested Anne. 'You're more mature, confident. You know what you want from a relationship.'

'Sex,' suggested Simone, and they all started giggling again.

'For heaven's sake. I'm sure Amanda's far too sensible to fall for someone just for sex,' Anne replied.

'Sshh,' commented Janine, 'I think that's her now.'

Amanda arrived, out of breath from dashing down the road to the off-licence, clutching a bottle of fizzy Australian wine.

'We'd better wait for her to tell *us*,' hissed Simone.

Amanda plopped down on to the last beanbag, a purple one. Five pairs of enquiring eyes fixed on hers. 'Have you started already?' She rummaged in her vast shoulder bag for *Memoirs of a Geisha*, this month's book. 'Well, I thought it was absolutely brilliant. I really felt, for the first time, I could understand the nature of erotic obsession.'

A small giggle escaped from Simone, which spread like wildfire around the group till they were all falling about with laughter, rolling off the beanbags and almost knocking over their glasses of wine.

'What?' Amanda asked, perplexed. 'What on earth did I say?'

'I think,' Simone explained, flicking back her long black hair and wiping sooty black mascara from her cheeks as she struggled to stop giggling, 'they assume you're referring to you and Luke.'

'Well, actually,' Amanda replied primly, 'there's more to life than sex, you know.'

At that moment, the bottle of Seaview Brut beside her suddenly popped its cork and showered the room with fizzy wine. Amanda started giggling too. 'Though, I have to say, it does help.'

Louise, emboldened by no lunch and two tumblers of Chardonnay, not that she needed much emboldening, prodded Amanda in the ribs. 'So, was my friend right? Is he a completely fabulous lover?'

'Fabulous,' Amanda endorsed. 'Compared to Giles, that is. But then almost anyone'd be fabulous compared to Giles. Giles's idea of foreplay was sticking his prick in my thigh and saying "Fancy a bit of nookie?" Five minutes later he was asleep.'

They all laughed uproariously again.

Except Ruthie. Somewhere, in the back of her memory, she was beginning to unearth the reason why she'd heard of Luke Knight.

And it wasn't because he was an incredible lover.

Chapter 18

Clio wrapped her Snoopy dressing gown tightly round her. She was dying for the loo but the bathroom was occupied by Luke having a bath. She could hear him singing some opera tune at the top of his voice as she hopped from one foot to the other. Hadn't her mother explained the bloody rota to him? The first fifteen minutes belonged to Amanda, then Sean, and finally, 7.45 to 8.15 was Clio's slot. Luke, with his arty-farty late-starting job, would have to go after that.

She rushed downstairs to protest. 'Mum, have you told Luke about the rota? He's in there now and I'm going to be late!'

Amanda suppressed a smile. She had, in fact, explained to Luke how the bathroom times were allocated, but suspected the give and take of family life was new to him.

'Luke!' She banged on the door, suddenly feeling more like his mother than his lover. 'It's Clio's turn for the bathroom and she'll be late for her work experience if she doesn't get in soon.'

Luke stopped warbling. 'Fine. I'll be straight out.'

Two minutes later he emerged, sleek and smiling like a rather smug cougar, wearing a bath towel round his waist. 'Sorry to steal your slot,' he apologised silkily to Clio. 'But I have left the water in for you.'

Clio scrambled into the bathroom, slammed the door and

ostentatiously ran the bathwater out. She reached for the bouquet-scented disinfectant her mother bought to clean the loo and spread it all round the bath in narrow purple streaks, to erase every trace of Luke's body. She opened the bathroom window wide even though it was still cold.

Downstairs, Sean was in a world of his own, sitting at the breakfast table reading the quiz on the back of the Cheerios packet. Amanda bustled about making packed lunches, and Luke nonchalantly helped himself to the last of the milk.

'You've finished the milk!' Clio accused when she arrived.

'You usually have toast,' he pointed out calmly.

'This morning I fancied cereal. And where the hell's my mobile phone? Sean, have you seen . . .'

'It's on the dresser,' Amanda reminded her. 'Jasmine rang you last night, remember?'

'The early bird gets the worm . . .' suggested Luke in a voice that hovered between teasing and taunting.

'This bird would have been a lot earlier if her slot in the bathroom hadn't been taken,' Clio replied acidly.

'And you wouldn't be in such a rush now if you'd packed your bag last night,' he pointed out.

It was a refrain her mother came up with constantly, but coming from Luke it was too much.

'I won't bother with breakfast. And by the way,' her voice had an edge of rudeness even she could detect, 'I'll be leaving early all this week. My work experience. Have to show I'm keen.'

Luke pretended to ignore the meaning behind this. 'Good. That means I can keep your slot in the bathroom.'

Clio gathered up her stuff as quickly as she could and started for the door. 'See you later.'

'Bye, good luck!' Amanda called, waving.

As Amanda's hand fell, Luke caught it and kissed it.

Clio turned away, feeling slightly sick. It was her mother's expression that did it. Flushed, excited, girlish, and, worst of all, disgustingly fulfilled. Sex was obviously the root of her mother's attraction to Luke, but she didn't want to think about it. Amanda was over forty, for God's sake! Surely it was Clio's turn to be experiencing the joys of sex, not her mother's. And all Clio had managed was a quick shag in Val d'Isère before being dumped and left with a pregnancy scare. It was all so bloody unfair!

'Do you think she's all right?' Amanda asked Luke after Clio had gone and Sean was upstairs getting his football gear. 'It's hard for her, you know, having someone she doesn't really know moving into her house.'

'You pander to her, Amanda.' Luke's loving look evaporated into petulance. 'She hasn't exactly made much effort to get to know me, has she? And I have been trying.'

'I know you have,' Amanda comforted him. 'She's just at a very uncertain age, and all that business with the boy in France didn't help.'

'Maybe she should have been more careful.'

Amanda was about to protest that Clio had been the innocent one when Sean came back into the room, loaded down with boots, pads, shorts and his treasured David Beckham home strip.

'Are you going to be Barthez today?' asked Luke.

'Hardly,' Sean replied loftily. 'Barthez is a goalie.'

Amanda saw Sean off to the bus stop, then turned her attention to Luke. 'Busy day?' Now that they were living together he didn't come and drag her off for beach picnics so often. That was romance, she supposed, and this was real life. Still, she rather missed it.

Luke seemed to read her mind. 'How about a quick bite at lunchtime? Pick you up at one?'

'Perfect.'

It was one of those glorious April mornings with just a hint of early summer in the air. As Amanda walked to work she noticed that their street was lined with feathery apple blossom. A few petals drifted through the air like confetti.

Amanda decided to take the seafront route. It would add five minutes to her journey but she could make it up if she walked fast. Besides, Louise had been in a good mood ever since Luke had moved in with Amanda. Maybe it was because she felt the field was now officially open for her to pursue Angus Day.

She wondered, as she quickened her step, how Clio would get on with her work experience and why she'd opted for Angus Day's company when she could have had an exciting time meeting artists and theatre people with Luke. As if she didn't know the answer. Clio couldn't stand Luke. She was using the Angus thing to deliberately provoke. Amanda sighed. It seemed so bloody mean that she'd finally found a man she wanted to get involved with and it was still as complicated and difficult as being on her own. Didn't she deserve some happiness after she'd spent the last three years holding the family together and never thinking of her own needs?

Clio would get used to the situation eventually. Amanda just hoped that for all their sakes it wouldn't take too long.

She had just rounded the corner below the Eastcliff Estate to make a shortcut past Rose and Betty's home to the gallery when she noticed that the painted 'To Let' sign in front of the boathouse had disappeared and been replaced by one that said 'Let By'.

Amanda felt as if she'd been kicked sharply in the stomach. Someone had rented the boathouse! She rushed towards it and stared in at the window. It seemed as empty and untouched as before. How could anyone rent it? It was hers! Until this moment she hadn't realised quite how much the dream of having a gallery mattered to her. Mentally she'd stripped it down, painted the walls white with duck-egg-blue windows, and filled it with carved birds.

Instead of going straight to the gallery, she dashed to the estate agent instead. A young man in a Next suit that he probably hoped people mistook for Armani was opening up the shop.

'I wanted to find out about the empty boathouse down by the harbour,' Amanda asked, trying to keep calm. 'Has it really been let?'

The young man turned on his screen and whizzed through their files. 'Yep. Here we are. Clients have made an offer but we're just in the process of checking their references.'

Amanda's heart leapt. The deal hadn't actually been struck yet then. 'Is there likely to be a problem with the references?' she asked, hoping her rivals would turn out to be money launderers or undischarged bankrupts.

'No. It's just a formality. We're due to sign soon.' He glanced back at his screen. Amanda pretended to look for something in her handbag while peering discreetly over his shoulder. Her rival seemed to be a firm called Computer Central. 'On Friday, as a matter of fact,' the young man added.

'If someone else were to put in a rival offer, would that make any difference?'

'Depends on the offer.'

'Right,' she said with all the decisiveness she didn't feel. 'Could you register that I am also interested in taking the lease and would like to put in a competitive bid?' She stopped herself from adding, 'Providing my bank will give me a loan.'

'Fine.' After she'd gone, the young man pondered on how odd it was in his line of business that a property could remain empty for two years and then, suddenly, in the same week, two people could decide they wanted it. Unless, of course, they knew something about the area he didn't. He'd better try and find out if anything interesting was happening to make the harbour more sought-after.

It was almost eleven by the time Amanda finally got to the gallery. Louise, in Valkyrie pose, was leaning against the shop doorway. And from the expression on her face, she wasn't there to enjoy the spring sunshine. She looked as if someone had pumped her up to twice her normal size. 'What the hell is going on, Amanda? I told you that Mr and Mrs Williams were coming to look at the large oil.' She gestured to a bank managerish-looking couple at the far end of the gallery, studying the only expensive painting in the shop. 'I found them standing on the pavement outside, on the point of giving up. And you hadn't even had the courtesy to let me know you'd be late.'

'I'm really sorry, Louise, I didn't know . . .' Amanda began. And then she realised she could hardly explain about the boathouse. For a start, Louise wouldn't exactly be thrilled at the prospect of Amanda opening up a rival gallery round the corner, even if it turned out to be possible.

'Sorry. Domestic problems.'

'Lying in with your new lover, more like,' Louise said loudly, swinging her shawl like Lady Ottoline Morell. 'Friendship or no friendship, I'll be watching you.'

And she did. All day. So much so that Amanda had to phone Luke surreptitiously and cancel their lunch, and it wasn't until 3.30 in the afternoon that Louise finally went to buy a sandwich and Amanda could phone the bank about the question of a loan.

When Clio, smart and self-conscious in her new office clothes, turned up at Day Properties, Angus was in conference with his assistant, Fay. The stylish, open-plan office was empty apart from the unstylish fixture of Laddie Smithson, wearing his usual woolly bobble hat and making himself a cup of Earl Grey. Clio tried not to smile at the incongruous sight.

Laddie got her drift immediately. 'Think I'm too rough for this brew, do you? Blame Angus's mother. I learned it from Isobel Day.'

Laddie fished out his teabag with a biro. 'Want me to give you a little run-down on the business before Angus joins us?'

'I'd love that,' Clio replied.

'Angus is the MD, obviously. Fay runs the office. There are also a couple of architects in training, young chaps who want to be developers, and a quantity surveyor – the brick counter we call him – who does the pricing. Then there's the accountant, myself, and the lads who do the hard work. We employ all of them more or less permanently.'

'And what is Angus's philosophy for the firm?'

'Some money-making projects and some projects like the Eastcliff Estate, which take up far too much of his time but that he believes in. Sometimes, to get a development off the ground we have to build stuff for the Council. Angus enjoys that.'

'Why don't all developers do what he does? It seems to make such sense.'

'Aye. But there's not much profit in it. And people distrust your motives. A lot of officials at the council wanted him to fail.'

'Thank you, Laddie,' cut in Angus's voice behind them. 'I hope you're not painting a picture of me as a selfless social reformer again. I did perfectly adequately out of the deal. Forgive Laddie.

He likes to think of me as some saintly figure – of which he largely disapproves, as a matter of fact – bent on improving the lot of mankind when basically I just hate lack of imagination. What I loathe is councils spending millions on estates that look like Colditz when, with the same money, they could create somewhere where people actually *want* to live. End of lecture.' He stopped suddenly and grinned. 'Now, let's see what we can do with you for the next week. Fay, my assistant, thinks work experience is a way of exploiting young people without paying them, and Laddie here thinks supervising them's a waste of his valuable time.'

Laddie blushed under his woolly hat. 'Maybe this young lady'll prove me wrong.'

'I'll do my best,' said Clio, taken aback by Angus's frankness. Still, she could sense the deep affection and respect between the two men, and realised her time here was going to be much more interesting than in some more glamorous industry. She would be learning about them as well as the business.

'By the way,' Angus asked Fay, 'did you get through to Shireton Council about their new scheme?' He turned to Clio to explain. 'Shireton is the local authority down the coast a little. They own a further education college that they want to build on. The contract'll be worth millions. I thought we might put in a tender.'

Laddie sighed. 'Weren't we going to do a private development this time and make some real money? The council'll give you peanuts and be bloody rude to you into the bargain.'

Fay shrugged apologetically, as if in confirmation of this. 'I'm afraid their planning officer, a Ms Melanie Westmacott, refused to even talk to me. Rude cow.'

'These people,' Angus shrugged. 'They think that because I'm a developer I'm beyond the pale. Tell you what,' he grinned devilishly, 'Clio, why don't you and I go and lure this Ms Westmacott out of her lair? It's a nice drive. Only about ten miles down the coast.'

'She'll never see you,' Fay pooh-poohed. 'She obviously reckons property developers are one stop from Jack the Ripper.'

'Then we'll have to show her how wrong she is. Did she have a tempting white throat?'

'Angus.' Fay shook her head. 'How should I know?'

Before they left, Angus pulled down a large red-bound book and looked something up.

Clio forgot all her professionalism when faced with the prospect of another drive in Angus's sports car. 'Can we have the roof down again?' she begged as soon as they got in.

'Have you passed your test yet? If so, you can drive if you like.'

Clio shook her head vehemently. 'I'm only sixteen. Besides, I reckon my family's done enough damage to your car already. Was it very expensive to mend?'

'Extremely. I expect your mother explained that your work experience is designed to help pay for it. I'm allowed to exploit you as much as I want for absolutely no pay.'

Clio looked taken aback.

'No, seriously, it didn't cost much. And I thought fifty pounds a week would be about right?'

Clio was stunned. 'I didn't expect to be paid.'

'Then you'll just have to show me you're worth it.' He paused fractionally. 'How is your mother, by the way?'

Clio, staring at the bus stop they were passing, hoping against hope that someone she knew might be at it so she could impress the hell out of them, almost said, 'Happy as a pig in muck now that *he's* moved in.' She remembered just in time that Angus might not know Luke was living with them. 'She's fine, thanks.'

It was a fabulous morning, and as they sped along the coast road both of them fell into a companionable silence, the wind whipping Clio's hair into willing rat's tails. She was almost sad when they reached their destination.

The Shireton Council offices were in a surprisingly romantic Gothic building reached via a long driveway. 'It used to be a convent before the vocations dried up,' confided Angus. 'We'd better park away from the entrance. One look at the BMW and it'll confirm all Ms Melanie Westmacott's worst suspicions about me being a fat cat out to fleece them.'

They parked around the corner from the imposing building and walked the last few yards to reception. 'Could you tell Ms Melanie Westmacott that Angus Day of Day Properties is here and wonders if he could have five minutes of her precious time?'

The receptionist didn't even look up. 'Ms Westmacott never sees anyone without an appointment.'

'Could you tell her that I'm the Mr Day who redesigned the Eastcliff Estate in Laineton?' He winked at Clio and they both waited.

After ten minutes the phone rang on the reception desk. 'I'm sorry,' replied the receptionist in a tone that implied she was anything but, 'Ms Westmacott says the Eastcliff Estate is exactly what she *doesn't* want for this development.'

'Ah well.' Angus seemed unabashed. 'It'll have to be an early lunch for you and I in that café we passed, Clio. I'll give you a crash course in the property industry.'

They walked back to Angus's car, Clio feeling a slight sense of disappointment that Angus's bold move hadn't paid off. She was just getting in when Angus suddenly hissed, 'Quick. Sit up on the back!'

'Isn't that dangerous?'

'Probably, but I'll drive very slowly. This is an emergency.'

Clio didn't even have time to ask why before she noticed a young woman walking in their direction. She looked positively fearsome to Clio's eyes. She was very tall, with dark hair and narrow black-framed glasses, the kind that used to look nerdy but were suddenly the height of chic. She was wearing a severely cut black suit and carrying a leather computer briefcase. The one unexpected touch of frivolity was that she was wearing sheer black tights and ludicrously high heels.

She didn't look the kind of person who would waste her own or anyone else's time.

'Ms Westmacott,' Angus greeted her. 'Angus Day of Day Properties. Ms Westmacott, have you ever heard of Pauline conversions?'

Clio could hardly bear to look. What on earth was Angus gabbling about? The planning officer stopped just next to the car. For a brief moment, the ghost of a smile flitted across her earnest features. 'No idea. Are they some kind of studio flat?'

'I'm sure a woman of your intelligence has heard of the road to Damascus.' He pulled her gently towards the car. 'You said the Eastcliff Estate is exactly what you *don't* want to achieve, but I wonder if you're judging it by its old reputation. Have you seen it recently? Just come with us for half an hour. I promise you won't regret it.'

Ms Westmacott looked at the road sign in front of them. 'I thought that was the road to Laineton, not Damascus.'

'Half an hour,' insisted Angus. 'That is all I ask out of your busy schedule.'

Clio could see that as challenges went, this one would be hard to resist. Ms Westmacott hesitated.

'Thirty minutes. I promise.'

Ms Westmacott glanced behind her, almost as if she were hoping there were no witnesses to her decision.

She had amazingly good legs, Clio noted, as she swung them into the car. And her smile, which she seemed to save only for very limited occasions, had an unexpected twinkle. 'I may live to regret this.'

'This is Clio Wells. She's with us on work experience.'

'Are you all right up there?' she asked Clio. 'You look rather precarious.'

'I'm pretending to be a Bond girl as a matter of fact.'

'Ah.'

Angus was as good as his word. Even though he drove slowly, in just under fifteen minutes they'd reached Laineton and driven into the Eastcliff Estate.

Lou Mills was out walking her dog on the green. She waved to them just as the dog shamelessly squatted down. 'No sense of timing, this animal.' Lou produced both plastic bag and pooper scooper.

'How's the flat, Lou?' Angus enquired.

'Bloody brilliant. Fancy a cuppa?'

Angus raised an eyebrow towards the planning officer. 'Want to see inside? Then, if you like, I could give you a guided tour and show you the community centre.'

In the end, it was almost an hour and a half before they were back on the road, but Ms Westmacott seemed to have forgotten the time altogether.

When they stopped outside the council offices to let her out, she shook Angus's hand. 'I had no idea how much you'd improved the place. It's always been one of the worst estates in the country.' The look she produced was almost flirtatious. 'You were right about St Paul. I'm entirely converted.'

Angus winked. 'You got the reference, then.'

'Actually,' her smile had real warmth now, 'I read theology at university. You don't get much call for it in planning. I liked your development very much indeed. If you don't mind, I'll bring my councillors down to see it.'

'Thank you very much, Ms Westmacott.'

'Call me Melanie. Here's my card.'

'And here's mine, countered Angus gallantly.

Angus watched as she teetered off on her surprising stilettos. 'Not such a dragon after all,' he commented.

'Only because she fancied you rotten,' accused Clio.

'Did she now? And I thought it was my development she was interested in,' added Angus, pretending to look wounded.

'Anyway,' Clio congratulated, 'you were amazing with her. How did you guess she'd understand all that stuff about Pauline conversions?'

'I went and looked her up in the council handbook before we set out. Before she worked here she read theology at Edinburgh University.'

'You really are an operator,' Clio marvelled.

'That makes me sound entirely cynical,' protested Angus, 'whereas I really did think she'd like what we'd done. Besides, in real life I'm an old softie. Just ask Laddie.'

'Don't worry,' Clio grinned, 'Laddie's been telling me all about you.'

'Oh God. I hope he hasn't been boasting about our turnover again.'

Clio shook her head. 'He didn't mention your turnover. But I think *you* should. I feel I ought to know.'

'All right then. About fourteen.'

'Fourteen thousand pounds? That's hardly . . .'

Angus laughed and shook his head. 'Fourteen *million* pounds.'

'My God,' breathed Clio. 'You're rolling in it.'

'It's only turnover. Don't tell your mother,' Angus teased, starting the engine. 'She already thinks I'm a filthy capitalist.'

Clio's smile faded. Angus so obviously cared about her mother. And Amanda had chosen to go and fall for Luke Knight instead.

Clio bit her lip, wondering if there was anything she could think of to do about it.

Amanda was waiting for her when she got back, eager to hear how everything had gone. 'So, how was your first day in the working world?'

'Fantastic,' Clio enthused, 'really exciting. We kidnapped a planning officer and converted her.'

'Good God, you make Angus Day sound more like a cult leader than a property developer.'

'Well,' conceded Clio, winding her mother up. 'He is pretty charismatic. And the planning officer fancied the pants off him.'

Amanda glanced at Clio sharply. There was something so admiring in Clio's tone. She hoped to God Clio wasn't going to go and fall for Angus Day. 'By the way,' Amanda changed the subject abruptly, 'I've decided to make a bid for the boathouse. I've got to draw up a business plan really quickly and I wondered if you'd help me with the spreadsheets. I know you're brilliant at IT.'

'You should ask Angus to help you. He's amazing at that sort of thing.' Again, the thinly veiled admiration.

'It's all right, thanks,' Amanda bristled. 'I just need help on how to lay out a spreadsheet.'

'Fine. Couldn't Luke give you a hand?' Clio asked mischievously. She knew Luke hated computers.

'I'm sure he would but he's not back yet.'

'I'll help you too,' offered Sean. 'I put the entire First Division into a table last week,' he said proudly.

'Thank you, darling.'

With Clio and Sean's help, Amanda learned how to design her business plan. She felt like a dinosaur in the company of two gazelles, but they made surprisingly swift progress. When they heard Luke's key in the door Amanda was amazed how the time had disappeared. She quickly switched off the computer.

Clio looked at her curiously. 'You don't want him to know, do you?'

Amanda seemed embarrassed. 'I want to put it to him gently. It's a bit of a risk, you know.'

'If we're behind you, what does it matter to him?' Clio insisted. 'Dad always discouraged you from going it alone and you always swore you wouldn't make the mistake of falling for someone like that again.'

'Well, I should never have said anything so disloyal,' snapped Amanda, wishing Clio wasn't so perceptive.

'Angus wouldn't mind. Angus would be right behind you.'

'That's only because Angus has money to burn,' Amanda said waspishly. 'Now let's go and have supper.'

'That planning officer really did fancy him, you know. I wouldn't be surprised if she gives him the contract just to see him again.'

'Clio, don't be so simplistic.'

'You weren't even there. She practically had an orgasm over the Eastcliff Estate. Or maybe it was over Angus.'

'Well, bully for her.' Amanda felt her irritation rising. Partly it was Clio's point about Luke's reaction to her gallery idea. Why didn't she just tell Luke – it was none of his business – he didn't even contribute to their finances anyway. Amanda certainly didn't want to see him as being like Giles. And on top of that, she didn't want to hear about Angus Day giving frustrated planning officers orgasms.

'Are you coming down for supper?' she asked Clio.

'I'd rather stay up here and tinker,' Clio insisted.

'Suit yourself.' Amanda was too tired for a fight. Technically, whether she opened a gallery or not was no concern of Luke's, but she'd want his help and his understanding. Later this evening she'd broach the idea with him. She was sure he'd be right behind her when he realised quite how important it was to her.

As it happened, she didn't get the chance to ask him. There was some crisis to do with his own work and he spent most of the evening on the phone, to Clio's great annoyance since she wanted to call Jasmine and tell her how great her first day had been and she'd run out of vouchers on her Pay As You Go phone. By the time the crisis was sorted, Amanda had fallen asleep.

The next morning was Isobel Day's session at the hospital for her treatment. Angus dropped her there but she hated him staying. 'One should be allowed to suffer in private,' was her great motto.

'Look,' Isobel suggested, 'since you're in town, why don't you do something useful and go and offer Clio a lift to the office, save her having to wait for hours at the bus stop.'

Angus suspected Isobel had an ulterior motive, that it was Amanda whom Isobel really hoped he'd see.

Soon he was outside Amanda's house, feeling foolish and excited, ringing her doorbell. To his intense disappointment, there was no answer.

On the spur of the moment, he rang it again. No reply. They must have all left already.

Angus turned away. He was halfway back to his car when the door opened.

But the person standing there wasn't Clio, or Amanda. It was Luke Knight.

And all he was wearing was a pale blue bath towel and the kind of possessive smile that made Angus want to hit him.

Chapter 19

Luke leaned against the frame of the door, as unfazed as a lion sunning itself on the heat of a rock. He brushed back his damp fair hair and smiled insolently.

'You're the property developer, aren't you?' The silky smugness of Luke's tone fanned all Angus's prejudices. He'd known people like Luke at university. Privately educated, confident to the point of rudeness, caught up in their own little world of privilege. They thought things belonged to them as a right. Now, it seemed, Luke thought Amanda was one of those things.

Angus fought the urge to get into his car and drive over him. 'And you're the freeloader,' he replied instead.

Luke's handsome face hardened. 'Don't make casual assumptions about me just because you've got a chip on your shoulder.'

Angus struggled to contain his fury. 'I came to offer Clio a lift, as a matter of fact.'

'A bit young for you, isn't she? Or is that the way you like them? Easily impressed.'

This time Angus's fist curled into a ball of fury.

'Of course,' Luke sneered, 'you'd like the mother too, wouldn't you? A little bit greedy, don't you think?'

Angus swung just as Luke stepped backwards and slammed the door. He fought a swift instinct to try and break the door down and reined himself in. What was he doing, for Christ's sake? That would be just the way to make Amanda see how he felt, wouldn't it? If Luke Knight was a bastard out for what he could get, there had to be some other way of exposing it. Not that Amanda would thank him for it.

He turned and walked to his car without giving Luke the satisfaction of looking backwards. There had been something else that had disturbed him. Luke's sexual innuendo. His suggestion that Angus wanted both mother and daughter. What sort of warped mind would have come up with that idea?

Even though he had a strong personality, a frission of fear shuddered through Angus. What if Luke started trying to persuade Amanda that his warped fantasy were actually true?

He drove to his office with none of his usual enjoyment in the balmy spring day or the expensive purr of the BMW's engine.

Clio, happy and smiling in her cheap New Look suit, was already there when he arrived. Although she jumped when he walked into the office, this was nothing to do with any seedy aspersions that might have been cast against him but because she was guiltily photocopying a document.

'Sorry,' she apologised, flushing faintly, 'it's something for my mother. I shouldn't really be doing it on your time. It's just that she and I were sitting up last night for hours and I promised I'd finish it and drop it in to the gallery at lunchtime.'

'Don't worry,' he reassured, pushing the thought of Luke's twisted implication from his mind. 'You're a very hard worker. I won't charge you – this time.' He looked round the sunny office. It was so bright that each individual mote of dust reflected in the sunshine like a million-sided diamond. 'Any sign of Fay?'

'She's getting something ready for the quantity surveyor.'

'Fine. I'll put the coffee on. Want some?'

Angus sat down at the semicircular desk, which he knew looked like a tribute to an enormous ego but he liked anyway, and whizzed up to the end of it on his office chair.

Fay always laid out anything he needed for the day in clockwise order. Clio, he noticed, was now hovering near him uncertainly. 'I'm not sure I should mention this . . .'

221

Angus's heart felt as if it had suddenly been put in a clamp. Was she about to tell him about Luke and Amanda?

'The thing is,' she began, embarrassed at burdening him with her personal life, 'someone else is trying to lease the boathouse. It made my mother see how much she wanted a gallery there herself. So she's decided to go for it.'

'Good for her. I'm sure she'll make a big success of it.'

'It isn't quite that simple. The other people may get there first. She's got to go and see the bank tomorrow with her business plan. I just wondered – she'd kill me if she knew I was doing this – if you'd look at it and see if it's OK. I mean, you're such a good nego-tiator.'

Angus smiled. 'Are you suggesting she should adopt my tac-tics? Kidnap the bank manager?'

'It seemed to work for you. Has Ms Westmacott been in touch?'

'She has, as a matter of fact.' Angus tried not to smile. 'She called me last night.'

Clio laughed. She was very different from her mother most of the time, but there were sudden flashes of familiarity that tore painfully into him. 'Maybe not quite that dramatic.'

Angus looked at the neatly bound file for a few moments. 'Who are the other people interested in the lease?'

Clio told him. 'They're called Computer Central. Mum saw the name in the estate agent's details.'

'And which bank is it?'

'The South-Eastern.'

'Hmm . . .' he began.

'Hmm as in yes, they'll give her a loan? Or hmm as in she must be joking?'

'Hmm as in they're bound to ask her for security. Does she have any insurance policies, pensions or anything?'

'I very much doubt it.'

'Then they'll probably require your house as collateral.'

'Oh dear. Mum'll hate that. Besides which, Dad still owns part of it.'

'And you don't think he'll agree?'

'If I know Dad, he won't want to risk his investment. Poor Mum.' Clio sighed. 'She's wanted to do something like this for years but Dad always said it'd be a good way of losing money. He's hardly going to change his mind. Especially as he's about to have twins with his second wife.'

Angus heard the sudden twist of pain in her voice. 'Poor you.' He reached out a hand of sympathy and touched her face. She suddenly looked about six years old, hurting like mad that her father might prefer a new brother or sister to her.

'Excuse me.' Fay had just appeared from the outer office. 'There's someone here to see you.'

Angus turned to find Amanda standing next to his secretary, her eyes narrowed in appalled suspicion at the scene she'd just witnessed.

'I've had a call from the bank manager,' she said, her voice like ice. 'He wants to change our meeting to today. Clio's got the documentation I need so I thought I'd come and pick it up in person.'

Clio looked confused at her mother's sudden iciness. 'Here it is. I'll put it in an envelope for you.' Some instinct of self-preservation told her not to mention that she'd shown it to Angus.

'Nice offices,' Amanda commented to Angus as he made a point of showing her out himself.

'Thank you. Your daughter's a fantastic girl.'

Amanda was watching him, her eyes like lasers. 'Yes, but she's still very young, don't you think?'

'In some ways she strikes me as incredibly mature and wise.' Too late he realised how self-justifying that could sound.

'Don't be misled. She's still very vulnerable.'

It was almost too much for Angus. Did she really suspect him of inappropriate behaviour?

After Amanda had left, Angus found himself so angry with her that he had to get out, so he took Clio and Laddie to see another of his developments down at the harbour.

The scheme was to rebuild a row of dilapidated shops, add a block of luxury flats above them and create a café-bar right down on the waterfront. It had already received the go-ahead from the authorities because it would also provide five free units of council housing.

Clio studied the artist's illustration. It was a brilliantly imaginative development. Along the harbour front, the now-dilapidated beach huts were to be repainted in bright colours, with the new shops and restaurants echoing the rainbow shades.

Clio glanced at the line of beach huts as they were now, faded and peeling and falling apart, their lintels crumbling and their wooden decks rotting away, a far cry from the raffishly colourful row in the illustration.

'They're nothing like the picture,' she pointed out.

'They will be, don't worry.'

'Won't some of the owners object? Those beach huts have been there from the year dot.'

'The council owns them. It has the final say as to what colours they're painted. Till now they've been grey and white. I persuaded them we needed bright colours.' He winked.

'And do you know what colours this madman has undertaken to repaint them?' Laddie chipped in. 'Only jade green, bright red and sky-blue-bloody-pink, that's what,' he harrumphed. 'It'll look like bloody Disneyland.'

'Ignore that harbinger of doom.' Angus shook his head. 'Laddie thinks magnolia is on the bold side. This area is going to be the most exciting and colourful in Laineton by the time I've finished. You just watch. There'll be a waiting list for those shops. And you'll have to hang on for five years before you get a beach hut.'

Clio studied the plans again, inspired by Angus's infectious optimism. She could see why he was an exciting person to work for. He had vision. He saw a site not how it was now, but for its potential. Then he persuaded other people to share his excitement, and even managed to get them to break the rules to achieve it. Clio had no doubt at all that he would persuade Melanie Westmacott to let him develop her land and that the development they would come up with would be the single thing she'd be most proud of in her career. Planners were not exciting people, but when they came into contact with Angus he brought out the best in them, a sense of excitement and possibility not usual in their line of work.

'Hey.' Clio glanced up from the plan to the real view in front of her. 'What's happened to Rose and Betty's chalet?'

'Yes, Angus,' Laddie cocked his head, his weatherbeaten face alive with sardonic amusement, 'where *is* Rose and Betty's chalet on this plan, exactly?'

Angus could have cheerfully smothered him with his own woolly hat. Laddie knew perfectly well that Betty and Rose had been offered, for free, the very best of the luxury new flats. Not only would they have hot water, central heating, a bedroom each and the best sea views in Laineton, but also a hefty compensation negotiated by Angus himself for leaving their chalet.

'It's going to have to be demolished,' Angus admitted. 'It never had planning permission in the first place.' Clio and Laddie exchanged glances as Angus, for once in his life, appeared to lose his cool a little. 'You have to see the council's point of view,' he floundered, 'it is a terrible eyesore. And Betty and Rose have been offered the pick of the new flats. It'll be worth a fortune.'

After the meeting on the seafront had finished, it was approaching 4.00 p.m. 'You can clock off, if you like,' Angus told Clio and Laddie. 'I'm going back to the office to make a few phone calls.'

'See you tomorrow, then,' Clio waved, wondering whether or not to tell Amanda about Rose and Betty's chalet.

Once he had the office to himself, Angus's first call was to the MD of the South-Eastern bank. If Angus knew anything about bank managers, this one would be keen to get some of Day Properties' business, and would happily listen to his proposition.

The next call was to Computer Central. He didn't leave a name this time, just a voicemail for the managing director asking him if he was aware of the wet rot problem at the old boathouse.

In fact, as Angus well knew, there was a little wet rot in the boathouse. But it was a small job and it could easily be put right. But there was no reason for Central Computers to know that.

*

When Amanda nervously arrived at the South-Eastern bank she saw someone much lower down the scale than the illustrious personage Angus had approached.

Not only did this representative of the bank look about sixteen, but to compensate he talked in a slow, pompous voice as if he were nearing seventy. His reaction as she took him through her business plan and how much she'd need to pay for six months' rent in advance plus modest decoration costs was deeply disconcerting.

'Oh for God's sake!' Amanda felt like saying when he went through her costings line by line, 'why don't you just say no in plain English?'

They weren't even in a private room. The modern banking suite was entirely open-plan, so that customers could be publicly humiliated for going five pounds over their credit limit and Amanda could have her business torn to shreds in front of a line of people all watching themselves on closed circuit TV as they queued up for the teller.

'I'm very sorry, Mrs Wells, but unless your husband agrees to the family home as collateral, we couldn't possibly lend you an amount like that without substantial guarantees,' the pipsqueak informed her.

Amanda felt like shouting that Giles was her *ex*-husband, that it was nothing to do with him, that he had sacrificed all rights to owning the house the first time he'd put his hand down Stephanie's pants, but she doubted this youth would be convinced by her arguments.

Instead, she snapped shut her Filofax, thanked him coldly, and took herself off.

She felt utterly miserable. Already she had mentally re-painted the boathouse, placed each individual carving, and offered her resignation to Louise who, in her imagination, had kissed her and given her a huge bunch of flowers and her blessing. In fact, Louise was more likely to scream at her that she was an ungrateful bitch and pour the flowers she bought weekly for the gallery over Amanda's head.

On her way home she couldn't bear to even go past the place. Now some stupid computer company would get the lease and with it her dreams.

'You look down in the dumps,' Luke greeted her when she got home.

'Yes, you do, Mum,' seconded Sean. She was incredibly touched when he abandoned his FIFA PlayStation game and came to give her a hug. She tried to cheer up. She was pretty lucky. Clio might still be being stand-offish with Luke but Sean had accepted him, more or less. And she loved the family feeling in the kitchen with Sean playing his football game and Luke reading the *Guardian* at the kitchen table.

'Why don't I pour you a glass of wine?' Luke offered. 'I've already started supper.'

Amanda kissed him. What bliss. Giles would never have offered to cook, except for barbecuing in the summer. And even then he left everything in such a mess it used to take Amanda hours to clean up afterwards.

Admittedly Luke hadn't yet offered to contribute to the family outgoings, which would help greatly, but still. One of these days she'd screw up her courage and suggest it. She was sure it wasn't meanness; he was just used to living on his own.

'So.' He began to stroke her neck. Sean glanced up, then busied himself once more with the PlayStation. Adults were weird. 'What is it that's upset you so much?'

She sipped her wine. 'I didn't tell you this before, but I've been thinking of starting my own gallery.'

'Have you?' Luke's eyes opened in surprise. 'No, you didn't tell me. Since when?'

'I've wanted to for ages. Louise and I have such different tastes but I worried it was too risky financially.'

'And?' His voice was neutral. 'What changed your mind?'

'I've had my eye on the old boathouse down by the harbour for a while and I suddenly found out someone else was after it too, and I just knew I had to try and get it. I know I could make a success of it.'

227

'Right.' Luke paused as if to consider the information. 'But you'd have to give up your job with Louise.'

'I'm sure she'd find someone else.'

'But how would you pay for it?'

'I'd borrow money from the bank.'

'Money borrowed from the bank has to be paid back. Plus interest.'

'Obviously.'

Although he wasn't overtly critical, he didn't need to be. His tone implied it all: that she was off her rocker. Where Giles might have screamed and shouted, Luke merely shrugged.

But the effect was the same.

Amanda fought back her disappointment. She'd so wanted his faith and encouragement. 'Don't worry. The whole thing's fallen through anyway. The bank manager will never lend me the money.'

Instantly Luke's attitude changed. 'Poor you,' he soothed. 'It's just, with my job being uncertain too, I'm not sure what we'd live on.'

'We'd have managed. Please don't say it's for the best,' warned Amanda, draining her glass of wine.

He slid his arms round her. 'I won't. I promise. By the way, that man, Angus Day, came round this morning after you'd left. Said he'd come to offer Clio a lift.'

'That was kind of him. She seems to be really enjoying her work experience.'

'Rather out of his way, isn't it? Didn't you say he lived outside Laineton in the country somewhere?' He paused, tellingly. 'I wondered if he wanted to get her into his car. Older man, fast car, you know the sort of thing. She's very young and impressionable. Remember the ski instructor.'

'I don't need reminding. But that was a one-off. Clio's incredibly sensible. And she's in absolutely no danger of throwing herself at Angus Day.'

'I didn't think she was. It was him I was more concerned about. How do you know he wouldn't try something to get back at you? The mother rejects him so he forces his attentions on the daughter. A tempting scenario.'

'Luke, this isn't *The Duchess of Malfi*, it's modern-day Laineton.'

'Passion doesn't change much. Especially lust and revenge.'

The memory of Angus touching Clio's face flashed into her mind. She'd better have a serious talk with Clio and make sure that Angus wasn't taking advantage of her innocence.

Except that Clio was hardly ever in. And tomorrow was her night for the book group. Amanda kissed him. 'Don't forget, I'll be out tomorrow till about ten or eleven. It's my book night, remember?'

'Fine. I'll put Sean to bed. Do you want me to save you some supper?'

Amanda sighed gratefully. He might be sceptical about the gallery but he certainly made life easier in another ways. And he was making a real effort to win over her children.

Chapter 20

Even though Ruthie had volunteered to host the book group again, she couldn't summon up her usual enthusiasm. The text they'd been studying was Donna Tartt's *The Secret History*, but the only secret history that was worrying her was a real-life one.

Ruthie sat curled up in one of the bright birthing beanbags and felt like issuing a primal scream herself.

Amanda was so happy. She'd had a shitty deal from Giles and it wasn't over yet. Giles's new wife Stephanie was due to drop the dreaded twins at any moment. But even that hadn't dented Amanda's happiness. She had a handsome live-in lover, was obviously getting some great sex, and was going around glowing like some ad for Oil of Olay. And Ruthie was going to have to be the one to spoil it all.

She wondered for the tenth time if the information she'd been given about Luke was either malicious or blown up out of all proportion. After all, she didn't know the source it came from personally. It was only hearsay.

Ruthie pulled herself out of the purple beanbag and made a cup of camomile tea. Maybe she ought to discuss it with some of the others first.

She stirred the teabag, biting her lip. On the other hand, Amanda was her friend, and didn't friendship mean that you ought to be prepared to take some risks if it was important enough?

The lovely April morning clouded over suddenly and she thought of her washing on the line. Ruthie dashed out to get it, breathing in the newly laundered scent as she did. She remembered how Amanda had mentioned the smell of Luke's denim shirts, fresh and clean yet wildly masculine.

What the hell should she do?

As the first spots of rain fell, she dashed for the kitchen. She'd made up her mind. Tonight, after the book group, she'd tell Amanda what she'd heard.

Even if it cost her their friendship.

But Amanda didn't get to the book group that night. Something far more exciting happened.

The day started as usual with Amanda opening the gallery, making the coffee, sorting out the post and reordering any gift cards they seemed low on. Louise was on her way back from London. One of her friends had been so struck with her Turkish delight decor at the New Year's Eve party that they'd invited her to interior design their new flat. Louise was as flattered as Fergie hearing she looked ten pounds thinner.

Amanda had just sat down to call the estate agent when an elderly lady arrived carrying an enormous canvas which she'd obviously transported all the way to the gallery on the bus.

'Sit down,' Amanda insisted, taking the picture and gently leaning it against the counter. 'Would you like a glass of water or a cup of tea?'

'Thank you, dear,' the lady shook her head, delving in her straw shoulder bag, 'but I'd prefer something stronger.' She produced a miniature of purplish liquid and downed it in one. 'Sloe gin,' she winked. 'Home-brewed. Sets you up a treat. Now.' She looked around the gallery hopefully. 'Where's the lady who came to our art class? She said to bring the painting down when it was finished and she might give me thirty pounds. I'm nipping straight round to the showroom to pay my electricity bill with it. Else I'll be cut off.'

'I'm afraid Louise is away this morning.'

'But she said Wednesday. I've come four miles,' she indicated the canvas, 'carrying that blessed thing. I'm not taking it home again. I'll have a heart attack.'

'Maybe I could have a look at it?' Thirty pounds was so little that even if the painting were truly terrible it would probably still be worth buying.

'You go ahead. My name's Sadie, by the way. Sadie Johnson. And maybe I will have that cup of tea.'

Amanda made her one, hoping she didn't mind Lapsang Souchong.

'No PG Tips?' Sadie asked. 'Only I always use my teabags twice, so it'd be nice to have a proper cuppa.' This insight into the life of a senior citizen in enlightened modern Britain came with no hint of self-pity.

'I'm sorry. Louise prefers China tea.'

'She would. You look a nice girl,' Sadie confided. 'To tell you the truth, I didn't much go for whatsherface.'

'Louise.'

'Bossy sort. Coming into our art class and saying I'll take this and that. We used to get women like her in Malaya. They were always the wives of the lower ranks. The officers' wives would never behave like that.'

Amanda would have loved to have heard Sadie's run-down of the class system among the soldiering classes in south-east Asia, but another customer had arrived in the gallery.

'Can I see the painting now?' She picked up the sharp knife they used to cut through packaging, snipped the string, which Sadie had painstakingly tied up into a dozen knots, and began to undo the brown paper.

'Don't tear it,' Sadie scolded. 'Had to go to the post office and buy that. It was nearly two quid. Daylight robbery. I'll use that for me next effort.'

Amanda removed the rest of the paper as carefully as she could and folded it up. Then she propped Sadie's painting against the far wall and considered it.

Amanda felt a small prickle of excitement in the back of her neck. The painting was wonderful.

One corner featured a sunny dining room with a bowl of fruit in front of an open window, with a seaside town, perhaps Laineton, down below. The middle section was a different space, bigger this time, and depicted a vase of flowers on another table and a bureau with a chair in front of it on which a diary sat open. Then, in the right-hand corner, there was yet another room, and another open window, looking out on to woods.

'It's called "Memories",' Sadie announced. 'Those are all the houses I've lived in over sixty years.'

'No wonder it's so full of life,' Amanda smiled, feeling an unexpected tear coming to her eye. Sadie's painting wasn't fashionable. It's Matisse-like colours and shapes wouldn't appeal to the snobby art world, nor would the figurative nature of the images, but the depth of emotion was extraordinary. It really did feel like a lifetime of wonderful moments.

Amanda loved it. 'Have you done any others?' she asked.

'Oh yes,' Sadie shrugged. 'Lots. Now, can I have that thirty quid so I can pay my electricity bill?'

'Certainly,' Amanda paused, thinking how Louise was going to kill her. She added, 'In fact, thirty pounds is far too little. I'll give you a hundred. And even then, it probably wouldn't be enough. You're a natural, Sadie. I'm sure a lot of people will love your paintings. Your art's like you, full of life.'

Sadie just laughed, pocketing the money. 'More fool you. You could have had it for a third of that.'

'I'd like to enjoy it without a guilty conscience. Do you mind if I buy it to keep rather than to show? I'd like to see the others too. And I'll talk to Louise about the rest of your paintings. That is,' she hesitated, hoping she wasn't moving in like some unscrupulous antiques dealer on Sadie's personal possessions, 'if you want to sell any of them.'

'*Any* of them? I'd like to flog *all* of 'em, dear. I paint because I don't know what else to do with all my feelings. They'll suffocate me otherwise. They're just eager to get out and on to canvas. What

I haven't been able to afford is the materials I'd like. Do you know, the price of paint is criminal?'

Amanda counted out the money. She'd been going to get herself a pair of linen trousers and some summer sandals, but something told her Sadie would be a much better investment.

'It's too much, dear.' Sadie tried to shake her head. 'I live very simply.'

'For more materials. With a talent like yours, you should paint as much as you can.'

'Do you know, dear,' Sadie squeezed her hand, 'seeing your face when you looked at my painting, *really* looked at it, gave me more pleasure than you could imagine. Here's my card. I painted it myself. Let me know if you want to come and look at the rest.'

Sadie's card was a work of art in itself – a bright-red background with green leaves bordering it in an intricate pattern. What an amazing woman Sadie was. Amanda could hardly contain her excitement as she waited for Louise to come back and hear about her discovery.

Louise didn't appear until the afternoon, looking mightily pleased with herself. 'You know,' she preened, tossing her scarf with skittish abandon, 'I think I might have quite a future in inte-rior design, now that that frightful minimalism's old hat. My friend even has a name for my style. "The New Bohemianism." She thinks it could be the next big thing after shabby chic. My God.' Sadie's painting was propped up behind the counter since Amanda was hoping to keep it. 'What's that hideous thing?'

'I think it's wonderful, actually. An old lady brought it in. She said you'd offered her thirty pounds for it at her art class.'

'My God! I thought it was going to be a view of Laineton, not have the rest of that crap in it. I couldn't sell that.'

'You already have. To me. I gave her a hundred pounds for it.'

Louise went deathly quiet. 'Are you questioning my judgement, Amanda?'

Amanda felt anger bubble up in her. Normally she'd say no. But today, having seen Sadie's brilliance, and Louise's patronising response, she knew she couldn't keep quiet any longer. 'Yes, yes I am. And your methods. Exploiting old ladies isn't one of your nicer qualities.'

'Oh for God's sake! All galleries exploit unknowns. It's the gallery that takes the risk. You know that.'

Amanda stood face to face with Louise, realising how much she'd been resenting Louise's methods for months.

'I think it's the end of the road for us, don't you?' Louise said quietly.

Amanda took a deep breath. Not only was her dream of her own gallery doomed, but she'd be out of work as well. 'I suppose it is. Would you like me to work out my notice?'

'I'd rather you didn't. It'd only be uncomfortable for both of us. I'll give you two weeks' salary from the till.'

Amanda would have loved to have thrown it at her, but she was the breadwinner and pride wasn't an option. She picked up her painting. 'Goodbye then, Louise.' She could hardly believe that after years of friendship and working together, it could end like this. The only good thing was that now she owed no loyalty to Louise. Louise might have asked Sadie to bring in her picture, but she had no understanding or respect for her work. If Amanda got her own gallery, Sadie would be the first painter she showed.

Louise had already turned her attention to another customer, so Amanda picked up Sadie's picture and left the gallery without another word.

It was too far to walk carrying the canvas and a taxi would be much too extravagant given her new status – or lack of it – so she decided to take a bus.

But no bus came, so she had to walk after all. Still, if Sadie could carry the canvas at her age, surely Amanda ought to be able to manage.

As it turned out, she was in luck. Angus Day was on his way back to the office after a site meeting and had left Clio to spend some time with Laddie to learn about the various building processes involved in constructing a house. Amanda could hardly see around the canvas and didn't notice him stop. She almost tripped over the open car door.

'That looks tricky to carry. Can I offer you a lift?'

After her conversation with Luke the night before, Amanda didn't know whether she should be suspicious of Angus. Maybe this would be an opportunity to find out more about his motives.

In the end they had to take the roof down to fit the canvas in.

Angus chatted easily during the five-minute drive, apparently oblivious of any coldness there might be between them. He even asked if Clio was enjoying herself. 'She's incredibly quick to pick things up,' he enthused before Amanda had time to answer his question, 'and she gets on with all sorts of people, from the council tenants to tricky officials. Everyone likes her. I think you'll be really proud of her, whatever she finally decides to do. It must be so exciting,' he added wistfully, 'to see a child emerging as a person in their own right, becoming someone who has a life of their own that you can't even predict or control.'

This was so much what Amanda had often thought herself, and had pointed out to Giles, that all she could do was nod. She had to admit, despite the scene yesterday, that Angus didn't strike her as the kind of man who'd get his revenge by trying it on with a young girl who clearly trusted and liked him.

'She seems to be really enjoying her work experience,' Amanda conceded.

'And you?' He suddenly turned his steel-grey eyes on her full beam. 'Are you happy with your new relationship?'

Amanda found herself flushing furiously.

'I was up your way yesterday, taking my mother for her treatment. I dropped in to see if Clio might like a lift.' Somehow, when Angus told it, it sounded entirely innocent. 'Luke answered the door. In a bath towel. He didn't seem that happy to see me.'

The image of Luke answering her door in a bath towel suddenly annoyed Amanda enormously. There was something so presumptuous, so coolly possessive, in the action. Why wasn't he dressed or wearing a robe? It must have been at least half an hour after she'd left, and he'd already showered by then. What had he been doing in all that time?

'Are you storing that for Louise?' he asked, filling the embarrassed silence that had fallen between them.

She glanced at the canvas. 'That's mine. As a matter of fact, I've just been fired.' And then she stopped. Why was she telling him that? She hadn't even broken the news to her family yet.

'Good. So there won't be anything to stop you opening up your own gallery. You're far more talented than Louise, you know.'

'I didn't get the boathouse,' Amanda began. 'Someone else is about to take on the lease.'

'Ah.' For some reason he seemed to be smiling.

'Look,' she began, conscious of the smallness of the space between them. 'That time on New Year's Eve . . . I behaved really badly.'

Angus stared into her eyes intently. 'No, you didn't. You behaved beautifully. It was just bad timing.' He reached out and stroked away a stray strand of her hair. 'In fact, probably the worst timing of my life.'

Amanda realised they'd stopped outside her front door. 'Let me help you with that.' He lifted the canvas for her.

She hoped Luke wasn't home, or anyone else for that matter, and the front door was reassuringly double-locked. Should she invite him in?

On the spur of the moment, she did. 'Would you like a cup of tea? Or a whisky perhaps.'

'At four-thirty?' he laughed. 'A bit early even for the drunken Scots. Tea would be fine.' In fact he had a meeting, but how often did he get an invitation from Amanda?

Her answering machine was flashing imperiously, telling her she had two messages. 'Would you mind if I just listened? In case they're important?'

'Go ahead.'

The messages boomed out via Amanda's ancient machine. 'Hello. This is Stephen Williams from South-Eastern bank to apologise that I misinformed you the other day. We are in fact happy to authorise your loan. Perhaps you'd like to come down as soon as possible to sign the forms.' Amanda pressed the pause button, stunned. She'd been convinced she had as much chance of getting the loan as winning the lottery without buying a ticket.

She pressed play for the second message. It was the estate agent, informing her that the rival client, Computer Central, had withdrawn from signing the lease. The boathouse in Laineton was hers if she wanted it. In fact, she could have the keys straightaway.

Amanda sat down on her aged sofa, lost for breath.

'Perhaps it's a sign,' Angus Day suggested, 'that you and the boathouse are meant for each other. Shall I make that tea? You look as though you've seen an army of ghosts. I thought a gallery in the boathouse was what you wanted.'

'I do. More than anything. It's just that I've got a family to support.'

'Surely your ex-husband . . .'

'Provides as little as he possibly can,' cut in Amanda. 'He takes them on holiday but forgets we need to eat and pay a mortgage. That's why I'm so amazed he agreed to this. The bank must have asked him.'

But Amanda didn't get time to pursue this thought because a key turned in the door and Luke appeared, his handsome face pale with anger at the sight of Angus. 'I've just been to the gallery. Louise said you'd resigned from your job.'

Amanda shrugged. 'That's one way of putting it. Louise told me it was time we parted company and I agreed.'

'You could at least have discussed it,' Luke accused. 'I passed up the offer of a lifetime to stay in Laineton, and you go and throw away your job without even talking about it first.'

'Then you'll just have to trust my judgement,' her chin went up combatively, 'won't you? Because I've had some rather good news.' For some reason, the knowledge that Luke wouldn't approve made her more determined than ever to go ahead. 'I've just agreed to take on the lease to the old boathouse down by the harbour. Luke, I'm going to open my own gallery and I've found the most fabulous artist for the very first show!'

Chapter 21

'You don't seem exactly ecstatic at Amanda's new project,' Angus remarked.

'Just piss off, why don't you?' Luke said nastily. 'And take that pretentious car of yours out of our driveway.'

'Luke,' Amanda began, 'there's no need to . . .'

'I think there is.' Luke was still looking at Angus, not Amanda.

'I take it you won't be joining the rest of us this weekend to start refurbishing the boathouse, then?' Angus asked coolly.

This statement was entirely outrageous and Angus half-expected Amanda to jump straight in and deny it. For some reason, she didn't.

'Nine o'clock on Saturday morning, OK?' Angus decided to go for it while he was ahead. 'Laddie will join us, and I'm sure Clio would like to see a refurbishment in action. I can get my guys to do the damp work this week, if you like.'

It didn't occur to Amanda till later to wonder how Angus knew about any damp work in the first place.

Luke followed Angus out to his car. 'I know what you're up to, Day. Even if Amanda doesn't,' he hissed. Angus ignored him and drove away.

Amanda watched him, appalled. 'What the hell is the matter with your attitude?' she demanded.

'Don't you see what this is all about? Clio's work experience fin-ishes this week. It isn't you he's doing the favour for. He wants to help you so he can carry on seeing Clio.'

In all the excitement over the lease, Amanda had forgotten that tonight was the book group. Her head was too full of lists and plans and jobs to go and talk about some novel. She knew Ruthie would tell her off for missing it, so she called Simone instead and asked her to pass on her apologies.

There were so many things to sort out. First she had to sign the lease. She could do that tomorrow. Since the area near the harbour was so run down, the rent was astonishingly reasonable. Even so, there would be costs to meet. She'd have to contribute to the deco-ration, even though she suspected Angus would try not to let her. Then they'd need a proper till system, though nothing too elabo-rate for the moment. Local advertising. Bookkeeping. Would she sell cards and arty gifts like Louise did?

Luke had decided to face the inevitable and be enthusiastic, so the next evening he looked after Sean while Clio and Amanda went down to assess the space.

The boathouse was just as spectacular as she'd remembered, but there were a few disappointments. The floor, for a start. It was lined with filthy linoleum dating from the 1950s.

'You need to work out how to use your space,' Clio announced eagerly. 'I'll draw you a plan, if you like. Angus says I've got a designer's eye.'

'Right.' Amanda thought about it. 'I'll need storage space at the back, screened off, and a till point on an island. I don't think I'll need a whole counter – I'd like to keep the feeling informal. I'm not sure about selling cards and gifts.'

'I suppose it brings people into the shop. You could easily fit in some display shelves down that end.' Clio gestured to the far end of the boathouse. 'In fact, with those fabulous sea views, you could even open a café.'

'Hang on,' Amanda laughed, delighted at Clio's enthusiasm, and at how much she seemed to have grown up during her work experience. The sulky, confused teenager of late had disappeared. 'One step at a time. I can't afford anything that ambitious.'

'Maybe later then, but you've got huge potential. Angus says you should always think about the next step.'

'Does he, indeed?' Amanda smiled at being quoted the wit and wisdom of Angus Day. A week ago Clio would have refused to believe anyone over twenty knew anything of use or value. 'Now.' Amanda gestured to the empty walls. 'This is something I do know about. How we should hang the pictures.'

'Pictures? I thought you were starting with carvings?'

'I am. And pictures as well. I've just discovered the most wonderful artist. You'll love her. She's a real character – seventy-seven years old. *And* she's local.'

'Ooh. Louise isn't going to be very happy, is she? Isn't the local angle her thing?'

Amanda shrugged. Louise wouldn't be very happy about her opening a gallery at all. 'Right. What are we going to call it? I wondered whether it had decided for itself The Boathouse Gallery?'

'Hmm. I'm not sure. Maybe a bit too much like The Wave Gallery. How about Marine Arts?'

'Marine Arts . . . yes, I rather like that. It sounds modern and new.'

'We could have marine decor.' Clio caught sight of Amanda's face. 'Not anchors aweigh and old fishing nets, like a crappy Italian restaurant, but sea tones and the odd tasteful artefact.'

Amanda felt herself melting with pride. Clio sounded so grown-up and knowledgeable.

Ruthie was delighted: so many people had turned up for the book group that they'd run out of beanbags.

'Wow! Even Louise is here.' Louise, as usual, looked like a cross between a Panamanian parrot and one of the Witches of Eastwick. 'Hello, Louise. Long time, no read.'

Louise tossed her earrings without a hint of apology. 'Been too busy I'm afraid.'

Simone was collecting everyone's bottles, putting the white in

Ruthie's overflowing fridge and assessing which one they should open first. They all looked equally dodgy – some with torn labels, some covered in dust. One even had a raffle ticket attached to it, clearly the prize in some ancient tombola. Just as well they weren't fussy. 'What do you fancy? Transylvanian Riesling or Hungarian Bulls Blood?' Simone enquired.

Louise shuddered and offered her own bottle of Safeway's Muscadet. 'I'll stick to this, thanks.' She squinted round the room. 'Isn't Amanda here yet?' Since their quarrel earlier on, Louise had begun to regret Amanda's sudden departure, mostly because she was having to do all the boring chores herself. She'd also forgotten what a sure touch Amanda had with hanging the pictures. They didn't look the same when Louise tried. What's more, she'd worked out that replacing Amanda with anyone as competent would be far more expensive than she'd realised. She'd rather hoped to do some bridge-building tonight. She certainly hadn't been lured here by literature. And even less by the wine.

'Oh, shoot.' Simone clapped her hands over her mouth. 'Forgot to tell you, Ruthie. Amanda's not coming tonight. The big news is, she's opening her own gallery and she's up to her ears in preparations.'

'The hell she is!' erupted Louise, furious at herself for even considering giving Amanda her job back.

Everyone stared at her.

'But I thought Amanda worked for Louise,' puzzled the unworldly Anne.

'She did until she walked out this afternoon. What a shitty thing to do. Especially when I gave her the job without any qualifications because her marriage was coming apart and she needed the money. And this is how she repays me! Something like this doesn't just happen out of the blue. She must have been planning it for months.' Louise looked as if she might explode in tiny puce pieces. 'What a snake in the grass! She's probably been writing down the names of all my customers.'

'For God's sake shut up, Louise,' Simone said dismissively. 'You've been taking advantage of Amanda and paying her a pittance

for years. It'll serve you right if she gives you a bit of healthy competition. Now, why don't we get on with talking about *The Secret
History*?'

Louise hadn't read the book anyway so she shut up for the rest
of the evening and thought of ways to get her own back on the
ungrateful Amanda. To think, she'd even gone to all that trouble of
fixing Amanda up with Luke. Now they were living happily ever
after and Amanda had turned round and thanked her by opening
up a rival gallery round the corner.

'More wine, Louise?' offered the gentle Anne, trying to pour
Riesling on troubled waters.

Louise noted sourly that her superior Muscadet had been polished off and they were down to the horrible Hungarian. 'No
thanks.' She covered her glass pompously.

All the others, she noted, were ignoring the label and knocking
it back, giggling as the discussion took a rather sexy tone. Rather
than sit and listen any longer, she gathered up the dirty glasses and
took them out to the kitchen.

Ruthie appeared at Louise's elbow, rather the worse for wine but
looking anxious rather than relaxed. There was obviously something she wanted to get off her chest.

Louise stiffened. She was damned if she was going to stand here
and be attacked again on the subject of poor, exploited Amanda.

'Look,' she began defensively, 'I really don't want to talk about
Amanda.'

'Too bad.' The wine was making Ruthie even bossier than usual.
'The thing is, I've found out something that's really worrying me. It
could just be unfounded gossip, but I think maybe I should tell
Amanda anyway.'

Louise listened, riveted. If Amanda hadn't betrayed her, she
would have insisted that Amanda must be told at once.

'You've asked me what I think,' Louise said when Ruthie had finished. 'And what I think is that you should stay out of it. If you go
and tell Amanda something like that, she'll never thank you. If you
ask me, you should get your facts pretty damn straight before you
say anything. Let me think about the best way to handle this.'

Ruthie nodded. Louise had known Amanda longer than anyone else in the group.

She just hoped to God that Louise's advice was right. There was a lot at stake if it wasn't.

On Saturday Amanda set her alarm for seven a.m. as she did on weekdays, but Luke rolled lazily over on top of her, wanting to make love. Although she was dying to get down to the gallery, she knew this was Luke's way of offering an apology. She almost gave him her *Men Are from Mars* lecture, explaining that women like the apology, *then* the sex, and that they don't see the sex itself as an apology as men sometimes do. But it was too early and she wanted to get on, so she just threw herself into it briskly and hoped he wouldn't notice the difference. Afterwards, she jumped out of bed and put on her painting clothes, which consisted of ancient bibbed jeans.

'You didn't tell me you owned dungarees. I'm living with a paid-up dungaree-wearing feminist!' Luke teased.

She swatted him affectionately.

'And very lovely she looks too!'

Sean was already sitting at the breakfast table, raiding the new cereal packet for free games. But there was no sign of Clio.

'Clio!' she shouted. Still no response. And when Amanda looked in her room it was as untidy as usual and the bed was unmade but her daughter was nowhere to be seen. Just as she was about to be worried, she spotted a note saying 'Got up early. See you later at Marine Arts'.

It was a glorious day and Amanda decided to do without a coat. May was very much in the air. She cut through the backstreets to the harbour, waving at Rose Miles who was making the most of the warm morning by hanging out her washing. It was a pity the area was so run-down, but she had to remind herself that she wouldn't have been able to afford the rent if the boathouse had been in the smart end of town. She would have to make the gallery so attractive that people came here especially.

As she rounded the corner, the sight that met Amanda made her stop dead. Clio, holding the plan they'd roughed of the interior, was directing a team of about eight different plasterers, painters, and chippies while Laddie Smithson looked on, smiling. 'She's got the knack of it all right,' he confided. 'Only a chit of a girl, but she's got them eating out of her hand. I'm the foreman and here I am feeling like a spare bridegroom at a wedding.'

'Hi, Mum,' Clio called. 'What do you think? They're going great guns with the painting. Which colour do you want for the windows? I thought this slatey-blue was really nice.' She shoved a paint chart at her astounded mother. 'Laddie here'll go and get it for us with his builder's discount card.'

Laddie grinned, looking like a cat who'd been stroked rather than a fifty-five-year-old man being ordered round by a teenage girl.

'Wonderful, isn't she? She'll be running Bovis before you can say starter-homes.'

Amanda felt a slight jolt of disappointment that there was no sign of Angus. 'He thought he might be in the way,' Laddie explained, which Amanda translated as he thought Luke would be here. Still, it was sensitive of him.

'The boys did the damp on Thursday, so we were able to plaster on Friday and paint today. Want to see how it's coming on?'

Inside the boathouse, every sign of its previous life as a tyre depot had vanished and been replaced by the pure, simple white walls she'd seen so often in her fantasy. 'Clio thought you'd rather keep the beams unpainted. That they gave the place some atmosphere.'

Amanda nodded. Clio was right.

'Here's the till island,' Clio pointed out excitedly. 'The guys have done an amazing job. All you have to do is decide on the colour. And Laddie's got a nice surprise. Tell her, Laddie.'

'It's a mate of mine who's a sign writer. Said he'd drop round and do you a sign, cheap like. Only I'd recommend you have a think about what you want now. He goes to the pub at lunchtimes, and after that his lettering tends to wobble like a ghost train.'

Amanda smiled and thanked him. Then a thought struck her. How was she going to afford to pay all these workmen?

Laddie read her mind. 'It's their sort of going-away present to Clio here. She's been giving them lessons in how to understand their teenagers.'

'Don't worry, Mum. They're enjoying themselves. Makes a change from being bossed around by Laddie here. When we've decided on the sign, why don't you go and stand everyone some fish and chips? This lot are like camels. They never stop to eat or drink. But today I think we should make them.' She clapped her hands bossily. 'Right gents, place your orders with Amanda here. Mine's a saveloy, chips and mushy peas. With plenty of vinegar.'

Obediently writing down the enormous order, Amanda felt a stupid tear mist up her eye that this efficient girl could be the same self-hating confused child of only a few weeks before.

Two weeks later everything was finished and they were ready to open. Clio had the inspired idea that if they moved the display shelves to the middle of the gallery they could effectively create two spaces, so they set up one with Natasha's seabirds and the other with Sadie's oil paintings.

The opening party was that night and they'd invited everyone they could think of. Luke had found a brilliant 'France for a fiver' offer on the ferry and nipped over and bought three cases of cut-price fizz at the local hypermarket. So now they were handing out glasses of Kir Royale, like a proper posh gallery.

Sadie had brought the whole of her art class with her and they were merrily toasting her as their biggest success story. Natasha was there with her invalid father, and Laddie and his team of work-men had dug out their best suits. They all stood, looking proud but flummoxed, discussing Sadie's pictures.

'What's that when it's at home?' the chippie asked, moving his head to try and decipher the large pink object on the canvas.

'That's my one attempt at an abstract, darling,' Sadie chortled. 'It's me in the altogether. Those are my tits and that's my . . .'

'Right, gotcha,' interrupted the chippie, hurrying off for a refill, with the air of a broken man.

Helen was showing off her knowledge of Impressionist art to a delicate-looking Isobel Day, who was clearly determined to hold her own despite being in a wheelchair.

Half of the Over-Sixties club were there in force, as well as Lou Miles from the Eastcliff Estate. Giles couldn't make it because Stephanie's waters had broken, but he'd sent a big bunch of sunflowers.

'Quite touching for Giles,' Amanda conceded. 'I hope he remembers to send Stephanie some too. Knowing Giles, he'll probably have negotiated a discount for two bunches.'

Rose and Betty Miles were both in the midst of the throng, deep in conversation with Luke. Betty, dressed in a sequinned stole from the 1930s, was knocking back the Kir as if it were the last liquid before the Sahara and flirting with Luke outrageously. It was amazing, Amanda mused, how sibling rivalry survived into your eighties.

Amanda, unsure of what to wear, had put on the sea-green dress from New Year's Eve, and, at the last minute, the bead necklace.

'I hope you didn't wear that deliberately,' said a quiet voice behind her, 'just to stoke up old memories.'

She turned to find Angus Day leaning on a pillar, watching her.

Amanda found her neck turning a fiery and unbecoming red. Why *had* she worn the dress? 'I wanted to thank you,' she willed her voice to stay calm, 'for all your help here.'

'Nothing to do with me. They did it all for your daughter.'

'That's the other thing I wanted to thank you for. I can't believe how much more confident she seems. She's a changed person.'

'That's all down to Clio herself. She really is an exceptional girl.'

Across the crowded room, she saw Luke's eyes lift from Betty's and take in who she was talking to.

She'd been through possessiveness once and she was damned if she was going to worry about who she spoke to this time round. If Luke wasn't confident enough to trust her then too bad.

'Thank you anyway.' She raised her glass to Angus. 'You're much more generous than you ever admit.'

There was a sudden commotion behind them and she turned to find Luke standing only inches away, with a startled Betty by his side. 'I wouldn't overdo the generosity bit,' Luke informed her, 'until you've heard what Betty has to say.'

Angus watched him, unmoved. 'And just what does Betty have to say?'

Luke raised his chin challengingly. 'Only that Mr Big-Hearted here wants them to move out of their chalet. After living there for fifty years. To make way for a grand new development. How generous would you call that?'

Chapter 22

Amanda stared at Angus. Surely he wouldn't do something like that?

'It's all right, Luke.' Rose had appeared in the middle of the group. 'Thank you for taking up the cudgels on our behalf, but Mr Day isn't forcing us out. There've been no nasty incidents in the middle of the night to put the frighteners on us. No rats through the letter box.'

Luke raised a sceptical eyebrow. 'No, I'm sure Mr Day's techniques would be far more subtle. He'd plead the good of the community. His scheme would help regenerate the town and provide employment. I'm sure his arguments were irresistible.'

'Well,' Rose conceded, 'he did show us the plans and the whole harbour did look lovely.'

'The beach huts are all so sad and neglected now,' Betty added. 'Not like in our day. Besides,' she smiled, unaware of the fact so many people were listening, 'he's giving us a nice new flat instead.'

Even though she knew Betty and Rose might be better off in a flat, Amanda was disappointed in Angus. The chalet had been their life, as well as part of the landscape of the town. It was obvious he just wanted the site and Betty and Rose were in his way. The fact that their scruffy chalet might be full of memories, and that their home was as much a part of Laineton as the pier or the breakwaters, would hardly be of importance to a property developer. To a businessman's mentality they were simply in the way of a profitable scheme.

But somehow she'd expected more of him than that.

Everyone was suddenly looking at Angus. In her corner by the window even Isobel was aware of it.

Angus wasn't about to start defending himself to a man he couldn't stand. 'I think it's time I took my mother home,' he said simply.

But Clio's passionate and headstrong nature wasn't prepared to leave it at that. 'You're all talking complete crap,' she announced angrily. 'It's an absolutely wonderful design. It'll bring the whole of the harbour back to life. Why don't you all look at the plans before condemning Angus?'

It was the worst thing she could possibly have done.

'So it's all right to chuck out two old ladies from the house they've lived in for most of their lives just to brighten up the harbour, is it?' Luke countered furiously. 'I think maybe you've been spending your time in bad company, Clio. A couple of rides in a nice sports car and you're seeing things his way.'

'Oh for God's sake, Luke,' Amanda cut in before Clio could answer. She might be disappointed in Angus but this was going too far. 'Don't be so ridiculous.'

'I don't happen to believe it is ridiculous.' His eyes narrowed as they held hers. 'I had you down as someone who believed in people and the community, like I do. All that recycling you go in for is a con. You're just as easily dazzled by a smart scheme as the rest of them. Well, I'm not.'

Luke turned to the old lady and held her firmly by the shoulders. 'You shouldn't go, Rose. It's your home. You shouldn't be pushed out to make way for a wine bar and some tawdry gift shops. If you face it out the whole scheme'll fall apart. There'll be plenty of people who'll support you.'

Angus could hold back no longer. 'Against the wicked forces of capitalism? I suggest you look at the plans before you accuse me. We'll be housing eight young families.'

'And putting two old ladies out of their home at the same time. Is that what the local authority calls "housing gain"? It sounds like housing loss to me.'

Angus noticed Isobel trying to get her wheelchair to move out of the corner. She looked not just shaken but chalk-pale. 'Excuse me,' Angus pushed past Luke, 'I need to get to my mother.'

'That was handy,' said Luke.

'Get lost, why don't you?' Clio snapped. 'You're a bloody hypocrite, anyway. You don't dislike Angus because he's a property developer. It's because he's richer than you and he fancies Mum!'

The room was pitched into sudden silence.

'Right,' Luke insisted furiously. 'That's quite enough from you. You're grounded.' He grabbed her wrist and pulled her towards the door.

'No, she's not.' Amanda's voice was shaking with fury. 'Clio is my daughter and I'll decide how to discipline her, if you don't mind.'

'Excuse me.' Angus pushed his mother's wheelchair towards the door of the gallery. Everyone stood back to let them through.

There was a moment, just in front of the doorway, when the two men came up against each other. Amanda wasn't sure what would have happened if the ludicrously jolly tones of her mobile phone hadn't suddenly broken the tension.

Amanda took the opportunity to step forward and open the door. 'Thank you both for coming. I hope you're better soon, Isobel.'

Then she covered one ear so that she could hear the call better above the growing noise of the party and answered the phone.

It was Giles, calling from the hospital.

Amanda turned to Clio and put her hand over her mobile phone, not sure how she felt. 'It's Dad. Stephanie's had her twins. A boy and a girl.'

'A boy and a girl,' Clio repeated. 'Perfect. One of each. Just like Sean and me.' Before Amanda could stop her, she opened the door and ran out of the gallery towards the beach.

'What an exciting party this has been,' commented Luke.

Amanda ignored him and said goodbye to Giles. On her way out

of the door she called back to Luke, 'Clio's had bad news. I'm afraid
I need to go after her.'

'Don't mind me,' Luke called back. 'Right. Rose, Betty, let me get
you another glass of that pink fizz.'

Half an hour later the party was about to wind down when Luke
found another three bottles of sparkling wine hidden behind the
counter. Betty had begun singing a duet of *A Nightingale Sang in
Berkeley Square* with Luke by the time Rose finally went to look for
their coats. There was just one other guest left, a man who was
very much the worse for wear, Rose noted with embarrassment.

'He's a brave lad, that one,' slurred the man, draining the dregs of
someone else's glass into his and pointing to Luke. Rose wondered
if she should point out that there was a cigarette end in the wine he
was decanting, but she'd never liked men who couldn't hold their
drink.

'She's quite harmless, really,' answered Rose, assuming he was
referring to Luke's closeness to Betty. 'Just likes the company of
young men rather than old ones.'

'Good luck to her. I meant the way he insulted Mr Bigwig Day
earlier.'

'And just who are you?'

'Gary Hodges. I work for the estate agent that let this place. You
see, the thing is, Mr Bigwig Day . . .'

'What about him?'

'Mrs Wells doesn't seem to know it but he's the chap who guaranteed the lease on this place. I hope he won't be coming round
tomorrow to cancel it.'

Rose watched Luke and Betty twirl about the gallery, Betty glowing with girlish excitement. Luke was extraordinarily handsome
and charming, and very good at making old ladies feel young.
She'd been delighted when Amanda and he had got together,
because she'd felt it was time Amanda had someone in her life
who appreciated her.

But there was something else about Luke Knight she wasn't so
sure of. A quickness to lose his temper, a jealous possessiveness
that hadn't been apparent when she'd first met him. And she

didn't like the look of it. Not one bit. It reminded her of her father. He had been the most Victorian of fathers and had liked his daughters to do everything he commanded, which was why they'd ended up as impoverished spinsters. And she wouldn't wish that on anyone.

'If I were you,' she hissed to Gary Hodges in a tone that even penetrated the clouds of Kir Royale, 'I wouldn't mention that fact to anyone.' She paused menacingly. 'Especially to Mr Knight over there.' She shoved him swiftly towards the door before he got the chance.

'I haven't had such a good time in years,' Betty sighed as they walked back to their chalet. 'That young man is a real charmer.'

'Yes,' mused Rose. Somehow Luke's charm had dulled for her a little tonight.

But why, she wondered as they walked back through the warm spring night, had Angus Day backed the gallery lease, and apparently without Amanda knowing it? Was he being generous or profiteering? The boathouse was bang next door to his new development and if the area went up greatly in value, which it was bound to do with the arrival of a café-bar, a new boardwalk and attractive new shops and beach huts, then somebody was about to make a lot of money. When he'd first told them about it, he'd made the scheme sound like such a good thing for the whole town. Yet if Luke was right, it was more of a good thing for Angus Day. And if that wasn't the case, why the hell hadn't Angus denied it? The whole thing was very confusing.

Just as they got back to their chalet she remembered the look of concern Angus had shown when he'd noticed his mother. There had been genuine kindness there.

But even Hitler had loved his mother.

Amanda finally found Clio sitting on the shingle under the pier.

She was sitting right in the most inaccessible part, hunched up, listening to the waves. There was a small pale moon in the sky which threw a narrow pencil of light across the sea. It took a moment to spot where Clio was in the faintly fish-smelling gloom.

'How did you know I'd be here?' Clio asked.

Amanda attempted a smile. 'You used to like coming here when you were small. Especially when you were cross with me. You knew I couldn't see you in here and I'd worry.'

'Not much has changed then.'

'Are you all right? It's a bummer about the twins, isn't it?'

Clio smiled a small smile. 'No one says "bummer", Mum. You only talk like that when you're trying to get on my wavelength.'

'OK, I'll talk like my generation. How dare the bastard walk out of our lives and think he can start all over again with bloody twins?' She threw a pebble furiously into the water. 'You know what the most depressing thing is?'

'What's that?'

'I bet you he'll go all New Man-ish and start saying he didn't know how enjoyable fatherhood could be, screw him. Fathers in second marriages always do that. It makes their first wives want to kill them.' She threw another pebble; it skipped into ten perfect skims. 'I'm sorry. I shouldn't talk like that to you.'

'It's all right. It helps actually. It's Sean you shouldn't talk to like that. He has some vague admiration for Dad still.'

'I know. And I suppose it's important he does. He's not all bad, you know. Giles has some good qualities.'

'Such as?'

Amanda paused. 'He's very good at negotiating cheap holidays.'

They both fell about laughing and clung to each other, wiping away tears which could have been of laughter or of pain.

Suddenly Clio pulled back. 'I'm sorry about Luke, Mum. I've tried to like him, but I can't. I don't even really know why. Why do you like him? Apart from the sex, I mean?'

Anger and guilt overwhelmed Amanda. Maybe it had been unfair for Luke to move in before he really knew them properly. But didn't she have rights too?

'I was lonely. You know that. So lonely I resorted to advertising for a midget! Luke is incredibly attractive and he's interesting, not your usual small town bore who talks about golf and Neighbourhood Watch. And, I suppose, he fell for me.'

'So did Angus,' Clio wanted to say. 'Maybe I should try harder to get on with him,' Clio sighed.

'And maybe he should. It's not his job to discipline you without talking to me first. I'll have it out with him when I get home.' She put her arm round Clio and Clio rested her head on Amanda's shoulder.

'Do you want to visit the hospital?' Amanda asked after they'd sat there for so long that she was beginning to stiffen up. 'Or would you rather wait until they're all home? You should only do what's best for you.'

'What if what's best for me is that Dad hadn't left and that he didn't need any other children to replace us? I hate him, Mum. I can't help it but I do!'

'I know. It's a horrible feeling. Really shitty. But you're very loved. By me. By Sean. And Gran. By Dad, too, in his way. He just finds it hard to see the pain he might be causing.'

'I've thought about visiting the babies, but I'd rather not. I don't mean to hate them. In fact, I'm sure when I see them I'll think they're gorgeous and go all gooey and want to hold them. But I don't want to feel like that either. I suppose what I really want is for Dad to understand how I do feel.'

Amanda hugged her tighter, wishing she could take all Clio's pain away. 'I'll explain to him, don't worry.'

'I wish you didn't have to. I wish he could work it out for himself.'

'Maybe he will.'

'When pigs can fly. Come on, let's go home before someone tries to flog us some drugs. This is their favourite hang-out.'

'And how exactly do you know that?'

'I am sixteen. Old enough to be somebody's half-sister.'

'Come on. I'll make you a hot-water bottle and a hot chockie.'

'In May?'

'The season's got nothing to do with it.' Hot chocolate and furry hot-water bottles worked no matter what the season.

Luke was still up when they got back, looking charming and contrite. 'I'm really sorry, Clio. That was entirely inappropriate of me. I was just furious on Rose's behalf and I took it out on you.' He smiled winningly. 'I've put Sean to bed and read *3,089 Football Stories* to him. Giles rang again. He's incredibly keen for you all to come down to the hospital tomorrow.'

Clio shot her mother a look and ran up to her room.

'Did I say the wrong thing again?'

Amanda shook her head. He was really making an effort to be sympathetic. 'No. She's just incredibly cut up about the twins. It's hit her harder than anything since the divorce.'

'I tidied the gallery before I left, too. I assume it's business as usual on Monday for the busy gallery owner.'

Amanda smiled. In all the turmoil of the evening she'd almost forgotten the pleasure of finally having her own gallery.

'Come on,' his voice was loaded with promise, 'let's go to bed. I've never made love to a gallery owner before.'

'I'm not sure . . .' she began.

'You need some tender loving care too.'

And despite the worry she had over Clio, and the pain she felt herself about the twins' arrival, Luke's version of TLC certainly took her mind off things.

'Do *you* think I'm being a bastard, persuading those two old girls to move?' Angus asked Isobel as he drove her home.

'Are you?'

'The new flats will be amazing and I've offered them the best. First-floor balcony overlooking the harbour where they can practically lean over and chat to passers-by, underfloor heating, a bedroom each, lift, porter on duty downstairs. I'd have thought it'd be perfect for someone of their age.'

'The old don't always want what other people think would be perfect for them. What would you do if it were me?'

Angus thought for a moment. 'It wouldn't suit you. You're someone who likes peace and quiet. You don't much like your fellow men. Betty and Rose are sociable. They've practically lived on the beach.'

'Would they have a washing line?'

'A washing line?' Angus was stupified. 'Wouldn't a nice new tumble-dryer do?'

Isobel shook her head. 'Our generation need somewhere to hang things out. It makes us feel at home.'

'Right. I suppose we could rig one up on the roof.'

'Tell them that. Do you think they really want to go?'

'I don't think they know themselves. They're canny like you. They can see the advantages. But they're always nervous of change.'

'How about your own motivation? If it weren't for the fact their chalet's holding up your scheme, would you still think it a good thing for them?'

'On every rational level, yes.' He glanced at his mother and saw that she was looking better. The chalk-pale pained look had left her. In fact, she was smiling at him. Even though he was driving along, he took both hands off the wheel as if in surrender. 'All right. All right. I'll see if I can talk the council into adapting the plan to leave their chalet. But for God's sake don't tell Laddie. He already thinks I've gone soft in the head.'

They reached Isobel's house and Angus opened the car door and lifted her out. She was even lighter than usual. A sudden sense of panic, of imminent loss, ran through him. 'Let me stay.' He felt as if a part of himself were being chipped away. 'Please. I promise I'll be no trouble and I positively won't nag you.'

Isobel smiled again. 'All right. Just this once.'

Angus carried her in grimly. This was the first time she'd ever agreed to let him stay with her.

Amanda woke to find sunlight streaming in the window. She sat up and groped for her watch. The space next to her in the bed was empty and the whole room was peaceful.

The bedroom door opened and Luke appeared carrying a tray loaded with coffee and croissants. He put it down next to her. 'Madam's breakfast.' He handed her the local paper. 'The write-up for the gallery opening's on page six.'

Amanda excitedly rifled through the paper to find it. It was only a couple of paragraphs about the opening party but next to it was a large photograph of Sadie, with whom the journalist had obviously got on as if they were long-lost sisters parted at birth. There were some fabulous quotes about Sadie's paintings. On the opposite page was the ad Amanda had placed inviting people to come and see Marine Arts for themselves.

Amanda bit into a croissant. This was as close to heaven as life got. Luke picked up the paper. 'It also says that the gallery will be well placed to benefit from the new harbourfront development proposed by the council and Day Properties, which explained why Mr Angus Day was at the party.'

'How dare they?' Amanda demanded furiously. 'My gallery is completely unconnected with Angus Day.'

'That man gets his oar in everywhere. Perhaps you should write and correct them,' suggested Luke, removing a crumb of croissant from beside her mouth and kissing her. 'I don't suppose there's time for . . .'

'Mu-um . . .' yelled a disembodied voice from downstairs. 'Where are my football gloves?'

Luke held up his hands in mock surrender. 'OK. OK.'

Amanda jumped out of bed. Now that she was working for herself she mustn't start slacking and opening the gallery late.

'Time to get up.' She kissed Luke and started to get dressed. 'You can lie-in for a bit though.'

Amanda pulled on some olive-green linen trousers and a stretchy lime-green twinset. She noticed her hair needed a cut and colour as she glanced briefly in the mirror, but it would have to wait. A moment of panic shuddered through her that she no longer had a salary, however pathetic, coming in but also had rent and overheads to pay. She mustn't think like that.

Downstairs, Sean was sweetly making his own sandwiches, which seemed to consist of jam, banana and Rice Krispies. 'They're really good,' he insisted. 'And incredibly healthy.'

'Of course they are,' Amanda agreed, shouting upstairs to Clio that it was time to go. 'I'll walk to the bus stop with you.'

'Why?' asked Sean suspiciously.

'Can't I just enjoy the pleasure of your company?' Amanda

asked. Actually she wanted to tell him about the twins and see if he'd come to the hospital with her to visit them. It might be easier for him if he chose to go for himself rather than having Giles spring their arrival on him.

'Adults always have an inferior motive,' Sean pointed out.

'Ulterior. It's a fair cop. There is something I wanted to chat about.'

'Is it serious? Something I won't like?'

Amanda didn't know how to answer this.

'Because if it is, we'll need to go via the sweet shop to get my consolation prize.'

Amanda considered whether to resist this obvious blackmail. What should the good parent do? Or at least the good single parent? To hell with it, she was about to break the news to her ten-year-old that his father had had twins with someone else. Even a giant-size Toblerone would be acceptable. In fact they settled on a Yorkie Bar, which Sean happily chomped as they walked along.

'Something exciting happened on Saturday night,' she began, ignoring the fact that he'd put two squares in his mouth at once and could hardly close it. 'Dad and Stephanie had twins. A boy and a girl.'

'Oh,' Sean shrugged, 'I knew that. Clio was talking to Jasmine about them. She called them the spawn of the she-devil and said she hoped they suffered from arrested development.'

Amanda tried not to laugh. 'Clio's a really naughty girl to say that.'

'No she's not,' corrected Sean. 'She's just really pissed off with Dad. She thinks he's a shitbag. So do I. Look, here's the bus.'

'Will you come and visit them with me in hospital? Dad would like it.'

'Yeah, but would *you* like it?'

Amanda was tempted to say she would have preferred the twins to have been drowned at birth, or better still never conceived at all, but if she wanted Sean to feel he still had a father, and that his father still loved him, she mustn't muddy the waters with her own resentment. 'I'd like you to come.'

'All right.'

'Thanks, darling.'

The bus had arrived and Sean spotted one of his friends on board. He rushed off, terrified that Amanda would do something terminally embarrassing like kiss him.

Amanda knew better. 'See you when I get home from the gallery.'

She almost ran the half mile between home and the harbour. Her own gallery! All the years she'd had to do what Louise wanted, with Louise asking her advice and then almost joyously ignoring it. Now she could follow her own instincts! The thought was wonderful yet terrifying.

Luke had been as good as his word about clearing up. The plastic plates and glasses had all been binned and the empty bottles lined up ready for recycling. He'd even hoovered. She smiled, allowing herself to think about breakfast in bed and what they might have got up to if it hadn't been a school day. And then she remembered the tension between Luke and Clio. And she hoped fervently they would work it out.

Clio waited until Luke was in the bathroom. As soon as she heard the bolt slide across she slipped out of her room and started tip-toeing towards the stairs.

She didn't even hear the bathroom door open again, but suddenly there he was in front of her, wearing nothing but a small bath towel. 'Why are you creeping around like that? I'm not the Big Bad Wolf, you know.'

Clio tried a smile but she just couldn't do it – there was something about Luke that gave her the creeps. 'Just off to school.' It was all she could think of to say.

'That explains the school uniform,' he answered, smiling. 'Do they all wear skirts as short as you?'

'Shorter.' Clio ducked under his arm and ran downstairs. 'Bye. See you later.' She was out of the door before Luke even had time to react.

She had double biology first period and they were due to have a test on human reproduction. There was more evidence than she wanted of human reproduction down at the hospital. She imagined her father clucking about uselessly, while Stephanie, bony and bossy in her pristine white nightie, informed him that the most useful thing he could do would be to book them a holiday in a five-star hotel with a crèche.

It was so bloody unfair. Why couldn't parents get on with each other and stick to their marriage vows instead of allowing people like Stephanie and Luke to barge into the picture? Neither Stephanie nor Luke felt like her family. They felt like squatters who'd broken into her home and were sleeping in her bedroom.

Clio bought a packet of chocolate biscuits and a carton of juice on her way to school. She'd never tell her mother, but working for Angus Day had put her off school. The working world seemed so much more enjoyable than slogging away at physics and biology. Yet she knew exactly how Angus would react if she asked to come and work for him full-time. His grey eyes would widen sardonically and he'd say he only employed people with qualifications, so if she wanted a job with him she'd better go off and get some. Plus a degree, preferably.

It was such shit being a teenager. You still didn't have any real control over your life, yet people were continually telling you to behave like an adult.

She munched her biscuits but instead of heading towards school and the biology test she turned down to the seafront, carefully avoiding the harbour and Marine Arts. She walked along the front for a while. It was very windy and the sea danced with white horses. Further up the prom an old lady was trying to get out of a deckchair but kept being blown back in. There was no one about under the age of about ninety.

An irresistible tide of loneliness swept over her. She didn't really feel at home anywhere. Before Luke had moved in she'd had her mum to confide in, but now she was the one who felt like a guest. He was always there. She couldn't relax or spread out, and even though he was so good-looking there was something about him she found unnerving.

Before she could stop herself she was crying again – big painful sobs that wrenched out of her narrow chest. Suddenly all she wanted to do was be comforted by her mother, the one person she was sure really loved her. She skittered along the promenade, her long legs flailing, and turned up Market Street, almost tripping over Louise who was standing outside The Wave Gallery and reeling in the canopy which was flapping in the wind.

'Hey,' Louise asked, 'what's the matter? Shouldn't you be at school?'

'I'm just looking for my mum,' Clio sobbed, and rushed on, leaving Louise creased up with guilt and staring after her. She had promised Ruthie faithfully that she would warn Amanda about the rumour they'd heard about Luke. And she hadn't done so.

She'd better go and ring Amanda straightaway.

Before it was too late.

Chapter 23

'Amanda, is that you?' Louise decided that if she was ever going to make the call, now was the time. The sight of Clio looking so distraught had pricked her rather jaded conscience.

'Hello, Louise.' The last person Amanda had expected to call and wish her good luck was Louise, but here she was on the line. 'How did you get the number?'

'You've got an ad in today's paper, remember? Look, I'm not actually calling about the gallery. I've just seen Clio.'

'But Clio's at school.'

'No she isn't. She's on her way to see you and she looks really upset.'

'Oh God, it's the bloody twins. Giles and Stephanie have had twins and it's hit Clio really hard.'

Louise hesitated. 'Are you sure that's all it is?'

'Absolutely. She was crying about it on Saturday. I had to make her a hot chocolate and a hottie. Poor thing. She feels well and truly replaced and Giles will be too proud of his own fertility to notice. I'm taking Sean to see them but Clio didn't want to come.'

'Oh. Right. You see, there was something Ruthie heard that I thought you ought to know. It's about . . .'

At precisely that moment Clio burst through the door.

'Thanks for ringing, Louise, I appreciate your concern.' Amanda put the phone down before Louise could say more. Clio would loathe it if she thought they were discussing her. At Clio's age, privacy was everything.

'Are you all right?' She folded her daughter into a bear hug. Clio was just taller than her. 'Silly question. No, of course you aren't or you wouldn't be here.'

'Oh Mum, I'm sorry. I'm being pathetic.'

'No you're not. You're being entirely sensible and reasonable. Do you want to take the day off school and go home?'

Clio wondered whether to tell her mother this was the last thing on earth she wanted to do. Amanda, wondering if she could re-organise her day to spend some time with Clio, didn't notice the hesitation.

'I suppose you could stay here if you wanted. Then go to school later.' She stroked the hair away from Clio's lovely face. 'I'm not pushing you, but the worst possible thing when you're blue is having nothing to do.'

'All right,' Clio conceded. 'I'll go in after break.' She looked round the gallery. 'It does look good here. Stylish and welcoming. I love the old lady who does the paintings.'

'Sadie? She's great, isn't she? Look, you hold the fort. I'll go and buy us a sticky bun. See you in a minute.'

A few streets away at her own gallery, Louise agonised. She suspected that this rumour about Luke was just silly gossip. But maybe she owed it to Amanda to let her decide for herself. She'd better try again.

But it wasn't Amanda who picked up the call. It was Clio.

'Never mind,' Louise spluttered. She'd never been able to talk to children, especially teenagers. 'Just tell her I called, will you?'

A couple of minutes later Amanda came back carrying a cake box. She handed Clio an iced doughnut covered in hundreds and thousands. 'There's only one known cure for heartache, backache, headache and soul-ache. Carbohydr-ache.'

Clio shook her head. 'Mum. You never make jokes.'

'I suppose I must be happy. I'm really sorry about Dad and the twins and I wish he and I could have made it work, for your sakes. But people do change, and Dad and I are better off apart. To be honest, I'm much happier with you and Sean, and Luke, and now the gallery. I feel my life's coming together at last. I suppose that explains the bad jokes.'

Clio turned away. How could she spoil her mother's chance of happiness by telling her what she really thought of Luke?

'Tell you what, let's have a hot chocolate. I bought some of that High Lights low-calorie stuff. I'll make us one. Maybe it'll cancel out the doughnuts.' She smiled guiltily at Clio. She shouldn't have gone on about being happy with Luke when Clio was distressed. Thankfully, she seemed to have cheered up now.

'There you go.'

Clio nudged her, grinning. 'Look, you've got a customer.'

An elderly gentleman was gazing raptly at Natasha's seabirds. 'What fantastic attention to detail. I'm a birdwatcher and I've never seen anything like them.'

'Lovely, aren't they? The artist sculpted them all locally.'

'I think I know that one.' The old man pointed to a particularly fierce seagull. 'He's got no manners. How much is that small fellow? The little wader?'

Amanda picked up the bird. It was one of her favourites. 'Forty-two pounds.' She had to stop herself from adding, 'I'm afraid.'

'Luckily I've just picked up my pension.' He delved around in his straw basket which was loaded with leeks and cabbages.

'Make it forty,' Amanda said. 'Then you can eat too.'

'Your first sale,' Clio hissed as the man left the shop, happily patting his basket where the bird was stowed. 'Congratulations.'

'Look, Clio love, I'm popping up to the hospital later with Sean to see the twins. He'll probably think they're deeply boring. Will you be all right at home?'

'Actually,' Clio said quickly, 'I'll probably go to Jasmine's.'

Amanda studied her for a moment. 'You would tell me, wouldn't you, if there was something else bothering you? If it wasn't just the twins arriving?'

Clio sighed. How could you tell your mother you didn't want to be left alone with her lover, especially when your mother seemed to be so ludicrously in love with him?

'Course I would. Isn't the arrival of the half-siblings from hell enough?'

Angus Day stood with the plans to the harbour development in front of him, propped up on a brightly painted fisherman's box.

'When I first came here,' Laddie said, 'they used to sell their catch on these things, all along the beach, twenty or thirty of them. Now there's only one or two fishing boats go out. And they aren't allowed to sell their catch. Against EC regulations. It has to be properly refrigerated now. If you want to buy fish in Laineton,' he joked, elbowing Angus, 'it probably has to come from Aberdeen! So,' Laddie enquired, knowing that, eventually, Angus would get round to explaining their presence, but impatient anyway, 'what are we doing down here staring at these plans for?'

'I've been wondering,' Angus mused, 'if the scheme could still go ahead if we kept the old girls' chalet.'

'The answer's no,' Laddie said. 'And you know it. It's right slap-bang in the middle of this poncy scheme of yours. The council are thinking of calling it Fisherman's Wharf, like they have in San Francisco, and did that have a chalet stuck right in the middle of it?'

'I could go and talk to them about it,' Angus decided.

'Much good it'll do ye.'

'I could walk away, you know, Laddie. Go and build some nice expensive flats or a golf course up the coast.'

'Except your heart wouldn't be in it. You're committed to this, Angus. This is a good scheme for the town. And, don't forget, there's ten million pounds involved.'

'I'll persuade them,' Angus said with more confidence than he felt. 'Though at this moment I don't actually know how.'

'If it's anything like the plan, it'll be a fine-looking spot,' Laddie conceded.

Angus looked stunned. 'You never praise the schemes we work on.'

'It reminds me of a town I visited when I was a merchant seaman. Portugal, I think it was. All bright colours and fishing boats. Made a nice change from all that granite at home.'

'Then I'd better try my best to make it happen.'

'Aye. You'd better. As a matter of fact, I've put myself down for a beach hut. And bloody expensive they are too, thanks to you.'

Angus was taken aback at how touched he felt. He liked his developments to mean something to people, and if the laconic Laddie was paying good money to be part of it, they must have come up with something really special.

Amanda looked at her watch: 5.25 p.m. She would be closing in five minutes. On her second day she'd made several more small sales and sold some assorted greetings cards, and lots of people had popped in to have a look around. It wasn't exactly a stampede but she was modestly hopeful that more people would come as the word got round.

The main problem was how tied she was to the gallery physically. Working with Louise, they'd been able to cover for each other when one had to go out for some reason, but there was no way Amanda could afford any assistance. If she got really desperate she'd have to ask her mother. But she could just picture that. Helen would start gossiping with the customers and forget to make any sales.

Now that she was living with Luke, Amanda had imagined he might help out with childcare, but Luke had turned out to be disappointingly unhelpful in this respect. He called it 'having a meeting he couldn't shift'. She called it having old-fashioned masculine values. She was particularly annoyed with him at the moment over the birth of the twins. He couldn't seem to grasp how painful this was to Sean and Clio. She wondered if he'd understand – or care – more if they were his own children, but there was something enduringly child-free about Luke, despite the attempts he occasionally made to be helpful.

Sometimes it exasperated Amanda to the point of questioning their whole relationship. Then she reminded herself that living with someone who had kids was probably very difficult for Luke. He might not be the icon of perfection she'd fallen for, but in these days of tricky relationships he was well worth hanging on to.

She was deep into these musings when her mother arrived with Sean, who was dressed in his favourite Manchester United football strip.

'I've given him his tea,' Helen announced. 'He had four sausages and a *whole* tin of beans.'

GG herself ate like an anorexic bird and considered anyone who consumed more than a teaspoon to be seriously greedy.

'Thanks for looking after him. We'd better get along to the hospital now.'

'How are the little bastards?'

Sean looked bemused. 'Aren't children only bastards if you're not married? Our teacher says William the Conqueror was a bastard.'

'Well, he'd have to be to shoot that nice King Harold, wouldn't he?' Helen said. 'But you're quite right, darling, it's just an expression to convey disapproval. In this case, of your father going and having another set of children when he's got a perfectly lovely set already. You and Clio.'

There was no point, Amanda realised, in trying to get her mother to be tactful. 'Here,' she asked Sean, 'will you help me wrap these up?' She took out two tiny knitted hats in the shape of strawberries.

'Mum,' Sean pointed out reasonably, 'they'll look really soppy in those.'

'That's the joy of babies,' Helen pointed out briskly. 'They're too young to know they look soppy. I'll say goodbye now.'

'Mum,' Sean said softly when Helen had disappeared and Amanda had closed up the gallery. 'I wanted to give them something of my own, something I really liked a lot.' He paused. 'Like my Action Men. Then I thought, Dad'll want to buy all that stuff for them himself.'

A sudden sob jerked out of him. 'Will they take our place, Mum? Will Dad love the babies more than us?'

'Of course he won't,' Amanda lied, holding Sean tight against the beating of her heart. 'You'll always be just as important to him as they are.'

On the way to the hospital they stopped so Sean could buy a comic. While he was in the newsagent Amanda called Giles on his mobile. 'Make a big fuss of Sean,' she whispered to her ex-husband. 'He's really worried you won't love him any more.'

Amanda straightened her shoulders, trying to ease away the tension of attempting to protect everyone else from pain. She tended to forget that she was hurting too. Pain had a habit of jumping out at you no matter how hard you tried to make yourself be practical and unemotional. Like now. Here she was, taking Sean to see Giles's new children, and yet if it wasn't for Sean she'd rather be anywhere else on earth.

As the hospital's automatic doors opened, a whole layer of memories tumbled out. This was where she'd had Clio and Sean.

Suddenly the image of herself, holding Clio wrapped in a white lacy shawl, imprinted itself on her mind. It was the morning after the birth and already she'd forgotten the pain and indignity of labour. All she could feel was the miraculous happiness of holding her firstborn baby.

'Are you all right, Mum?' Sean asked.

No, she wasn't all right. The sense of loss was overwhelming. How had it all gone so wrong?

'I'm fine,' Amanda lied, willing herself to be strong. All she could do now was limit the fall-out. And if she felt pain in this situation, how much worse must it be for Sean?

Fortunately they didn't have to hunt around for the twins. To Amanda's startled amazement, Giles was standing in the middle of the ward holding them both, a muslin nappy liner thrown over each shoulder to protect him from any stray puke. He reminded Amanda of a smug TV chef, boasting, 'And here are two I made earlier.'

'Hello, son,' he greeted Sean with a rare flash of tact. 'Scored any more goals for Man U lately? I hope this little lad's going to be half as good at free kicks as you are.'

Amanda smiled at him gratefully.

'What are you calling him?' Sean enquired.

'I thought maybe Beckham Giggs Keane Barthez Wells.' Giles suggested. 'What do you think?'

'Nah,' Sean advised seriously, 'it'd be dead embarrassing for him. The players might have all changed by the time he's grown up. Had you thought of that?'

'You're absolutely right. How about Jack?'

Sean mulled it over. 'Yeah. That's cool, actually. How about her?' He jerked his head towards the other twin.

'We thought Jill. What do you reckon?'

'Da-aad! Everyone will laugh at her something rotten.'

'I hadn't thought of that. Emily, then?'

'Hmm. It's OK. For a girl.'

Amanda felt a disconcerting wave of tenderness towards Giles. Would they have had more children themselves if they'd stayed together? Sean was only ten. Plenty of mothers had last-chance babies when their youngest was older than Sean.

Amanda dragged herself back to reality. If they'd had another baby Giles would still have left and she would have had to bring it up on her own.

Stephanie, Amanda noted, was sitting up in bed looking as if a photographer from *Harpers & Queen*, circa 1950, were about to turn up at any moment. She was wearing more make-up than a weather girl and her hair looked as if Nicky Clarke had nipped in and done a blow-dry.

'How are the babies sleeping?' Amanda enquired.

'Oh, they both sleep right through the night,' Stephanie announced calmly.

Amanda gulped. Her own babies had never given her more than three hours' sleep for weeks. 'At four days old?'

'What Stephanie means,' translated Giles, 'is that she puts them in the nursery and ignores them until a nurse or one of the other mothers gets so fed up they give them a bottle.'

'Aren't you breastfeeding?' Amanda asked.

'With two of them? Good God, no. I'd end up with two deflated beach balls on my chest. Actually, Giles has proved quite useful. He can even feed them both at once. I suppose it must be all his previous experience.'

Amanda tried not to cough into her plastic cup of coffee. Giles had never fed either Sean or Clio once, even when Amanda had had flu. Her mother had been more use than Giles, which was saying something because Helen had about as much maternal instinct as Cruella de Vil.

The tenderness she'd felt earlier turned to fury. How bloody typical that Giles hadn't done a hand's turn with their children, even managing to miss Clio's birth, and now he was going for Olympic gold in New Fatherhood. 'And I suppose he's changing nappies too, is he?' she asked.

'There are limits,' Stephanie conceded. She dropped her voice and leaned forward. 'He draws the line at nappies. But that doesn't stop him criticising me. Apparently I don't put enough Sudocrem on their bums when I do it.'

Amanda wondered if she could really be hearing this. The old Giles would have thought Sudocrem was a German province.

'Oh yes,' sighed Stephanie, 'he's an absolutely wonderful father.'

Amanda was about to quip sarcastically, 'Well, there's always a first time for everything,' when she remembered Sean's presence. She winked at him and Sean winked back.

'Can I pick them up?' Sean requested.

Giles held out Emily. 'She's the firstborn. She's a bit more robust. Now, remember, put a hand under her head and hold her tight against your chest. Babies like to feel as though they're still held safe in the mother's womb. That's why they like being swaddled up tight.'

The sight was almost too much for Amanda to bear. If things had been different, this would have been Sean's baby sister. 'We ought to go now,' Amanda reminded Sean gently. 'School tomorrow.'

Sean handed Emily back as if she were made of exquisite crystal. 'She's very sweet.' And then he added, as if to redeem his masculinity, 'For a baby.'

'No Clio?' Giles enquired.

'I'm afraid she didn't want to come.' Amanda was damned if she was going to protect Giles from the truth.

271

'Thanks for bringing Sean anyway,' Giles said quietly when Sean went to help himself to water from the water cooler. 'It must be difficult for you but it means a lot to us.'

Amanda nodded, taken by surprise by this sudden streak of sensitivity. During their marriage, Giles had been about as sensitive as an insurance salesman closing a deal. 'It means a lot to Sean too. Thanks for making him feel special.'

'I'll give Clio a ring, shall I? Maybe she'll see them when they're at home.'

'Perhaps. She's acting tough but she's actually quite vulnerable at the moment. She's really quite fragile under all the bravado.'

'You're a good mother, Amanda.'

Amanda felt her eyes blur at Giles's unexpected compliment. If she wasn't careful she was going to cry.

She was saved by the reappearance of the old, controlling Giles. 'Watch out, Steph,' he suddenly ordered his new wife, who was attempting to put Jack back in the transparent plastic cot by the bed. 'You haven't even burped him yet. He'll just throw the lot up.'

As if on cue, Jack produced a stream of yellow posset.

'What did I tell you?' demanded Giles with satisfaction.

Amanda smiled to herself. Giles the caring new dad was actually Giles the grumpy old dad in disguise.

What's more, his new-found expertise in matters of childcare could get more than a little irritating.

'Bye, Dad,' Sean waved. 'Bye, Stephanie. Bye, babies.'

On the way home neither of them talked much, both lost in their separate thoughts.

'They're a bit boring, aren't they?' Sean volunteered just as they got to the end of their road.

'Emily and Jack?' Amanda asked, relieved. At least he didn't sound too hurt by their arrival. 'Well, babies are a bit boring.'

'I didn't mean the babies. I meant Dad and Stephanie.'

They got home a few minutes later to find Clio sitting on the wall across the road.

'What on earth are you doing there?' Amanda asked. It was getting quite dark and the house was lit up invitingly.

'Forgot my keys.'

'Luke must be in. Didn't you try the door?' She cast a swift look at Clio. 'Are you all right?' Amanda asked softly. 'Why on earth didn't you just ring the doorbell?'

The door suddenly opened and Luke stood there, barefoot, in blue jeans and a white T-shirt. Even after a day's work he looked just-washed and sexy.

'Clio forgot her keys. She was sitting on the wall.'

'That's a funny thing to do, Clio,' he said lightly. 'You must have known I was here. All the lights are on.'

But Clio didn't reply. 'How was Dad?' she asked. 'And the twin spawn of the she-devil?'

Isobel Day woke up hoping she would never have another night like that. The pain had been intolerable. So much so that she had allowed Angus to stay again. She knew she only had to say the word and her morphine dose would be doubled. Or tripled. But to give in to the lures of morphia would mean slipping into a half-world from which she knew she wouldn't emerge.

Isobel wished she had some religious faith, but God, it seemed to Isobel, was for the faint-hearted. A comforting invention to distract the world from the cruel and crippling blows of fate. She had tended, during her reasonably long lifetime, to believe in Man instead. And she hadn't always been disappointed.

She had also taken enormous pleasure in nature. She could hear it now, outside her window. The sounds of spring. Wood pigeons cooing. A lawnmower. She could imagine the garden. Bluebells everywhere, the first early roses, blossom on the trees. Birds trilling extraordinary songs either to protect their young or attract mates. It was all, it seemed to Isobel, about the future. Bees pollinating flowers, bluebells self-seeding, birds producing eggs. The job of nature was to reproduce.

A wall of silent sadness surrounded her. Not because she was dying. That, in its way, was part of nature too. She would soon be part of that process and the idea rather appealed to her. She would be buried, not cremated, because she wanted to join in that regeneration.

Her deepest pain was about Angus. In the world's eyes he was a success. He had made money and he had made a difference. Both these things mattered to Isobel. And he also had the people who worked for him to offer respect and loyalty.

But he didn't have a wife or family of his own.

And, perhaps more importantly, he didn't have the woman she knew he loved.

She glanced over at the courting herons on the windowsill and for the first time they seemed to her unutterably sad, their wooing arrested, frozen for ever in desperate longing.

And Isobel, a tough, unsentimental woman who had fought her illness with strength and dignity, found the pillow she leaned on to be wet with her tears.

'What's all this?' Angus's voice, jagged with love and emotion, penetrated her consciousness. 'My mother crying?' He sat gently down on the edge of the bed. 'Bad night?'

'Not good. It won't be long, you know.'

He took her hand and stroked the prominent blue veins. 'Is that why you're crying?'

'If you must know, I was weeping with frustration.'

'What about? I'll get you anything you want. Would you like to go outside? Spring's bursting out in the garden.'

'Forget the bloody garden! It's you I'm frustrated with. There's someone in your life you love and yet you're letting her throw herself away on a good-looking lightweight.'

'So what do you suggest I do?'

'Tell her. Tell her you're in love with her. Tell her that if she ever needs you, you're there. That life isn't a rehearsal, that you don't happen to have world enough and time, and that she ought to bloody well wake up and see that you're the best man . . .'

'And the best man wins . . .'

'Don't crack stupid jokes. I'm serious. I'll die peacefully if I know you've at least stopped pretending to be civilised. The English are civilised, they specialise in it. You're a Scot.'

'So you think I should paint my arse with woad and go into the fray like Mel Gibson in *Braveheart*?'

'Yes. As a matter of fact, I do. Now where are my wretched pills? This pain is killing me.' She reached a hand up to his face. 'Promise.'

'Promise what?'

'That you'll go today. If not today, then as soon as possible. Tell her how you feel.'

'Not today. I've got to spend all day negotiating with the council. Trying to get them to leave that chalet. I blame you for that.'

'Good for you. Tomorrow then. Promise. Repeat after me – I will tell Amanda Wells that I love her, that she is living with the wrong man. I will then kiss her.'

'For God's sake, Maw.'

'Repeat.'

Angus repeated.

When he looked into his mother's room half an hour later, after her nurse had arrived, he saw that she was sleeping. With a smile on her face.

He supposed he owed her this.

But he was going to feel damn stupid doing it.

Chapter 24

Amanda had only just opened the gallery and made herself a large cup of bracing coffee when Sadie exploded through the door, enveloped in a bright blue kaftan with matching African-style turban, grinning like a mad woman.

'You're never going to believe this,' she fizzed, 'but I've been invited on to a radio programme. By the BBC! In London!'

'Sadie, that's fantastic! What do they want you to talk about?'

'What made me decide to become an artist at seventy-seven. They reckon I'm the Mary Wesley of the visual arts! It's going to be broadcast tomorrow, live at eight o'clock. And Amanda, I said I wouldn't consider doing it unless you came on the programme too!'

'Me?' The utter horror of being live on radio made Amanda feel faint. But she was a businesswoman now. Louise would have jumped at the chance. 'Will they credit the gallery?'

'You'll have to mention it yourself. If it's live they can't edit it out then, can they?'

After Sadie had left, Amanda didn't have much time to think about the horror of the broadcast. She had a steady stream of browsers and card buyers all day, as well as one lady who stood in front of a picture of Sadie's for so long that Amanda finally went up to her. 'She's going to be interviewed on the radio tomorrow night. Eight p.m. on Radio Four.'

'I'll make a point of listening,' the customer answered. 'And maybe I'll come back and buy the picture.'

There was something about the woman's intense demeanour that convinced Amanda she was serious. Things were really taking off!

'Guess what,' she boasted nervously to Clio next morning. 'I'm going to be on the radio tonight.'

'What on earth for?' Clio demanded, looking up from the TV programme she was watching instead of getting ready for school. 'It's not something to do with your ghastly book group, is it? If so, could you not say your name's Wells?'

'Actually, it's to do with the gallery. It seems I may have discovered a rather important new artist.'

'The seagull woman? I've always quite liked her stuff.'

'No, actually it's Sadie, my seventy-seven-year-old prodigy.'

'Prodigies have to be young, Mum,' corrected Sean.

'Like Ruth Lawrence, the maths girl, and all those horrible six-year-olds who can beat Kasparov?'

'I was thinking of Michael Owen actually,' Sean admitted.

'You would be.' She hugged him till he struggled. 'You've got a football where your brain should be. Anyway, it means I'll be out till late. GG is going to have you for the night.'

'Oh, Mu-um,' Sean complained. 'I hate going to Gran's during the week. She makes me go to bed at seven-thirty and eat peas 'n' stuff.'

'It'll be good for you. How about you, Clio? Do you want to go to Gran's?'

'God, no.' Clio jumped up, exhibiting four inches of silky midriff as she did. She was getting more stunning every day. She'd even been stopped when she was out on the pier with Jasmine by a man claiming to be a photographer. Amanda didn't know whether the man was genuine or not but Clio was certainly at that child-woman stage that some men found incredibly attractive. And not always the right men, either. Unfortunately, boys of Clio's own age seemed as if they came from the planet Pimple.

'Luke might be in. You could stay here with him.'

Clio hesitated. 'Maybe I'll go to Gran's then.'

Amanda almost lost her temper. This thing with Luke was getting silly. 'Look, Clio, what exactly is your problem with Luke?' Amanda couldn't keep the irritation from her voice.

Suddenly all the tension and pain of holding her family together, of being the strong one for everyone, was too much for Amanda. 'I think you're jealous,' she flashed. 'You don't like me being involved with Luke because you want all my attention yourself. But I am, Clio. Luke makes me very happy. It may be annoying and inconvenient for you – but at least I haven't had twins.'

Clio flushed and Amanda caught the glint of tears in her eyes. Amanda was immediately grief-stricken. 'I'm sorry. I shouldn't have said that. It's just that sometimes it can be quite hard to keep everyone happy.'

'Don't worry. I'll be fine with Luke. As long as he promises not to watch one of those black and white films with subtitles.'

Amanda smiled gratefully. 'I'll make it a condition.' She loved Clio so much, but she had to have her own life too.

'I'd better get off to school.' For once Clio had her school bag packed and ready.

'See you tonight. I should be back by eleven-thirty.'

After Clio had left, Luke came into the kitchen. He was wearing blue jeans and a denim shirt that had that lovely just-washed smell to it. Unlike Giles, Luke did all his own shirts, which made the scent all the sweeter.

He came up behind Amanda and kissed her neck.

Sean concentrated on reading the Cheerios packet.

'You look gorgeous today,' Luke murmured.

'It's for the radio interview. And don't tell me you don't need to dress up for radio, Clio's already pointed it out. I need to look my best to be able to open my mouth. Irrational, but true.'

'What was the row with Clio about? I've hardly ever heard you shout.'

'She was being a bit funny about tonight.'

'Funny in what way?' He put some bread in the toaster.

'Oh, you know, she didn't want to go to my mother's with Sean.'

'Why couldn't she just stay here with me?'

Amanda struggled to find words that wouldn't offend him.

'She doesn't like staying in with you,' Sean announced, still reading the cereal packet. 'She says you always watch black and white films with subtitles.'

'Is that all?' There was a curious edge to Luke's tone which Amanda would have picked up on if she hadn't been so preoccupied with childcare and the interview. 'In that case, we'll watch something completely different. In fact, I'll get a takeaway and a video she *will* like.'

Amanda heard the last bit of his speech and was touched at how hard he was trying to forge some kind of relationship with Clio. And how unlikely it was that Clio would appreciate the effort. She must have another talk with Clio about Luke. But not today.

Angus Day was discovering that once a local council decides to purchase a property – in this case Rose and Betty's chalet – they could be very stubborn about changing their minds. Rose and Betty would have to launch a formal appeal, he was informed, and the whole project would be delayed for months, maybe even years. But the complexity of that was nothing compared to his other obligation, the one he'd made to his mother.

It was one thing to agree for his dying mother's sake that he would tell Amanda how he felt about her, but it wasn't at all easy to see how he could actually do it, or how she would react if he did.

'You look as if you've just seen Tam O'Shanter's ghost,' Laddie commented. 'You've been sitting at yon desk for ten minutes now, staring at a brick wall. Does it have any answers for you?'

'None at all,' Angus smiled. He hadn't been aware he'd been looking so preoccupied.

'So what's the problem, if you don't mind my asking? We're not going down the Swanee, are we?'

'No,' reassured Angus. 'Not yet, anyway. Though if this harbour development gets well and truly snarled up, you never know. But it's not that I'm thinking about.'

Laddie hadn't known Angus for twenty-five years for nothing. "'My love is like a red, red rose,'" he quoted, dropping down on one knee. "'That's newly sprung in June.'"

Angus laughed. 'And what if my love happens to prefer someone else? I'm not sure even Burns had an answer for that one.'

'Pity mortal combat went out of fashion.' Laddie struggled back to his feet. Years of working on freezing building sites had stiffened his joints. 'It made affairs of the heart so much simpler.'

'So you think I should call him out, do you?'

'Or find a way of showing that you're the better man.'

'And how the hell am I going to do that?'

'Angus, lad, you're the one with the education. I'm a humble navvy. This type she's involved with, appeared on the scene out of nowhere, didn't he, and moved in with Mrs Wells pretty damn quick. Maybe you should find out a little bit more about him.'

'Laddie, you're a genius. Do you know what my old dad used to say? "Never trust a man who's too good-looking or too well-dressed".'

'And Mr Luke Knight is a good-looking man, right enough.'

'Not to mention ludicrously well-dressed. If you like denim.'

'Your honour,' grinned Laddie, 'I rest my cast.'

There was only one problem: how the hell was he going to find out more about Luke Knight? He wondered how Amanda and he had come to meet in the first place. Luke Knight wasn't from round here. He had that slightly supercilious London air about him. Had they met through one of those crazy ads she'd placed?

He smiled, remembering the tiny man in the wine bar, and her obvious panic when she'd realised he was her date. Had Luke Knight replied to a similar ad? Somehow he didn't seem the type.

A snatch of conversation he'd had with Clio came back to him. He dimly remembered Clio telling him that Louise was boasting that she'd brought them together. Luke Knight had been due at the New Year's Eve party where Angus had so nearly made love to Amanda. How ironic.

Angus looked at his watch. It was 4.30 in the afternoon already. Would Louise still be at the gallery?

*

Halfway through the afternoon, Amanda began to feel palm-sweatingly, nail-bitingly, nauseatingly nervous. She'd never done a radio interview before, let alone a live one, and certainly not on a national radio station that was listened to by almost everyone she knew. Would she dry up altogether? Or gabble on incomprehensibly? Or find some entirely novel way of putting her foot in her mouth? Sadie would be fine; she was a natural and old enough not to give a stuff about what other people thought of her.

Amanda was just considering the option of a diplomatic illness, and realising that Sadie would probably drag her there bodily if she tried it, when Luke appeared at the door of the gallery carrying a bunch of roses. They were those slightly withered roses that were sold at the side of roads, but the thought was there.

'For you.' He smiled his warmest, come-into-my-arms smile. 'To wish you good luck. You're going to be great.'

All her feelings of irritation at him dried up. He might not be the most natural family man, but he was trying.

'Thank you.' She hugged him gratefully. 'I'll put them here next to the till. They can remind me of the kind of gallery Marine Arts will be one day, with huge vases of fresh flowers everywhere.'

'And loads of customers.' He glanced round the deserted room, but there was no suggestion of criticism in his tone.

'With bulging wallets,' Amanda added.

'And lots of rich friends. See you later.'

After his visit, Amanda calmed down a lot. There was nothing like feeling loved to make you get things into proportion.

She combed her hair, touched up her make-up and slipped into the tiny loo to get changed, carefully locking the till before she did.

When she emerged, looking what she hoped was smart and Londonish, her mother was just arriving with Sean in tow to mind the gallery. Amanda did a double-take. Her mother was wearing an artist's smock.

'Hello, dear,' Helen greeted her. 'Aren't you a little late?'

Amanda thought about explaining that the reason she was late was because she'd been waiting for Helen to arrive, but decided not to. It was kind of her mother to gallery-sit.

She grabbed her bag and kissed Sean. 'Thanks for looking after him, Mum. I may be a bit late back.'

In the end, Sadie and Amanda had to make a mad dash to get the early evening train. As she sat in the carriage, Amanda thought about Clio's attitude. Tomorrow she'd have a real heart-to-heart with her and see what could be done to improve things.

'Look,' Sadie interrupted her thoughts, 'here's the nice man with the drinks trolley. I don't care if it's only teatime. I'm gong to have a large Bloody Mary. It isn't every day one gets catapulted to fame at seventy-seven. Besides, it'll relax me.'

Sadie was so relaxed by the time they got to Victoria Station that she had to go into the ladies' toilets to have a wash and brush-up.

'Twenty pence!' Sadie announced indignantly when she re-emerged. 'They wanted twenty pence just for me to use the ladies! Whatever happened to spending a penny? They'll want damn credit cards next. I shall write and complain.' With great dignity, only dented a little by the fact that her skirt was caught in her knickers, Sadie walked over and demanded the name and address of the duty manager.

They finally arrived at the studios just before seven. The programme's researcher turned out to be nothing like her posh voice. She had blue hair and a nose stud, not to mention studs in quite a lot of other places. She was extremely friendly and obviously intrigued by Sadie.

'My grandmother's just like her,' the blue-haired girl confided to Amanda, 'absolutely outrageous. The only people she says are worth listening to are her horse and her dog. I love her to bits.'

To Amanda's relief and delight, when it was her turn to be interviewed she managed to be quite entertaining and even to get in a plug for the gallery.

Sadie, as Amanda had known she would be, was a star. She had the presenter in fits of laughter with her stories of life in the OAP-belt and told some wonderfully unsuitable tales of posing as an artists' model for life classes in a men's prison.

'They'll be handing you your own show,' whispered Amanda as the programme finished.

'That was absolutely amazing,' enthused the blue-haired researcher. 'I was going to offer you a coffee in the canteen, but after all those stories of you popping out of a cake wearing only sequins I think we'd better go somewhere a bit more stylish.'

She led them over busy Portland Place to a very smart hotel where they sipped dry martinis in the Palm Court, surrounded by rather shocked businessmen.

The researcher, whose name was Marianne, seemed totally unmoved by the glances her hair was attracting. Amanda hoped Clio would share the girl's effortless confidence one day.

'I used to have hair your colour,' Sadie teased, ordering herself another dry martini. 'Only I gave it up. Too conventional!'

Marianne roared with laughter.

In fact they had such a good time that it was after ten before Amanda looked at her watch. The last train was in half an hour. If they weren't careful, they'd miss it.

'So you've finally got round to giving me a call,' Louise purred. She and Angus were sitting on the terrace bar of the Grand Hotel, with the best sea view in the town stretched out before them. Even though it was early in the season, the good weather had brought out the first sunbathers, who were lying on brightly coloured beach towels catching the last of the early evening rays.

Angus would have preferred somewhere more discreet but Louise insisted on sitting here, where the whole of Laineton could see them, and then ordered a large jug of Pimm's.

'I never drink anything else between the months of May and September,' she announced grandly. 'It makes me think of cricket matches and rowing at Henley and picnicking at the Derby.'

'I've only ever had tea at cricket matches, or extremely cloudy beer,' Angus observed. 'Henley is full of Hoorays drinking cheap champagne, and the only time I've been to the Derby I was mooned at by a drunk with a rose up his bum. I think I'll stick to malt whisky.'

'All the more for me, then. How's the world of property development? Are you still making obscene profits out of throwing old ladies onto the street?'

Angus flinched.

'Silly me, I was making a joke. I'd forgotten you actually *are* throwing old ladies on the street.'

'Not on the street. Into a luxury two-bedroom flat with wrap-around balcony and magnificent sea views.'

'Pity. I rather liked the thought of you as a ruthless capitalist, deaf to the cries of those too weak to resist you.' Louise batted her heavily mascaraed eyes.

She studied Angus Day's expression. What did those flinty grey eyes of his reveal? There was a subtle strength about Angus that she'd been drawn to from the start. He was self-contained, certain about himself. The kind of man who knew exactly what to do in life. And in bed.

'I'd never describe you as weak, Louise. I think you're probably tougher than I am.'

'Any time you want to put it to the test . . .'

'I'll bear it in mind. If you're still speaking to me.'

'Why would I not be?'

'Probably when I confess why I really rang you.'

Louise's glass froze halfway to her lips. He'd called her because he had an ulterior motive. For a second she considered throwing her Pimm's over him. Of course he hadn't rung her because he wanted to invite her out for her own sake. How dumb could a woman be? 'You want to talk about Amanda,' she said coldly.

'Not Amanda. Or at least not directly. I wondered how well you knew Luke Knight.'

Louise hesitated. 'Not very well at all really. He used to go out with someone I know and she told me he was coming to Laineton. Amanda was lonely. Luke was gorgeous. What could I do?'

'That was very unselfish of you.' His grey eyes held hers. 'Weren't you interested in this paragon yourself?'

'Luke's the boyish type.' She held his gaze. 'I prefer men.'

'And that was all you heard? That Luke Knight was gorgeous?'

Louise looked away, her eyes focusing on a lone bather who was striking out for the horizon. If she kept quiet, Angus might get over Amanda.

Amanda wasn't that much more attractive than she was. Why should she have two men pursuing her when Louise spent night after night alone? She suddenly felt furious with Amanda, who had a lover as well as a family, for the fact that she'd so thoughtlessly set up her own gallery so near to Louise's, no doubt stealing half of Louise's clients.

'I did hear something else,' she added maliciously.

'And what was that?'

'That Luke Knight is incredible in bed.'

If she'd expected to see pain in Angus's grey eyes she was disappointed. He simply put down his glass and stood up. 'You stay and finish your drink. I'll settle up at the bar. Thanks for your time.'

Louise stared out at the horizon again, biting her lip. She drained her glass in one long gulp.

On the beach a young girl stood up and shook the sand from her towel. She was about sixteen, slender, with a stud in her belly button. Young girls these days were tough and confident, they took so much in their stride, even harsh things, she told herself. Then she remembered Clio coming into the gallery over the years, growing from toddler to child, and how sometimes she'd imagined, if things had been different, that she might have had a daughter like her.

She stood up and hurried over to the bar.

'Before you go, Angus, there was one other thing I heard about Luke. It's only hearsay, something Ruthie from our book group told me. Apparently, a while ago, Luke got involved with someone Ruthie knew slightly from her college days. Ruthie's friend and Luke were very happy together, then the whole thing broke up.' She paused, as if still uncertain whether to go on.

'Why did it break up, Louise?'

Louise hesitated, her usual domineering confidence temporarily deserting her. She had the sudden air, it struck Angus, of a plucked parrot.

'Because Luke tried to seduce her teenage daughter.'

Chapter 25

'Bloody hell!' Amanda was pulling Sadie along the platform, which wasn't easy given that Sadie had had more to drink than a squaddie on leave and kept tripping over her kaftan. 'There goes our train. Just sit here and I'll find out if there's another we can catch.'

Amanda ran back along the platform as fast as her rather too high heels allowed her. The station concourse, usually bristling with commuters and tourists, had just a few drunken revellers in one corner and some crumpled backpackers asleep in another. A cleaner was desultorily picking up fast-food wrappers. The ticket office was firmly closed and there was no sign of a rail official anywhere. Amanda surveyed the departure board. There were no more direct trains to Laineton tonight. Her heart leapt when she saw there was one last service to Maynard's Heath. That was two-thirds of the way to Laineton. At least if they had to get a cab from there the cost would be nothing comparing to hiring one all the way from London.

'Come on, Sadie, we've got to rush to another platform. The last train leaves in five minutes,' she gasped breathlessly as she returned to her friend. But Sadie, finally overcome by fame and liquid refreshment, had fallen asleep.

Amanda fought back panic. She was a grown woman, she had a

credit card. They weren't marooned in the Sahara desert without a compass.

She was about to give up and head for the taxi rank when a voice behind her said, 'Can I give you a hand, madam?'

It belonged to a young Ethiopian man with a wide, bright smile.

'Thanks a lot,' Amanda said gratefully. 'I just have to get her to platform six.'

Together they half-carried Sadie across the main concourse, past the closed-up Costa Coffee and magazine stall, and on to the train, just moments before it departed.

'That was incredibly kind of you,' Amanda gasped.

'It was a pleasure,' the young man said in his slightly formal English.

Sadie sat up suddenly and looked around. 'Where are we?' She caught sight of the smiling young man. 'Addis Ababa?'

'Sadly no.' He smiled again. 'Victoria Station.'

He stood waving as they left the station, a startling figure of forlorn dignity, his eyes taking on a hint of sadness as the train disappeared into the darkness.

'Thank God for that,' breathed Amanda. 'I'll just call home and let them know we'll be late.'

She hit the buttons on her mobile. She heard eight or ten rings but no one picked it up, yet the answering machine wasn't switched on either. A slight feeling of panic shuddered through her. It was just possible they were asleep and hadn't heard the phone, but Luke rarely went to bed early. In fact, as Sean had pointed out, he quite often stayed downstairs and watched his beloved black and white classics while she went up on her own and read in bed.

Damn it, her battery was low. She only had half a bar left. In desperation she rang her mother. Helen would be furious but she'd just have to take the risk.

'Hello,' said a sleepy voice. 'This is Helen Mason speaking.'

'Mum,' Amanda blurted, 'I'm sorry to call you so late but we missed our train and we're having to catch one to Maynard's Heath. I'll find a taxi there. The thing is, I've tried to call Luke or Clio to tell them and I can't get through. No one's picking up and now my bloody battery's going. Could you keep calling them for me?'

'They've probably gone to bed, like any other sane person,' Helen said irritably.

'No. Luke never goes to bed this early. He must be up. Please, Mother.'

'You're such a worrier, Amanda. You always were. I'll try a couple of times. After that I'm going to sleep.' The phone clicked as her mother hung up. Amanda's battery had gone completely dead now. She wouldn't even be able to call for a minicab. So much for modern global communication. Still, they'd have payphones at Maynard's Heath. She'd be home soon, tucked up in bed, realising how silly she'd been to panic.

Beside her, Sadie snored peacefully. Fortunately Maynard's Heath was the end of the line and she'd have plenty of time to get Sadie off the train and on to her feet.

Angus ran along the seafront back towards his BMW. It staggered and disgusted him that Louise could consider herself a friend, or even an ex-friend, and not tell Amanda the rumour about Luke.

Louise had tried to suggest that to do so would be interfering. It wasn't as if, she'd argued, Clio was a toddler prey to some pervert. She was a strong personality who'd be more than able to stand up for herself if anything were to happen.

Angus climbed behind the wheel and wondered what the hell to do next. The thought occurred to him that he might be wrecking his own chances with Amanda if he interfered and that she might try and dismiss his allegations as jealousy. But surely, if what Louise had just told him were true, she must have *some* suspicions about Luke.

Angus put the car into gear and drove out through the town towards the Downs and his home. His mother's light was on, he noticed as he passed her cottage, which meant she was probably not sleeping. The nurse's light, on the other hand, was out.

He parked outside Isobel's house and let himself in with his own key.

The nurse was sitting by the television, fast asleep.

He went quietly upstairs.

'Hello?' said his mother's voice, with a tiny edge of fear in it.

'Don't worry, Maw, it's only me.'

She smiled faintly. 'Well I knew it wasn't the Grim Reaper; he doesn't usually arrive by car.'

'How are you feeling tonight?'

'Woozy. I took some extra tablets for the pain but I still can't get off to sleep. So now I've got the pain and insomnia. Nice evening?'

'Not really. I've been thinking about my promise to you.'

'About Amanda?'

'Yes. And it struck me that I've always distrusted Luke Knight. Dad used to say that if you think you don't trust someone you're usually right so I did a little bit of investigating. Luke Knight was thrown out by a previous girlfriend because he made a pass at her daughter.'

'Oh, Angus, what a horrible situation. And you're concerned about Clio.'

'She's such a fantastic girl, Maw. Everyone liked her when she came to work with us; she even had the electricians eating out of her hand and you know how tricky they can be. But she's vulnerable too. I'm not sure she's really over her parents' divorce.'

'And you feel you've got to tell Amanda?'

'Of course I've got to tell her.'

'She may not thank you.'

'No. But she may not thank me if I *don't* tell her either.'

'Poor Angus. You don't have much choice, do you?'

'Poor Clio. If that bastard were to lay a hand on her . . .'

'The sooner the better then, I suppose. You are sure? It's a pretty unpleasant charge to bring.'

'I know.'

He dropped down to his knees next to the bed and very gently kissed her forehead.

'You're a good son. I just wish your life wasn't so complicated.'

Angus smiled. 'Maybe I like it this way. I've never been the slippers and pipe type.'

'There is a middle way.'

He stroked her short grey hair tenderly. 'I could have settled down, you know, if I'd wanted. You and Dad were so happy, despite all the knocks you had. I just didn't want to go for something less.'

'That's the best defence I've heard yet of being too fussy.'

Angus laughed. 'You could be right. I'm going to wake the nurse on my way out.'

He shook the nurse awake, trying to convey his irritation without making her resentful. 'I'd like you to increase her dose tonight. Just so that she can sleep.' His mother was in too much pain not to get any rest. And now he'd given her even more to lie awake and worry about.

As he turned down the drive, his house loomed out of the dark at him, huge and empty. He always asked his cleaner to leave lights on so that it would seem welcoming when he got home, but his mother had hired him a parsimonious Scot, like herself, who always took pleasure in turning every last one off.

Angus went round switching them all on again so that the house blazed like Versailles on a ball night. Then he sat down in his comfortable kitchen and poured himself another whisky. What if the rumour about Luke was indeed fabrication? Some malicious slur against him by an abandoned lover? Should he go round now? He pictured himself rousing them all from their beds and assembling them like in a third-rate Agatha Christie. There'd be no harm in driving past the house. It would probably be as normal as apple pie.

Before he could remind himself that driving past your lover's home for no apparent reason was the act of a seriously disturbed person, he was in the car and speeding back towards Laineton.

It wasn't even ten o'clock by the time he drove through the town and yet the place was deserted. Amanda's house was about halfway down her street. It was tall and pastel-coloured and had always reminded him faintly of a doll's house. There were no lights on and no sign of life.

Sitting outside, Angus felt a chill of apprehension. Was he certifiably insane, waiting here like a misguided guard dog?

Trust your instincts, his father had said.

Angus, suspecting he might regret this step for the rest of his life, got out of his car and opened the gate.

Chapter 26

Luke wandered around the empty sitting room, tidying up. He wanted the atmosphere to be calm. He plumped up the cushions, telling himself he was behaving like a jumpy housewife, and lit one small scented candle. Nothing too obvious. Tonight would be special. Just the two of them.

He couldn't wait.

'So what are you going to do tonight?' Clio's friend Jasmine asked her. 'Are you sleeping over or what?'

'I'd rather stay at your house. My mum's boyfriend gives me the creeps.'

'What, the good-looking one? What does he do? Drool over you?'

'I've just caught him looking at me a few times.'

'Well, you can stay if you want. The only thing is, my mum and dad are in so we'll have to be quiet.'

'Fine by me. Better than Luke giving me one of his smouldering looks.'

Jasmine's bedroom was on the middle floor, just above the TV room where her parents were watching *ER*.

'So, when's your mum on the radio?' she asked.

'At eight, I think. But we don't have to listen.'

'I suppose you'll get all posh now that your mum's been on Radio Four,' Jasmine teased.

'No, I won't!'

'Bet you will.'

Clio reached for one of the pillows on Jasmine's girlie-girlie bed. 'I will not.'

'Girls!' shouted Jasmine's mum. 'Shut it, will you? We're watching the telly!'

'Silly old bat.' Jasmine jumped up on to the bed and picked up another pillow and thumped Clio with it. 'They've seen them all before anyway. My mum just fancies the foreign one.'

Clio replied in kind while they both squealed with laughter.

'Right,' Jasmine's father shouted from downstairs, 'don't be so bloody selfish.'

'Sorry, Dad.' Jasmine tended to listen to her father because he was the one who paid her allowance.

The two girls sat on the bed. Jasmine reached for her school backpack and rummaged round in it. 'Fancy a bit of this?' She pulled out a badly fashioned joint from one of the bag's many pockets.

Clio looked at it. She'd had a puff a few times after school, but never a whole joint. The joint looked as if it had been in Jasmine's bag for months and might fall apart at any moment.

'You can't!' Clio hissed, scandalised. 'Not with your parents downstairs. They might smell it.'

'Silly old farts,' Jasmine dismissed. 'Anyway, I'll get the air freshener from the bathroom. They'll never be able to tell then.'

She returned with a can and a box of matches. 'They light a match when someone's done a stinker. Usually my brother.'

While Clio looked nervously on, Jasmine lit the joint and started to inhale the sweet-smelling smoke. She promptly had a coughing fit and handed it to Clio.

'What the bloody hell do you think you're doing?'

Neither of them had noticed the TV go quiet. Jasmine's father was standing in the doorway, so angry he was hardly recognisable as the mild man who seemed to spend most of his time mowing the lawn. 'You'd better go home right now, young lady,' he instructed Clio.

'And, Jasmine, you are hereby grounded for the next month. No phone calls. No friends. Not even any texting. You'd better learn just how serious it is to take drugs and you might as well start now.'

There was no point trying to argue. Clio meekly picked up her bag. 'Sorry, Mr Mondi. It was a stupid thing to do.'

'Too right it was. Off you go home. In fact, I'll call your mother this minute and get her to come and get you. I'm sure she'll be as angry as I am with you stupid little girls.'

'I'm afraid she's in London this evening. But I can make my own way home.'

'Right. But don't think you're off the hook.'

Clio didn't even dare speak to Jasmine. She just took her coat and bag and left. She wandered miserably along the prom for a while, then went to the pier. Would Jasmine's father really get in touch with her mother? She shuddered at how much it would upset Amanda. How bloody, bloody stupid of them. What had she been thinking of, when Jasmine's parents were just downstairs? It had been asking for trouble.

Eventually she sat down with a group of pensioners who were going to play bingo.

'Want to join us, love?' asked one old lady. 'You'd bring the age range down by about forty years.'

'I'm afraid bingo really isn't my thing.'

She played the arcade games and very nearly won on the machine where you pick up a revolting teddy bear with a mini-crane, but her money ran out just too soon.

So she told herself not to be silly and walked slowly back towards home. For some reason she counted the paving stones between the seafront and their house. There were 3,742, and Clio didn't stand on a single one of the cracks.

She turned her key in the lock and stood in the hall, listening.

'I'm in here,' called Luke. 'I thought we might order a takeaway. Your favourite. Chicken korma.'

It all sounded so boringly normal that Clio relaxed.

It was surprisingly dark in the sitting room and Luke was seated on the sofa.

'And what about some Häagen Dazs for afterwards?'

He sounded like one of those men your mother told you not to take sweets from.

Clio put down her backpack and sat as far away from Luke as possible. 'Thanks. Just a chicken korma would be great.'

He ordered the takeaway, then came and sat down beside her. 'It'll be half an hour. Any thoughts on how to spend it?'

'Whatever you're watching on the video will be fine.'

Luke leaned forward to press the play button, even though the remote control was well within his reach. As he did so, his knee brushed hers. Clio breathed in sharply.

'Don't worry.' Luke was suddenly on top of her, trying to kiss her, his hand lunging for her buttons. 'This is going to be the best moment of your life.'

Clio wanted to scream. It was just like with Gilles, only a hundred times worse because this was the man her mother was in love with.

She struggled to push him off and they both fell to the floor, knocking everything off the coffee table. With all her strength Clio pushed him off and ran towards the door.

But Luke got there before her.

'So.' He leaned on the frame, barring her way and smiling threateningly. 'Who's been a naughty girl, then?' he demanded. He grabbed her shoulders and pulled her towards him.

Clio fought to get out of his reach. 'What the hell are you talking about?'

'I've just had your friend's father on the phone. Smoking joints at your age. Tsk tsk. What other illegal things do you get up to, Clio?'

A panicky fear came over Clio. What should she do now? She tried to remember if her mother had taken her mobile with her. Or could she call her father? Except that he might just laugh. Or ask her to call back after he'd burped the babies.

'If you're very nice to me,' Luke tried to grab her breast again, 'I might promise not to tell your mother. What will you do for me, Clio, if I keep our little secret?'

For an answer, Clio swiped him hard with her backpack, which she'd dumped behind the sofa. It was heavy with schoolbooks.

While Luke swore and nursed his shoulder, Clio made a dash for the front door.

To her stunned gratitude, she found Angus Day outside it.

'Clio, for God's sake!' Angus put a firm hand on each of her shoulders and stopped her in her tracks. 'What the hell's happened?'

'It was Luke . . .' she began, and then started to sob. Had all this been her fault? What would her mother feel? On top of the business about the joint as well.

But Angus didn't wait for any more explanations. 'Here.' He handed her the car keys. 'Get into my car.'

He ran into the house. The sitting room looked as if it had been burgled, with cushions from the sofa and magazines littering the floor.

'What did you do to that girl, you bastard?'

Luke shrugged. 'Don't worry. I didn't even touch her. She's still fresh for you.'

Angus grabbed Luke's shirt collar with one hand and swung a punch at him with the other. He had the satisfaction of seeing blood in the corner of Luke's mouth. 'You'd better get out, Knight.'

Luke just laughed. 'I think I'll wait for Amanda.'

'Tell her Clio will be at my mother's. I'm sure she'll want to hear why from Clio herself.'

He ran back to Clio, who was already sitting huddled in his car. 'For God's sake, where's Amanda?'

'In London. Doing a radio interview.'

'Have you got a mobile number for her?'

He dialled as Clio told him the number. 'Absolute zero. Let's just go to my mother's house. Will you be all right?' He looked at her searchingly. 'Did anything actually happen?'

'He put his hand on my breast and tried to kiss me.'

'Poor Clio. What a shit that man is.'

'Poor Mum. She thinks she loves him.'

'Not after this.'

She smiled faintly. 'I suppose there is that.'

Luke cleared up all the mess and straightened the cushions just as the takeaway arrived. Angrily, he stuffed the cartons into the bin. Amanda would be back soon and he would have to explain Clio's absence. What a silly little girl she'd been. It wasn't as if he'd intended anything serious. Just a little harmless fun.

'How much will that be?' Amanda asked the minicab driver, dreading the reply, when he stopped outside her house.

'Thirty-two pounds, love. Extra rates after midnight.'

Amanda counted out the money. It was literally all she had on her. 'Sorry, I'm afraid I haven't got any over for a tip.'

The driver roared off grumpily. Most drivers at least waited to see that you got inside your own front door, but not this one. So much for generosity of spirit.

Amanda had expected the house to be in darkness but the living room light was on. Luke must be watching one of his famous black and white films. She smiled, remembering Sean's comment about this studenty habit of Luke's.

She was about to get her keys out when the front door opened. Luke stood there, smiling his familiar disarming smile, his fair hair rumpled. He looked like a rather naughty choir boy.

'Hi,' she greeted him. 'I wondered if you might still be up.'

'How did it go? Can I make you a cup of tea?'

'It went brilliantly. Sadie was hilarious. And I even managed to get a plug in for the gallery. And yes, I'd love some tea.'

'You're in later than I expected.'

'Yes,' Amanda admitted, feeling guilty. 'We went to have a few drinks at a posh hotel with the researcher and suddenly it was ten-thirty. I nearly had a heart attack.'

Luke slipped his arms round her. 'Don't worry. You're entitled to a good time, you know.' Amanda sighed, wondering why she ever felt annoyed with him. Giles would have been livid and accused her of being an irresponsible mother.

Amanda sniffed the air, conscious of an unfamiliar but pungent aroma.

'We had a takeaway. Chicken korma.'

'Clio's favourite. You are thoughtful. What time did she go to bed? I hope she didn't go all teenage and bolshy and "I'm too old to have a bedtime" on you.'

'No.' This time it was Luke's turn to look guilty. 'As a matter of fact, she didn't go to bed at all. She went out.'

'*Out?* Where on earth did she go out to at this time? She didn't quarrel with you and storm off?'

'She went off with Angus Day. In his sports car, about ten o'clock.'

'Why would she want to do that?'

'Isn't that obvious? I've been telling you for weeks, Amanda. There's something going on between them. She got very shirty with me when I confronted her about it. I tried to tell her he was too old for her, and that he was exploiting her innocence, and she said that if I didn't shut up she'd tell you that *I* was the one who'd tried it on with her.'

'Clio wouldn't be malicious like that.'

'She would now that she's involved with Day. Older men can be very seductive when they catch girls young enough. He probably worked on her during that stint in his office.'

Amanda had never felt angrier or more revolted by anyone in her life. Angus had known that Clio was vulnerable, that she'd lost her father and been rejected by some sadistic young ski instructor. 'I'm going to see him now, this minute.'

'Amanda . . .' Luke said quickly. 'I really don't think that's a good idea. She probably believes she's wildly in love with him or something. She is sixteen. Maybe if you're too heavy in your opposition it'll backfire. It might make her decide to go and live with him. Surely it'd be better to let her cool down? If you go now she'll probably concoct some cock and bull – sorry, not very tactful use of language – story about it being my fault just to cover her tracks.'

Amanda stopped searching in the bottom of her bag for the car keys. 'Why the hell would she do that?'

'Because she doesn't like me. She's resented me from the moment I moved in. She wants me out. She'd like you to believe the worst of me so you'll send me packing. It's also a handy diversionary tactic from her relationship with Day.'

'Look, Luke.' Amanda felt as if she'd wandered into the plot of some Kafkaesque play. 'I don't really care what Clio says. It's Angus Day I want to kill.' She finally located the keys and brandished them triumphantly.

'OK. But don't expect him to just admit it. Though from what I've heard, it isn't the first time.'

'What do you mean?'

'Oh, just something his foreman said. I should've told you but I didn't want to worry you.'

'What did Laddie say?'

'That the work experience idea would be nice for Angus because he appreciated young girls. "Get her to wear her school uniform, like one of those girls from Saint Trinian's," he said. "That'll have Angus in seventh heaven."'

Amanda felt sick. What if Angus had pursued her when Clio had been his real target? She'd heard of men like that. Yet he'd seemed so generous, so kind to his mother.

'Why didn't you tell me any of this?'

'I thought I was making too much of it, that it was just a joke, but it's obviously gone further than that. Look, Amanda, you're tired. As you said yourself, you've had a drink. Leave it for tonight. She may come back.' He put his hands on her shoulders and smouldered at her like some Calvin Klein male model. 'Come to bed instead. I'll give you a massage. It'll take your mind off it.'

'Leave it alone, Luke!' Amanda snapped. 'As you didn't warn me that my daughter was in danger, you could at least have some sense of occasion now!'

She had already been driving for a couple of miles when she realised the light was flashing on the petrol gauge. How long had it been empty? Panic filled her at the thought of breaking down miles from anywhere. There was an all-night garage out on the bypass but it was in the opposite direction to where she was heading. Would she get to Angus's house before the car ground to a halt?

Swearing at her own incompetence, she did a U-turn and headed for the garage. It wasn't more than four miles away and the tank held enough petrol for fifteen. Surely she'd be all right?

The town was entirely deserted. Even the clubbers seemed to be tucked up in their own beds, or someone else's that they'd picked up. In the distance she could see the bright lighting announcing the Shell station and uttered a huge sigh of relief, just as the car started hiccuping as it gulped the very last dregs of petrol.

'Shit!' Amanda yelled. She even got out and yelled, 'Shit, shit, shit!' at the car.

She was so preoccupied that she didn't notice the unmarked police car that silently drew up behind her.

'Does there seem to be some problem?'

Amanda swung round. 'It's incredibly stupid, I know, but I'm afraid I've run out of petrol.' She tried not to breathe in his general direction. She'd had too much to drink tonight and there was no way she should be driving. Under normal circumstances she would never have dreamed of doing so, but tonight was anything but normal.

'We're not really supposed to help, but as there's no one around I'll get you a gallon.'

The policeman disappeared, leaving Amanda scrabbling round the car in a desperate search for an Extra Strong Mint. There were none. Sean must have polished the last one off.

Ten minutes later the policeman was back with a red plastic safety container of petrol. He poured it in.

Amanda got back in the car and gave him her most alluring smile. 'Good night. Take care now.' Thank God, she'd got away with it. She swore never to drive after drinking again.

She turned on the ignition key and thanked whoever was watching over her.

'Hang on,' the policeman added. 'You've got your seat belt stuck in the door.' He opened the door, released the belt and handed it to Amanda. As he did so, he caught a whiff of Palm Court dry martini and his face changed as swiftly as a child's magic slate. 'I'm sorry to have to say this, but would you mind getting out of the car, please?'

Chapter 27

Clio sat silently hunched up in Angus's car, holding her backpack to her chest like a refugee clinging to her last few possessions.

'Would you like some music on?' Angus asked gently. 'I can just about pick up Capital.'

Clio shook her head and went on staring out of the window. 'What am I going to tell Mum?'

'I don't think you have a lot of choice, do you?'

'But she loves Luke.' He could hear the start of a sob vibrating in Clio's voice.

'Not as much as she loves you.'

'What if she doesn't believe me?'

'Clio.' Angus's voice had all the certainty that had been missing from Clio's life since her parents had split. 'She'll believe you.'

'But she'll be so hurt.'

There was a tiny beat of silence as they sped past the dark outlines of the Downs. 'Yes. She will be hurt. But that's not your fault. Amanda is an adult. She'll recover. And her first concern will be that you're all right. We're almost at my mother's house now.'

Clio could make out the familiar exterior of the gatehouse with the driveway beyond. Angus opened the car door for her and she followed him up Isobel's front path. The night nurse answered the door.

'How's my mother?' Angus asked, beckoning to Clio to follow him.

'Frail, but she's been sleeping well.'

'There's a spare room here, Clio.' Angus led the way upstairs and opened a door off the landing. 'I thought you might feel more at home here than up at the big house. It can be a tad scary there at night. Would you like a hot drink or anything? Milk and biscuits?'

This time Clio didn't mind being treated like a child. 'That would be lovely.'

'I'll ask Mrs Northam to bring you some. She makes them herself and my mother has the appetite of a midge. What about a hot-water bottle?'

Clio smiled tentatively. The dirty, frightened, desperate feeling that had invaded her after Luke's behaviour was finally beginning to subside. There was an incredible sense of security around Angus. The phrase 'safe as houses' came into her mind. It seemed more than fate that he built them for a living. 'Thank you.'

'Goodnight, then. Try and get some sleep. I'll be up at my place but there's a connecting phone in all the rooms. I'll try and call your mother too. She'll be wondering where you are.'

Clio was just considering what sort of crappy story Luke would make up to explain her absence when the milk and biscuits arrived along with the hot-water bottle. In five minutes she was asleep.

Angus put his head round his mother's door to check she was comfortable. From the dark his mother's voice asked, 'So, did you tell Amanda what I told you to?'

'Not yet, Maw.'

And Angus had a horrible twisted feeling in his stomach that now, with all that had happened, she would never be able to forgive him, let alone return his feelings for her.

Chapter 28

Amanda couldn't believe the nightmare she'd stumbled into. If everything she'd heard was true then her daughter had accused Luke of making a pass at her and had run off with Angus. Now Amanda had just failed the breathalyser and was sitting in the police station waiting for the results of her specimen. If she failed that she'd be prosecuted for drunk driving.

'Mrs Wells?' A middle-aged man wearing a tweed jacket with leather elbows addressed her. 'I'm the police doctor.' He looked like a kindly schoolmaster about to break terrible news to some parents.

Amanda struggled to hold on to her emotions. What she really wanted to do was sink to the floor and weep. Was it any defence that she had never done this before? That her life, which had finally seemed to be coming together after three years of misery, was suddenly coming apart again at the seams?

The man waved a piece of paper at her.

'The fact is, you were lucky this time. Your urine test is under the limit. But I'd like you to think about how serious an offence this is. If a child ran in front of you, you might not react quickly enough. Now, I suggest you have a cup of coffee and go home to bed. And next time you're going out for a drink, take a minicab. Or walk. Good for your health too.'

Amanda thanked him. 'I will. Believe me.'

She accepted the cup of coffee and went to her car. One instinct told her to do what the doctor had said. But the instinct to find Clio was stronger. In the battle of good sense versus maternal terror, maternal terror won. If she hadn't been over the limit in the first place, and she'd just had a cup of coffee, then she should be sober enough to drive in an emergency like this. She'd do so very slowly and carefully indeed.

Amanda had never been to Angus's house but she knew roughly where it was, just outside Laineton in an area known as High Down.

It was deep countryside here, with very few dwellings. No one would believe the bustling seaside town of Laineton was just out of sight over the hill.

She came to the gatehouse. A floodlight immediately flashed on at her approach, bathing twenty feet around the house with blinding white light. Surely quite so many volts weren't necessary? But then the house was isolated and must sometimes be frightening.

Amanda banged on the door and waited. The silence was enveloping and, despite the bright light, unnerving, like finding yourself in the sights of a gun barrel. She banged again, half-expecting Angus to appear in a dressing gown, smiling dangerously like Rhett Butler after a night on the bottle.

But the person who eventually came to the door was a bleary-looking middle-aged woman with a grumpily bewildered air.

'I'm looking for my daughter, Clio. I understand she's here.'

The woman stood back, still half asleep. 'You'd better come in. I'll ask Mrs Day what to do.'

Amanda was shown into the sitting room, where she struggled to work out what the hell was going on. If Isobel was here then there could hardly be any untoward behaviour going on.

The room she'd been left to wait in was green and peaceful with a faint smell of medicines about it; hardly the scene of rampant seduction or underage sex. Amanda looked around her, confused.

She started, her eyes fixed on an object on the windowsill, illuminated by the still-blazing floodlights outside. The two courting herons. She scanned the rest of the room. On an oak mantelpiece over the fireplace the swan took pride of place. The ground suddenly fell away in front of Amanda as she guessed the truth. The recipient of those carvings hadn't been Angus's girlfriend. It had been his mother.

'I hope you'll forgive me,' a soft voice behind her said, 'but I don't feel we should wake Clio. She's had a horrible experience and it might be best to let her sleep for as long as possible.'

Amanda whirled round, dizzy with confusion. Isobel Day looked almost like a ghost, so pale and translucent was she in her long white dressing gown.

'What horrible experience?'

'Oh, my dear, don't you know?'

'Don't I know what? All Luke told me was that she'd gone off with Angus and I've come here to tell him that any relationship between him and my daughter is out of the question. She's only sixteen and he's forty.'

'Mrs Wells . . . Amanda . . .' Isobel looked at her as if she were speaking a foreign language and needed a translator. 'You can't really think there's anything between my son and Clio. She's a baby. Besides, you're the one he's in love with. You must surely know that, even if he hasn't had the nerve to tell you directly. He would never dream of laying a hand on Clio.'

Fear grabbed Amanda's heart and twisted. 'So what is this horrible experience you're talking about?'

'Amanda, dear, I think you ought to go and talk to Angus about this yourself. He can answer all your questions. You'll find him in the house at the end of the drive.'

'But Clio's all right?'

'She's fine. She had some warm milk and some of Mrs Northam's biscuits – quite a lot of biscuits as a matter of fact. You can glance in at her if you like.'

Amanda ran up the stairs and opened the door to the small spare bedroom. Clio had curled herself up in a ball, as she always did in bed, clutching a furry lilac hot-water bottle. Her long hair was sprayed out around her and her face was faintly flushed in sleep. Her mouth was open a little, showing her top teeth. She seemed so peaceful that Amanda's racing pulse began to calm.

'Thanks. I'll go and find Angus.'

Isobel waited until she heard the engine start, then immediately picked up the phone.

Angus answered it almost at once. 'Maw! What is it? Are you all right?'

'I'm fine.' This wasn't strictly true as she had a considerable pain in her stomach. 'Amanda Wells is on her way to see you and she seems absolutely furious. Maybe this could be your moment.'

'And maybe not. You never did have a sense of the right occasion.'

'At least I don't put things off because I fear rejection.'

'Thanks for that, Maw. Now get back to bed.'

'Just try and stop me.'

Angus could already hear Amanda's car approaching. She paused for a moment, presumably taking in the enormous size of the house and reinforcing her prejudices against him as a fat-cat developer.

The doorbell rang.

Angus dressed hastily in cords and a sweatshirt and answered it on the third ring.

'You're dressed,' Amanda accused.

'My mother rang. She said you were coming.'

'I want to know what the hell's going on.'

Angus's face was like granite. 'You mean about Luke?'

'No, not about Luke. About you and Clio.'

'Nothing whatsoever is going on between me and Clio. She's a child, for God's sake!'

'Then why did you take her from her home at ten o'clock, for God's sake?'

Angus's face was grimmer than she'd ever seen it. It almost frightened her with its scowling disapproval. 'So Luke Knight didn't fill you in, then, on why Clio ran away? Why am I not surprised?'

Amanda felt so tired she could hardly stand up. 'He told me some wild story about Clio accusing him of making a pass at her.'

'It wasn't a wild story. Why don't you believe your own daughter? Luke did make a pass at her.'

Amanda felt sick to her soul. Surely it couldn't be true. 'Oh for God's sake, Angus. Luke would never do that.'

'Amanda, I'm sorry. But it's not the first time.' Angus hesitated. He loathed Luke but he knew how much the real story would hurt her. 'Luke's done it before, apparently. In a previous relationship. The mother sent him packing.'

'Oh my God! How do you know that?'

'Louise told me. Ruthie heard the rumour and she made Louise promise to tell you about it. Louise conveniently forgot. He'd just tried it on when I went round to your house tonight.'

'But why did you go round to my house anyway?' Amanda asked, bewildered. She ran a hand through her hair tiredly. Her eyes were red and puffy with exhaustion.

'Because I'd promised my mother I would.'

'Your mother? What's this got to do with Isobel?'

'My mother's very ill. She made me promise her something. I didn't get the chance to fulfil my promise, which is fortunate for me as you clearly came here believing Knight's story that I'd tried to seduce your daughter.'

She'd never before seen an expression like that in his eyes, halfway between fury and disgust.

'It was Luke who made the pass, Amanda. He tried to kiss Clio and he put his hand on her breast. Not surprisingly, Clio completely went to pieces.'

Amanda froze. There was something about Angus's assertion that rang true. Clio had been behaving very strangely lately where Luke was concerned. She never wanted to be alone with him and made almost any excuse not to be in the house when he was there. Amanda had put it down to her resentment that Luke was taking her mother away. But what if it were something worse?

'I'd better get back and have this out with him.'

'If you aren't sure I'm telling the truth, call Ruthie. She seems to be the one who knows about it.'

'Maybe I'll do that.'

She drove back like a zombie, shaking with cold and tiredness. But most of all, she felt a murderous, incandescent rage.

Chapter 29

The sitting room was quiet and dark, and there was no sign of Luke. She noticed that the cushions were in the wrong position and stooped unconsciously to straighten them. Something was stuck down the back of the sofa. It was Luke's wallet. She opened it and rifled through. It was full of standard stuff – receipts, credit cards, the corner of an envelope with a phone number written on it, a raffle ticket. She was about to put it on the dresser when she opened the final compartment. Inside, tucked under Luke's driving licence, was a photograph of Clio, stolen from the family album. It was a picture Amanda particularly disliked, because Clio was dressed for a school disco, looking bold and knowing and far older than her years.

It was so clear, now that she'd found out the truth. All those insinuations that Clio must have provoked the ski instructor, and the grubby hints that she was encouraging Angus Day, when all the time the one who had really been obsessed with Clio was Luke.

She slumped on to the sofa and got out her address book, searching feverishly for Ruthie's number.

The phone rang perhaps ten or twelve times before Ruthie answered it.

'Yes?' Ruthie asked, her voice spiked with the anxiety of any parent rung unexpectedly in the middle of the night.

'It's Amanda. Ruthie, I'm sorry to call so late, but is it true you know someone who was involved with Luke? Someone who had a teenage daughter?'

'Oh God, Amanda.' Ruthie's sharp tone acknowledged the truth of her words. 'Has something happened with Clio?'

Amanda felt herself shrivel up. There was no doubt, then. She had failed to protect her own daughter. She'd even been the one to put her at risk.

'Yes, it's true,' Ruthie said. 'Didn't Louise tell you? Why the hell did I trust the bitch? It's just that you didn't come to the last book group and I didn't want to talk about it on the phone. I should have come to see you. Louise said we shouldn't get involved but I knew that was nonsense. I'm so sorry.'

'Look, Ruthie, one thing. This friend of yours.' Amanda knew this mattered only for her own pride. 'Did she think Luke targeted her deliberately because of her daughter?'

'No,' said a voice behind her. She swung round. It was Luke. He was still wearing his jeans and denim shirt and had that wholesome just-washed look that she now knew was so deceptive. He ought to look like a dirty old man.

'I'll call you later, Ruthie. Goodbye.'

'It wasn't like that.' Luke ran a hand through his fair hair. 'For God's sake, it was you I fell for. It was just that Clio was so bloody gorgeous, and she didn't even know it. I didn't mean to. I couldn't help myself.'

'And you didn't think for one moment that Clio might be vulnerable because she'd already lost her father and he'd just had twins with another woman?'

'Maybe I could have helped. Been a kind of replacement father.'

Amanda stood up and hit him as hard as she could, so that her hand left a weal, red and livid, where her ring caught his cheek. 'Fathers don't try to seduce their daughters; at least not decent fathers. You exploited her. You knew she wouldn't want to tell me about it, that she'd know how humiliated and disgusted I'd feel.

Stop trying to pretend this was some harmless little incident. It could have damaged Clio for ever. Now, I want you to leave. Now, this minute. Just get out.'

'So this is goodbye then?' Luke attempted a charming smile.

'No, Luke, this is fuck off and leave Laineton. This is I'll be watching you, so keep your hands off vulnerable young girls. This is I'd like to kill you, Luke, for doing that to my daughter.'

'Think about it this way, Amanda,' Luke challenged. 'If you hadn't been so desperate you might not have let me move in so easily. Goodbye – I'll collect my things while you're out.'

'You'd better do it soon. I'll have the locks changed next week.'

Amanda heard the front door slam and she sat back down in the dark, shaking, stupefied by grief, drowning in her own sense of failure. She'd been offered the love of a good man and a worthless one and with unerring skill she'd chosen the worthless one. And there wasn't just pain but guilt that she hadn't protected her daughter. But there was also something darker and more shameful. A powerful sense of rejection that her lover had wanted her own daughter more than he'd wanted Amanda herself.

She sat staring ahead as the darkness softened into dawn. The cat jumped on to the sofa and sat on her lap, sensing some desperate need in her owner and trying to offer affection and reassurance. But Amanda didn't notice. Eventually, exhausted by emotion, she fell asleep.

It was the cat, purring like an engine, that woke her up when morning finally came. It took Amanda a moment or two to surface and remember all that had happened last night. Then, like a curtain being drawn back to reveal blinding, painful light, she recalled every moment in humiliating, agonising detail. Last night was the night her life had fallen apart. For the second time.

But at least one thing was clear. She must go and fetch Clio and bring her home. Now that Luke had gone there would be no more risk.

A faint smell of cumin and spice still hung in the air and Amanda knew she'd never be able to taste curry again without thinking of last night. She looked at her watch. It was 8.30 a.m.

Was that too early to turn up as Isobel's, given how ill she was? But Amanda knew she had to see Clio, to hold her tight and promise her that nothing bad like that would ever happen again.

But could a mother ever promise that? Especially one who had already failed to protect her child once.

It was the kind of morning that would normally have lifted her spirits. The sun was moving through a sky of clear blue as she drove over the Downs to Isobel's house. The trees still had the pale green of spring about them, and the fields, not yet worn out by enthusiastic walkers, were lush and inviting. But Amanda didn't notice any of it. She was numb with horror and shock.

Isobel's carer, Mrs Northam, answered the door, cheerful and bustling in a blue nylon overall, as if today were the most normal of days. 'Would you like a cup of coffee? Mrs Day is sleeping in and Clio's gone for a walk.'

A small beam of light penetrated the darkness in Amanda's mind. If Clio had been really damaged, surely she would have stayed in bed, too depressed to get up?

Amanda realised how bone-tired she still felt. 'A coffee would be lovely.'

Mrs Northam arrived back almost at once with fresh coffee and a tray of her home-made biscuits. 'Mr Day usually pops in any moment now to see that his mother's all right.'

Amanda felt herself flush at the thought of the encounter ahead. She would have to apologise to him.

A moment later his blue BMW, the very one she'd backed into, appeared in the driveway.

'Hello, Angus,' Amanda faltered. 'I wanted to say how very, very sorry I am . . .'

'. . . that you thought I was trying to seduce your sixteen-year-old daughter? Someone I happen to greatly like and admire.' His voice was still as cold and sharp as a chisel on flint. 'Yes, well, character assessment doesn't seem to be your strong point, does it?'

Amanda flinched. He was right of course. She was a lousy judge of people, especially lovers. 'Luke's moved out. He's promised he's leaving Laineton.'

'Good. Where is Clio?'

'I'm here.' Clio was standing at the door to the sun room at the side of the house, pulling off an outsized pair of Wellington boots. She glanced from Angus to her mother. 'Look, I'm all right. I might have decided all men are bastards, from Dad onwards, but maybe that's a useful lesson.'

Amanda's heart turned over that her beautiful daughter should already be so cynical before she'd even had the chance to grow up and fall in love.

Amanda noticed that she'd wiped off every sign of make-up and adulthood. A small, sad smile lit up Clio's pretty features. 'Are all men bastards, Angus?'

Amanda wanted to hold her and tell her that love was out there waiting for her.

'Only the ones your mother chooses,' Angus replied. It could have been said as a joke, but Angus's expression was stony.

'If you're such a perfect judge of character, what went wrong with your own marriage?' Amanda flashed, and immediately regretted it.

Angus didn't answer.

'We ought to go, Clio love,' Amanda said, desperate to get away to try to rebuild some normality in their lives.

Clio sighed. 'It's so lovely here. Can I just go and say goodbye to Isobel? On my own?'

If Clio was deliberately leaving them together, Angus wasn't having any of it. 'I'll go and move my car. It's blocking the driveway.'

For a moment Amanda hoped he might add, with that old familiar smile of his, 'And I don't want it driven into again.'

But he simply walked out of the room.

Clio came back, striding confidently, apparently undented by her experience. 'I really like Isobel. She's so ill and yet she never complains. I've left her my mobile number and she's going to let me know when I can come again. I'd like to keep visiting her, if that's all right.'

'Of course.'

By the time they got out to the car, there was still no sign of Angus.

'I think he's avoiding you,' Clio pointed out.

'Yes,' conceded Amanda. 'And you can't really blame him, can you?'

'Don't worry, Mum. Now you know you have terrible taste in men, maybe things'll look up.'

Clio was silent for most of the journey home.

'Are you really all right?' Amanda knew it was a silly question. One that Clio herself probably didn't know the answer to.

'Yes, I am. Just relieved that Luke's not going to be hanging round our home any more.'

Amanda closed her eyes for a moment. 'I should have seen what was going on. I should have noticed the signs, the things he said about you, the accusations about Angus.'

'It was easy to miss. You wouldn't expect someone so charming and good-looking to behave like that. I don't think he was a pervert, really. Just used to getting his own way. When he wanted something he didn't see why he shouldn't have it.'

'Of course he was a pervert! He abused your vulnerability. Oh Clio, I wish you didn't have to be so grown-up about this. I'm the one who should have seen all that.'

'He was pretty clever at hiding it. Even Rose was fooled and she's one of the shrewdest people I know.'

'Clio, I'm really, really sorry.'

Clio glanced at her mother. 'Forget about me. Are *you* all right? In some ways he's hurt you more than me. At least I've got some good gossip for Jasmine.'

Amanda laughed, even though she felt like crying. 'I think I'll give up on men. I got him so wrong. I can't bear the idea of you judging all men by him.'

'Funny, you thought he was so different from Dad, but he isn't really. They both think they should get what *they* want and screw everyone else.'

Amanda was shocked. 'Your dad isn't anything like Luke.'

'OK, he didn't feel up my friends. But he was only thinking of himself when he buggered off with Stephanie. He didn't want to be a middle-aged old fart so he went and got himself a new wife to prove it and sod the rest of us. He isn't exactly Mr Sensitive, is he?'

'Not many men are.'

'I can think of one who is.'

Amanda found herself flushing. She didn't want to be reminded of how stupid she'd been all over again. 'Clio, don't. I've had it with men. I've got you and Sean, my friends, my gallery. It's more than a lot of people have.'

'Fine. So you're going to settle for nights out with Gran and a subscription to *Art and Artists*?'

Amanda almost drove into the car in front. Clio seemed to have recovered from her ordeal astoundingly quickly. It was going to take Amanda rather longer.

'I love you, Clio.'

'And I love you too. Now for God's sake concentrate on your driving. We all know it isn't your strong point.'

Without Luke around, the household seemed to take its shoes off and relax. Sean left his football gear all over the floor, Clio lounged on the sofa in a towel without a hint of self-consciousness – even Kinky seemed more at ease. How did other women manage to introduce a man into their households, even if, unlike Luke, he was nice and normal, when they had so many established habits and unwritten little rules?

Luke came and collected his things the following Monday while they were all out, removing every trace of himself except for one snowy linen shirt which Amanda took great satisfaction in ripping to shreds. She then changed the locks. It seemed symbolic. The end of an era. Least said, soonest mended, as her mother always said. As if it were that easy.

The worst thing, Amanda decided, was that it had robbed her of any belief in her own judgment.

Chapter 30

High summer was coming to Laineton. It was turning back into a tourist town, as it did for three months every year. The promenade was suddenly crowded with people eating candyfloss and wearing cowboy hats declaring I LOVE LAINETON or T-shirts saying I'M A VIRGIN – WELL, ALMOST. The gallery was getting more crowded every day. Clio and Sean's school activities had multiplied as the end of term approached. It would soon even be the finish of the football season. 'I don't know what Sean's going to do with himself,' Amanda had remarked to Ruthie, who'd dropped in to console her.

'Don't worry, Mum,' Sean had pointed out brightly. 'The new season starts two weeks afterwards.'

At least Amanda could feel grateful that things had gone swiftly back to normal. Clio had immersed herself in magazines and television. Sean continued to make lists about Man United and her mother still nagged her about meeting men. Personally, Amanda wouldn't have minded if she never saw another man again in her life.

Except perhaps one, and he obviously despised her. What's more, he seemed to have done a disappearing act. Normally she at least saw his car parked somewhere in the town, gleaming pretentiously in the summer sun, but recently even that seemed to have gone to ground. Maybe he was on a long holiday. Or avoiding her.

Several weeks later she was walking from home to the gallery, enjoying the sun on her back and allowing herself to feel fractionally less dismal, when she noticed a swarm of workmen, including one with a tell-tale bobble hat, down on the boardwalk near Rose and Betty's chalet. Just for a moment, excitement fizzed through her.

Even from a distance she could hear Betty's girlishly petulant tones complaining about something to Laddie.

'She's just cross with Angus Day,' Rose whispered to Amanda as she stopped next to them.

'Why's that?'

'Because he's persuaded the council to let us keep our chalet after all,' Rose explained. 'And Betty was only pretending she wanted to stay. The truth is, she'd much prefer a luxury flat with underfloor heating and a wraparound balcony.'

'Oh, Betty!' Amanda had to feel for Angus. He'd clearly been to hell and back to save their chalet from demolition.

'And now we're stuck here in this pokey, freezing place,' Betty carped.

Trying not to smile at Betty's fickleness, Amanda glanced round and saw Laddie Smithson struggling with a large plan that was being whipped by the lively sea breeze.

He raised his eyes to heaven as Amanda approached. 'Has Angus really managed to save their chalet?' she asked.

'He's moved mountains so they can stay. Pissed off everyone at the council. You might ask that wee woman if she's read the tale of *The Old Lady Who Lived In a Vinegar Bottle*? Because that's where she'll end up if she doesn't stop moaning about her blessed chalet.'

'He's been to a lot of trouble on your behalf, Betty,' Amanda told her sternly. 'I think you really ought to be thanking him.'

'Amanda,' Betty cut in, 'do you think there's any chance, if we asked him *very* nicely, that Mr Day would let us have the flat after all?'

'I've no idea,' Amanda said more brusquely than she'd meant to, 'and I don't know why everyone seems to think I've got an inside line to Angus Day's mind.'

316

Amanda said goodbye and hurried away to open up the gallery while Laddie and Rose Miles exchanged significant glances.

'What I want to know,' Isobel Day asked her son as they sat in Isobel's shady garden, 'is how long you're going to sulk in your tent?'

'I'm not sulking in my tent. You seriously expect me to pursue Amanda Wells when she thought me capable of child-molesting?'

'Hardly child-molesting. Clio is sixteen.'

'Well, then, of taking advantage of a vulnerable teenager whom I happen to admire and respect? I feel used and abused and I've just about had enough.'

'Oh, come on, Angus, don't be so pompous. Just because she preferred someone with a pretty face to you. Imagine how *she* feels? She's been stupid and reckless and she knows it.'

'I'm sorry, Maw. That's it. Compassion fatigue. I'm not interested any more. But if all you care about is that I find a female, you can cheer up. I've asked somebody out to dinner on Saturday.'

'Not the frightful woman from The Wave Gallery?'

'Louise? I do have some judgment, you know.' Even sitting in the shade, Isobel looked luminous, almost like a translucent statue. 'Louise would eat me alive. No, her name's Melanie Westmacott. She's a planning officer from Shireton.'

'Isn't that rather dipping your pen in the company's inkwell, given your line of work?'

'Hardly.' Angus was surprised at his mother's crudeness. 'I suppose I could be accused of trying to charm the council into giving me a deal. But actually Melanie's a lovely girl, and very interested in all my projects.'

'I see. And, of course, you can discuss planning together. That must be a bonus.'

'Stop it, Maw. She's got a very lively mind. She studied theology at university. I find her very restful company.'

'*Restful?* Now there's an interesting adjective. Shouldn't you be feeling a bit more passion at this early stage of your relationship?'

'Where did passion get me? Now, have you taken your medication?'

Isobel nodded, but actually she hadn't. If she took the amount of morphine the doctor recommended she felt both sleepy and sick. 'Does she like herons, this Melanie?'

'Herons? I've no idea. Look, Maw, I wish you'd stop interfering.'

'Interfering? Me? I just never had you down as a quitter, that's all.'

'Well, maybe you don't know me as well as you think.'

Isobel watched her son's departing back thoughtfully. He'd accused her of interfering. *Was* she? Didn't you have a right to interfere when you only had a brief whisper of time left to you? She thought of Clio and how much she liked the girl, and what a rotten time she'd had in her brief foray into the adult world. Clio deserved a decent father figure in her life.

Before she had a chance to change her mind, Isobel dialled Clio's mobile phone number. Clio had told her to ring any time, but maddeningly all Isobel got this time was an answering service inviting her to leave a message instead.

Isobel took a deep breath. 'Tell your mother that she's got competition. If she's the slightest bit interested in my son she'd better do something damn quick.'

Amanda gazed tenderly at the display of seabirds.

To think that she hadn't realised the carvings Angus had bought were actually for his mother. She'd jumped to so many wrong conclusions about him.

For a split-second, hope soared in her like a bird rising into cold clear air. His mother *had* said that Angus was in love with her and he'd admitted coming to her house in order to tell her something. And yet, when she'd last seen him he'd seemed to have anything but tenderness for her. Contempt would have been a more accurate description.

At least the shop had done well today. The lady who'd admired Sadie's paintings had just come back and bought one of her largest pictures. The amazing thing was, Amanda thought as she swathed the canvas in bubblewrap and carried it out to the customer's car, the night of the radio broadcast had only been a few weeks ago. And yet it had changed everything.

She tucked the canvas into the boot and closed it.

'Do you think you could direct me out of the parking space?' asked the customer nervously. 'Only this is my husband's new car.'

'I'm not sure of her credentials for that,' a voice behind them volunteered.

Amanda whipped round, dizzy with relief that it was Angus and the coldness seemed to have disappeared from his tone.

Then she saw the reason for his change of heart. She was holding on to his arm. A rather studious young woman in a sensible suit and rimless glasses. Amanda noticed immediately that she had lovely, luxuriant hair, which she probably kept tied severely back when she wasn't with Angus, and ludicrously high-heeled shoes. She also had the kind of adoring smile usually confined to prime minister's wives.

'Sorry,' Angus apologised. 'This is Melanie Westmacott. Melanie is chief planning officer for Shireton Council.'

Amanda longed to snap, 'How very convenient for you,' but it would be undignified and she would sound like a shrew.

She drew herself up, trying to remember the advice from a magazine article she'd read about proper posture giving you inner calm. 'Hello, Angus. Nice to meet you, Melanie.'

She directed the customer out of the tight space without a scratch to the car's shiny new paintwork.

Behind her she could hear Melanie's ludicrous heels trip-triptrapping down the street, and she found herself fervently hoping that Shireton's planning supremo would fall flat on her face and do herself a mischief.

It was almost funny, Amanda told herself as she walked back into the gallery, that seeing Angus involved with another woman felt so painful. What a cliché. What timing.

In fact, she was amazed at how easily her life had settled down, give or take the odd twinge of pain or regret. Her mother had only once asked her what had happened to Luke, and when Amanda had offered a highly sanitised version of the truth, Helen had commented: 'I never trusted him. His hair was too fair for those eyes. Do you think he dyed it?'

She was almost – provided she stopped looking out for Angus Day's blue BMW – back to normal.

Clio pressed the buttons on her mobile and replayed Isobel's message. She felt she'd been trusted, taken into Isobel's confidence, and that it was down to her to take some action before it was too late.

The trouble was, what?

She rounded a corner by the harbour and stopped in surprise, staring at Betty and Rose's chalet. Its rotting woodwork had been replaced by brand new clapboard and the whole thing had been painted an eye-catching fuchsia pink.

'What do you think?' Rose asked her. The old lady was standing on the stoop, smiling proudly.

'I think it's glorious. Outrageous but gorgeous. Just like you two.'

'How's your mother?' Rose felt for Amanda. She'd trusted Luke too.

'Oh, fine. Business is booming at least.'

Rose considered this thoughtfully. 'Angus will be glad. I expect he believed in your mum's talent. That's why he backed her lease.'

'Rose,' Clio replied, puzzled. 'What are you talking about? Angus didn't back Mum. Dad did. Or at least,' Clio paused, her mind whirring with sudden possibilities, 'that's what Mum thinks.'

But the more Clio thought about her father's attitude to taking risks with money, the more unlikely it seemed that he would have backed the gallery.

'How do you know this, Rose?' Clio asked suddenly.

'The estate agent told me at the opening party.'

'I wonder why Angus would have done that?'

'I'd have thought that much was obvious.'

'I'd better get on, I suppose,' Clio said thoughtfully. She'd had an idea. Admittedly it was an idea that might easily backfire. But she had to do *something* . . .

'Give my love to your mother.'

'I will.'

Clio crunched back up the shingle to the new boardwalk.

Her idea was turning into a plan. She didn't know if it would work, but it was worth trying. She'd call her father and attempt to enlist his help as soon as she got home. It was time he did something constructive.

'You're looking very pleased with yourself,' Amanda pointed out when Clio arrived at the gallery.

'Am I? By the way, I just wondered, have you heard from Angus Day at all?'

'Angus?' Amanda managed to sound as though to hear from anyone called Angus would be highly unlikely, not to mention rather irritating.

'Yes,' Clio agreed. 'Scottish bloke. Rich. Drives a sports car with the top down in order to look at himself in shop windows.'

'Ah. That Angus. No. He's probably preparing planning applications with his new girlfriend.'

'What new girlfriend's that?' Clio asked disingenuously.

'I think he said her name was Melanie and that she was a planning officer or some such charismatic occupation.'

'Melanie? Gosh, sounds like the woman we kidnapped.'

'It obviously worked. She must like the rough stuff. They seem to be an item now.'

'Well, I suppose those high-heels might have been the sign of a frustrated *femme fatale.* Anyway, tsk, tsk. Don't be jealous.'

'Jealous, *me?*'

'Yes, the very one,' Clio insisted. 'Anyway, it wasn't just the rough stuff. He wooed her with theological allusions as well.'

'What a man of many parts he is.'

'*Now* she notices. Come on, it's five-thirty. Why don't we shut up shop? Gran will be back with Sean by now. Let's order pizza.'

Amanda was about to say that there was a large and infinitely cheaper pizza already in the freezer but she realised Clio was trying to cheer her up.

'Thanks. You're a lovely daughter.'

'And you're a lovely mother.'

'Who needs men, eh? We don't!' Amanda warbled, trying to convince herself she actually meant it.

She felt a little more cheerful the next day when one of Natasha's birds sold for the largest sum they'd made so far. On top of that, Clio appeared mid-morning with an unexpected coffee and croissant.

'By the way,' Clio casually enquired, 'did Dad get hold of you?'

'Giles?' Amanda repeated. Giles's visits were rarer than the Pope's. 'No. Did he say what he wanted?'

'To drop in and show you the twins today. Apparently they're the brightest, most charming and brilliant babies that ever puked or gooed.'

'They don't take after their father then?'

Clio put her arm round Amanda. 'Glad you're cheering up a bit.'

'Hey-ho,' Amanda grinned. 'Life's hunky-dory as long as I'm happy with poverty, celibacy and videos with Sean every Saturday night.'

'Could be worse. Gran could move in.'

'That would *really* scare me.'

'Now that's what I call a nice family scene . . .' Giles had arrived and with a great amount of huffing and tutting had managed to get the double pram through the door of the gallery. 'Really, Amanda, you ought to be a bit more baby-friendly in this place.'

She was about to tell him that on her budget she'd had other priorities when she remembered he'd been generous enough to guarantee the lease.

'By the way, Giles,' Amanda began. 'I never really thanked you properly for backing me in this place. You could have been quite difficult about it if you'd chosen to.'

Giles looked bemused and bent down to mop a minuscule fleck of milk from Emily's chin.

'What on earth are you talking about, Amanda?' he asked. 'Wherever you got your backing from, it certainly wasn't anything to do with me.'

Amanda couldn't believe what she was hearing. 'I thought your second marriage had mellowed you. Why the hell did the bank change its mind and lend me the money, then? They almost laughed in my face at first, then suddenly they agreed to let me have it. I assumed you must have guaranteed the loan.'

Giles looked like a man who'd been conned into an act of generosity without knowing it. '*Me?* I wouldn't dream of doing such a foolish thing as guaranteeing your gallery.'

Amanda shook her head. 'I don't understand this.' There was only one thing for it. She'd have to go and find out what had happened from the estate agent. 'Would you and the twins mind holding the fort for a little while? There's something I need to get sorted out.'

When Amanda had left, Clio and Giles started to laugh.

'Thanks a million, Dad. I only hope Rose got it right that Angus is the real backer.'

'And that he takes it as a come-on in disguise when she accuses him of being a complete shit for not telling her.'

'Oh, he'll know what to do,' Clio grinned conspiratorially. 'I've got to know him pretty well.'

The estate agent was just closing for lunch when Amanda arrived, irritated and out of breath from running all the way from the gallery. To make things worse, the man who'd overseen the signing of the lease was away on leave.

'Please could I just have a quick peek in your files?' Amanda begged. 'It won't take a moment, I promise.'

The spotty youth who was temporarily in charge of the office surveyed her. She was pretty attractive, in an older woman sort of way. He wondered idly what it would be like to be seduced by someone experienced and eager to impart her sexual wisdom to you. Opening a file wasn't much to ask in return for an erotic awakening. 'You're on.'

Amanda sat down at a desk and took a deep breath. The lease was between a Mrs Granville Bowling, who owned the boathouse as part of an estate she'd been left, and Mrs Amanda Wells.

But the guarantor wasn't Giles.

It was Day Properties of 23 East Street, Laineton.

'Thank you very much,' Amanda said coolly.

The young man was just building himself up to inviting her for a lager and lime in the pub over the road. But Amanda had already left.

She stood outside the estate agent and rang Day Properties.

Fay told her Angus wasn't there. She believed he had gone to the Eastcliff Estate for a site meeting with Mr Smithson.

In minutes Amanda was marching up the hill towards the Eastcliff Estate. Ahead of her, Melanie and Angus were saying goodbye to each other on a street corner, then Melanie clacked off down the street in her silly shoes. Melanie had only gone a few yards when she turned and smiled at Angus once more. It might have been touching had Amanda not discovered that she was insanely jealous.

'Angus!' she yelled as soon as Melanie had disappeared out of sight, 'I need five minutes of your valuable time.'

Angus, who had been about to join Laddie to discuss the exciting topic of guttering, stopped and waited.

'Yes? What can I do for you?' His grey eyes looked at her unsmilingly, quite unlike the old Angus.

'It's very simple. What the hell did you think you were doing backing my lease without even telling me?'

Angus was infuriatingly unfazed. 'It's pretty simple. Without my backing you wouldn't have got the lease in the first place, which would have been a waste since I was pretty sure you'd make a go of it. And, as I understand it, you are.' His eyes were chips of granite now. 'Did you think I was out to exploit your commercial inexperience? Just as I exploited Clio's sexual innocence?'

Amanda flushed uncomfortably.

'Or perhaps you thought I intended to make money out of you? Grow up, Amanda, and stop seeing villains behind every tree. There's such a thing as believing in someone for no other reason than that they deserve a shot. That's it. End of story. Now, if you'll excuse me, I've only got half an hour to talk to Laddie before I meet Melanie in town.'

A voice was screaming into Amanda's ear that it was now or

never. She realised it was her own voice, or rather the voice of the bold, brazen, roll-me-up-in-a-rug part of her. 'I think that would be a serious error of judgment.'

'Talking to Laddie?'

'Meeting Melanie in town.'

'Well, you'd certainly know about errors of judgment.'

'How dare you insult me when I'm trying to tell you . . . to tell you . . .'

She could hardly tell him the truth – that she'd just realised she loved him desperately and wantonly and that her plans to spend the rest of her life alone in celibacy would be fine if he didn't keep popping up in her memory, usually dressed as a sheik.

'What?' Angus pretended to look at his watch. 'What are you trying to tell me?'

Neither of them noticed that Lou Wills had just opened her window, or that Laddie Smithson, plus his gutterer-in-chief, had drawn imperceptibly nearer.

'That . . . that . . .' Amanda struggled.

Laddie, standing only a few feet behind her, was silently willing her onwards.

'That what, Amanda? That you're going to cancel the lease because you're too proud to take favours from me? Even though you seem to be doing well?'

'That I owe you an apology.' Laddie and Lou Wills breathed a sigh of relief. At last. 'The thing is, I've made some stupid assumptions about you.'

She was so intent on being truthful this time that she didn't take in the arrival of Clio, Giles and the twins.

'I thought . . .' she still felt embarrassed to admit this '. . . you were like Giles, my ex-husband. Charming and selfish.'

Giles was about to protest in the strongest possible terms when Clio put a finger to his lips. 'Shut up, Dad. You *are* charming and selfish.'

'But actually,' Amanda continued, oblivious of her audience, 'you're one of the least selfish men I've ever met. As a matter of fact, I think I may be in love with you.'

Angus stopped pretending to inspect the flashing on the roof above her head and looked at her. 'But are you sure you know me? First you think I'm a capitalist bastard, then you think I'm like your selfish ex-husband, and then you accuse me of trying to pursue your teenage daughter . . . What is it you've decided you like about me this time?'

Her audience waited with bated breath.

'That you're kind, and shrewd, and try to give people their dreams. That you pay for the damage to other people's cars even when you know it's their fault . . .'

'What a paragon of dull virtue I sound.'

'I haven't finished yet. That you're charming and intelligent and extremely sexy when dressed in Arab clothing . . .'

Angus took a step nearer to her.

'I can't go round in a djellaba for the rest of my life, you know.' He was standing right in front of her now. 'Even for you.'

'I'm sure we could find a compromise.'

And then she felt Angus's arms closing around her and she remembered the delicious feeling of New Year's Eve and how much she'd wanted him. Before Giles had so rudely interrupted them.

'Will you look at that?' She vaguely heard Giles's voice in the back of her mind and decided she must be hallucinating. 'She's got her sheik after all.'

Amanda came up for air to find Clio, Lou Wills, Laddie Smithson, the gutterer and Giles all watching them with ludicrously indulgent smiles on their faces.

'Just fuck *off*, Giles! It was all your fault things went wrong last time.'

Giles looked wounded.

'Mum's right, Dad,' Clio endorsed. 'For once in your life, just fuck *off*, will you?'

An hour or so later, Isobel Day was roused from her usual doze in front of the television by the approach of a sports car. But Angus didn't come in. The sound of laughter outside propelled Isobel haltingly from her chair to the window. She was sure the worthy Melanie wouldn't have a laugh like that.

Angus and Amanda were sitting in the car with the roof down.

With great difficulty, Isobel pushed open the window and leaned out. 'Did he look in any shop windows on the way?' she called to Amanda.

'No,' Amanda shouted back, 'but I did. I wanted to see us together.'

'And don't tell me I'm moving too quickly, Maw. If I wait any longer Amanda may discover some new character flaw she hasn't seen already.'

'Too *quickly*?' Isobel echoed, stunned. 'I thought you'd never get round to seeing what was completely obvious to everyone else. That you are absolutely perfect for each other.'

'As a matter of fact, I do have some confessions to make,' Angus admitted to Amanda. 'For a start, I'm rather rich. Are you going to hold that against me?'

'I expect I could get used to it.'

'And I'm not at all green.'

'I'll teach you to be.'

'And the honest truth is, I can't stand Manchester United. I've always been an Albion supporter.'

'Now that *is* serious. But would you be prepared to convert?'

'How long would the instruction take?'

'Oh, I think an afternoon with Sean should do it.'

'You drive a hard bargain.' Angus pulled her into his arms again.

As she closed the window to leave them in peace, Isobel caught sight of the two courting herons on the windowsill. She didn't know whether her son and Amanda would make each other happy, but her instinct told her they had a good chance. They'd waited long enough.

She just hoped someone had remembered to tell Melanie.

Acknowledgements

A number of generous people helped me to tell a hod from a frog, not to mention a truss from a stud . . . and other fabulous expressions from the building trade. Special thanks to Jane Atkinson, Philip Fry, Harry Handelsman, Crispin Topping and Roger Zogolovitch for explaining the fascinating world of architecture and development. Any insights are theirs; any inaccuracies are mine. Also to my friend Barbara Cook for her wisdom and sense of humour on the subject of men.

Thanks to my agent, Carole Blake, and my editor, Barbara Boote. We had endless fun discussing who would (and wouldn't) make good husband material. Send personal recommendations to the author . . .

Thanks also to my desk editor, Joanne Coen, for her calmness and insight, to Tamsin Barrack for brilliant publicity and to all at Time Warner Books for their endless enthusiasm and skill in design, sales and marketing.

Lastly to Alex, Georgia, Holly and Jimmy, who make my life the happy and chaotic experience that it is.